W9-CFV-641

PRAISE FOR JENNIFER PROBST

"For a sexy, fun-filled, warmhearted read, look no further than Jennifer Probst!"

—Jill Shalvis, *New York Times* bestselling author

"Jennifer Probst is an absolute auto-buy author for me."

—J. Kenner, *New York Times* bestselling author

"Jennifer Probst knows how to bring the swoons and the sexy."

—Amy E. Reichert, author of *The Coincidence of Coconut Cake*

"Jennifer Probst never fails to deliver romance that sizzles and has a way of tugging those emotional heartstrings."

—*Four Chicks Flipping Pages*

"Jennifer Probst's books remind me of delicious chocolate cake. Bursting with flavor, decadently rich . . . very satisfying."

—*Love Affair with an e-Reader*

a
brand
new
ending

OTHER BOOKS BY JENNIFER PROBST

Nonfiction

Write Naked: A Bestseller's Secrets to Writing Romance &
Navigating the Path to Success

The Billionaire Builders Series

Everywhere and Every Way
Any Time, Any Place
Somehow, Some Way
All or Nothing at All

The Searching for . . . Series

Searching for Someday
Searching for Perfect
Searching for Beautiful
Searching for Always
Searching for You
Searching for Mine
Searching for Disaster

The Billionaire Marriage Series

The Marriage Bargain
The Marriage Trap
The Marriage Mistake
The Marriage Merger
The Book of Spells
The Marriage Arrangement

The Steele Brothers Series

Catch Me
Play Me
Dare Me
Beg Me
Reveal Me

Sex on the Beach Series

Beyond Me
Chasing Me

The Hot in the Hamptons Series

Summer Sins

The Stay Series

A Brand New Ending
The Start of Something Good

Stand-Alone Novels

Dante's Fire
Executive Seduction
All the Way
The Holiday Hoax
The Grinch of Starlight Bend

3 1526 05217355 3

a
brand
new
ending

JENNIFER PROBST

Montlake
Romance

This is a work of fiction. Names, characters, organizations, places, events, and incidents are either products of the author's imagination or are used fictitiously.

Text copyright © 2018 by Triple J Publishing Inc. / Jennifer Probst
All rights reserved.

No part of this book may be reproduced, or stored in a retrieval system, or transmitted in any form or by any means, electronic, mechanical, photocopying, recording, or otherwise, without express written permission of the publisher.

Published by Montlake Romance, Seattle

www.apub.com

Amazon, the Amazon logo, and Montlake Romance are trademarks of Amazon.com, Inc., or its affiliates.

ISBN-13: 9781503904873
ISBN-10: 1503904873

Cover design by Letitia Hasser

Cover photography by Lauren Perry

Printed in the United States of America

To all of my beloved readers who struggle with addiction and believe there is no hope.
You can change your path any day, anytime, any moment—it is simply never too late.
You just have to take the first step.

"The weak can never forgive. Forgiveness is the attribute of the strong."

—*Mahatma Gandhi*

The Victory of Surrender: "We perceive that only through utter defeat are we able to take our first steps toward liberation and strength. Our admissions of personal powerlessness finally turn out to be firm bedrock upon which happy and purposeful lives may be built."

—*Twelve Steps and Twelve Traditions*

Prologue

The crickets screeched a symphony she ached to sing along with, but Ophelia kept quiet as she crept through the thicket of woods and searched for the pinprick of light. Her sneakers were soundless over the pine needles, and the full moon guided her way to the edge of the path.

Already, her heart pounded rapidly in her chest, and her palms were sweating.

Why did he always incite such a strong reaction? When had a tight childhood friendship turned so rapidly into something so exciting and lustful and . . . forbidden?

A beam of light swerved in a full circle, then flashed twice.

There.

She headed over. In moments, he was pulling her into his arms.

Her soul sighed. The clean scent of washed cotton and hay surrounded her. Kyle held her tight: chest to chest, legs tangled together, his breath warm against her cheek. Seconds dragged without either of them speaking. They shared a rare form of communication—the years spent together as children and then teenagers created an extra foundation allowing them to be comfortable with silence.

Finally, she lifted her chin and looked into his forest-green eyes that held the power to stun her with their intensity. "Did you tell your father about our plan?"

His face set to stone. "No. I tried, but he didn't want to listen. I don't care anymore, Ophelia. I don't owe him shit."

"You're right. You don't." The relationship between Kyle and his father ripped at her heart, but she knew the emotional abuse Kyle had dealt with over the years had taken its toll.

"What about you?"

"I wish I could tell Ethan, but my brother's been so pissed since he found out about us. I'm afraid he'll tell Mom and Harper. They expect me to start college, and I know if they find out our plan they'll try to stop me from going."

Kyle and she had just graduated high school and experienced the most idyllic summer together. But things were about to explode. Instead of getting a college degree, helping her mother run the inn, and doing the stable thing, she'd be ditching college, leaving her entire family behind, and jumping into the unknown.

"They'll understand. When we get there, we'll call your family and explain that we made some important contacts in California and had to move out there for a while. It won't be a lie because we're going to make this happen. Once they see our success, they'll forgive us."

"What about Ethan?" she said, her fingers interlacing with his in a quest for strength.

God, she hated sounding so unsure.

She was eighteen years old and knew exactly who and what she wanted, but her older brother was Kyle's best friend. He'd lost his mind when he found out they'd been secretly seeing each other in a romantic way. They'd been the three musketeers for so long, it'd never occurred to any of them there could be anything more than friendship.

Until it had.

Kyle stroked her hair back. "Ethan will forgive us, too. He'll barely be able to breathe the next three months in basic training. By the time we're married and settled in our careers, it won't matter anymore. We've been working toward this forever, Ophelia, and we're going to get it all.

Between your singing and my writing, we're both going to be famous. But none of it can happen if we stay here or suffer through four years of college for a meaningless degree. We have to make our opportunities—not wait."

Excitement shivered down her spine.

Yes.

Everyone knew Kyle was meant to be a famous writer. He'd been writing forever, and even placed first in a national writing contest.

And hadn't she been told by every music teacher that her voice was special?

Now that her sister, Harper, was helping out with the horse farm and her brother was entering the military, it was finally her time to focus on Kyle and their careers. She couldn't imagine a world outside of their small town; though she was nervous, Kyle would be with her. And Kyle was meant for bigger things than working a farm with a father who despised him.

"You're right." She smiled up at his beloved face. She never got tired of studying him. From his shaggy, white-blond hair that covered his slightly crooked brows to his sharp blade of a nose and those lush lashes that should have been bestowed on a girl, he had always been good-looking—and the most sought-after boy in high school. His square chin and dimples were the knockout punch.

But he'd never been interested in anyone else. Just her. A buzz of satisfaction and joy shot through her veins like the fizz from a newly opened soda can. She had nothing to worry about. She just needed him.

He smiled back, lowered his head, and kissed her.

The sweet thrust of his tongue against hers weakened her knees in the biggest cliché of all. His lips moved over hers with a familiarity and expertise that had been practiced for endless months in secret—the thrill of getting caught only adding to the pleasure.

"I love you," he whispered against her mouth.

Excitement shot through her at the raw emotion of his voice, the glint of savage intensity in his eyes.

"I love you, too."

"We leave in the morning. I have enough money saved to hold us over for a while."

His words spun around her and created a warm web of protection. She refused to show any doubt. Besides, he hadn't convinced her to do anything she didn't want. They were strong and they'd make it—together. She tilted her chin up.

"I can't wait."

He flashed a grin. "This road trip will be our first adventure together, with many more to come. Just you and me."

His second kiss drove the promise home—a kiss filled with a burning lust that made her feel all woman. "Kyle . . ." she breathed, his name a symphony on her tongue.

"I can't wait till you're my wife," he murmured, licking her lower lip, then biting it gently. "Can't wait till you're truly mine."

"I already am."

"Not in all ways. Not yet."

Kyle wanted to wait until they were married in Vegas before making love. She'd begged him to change his mind, but he had a core honor about her first time and wouldn't budge. The idea of finally not having to stop shot tingles down her spine. Soon. Very, very soon, she'd have everything she ever dreamed of.

They both would.

If only she'd known the road ahead that looked so bright and promising was really choked with weeds, thorns, and poison ivy. That it led not to happily ever after, but to a cliff dive over shallows filled with rocks.

If only she'd known how quickly the love of her life and new husband would betray her.

If only she'd known her dreams would shatter and leave her to return home with nothing but emptiness and regrets.

If only she'd known.

Ophelia kissed him back and believed.

Chapter One

Ten Years Later

Kyle Kimpton drove up the familiar curving driveway of the Robin's Nest B & B. The trees swayed almost in welcome, branches bent under a thick coating of ice. But with every foot gained, his breath squeezed a bit tighter in his lungs.

He was back.

His gaze swept over the inn, noting the extensive renovations and the care taken with each detail. The bright-blue trim of the Victorian farmhouse shone clearly even in the January gloominess. Mounds of snow covered the landscaping, but he had a feeling come spring the flowers and plants would be as impeccably groomed as their owner. The wraparound porch was brand new, sporting an array of wicker furniture with bright cushions and plush afghans set around a mobile fireplace. Silvery lights wrapped around the porch railing, twinkling merrily. Beyond the inn, the endless blanket of white broke open to reveal the thrust of the mighty mountains in the distance, sitting arrogantly between the fat wisps of misty clouds. A perfect winter wonderland. A peek into what he'd always believed Narnia could be.

He parked the car and cut the engine.

Ten years.

Ten years since he'd come home to the small upstate New York town of Gardiner and gazed upon the staggering Shawangunk Mountains. Ten years since he'd touched snow. Ten years since he'd been surrounded by the eerie beauty of nature's silence.

And too many years since he'd seen the only woman he'd ever loved.

They'd been the three musketeers—Ethan, Ophelia, and him— caught in a world of their own making. Memories assaulted him. Of running through the woods when they were young and racing horses barefoot as the green meadow flashed below. Of moonlight walks and late nights at Bea's Diner, squeezed into the cracked red-vinyl booths as they spun dreams of the future and feasted on greasy burgers. Of his first kiss with Ophelia. The taste of innocence and passion mixed with Juicy Fruit chewing gum.

He closed his eyes, staggering under the raw emotions the images brought. Some of those dreams had come true for him, but the price had been brutal.

It was time to make things right.

It was time to reclaim what he'd lost.

Kyle glanced at the passenger seat, his fingers already reaching to stroke the leather laptop case. He'd left a fancy mansion behind, along with rooms filled with expensive trinkets meant to amuse, entertain, and distract the masses. He'd walked away from a gourmet chef, housekeeper, and personal trainer. His garage still held the laser-blue Lamborghini and the sleek black Hummer. He'd left the tuxedoes and designer clothes in his closet; the cedar wine cellar still filled with rare, expensive wine; and the four-poster mahogany bed that had seen too many lonely nights.

Now all he had to his name was one battered suitcase, his laptop, and a Ford Fusion rental car.

And for the first time in way too long, he felt the beginning of a creative spark—the sexy wink of his muse beckoning him closer to his childhood home, where he'd sworn he'd never return.

He grabbed his phone and tapped out a text to Ethan.

I'm here. How bad is she going to take it?

He waited a bit, until the familiar gray bubble with ellipsis popped up.

Don't know—depends on how pathetic you look. Still have no clue why she's mad at you.

Kyle winced as guilt punched through him. Falling in love with your best friend's younger sister was a no-no. Running away with her was even worse. But eloping and not telling his friend about it?

There was no making amends for that one.

He cursed, then tapped his fingers again.

Maybe this wasn't such a good idea.

Don't be stupid—it's a great idea! The inn isn't booked up and she's just being stubborn. Go inside, make nice, and I'll be there in an hour.

He groaned and resisted the urge to bang his head against the steering wheel. When he'd asked about staying at the inn for three months to work on a new project, he'd worried Ophelia would refuse. When Ethan told him to book his ticket, he'd been relieved.

Until he found out on the plane ride that Ophelia had actually said no. Ethan had conveniently left that part out, citing in true guy code it would all be *fine*.

Her refusal to see him hurt more than he'd imagined it would, but now he had no choice. Everything was set in motion, and he wasn't about to return to LA. Not only had he committed to writing this screenplay surrounded by his memories, he'd sworn to fight for a second chance with Ophelia. It was time they both faced the past, put some ghosts behind them, and figure things out. After all, it had been eight years.

She had no idea he was about to walk through her door with the intention of staying for the next three months—in the dead of winter.

That'd be bad enough, but when she heard his other piece of news?

Things were gonna get a hell of a lot worse.

He stayed in the car a few more minutes, trying to psych himself up. Maybe she'd surprise him and be open to talking things through. Maybe she wouldn't be horrified when he told her about what he'd discovered a few months ago. Maybe it would all work out fine, just like Ethan said.

Even better?

Maybe he'd find himself again.

Grasping at all those positive possibilities, he gritted his teeth, grabbed his bag, and got out of the car.

Chapter Two

Ophelia Bishop floated through the rooms singing "The Impossible Dream" from *Man of La Mancha* in full-blast mode while she attacked each wooden surface with lemon-scented polish. The first week after New Year's was always dead at the inn, and as of today, she had exactly zero guests.

So it was party time.

Not caring that her love of old musicals was geeky and embarrassing, she belted out Broadway tunes and got rid of her mortal enemy: dust. So many people sank into the winter blues after the holidays, but Ophelia loved every moment of the winter. The way the snow piled up and weaved a web of sensuality and coziness around her home. The luxury of ignoring the usual rush of productivity nipping at her conscience to *get things done*. The comfort of indulging in lasagna and hot chocolate under a fleece blanket. Today she'd slept late, had a light breakfast all by herself, and didn't have to make anyone fancy French toast or omelets or scones. She hadn't even brushed her teeth till noon! Her big plans after cleaning consisted of lounging around in her yoga pants with messy hair and binge-watching Hallmark Channel Christmas movies with a big bowl of popcorn.

Two couples were checking in at the end of the week, but she would have five entire days alone before that.

It was almost . . . orgasmic.

A giddy giggle broke from her lips. Again, she didn't care. She spent her entire life serving her guests, and it had become a stubborn point of pride to give the very best to each of them. Just like her mother had.

The thought of her mom brought a pang. It had been five years since cancer had finally won the battle, but Ophelia knew her mother would be proud of her for carrying on the inn's traditions. She'd made the Robin's Nest B & B her very own, bringing her personal style and flair, finding the delicate balance between her own life and the career of sharing her home and daily existence with endless strangers.

Memories stirred, but she refused to poke the beehive. Yes, once she'd imagined a different life for herself—one more glamorous and creative. She refused to deal with regrets. Her days were happy, mostly stress free, and the family legacy gave her a satisfaction she'd never take for granted.

She had enough.

She stepped back to inspect the living room, enjoying the look of antique furniture paired with bright colors and comfortable fabrics. The balance was key—high end with a welcoming warmth. First impressions were important, and every room reflected her vision. Of course, she didn't intend to use this room until the weekend, but she had terrible OCD tendencies about having things perfect, just in case. She'd mostly be living in the kitchen and her own private rooms in the back, but she loved the sight and scents of a well-cleaned room. Now she wouldn't have to worry about it till Friday, when her first guests of the new year arrived.

She headed to the closet to grab the vacuum and morphed into the haunting strains of "If Ever I Would Leave You" from *Camelot*, her mind filled with moody visions of Lancelot and his queen.

That's when she heard the knock on the door.

She cocked her head and frowned. Her family never knocked, and she didn't expect any drop-ins since the town was pretty much shut down.

She put down the vacuum, eased toward the door, and peeked out from behind the lace curtain.

No.

Shock barreled through her, along with a burning pain and emptiness she'd thought was impossible to ever feel again. She stumbled back a few steps and mashed her fingers against her trembling lips.

Kyle was here. At her front door.

Why was he here? What did he want?

Maybe he'd go away.

She kept silent, as if a mass murderer was waiting to attack her rather than her childhood friend-turned-lover. Another round of pounding rose in the air, this time with more demand.

"Ophelia! I saw you through the curtain, so it's too late to pretend you're not home."

She closed her eyes and mentally cursed.

Unbelievable.

She'd been crooning sappy love songs—and conjured up the one man she never wanted to see again.

"For God's sake, I'm freezing my ass off out here. Can you open the door?"

Damn, damn, damn.

She held her breath. She couldn't let him in. Wasn't there a law against ex-lovers seeing each other after nearly a decade—especially when one wasn't looking hot? Right now, she was so far from hot she was on the edge of the mental-patient look. Her hair was tangled and stuck up in a clip. She had no makeup on and was wearing old, dirty clothes with no bra.

His fist shook the door. "Ophelia, I have nowhere else to go right now. You can yell at me and throw me out later, but I've just had a three-hour drive from the airport and I need a bathroom. Please."

It was the last word that sealed her fate.

Guess even all this time couldn't dull the effect of Kyle Kimpton asking her for what he needed.

She shoved away the memory of him saying that same word over and over while she was on her knees.

Dear Lord. She had to open the damn door.

It took her a few moments to force her feet forward and her stiff fingers to turn the knob. The blast of icy air hit her full force, and she reveled in the shock, preferring frostbite to the silly leap of her heart when she gazed at the familiar, solid body before her. She schooled her features into resting bitch face and hoped she'd finally pulled it off. How badly she wanted to be one of those women like Mia, her brother's girlfriend, who could command a room with an icily lifted brow. Ophelia's emotions were always too close to the surface—especially around Kyle.

"Come in."

He stamped his boots a few times and pushed through, closing the door and dropping his bag at his feet. When he turned back to face her, Ophelia thought she was prepared. Defenses firmly up, bitch face arranged, breath firmly dragged into her lungs, she met his gaze head-on.

And found herself dragged back to being that helpless, lovesick, teenaged girl.

The years had been kind to him. His face now held carved lines that took away the pretty-boy looks from youth and added character. Those famous dimples and classic square jaw were now covered by scruff that emphasized the sharp, almost aristocratic, blade of his nose. His white-blond hair had turned a softer dark gold, the burnished strands a bit on the longer side to spill over his brow and cover his ears.

He used to wear old jeans and T-shirts, and had no idea what designer clothes were. Now, it seemed he had his own tailor. He wore a black wool coat that fit his trim frame like it was custom made and a plaid Scottish wool scarf wrapped around his neck. Rich leather gloves hid his long fingers. Snow dusted his hair and the shoulders of his coat. But it was his eyes that told her how he'd really changed.

Those forest-green depths were still highlighted by lush lashes, but instead of the zeal and inner light that had always shone like a beacon, there was a weariness that halted her breath. His force had dimmed. The knight who'd promised to fulfill all her dreams now wore tarnished armor, and the familiar passion seething under the surface throbbed with something brand new.

Disillusionment and the faint waft of regret.

A cocktail she knew too well.

Emotion surged upward from her very core, but this time, she'd had nearly a decade to practice blocking any chink in her defenses. She stared back at him, refusing to retreat from the raw chemistry that still crackled between them. It would always be there, but her calm acknowledgment hopefully gave him the message she was finally in charge.

"Ophelia." His voice seemed deeper, more gravelly, but it still stroked all the sweet spaces between her spine like one long shiver. Trying desperately to mask her reaction, she allowed herself a few steps back, her name lingering in the air like a question. "It's been a long time."

She crossed her arms in front of her chest to hide her braless state. Best to keep the conversation polite, yet cold. He'd use her bathroom, and she'd throw him out of her inn.

"What are you doing here?"

He rubbed the top of his head. It was a signature move that always told her he was frustrated or uncomfortable. Right now, he looked both. "You're not going to like it."

She kept quiet, cocking her head with a touch of impatience that Mia would be proud of. Maybe it would intimidate him.

"Ethan invited me to stay here for the next few months."

Ophelia blinked.

Impossible.

On Thanksgiving weekend, her brother had brought up the idea of Kyle staying at the inn to write some script, but she'd quickly shut it down, telling him in no uncertain terms that Kyle was not welcome. He'd been confused by her vehemence, but Ophelia had pushed back hard. Ethan had finally agreed to find Kyle another place.

"There must be some kind of mistake. I specifically told Ethan you couldn't stay here."

Kyle rubbed his head harder and muttered something under his breath. "I swear, I'm going to kill him for this."

"For what?"

His jaw clenched. "Ethan never told me I wasn't welcome. He said he spoke to you and you had a room specifically set up for me through March."

Her voice rose a few pitches. "He *lied*?"

"Yep. When I called from the plane to tell him I was landing, he confessed you had no idea I was coming. Said he was sure you would change your mind and it wouldn't be a problem."

Oh, she was going to murder her brother. Painfully. But right now, she had to deal with the fallout of his dumbass decision.

"I'm sorry, but I can't offer you a room. You can't stay here."

"You're booked up, then?"

She opened her mouth to lie, but nothing came out. All she had to do was say yes. It didn't matter—he'd never really know, and she'd threaten Ethan if he breathed a word of the truth. "I'm very busy," she said, hoping she sounded convincing. He nodded, and relief coursed through her. "Maybe you can stay with Ethan tonight and catch a flight back tomorrow?"

"No, I can't go back to California. I have to write this script here. In Gardiner." He paused, his gaze delving so deep she felt captured. "Every single room is booked?"

She wet her lips and looked slightly to the right. "I'm sure you can find a local hotel or stay at your father's."

He flinched, and his voice turned stone cold. "My father doesn't know I'm back. I intend to keep it that way."

How many times in the past had she tried desperately to help the two men mend their relationship? Kyle's pain from his father's verbal and emotional abuse broke her heart, but she knew how important family was, and she had always been hopeful one day his father would make amends. Of course, that was no longer her business. Her old need to fix everything bad in Kyle's life was permanently deleted, like a corrupted computer file.

Unfortunately, there were still aftershocks.

Why did he still smell the same? A delicious combination of washed cotton, soap, and sunshine? Why was there still this tightening awareness that practically vibrated in the space between them? Why did he still affect her on such a basic level of lust and want?

"I'm sorry," she said again. "Maybe Ethan can help, since he got you into this mess. He moved into the old cottage down the road with Mia. Why don't you drive over? I'll let her know you're on the way." She knew the cottage was too small for guests—they had plans to renovate and expand it in the spring—but she needed to get this man out of her house so she could breathe again.

"Ophelia."

The quiet way he spoke her name seared through her. It was the same intimate growl he used to whisper in her ear while he pinned her beneath him, driving inside her over and over in a quest for pure possession, wringing endless cries from her lips.

Her palms grew damp. She didn't want to dredge up the past or make polite chitchat as if nothing mattered. She wanted to get back to her cleaning and her empty inn and forget that the man she'd once loved and trusted with her entire soul was here.

She motioned to the hallway. "The bathroom is the second door on the right. I'll call Mia now. I can put some hot coffee in a thermos for you to take with you."

17

"Stop."

Her gaze slammed to his, those dark-green eyes burning into her.

"Stop treating me like some guest. I know you're pissed. And I know you're lying to me about there not being room at the inn."

She flinched but held her ground. How dare he? It wasn't her responsibility to make things right. She refused to give over her safe haven to the man who had almost broken her.

Ophelia straightened up to her full height, unpinned her arms from her chest, and welcomed the prick of glorious, clean, hot anger heating her blood.

"Fine. You want to push? Want to know the truth? You're right, Kyle. I have plenty of available rooms, but space has nothing to do with it. I don't want you here."

Pain flashed in his eyes, but she refused to let him affect her. Not this time.

"I can't pretend to be best buds reunited while we drink beer and talk about the good old days. I'm not comfortable with you sleeping under my roof while you create another hot screenplay to make you more millions. Go back to California. Go back to your sun and fake smiles and cutthroat deals and your real life. Leave me my damn memories. How's that for the truth?"

She waited for him to either turn and leave or pummel her with his own accusations. Instead, he laughed. The sound came out dry—it contained none of the joyful buoyancy she'd known so well.

He closed the distance between them, forcing her to lift her chin to keep his gaze. "There you are," he murmured. His body practically crackled with heat and anticipation, like fur boots dragged over a carpet, ready to ignite a shock. "That's the girl I remember. The one who looked at you straight and told you the truth whether you liked it or not. The one whose temper simmered beneath the surface and kept me off guard. God knows I'm starting to lose my instinct on what's real or fake anymore."

She refused to engage in memories of who they'd once been. He'd chosen to stay across the country and carve out a new life in Hollywood alone. Her voice dripped icicles. "Yes. Karma can be a real bitch. And don't think you can pretend to be the cynical, rich screenwriter who suddenly tires of his plastic life and returns home to find himself again—along with his first love he hasn't forgotten." A touch of meanness flared inside. "Trust me, it's been done to death. I'm hoping you'll at least be original."

"Maybe that's what I'm really afraid of," he said quietly. "That I've been kidding myself all along. That I'm really just a trope."

He'd only been here a few moments and already she was choking on emotion. She wouldn't allow him to torture her for the next few months. She might not live through it.

"Go home, Kyle."

"I know I hurt you. We hurt each other. Together, we're a tangled mess. I have no right to ask this of you, but I am. I have a screenplay I need to write and I have to do it here, surrounded by the memories of my childhood and what it means to return home. And you're part of it, Ophelia. I need to sequester myself from the world and see if I can really do this thing, or I'll regret it for the rest of my life."

She gritted her teeth against the anguish. His regrets would always revolve around his career, but she had no right to feel bad about it. She was only part of his past. They may have loved each other once, but he hadn't come back to make amends. His reasons were purely selfish. At least now she knew the rules so there would be no false expectations. She despised the brief disappointment she felt but swore she'd never let him tip her off balance again.

"You can stay at another B & B or hotel. Go to Mohonk Mountain House." The popular resort attracted visitors from all over for its gorgeous views of the mountains, shimmering lake, and endless activities set around the giant, rustic lodge.

"It's too commercial and crowded. The nearest B & B or hotel is almost an hour away. It won't work." He half closed his eyes, as if fighting to try and explain it right. "I need to be near Ethan and the farm. I've never felt safer anywhere in my life than this inn, where your mother cooked for me and made me feel like family. Where I found my best friend and my first love."

She couldn't help the grunt that escaped her lips.

He forged on, his voice a touch pleading. "Somehow, I've lost a part of me along the way. I stopped writing." He lifted his hands up. "I've been blocked for almost a year now, and I know if I can stay here this winter to connect with my past and write this script, I can get my life back. I'm asking to stay."

His final words exploded in the air like fire and dissipated slowly like smoke. After eight years, he was at her doorstep. He needed her help. She'd dreamed of this day, but it usually occurred in a fantasy where she looked really hot and wore spiked heels and tossed her hair over her shoulder in dismissal while he begged for forgiveness for letting her go.

Instead, he stood in her home with his fancy boots and briefcase and requested to spend the winter so he could write the script of his dreams. Then he'd return to Hollywood in restored glory, leaving her without a backward glance.

Ophelia dragged in a breath. Then another. Soon, calm radiated from her core, soothing the rough edges and the wicked emotional roller coaster he always took her on.

"I understand," she said.

Relief skittered over his features. His shoulders relaxed, and a slow smile curved those luscious lips that used to plunder hers with such sweet, spicy passion. "Thank you, Ophelia. I cannot tell you how grateful I am. Where can I bring my things?"

She smiled back, stretching out the glorious moment so she could savor it over and over in her dreams. "Back out to your car."

The confident expression on his handsome face vanished. "What?"

Her smile grew brighter. "I heard you, and I understand your dilemma, Kyle, but you can get your life back on somebody else's property. Good luck with your project. I'm sure it will be another *Fast and Furious* hit."

"I didn't write those screenplays."

"Oh, sorry. Sometimes they all seem the same." His wince confirmed she'd made a direct hit to his ego. "I am not now and will never be your consolation prize, or the vehicle needed to reconnect with your past. Whatever we felt for each other died long ago—including our friendship. I'd advise we leave the dead untouched. Don't you agree?"

She walked past him, opened the door, and waited.

Slowly, he backed up, took his briefcase, and stepped into the cold. He paused only briefly. His gaze pierced hers, holding her captive. Those dark-green depths mixed with seething, raw emotions.

Then Ophelia shut the door.

Her fingers shook. She held her breath and counted.

One. Two. Three. Four. Five. Six. Seven . . .

Footsteps clattered down the porch steps. Soon, headlights cut through the side window, arced high, then disappeared into the night.

It was like he'd never even been there.

He was gone.

Relief sagged her muscles even as her stomach turned. Ethan would be pissed. She hadn't acted as a gracious, calm, centered hostess. She'd turned a childhood friend out in the cold after he asked for help. It was against everything she'd practiced and become since returning home—a woman who not only accepted but also tried to embrace her new life and find joy in all the hidden parts.

Today, she'd acted like a lover scorned. A mean-spirited bitch. A woman bent on a little revenge.

God, it felt so damn good.

She headed toward the kitchen to open a bottle of wine.

Vacuuming was definitely done for the day.

Chapter Three

Ethan stared at him in shock. "She threw you out?"

Kyle sat back in the leather chair and sipped his coffee, enjoying the added touch of cinnamon that elevated Ethan's usual black sludge. Of course, Mia had probably made it. The petite, attractive woman perched by his friend's side was comfortably notched against his chest, her head barely reaching Ethan's chin. From her fashionable bobbed honey hair, manicured French nails, sleek black pants, and trendy sweater, he knew she'd definitely been the one to upgrade both the coffee and bungalow.

Ethan was a minimalist. Even though the bungalow was small, Mia's special contemporary touches made it homey, from the canvas watercolors of Saratoga horse racing, Tuscan pottery vases sprouting wild blooms of color, and scattered throw rugs, afghans, and matching pillows in rich earth tones.

Though it was the first time they'd met, Kyle took an instant liking to the woman who had stolen his friend's heart. Ethan's leg had almost been blown off during a Special Forces mission, and he'd suffered some wicked PTSD. Finding love with the right woman had softened all his hard edges and put a joy back in his eyes that seemed to make all the bad worth it.

Kyle reached down to pet the dogs curled at his feet. He couldn't believe Wheezy was still around. The family hound had howled in welcome after catching his scent, his white face evidence of an advanced age. The dog had been part of many of their adventures on the Bishop farm, and well loved. He'd found a companion who seemed to be his shadow—a small brown-and-white terrier mix named Bolt. Currently, the pup was snoring on top of Wheezy's back.

He put his coffee mug on the table. "Let's just say she made it clear I wasn't welcome."

"What happened between you two?" Mia asked, brow arched in curiosity. "Ethan said you guys were all tight friends growing up."

"I've been wondering the same thing," Ethan said. "I went into the military, and you both took off to California. By the way, I'm still not pleased with that move."

Kyle winced. When his friend had found out from Harper they'd run off, their friendship had taken a hit. Thank God, after some time, Ethan had forgiven him. "Sorry."

Ethan snorted. "Yeah, right. Anyway, they were in California for a while. Then suddenly Ophelia comes back, declares she's done singing, and wants to run the B & B with Mom. When I asked what happened with you, she said it just didn't work out. I figured she didn't like the lifestyle out there, but I never realized there was bad blood between you two. What happened, dude?"

Kyle took another sip of coffee to buy time. If only there was one answer to that question. Instead, a million responses whirred in his head, hurting his heart.

He'd been too young. Too sure of the world around him. Too selfish. Too ready to sacrifice anything for his dream, even if it was love.

He'd spent enough nights racked with regrets but always pushed them away to chase the next film project. He'd gone from a poor farmer in a small town to a big-time Hollywood screenwriter. He'd morphed from a kid whose own father despised him to a famous writer with an audience of millions who reveled in his talent. It had been easy to get lost.

And Ophelia?

The image of her slammed into his vision. How many times had he imagined her in his dreams? The milky white of her skin. The thick coarseness of her strawberry-blonde hair. The sprinkling of freckles on her cheek that looked like a heart. The bee-stung lushness of her mouth. Once, he'd known every inch of her body, able to pleasure her by just a touch.

The woman he'd met today was so much better than his memory.

Clad in those tight yoga pants that cupped the perfect curves of her ass and hips, heavy breasts that he could see were braless no matter how hard she tried to hide it, her face bare of makeup—which only emphasized the freckles she despised—he'd been thunderstruck. Those sky-blue eyes flashed with a confidence and challenge that practically begged a man to tame her.

Once, he'd risen to that challenge. Now, he had no right.

But the moment he stepped close, his gaze delving deep into hers, he'd been hit by a surge of pure electricity that almost knocked him on his ass. He'd caught her tiny hitch of breath; the way her pulse beat madly beneath her pale, delicate skin; the dilation of her pupils. Their chemistry had always been red-hot. Their connection ran deep. He knew if he reached out to touch her, she wouldn't be able to fight her reaction. Their bodies still belonged to each other, no matter how many years had passed.

Instead, he'd clenched his fists, ignored his straining dick, and tried hard not to remember how she was the only one who'd ever made him feel whole.

She accused him of running away.

But who'd been the one to jump on a plane and return home without a look back? Had he been that easy to forget?

She gave up on him, her vows, and her own dreams to retreat back to safety.

But he couldn't tell Ethan any of it. It would rip his heart out to know the truth.

Kyle refocused on the conversation. "We had a big fight in California. She came home, and I stayed. Guess we never really had time to settle the argument."

Mia cocked her head. She raked her gaze over him in a way that was way too shrewd for his comfort. "Ophelia doesn't fight. She's the calmest, most centered person I've ever met."

Kyle barely managed to clamp down a laugh. The girl he'd known was a spitfire. Mischievous. Passionate. Stubborn. She gave with her whole heart. "She must've changed, because that's not the woman I knew."

Ethan laughed. "Yeah, Kyle always knew how to push her buttons. Tink has definitely settled in. Now she's happy to run the inn and control her own environment. Just like Mom."

Kyle smiled at the nickname Ophelia's brother had bestowed on her from their shared love of Disney movies. With her looks, she was definitely fairy material—and she also had the famous Tinkerbell temper.

Mia shook her head. "That still doesn't make sense. It's been almost a decade—how long can a fight last? I'm sure once you guys talk it out she'll offer you a room. For now, you're welcome to stay with us if you don't mind the couch. We have big plans this spring to build my office and a few more bedrooms, but for now you can share my amazing closet." She pointed to the small area where she'd crammed a desk, computer, and a file cabinet.

"I can't impose like that. You're still in the honeymoon phase."

Ethan snorted. "You're sleeping on the couch, dude. Don't think you're gonna bother us in that department."

Mia punched him in the arm, making them both laugh, but the intimate glance they shared socked Kyle straight in the gut. Once, he and Ophelia had been as close, practically finishing each other's sentences, falling into each other like a beautiful poem or symphony that made sense. All their pieces slid into place. Now, she was a stranger.

Frustration simmered. He *had* to stay at the inn. The only way he'd be able to do this story justice was by steeping himself in the past. It was also his last shot at career redemption. Finally, he'd be able to walk away from the trap of canned action movies that had eroded his creative soul, leaving nothing but a shell. His agent had been a wreck about Kyle's writer's block, and he was delirious with glee when Kyle promised to deliver a new script in three months. He was in the process of assembling a dream team they could pitch it to, and Kyle would get one shot to convince everyone to take a chance on something completely fresh—the next great romance to rival *The Notebook*.

Yeah. They'd laugh him out of their offices if they realized that instead of another hot action movie, he was pitching a second-chance love story for the ages.

But every part inside him screamed he could pull it off if he got the chance.

If he got to write it here, where his story began.

He had to find a way to convince Ophelia to let him stay at the inn.

"Well, I appreciate the offer," he said, tugging affectionately on Wheezy's long ear. "Hopefully it will only be for a few nights."

"Of course," Ethan said. "I'll talk to Tink and get it straightened out. You know how hard it is for her to say no to me."

Mia groaned. "Think much of yourself, horse man?"

He pulled her onto his lap and kissed her fully. "Yeah. 'Cause of you."

Kyle made a retching sound. "You have officially become whipped. Congrats."

"Worth every lash," Ethan threw back.

Kyle rolled to his feet. "Let me grab the rest of my stuff. Can I take you both out to dinner tonight? I'm looking forward to going into town."

"Sounds good," Ethan said.

"Great, why don't I—holy shit, what is that?"

He stared in shock at the giant creature that had just strolled out of the bedroom. The monster had crazy white feathers that stuck up in various directions from his massive head. Red, fat jowls hung under a wicked sharp beak. His body was a mottled, inky black. It must've been surprised by the new visitor, because his beady eyes seemed to widen in mirrored shock, and it let out a wild screech that froze Kyle to the spot. He drew his wings back, and his clawed feet scratched at the floor like a bull revving up. He launched himself across the room in a fowl attack.

Kyle was used to farm animals, but he had to admit, he had to tamp down the yelp that rose to his lips.

"Hei Hei! Stop that now!" Mia's voice whipped out. Magically, the creature halted just a step away.

Feathers bobbing up and down like mad, it let out a series of outraged squawks directed toward Mia.

"Don't talk back to me like that. Kyle is a friend, and he's staying here. Charging him is not appropriate behavior."

The creature thing regarded him with a touch of resentment, then headed toward Mia. He rubbed his head like a cat over her legs, making low screeches as his beak tried to peck at her feet.

She giggled, stroking his crazy feathers with pure affection. "Good boy. Did you enjoy your nap?"

Kyle's mouth dropped open. "What the hell is that thing?"

"A Polish chicken," Ethan said, shaking his head. "He was one of Harper's rescues, but the moment he saw Mia he fell in love. Now he's her slave for life."

"At least one of the men in my life is," she said, giving him a wink. "His feathers are very delicate, so in the winter he has to stay inside the house. Don't worry. He's cranky but completely manageable."

Ethan shot Kyle an amused look. "Hey, maybe he can be your new muse."

"Sure. How'd you know I'm writing a fowl romance?"

They both cracked up. Ethan was the brother he'd never had, and he enjoyed their quick regression into juvenile humor.

Mia groaned, rising from the sofa and grabbing his empty coffee cup. "I have one conference call, then we can head out. I'll leave you two to some male bonding time." With a grin, she headed toward the kitchen. Hei Hei raced after her as if terrified she'd disappear.

"He's a bit codependent," Ethan said.

"You think?" Kyle paused, staring at his friend. "You scored, dude. She's cool."

"I know. Not sure how I got so lucky, but I'm not dumb enough to fuck it up. Even though I was engaged before, I didn't know what love really was until I met Mia. Ever have that happen? Where you had this idea of how things should be, but you realize later you had it all wrong?"

He wished he could confide in Ethan about Ophelia. God knows his friend deserved every bit of happiness he'd found with Mia. Kyle craved that same type of fulfillment. Ophelia had been the only woman to give him a taste, and he'd lost her. Kyle winced and tried to push Ophelia out of his mind. "Yeah. That's why I'm excited about this new project. I need to figure some shit out."

"Well, I'm here if you need some help. Been down that road."

"I know you have." He paused. "I missed you, man."

"Back atcha. Now before I give you a big-ass pansy hug, get your stuff and let's set you up."

"Thanks."

Kyle headed to the car. For the first time in a long while, he felt the stirring of hope that everything would finally be different.

Chapter Four

"Tink, I'm begging you. Please help us out."

She bit back a groan and tried not to look at her brother's puppy-dog face.

Dammit.

He'd been insistent that he treat her out before she got slammed with guests, bribing her with the wickedly delicious homemade pasta at Lombardi's. It was one of her favorite restaurants in town. The pasta and bread machine worked overtime, and the rich scents of garlic, red sauce, and olives saturated the air.

She hadn't realized she'd be ambushed.

"You reap what you sow," she retorted, grabbing a hunk of Italian bread drizzled with olive oil. "I told you he couldn't stay at the inn, but you ignored me."

"Your sister's right," Mia interrupted, coming to her rescue. "If I had known about it, I would've warned you to sit down and have a talk, not invite him and figure it was all just going to work out. But now we have a problem." Her eyes glowed with worry. "Things are getting a bit . . . challenging."

Ethan glowered. "Challenging? We're dying over there, Tink. There's nowhere to sit anymore. He writes on his laptop on the couch, muttering stuff like some kind of whacko at all hours of the night."

"Well, he's a writer. He's always been that way when he's involved in a project."

Mia cleared her throat. "Yes. With more room, it would be fine. But there's the issue with one bathroom. Since there's not a lot of privacy—"

"Mia saw him naked!"

Ophelia choked on the bread. "What?"

Mia stroked her brother's shoulder as if soothing a wounded beast. "Not completely, baby. See, we started to do some renovation on the bathroom, and the door doesn't close properly. Wheezy and Bolt wanted to see him, so they bashed their heads against the door and it flew open—"

"And Mia saw him naked!"

Mia sighed. "I saw his rear. That's it. And it was probably more embarrassing for him than me."

"I doubt it. Mia can't get any work done because they're on top of each other, and he seems to emerge at midnight like some kind of wombat and eat everything in the damn refrigerator."

Ophelia winced. Yeah, Kyle was a bit of a night owl. He'd miss too many meals during the day because he'd be immersed in his work, then raid the fridge in a crazed orgy of food. She'd gotten used to it, but at the bungalow where every sound echoed, she bet it wasn't easy.

Not her problem. Not her problem.

She kept the mantra up and tried to concentrate on the perfect firmness of her ravioli with creamy ricotta cheese filling. "I'm really sorry, guys. Do you think he can stay with Harper?"

Their sister lived in a small apartment down the road from the horse stables. Her Spartan lifestyle lent itself perfectly to caring for and training the horses, since she preferred practically living at the stables rather than her own place.

Ethan shook his head. "Already checked with her. She likes Kyle, but isn't comfortable sharing her space. You know how she relishes her privacy and solitude."

Yeah, their sister was really only social with creatures who had four legs.

Ethan continued his entreaty. "I know you said you had some type of fight back in California. But that was what, eight years ago? We grew up with him. Why won't you be reasonable and give him a chance to make amends?"

"We don't want to push you or make you uncomfortable, though," Mia said firmly, forking into her salad. "It's none of our business why you don't want him to stay with you. If you don't want to change your mind, we respect that. Right, Ethan?"

"No." Her brother stabbed his fork in the air. "You're one of the most forgiving people I know, and it's time to put words into action. If you don't take pity on us all, Kyle is going to get seriously hurt."

Ophelia rolled her eyes. "Dramatic much?"

Mia shifted in her seat. "Umm, well there's one additional problem."

Wariness cut through her. "What is it?"

"Hei Hei hates him," Ethan said flatly.

Ophelia burst out laughing. "Funny."

"He's serious," Mia said. "I know it's crazy, but I think Hei Hei views Kyle as some type of intruder rather than a guest. Hei Hei is stressed out and always on guard. I think he's trying to protect me."

Ophelia reached for her wine and took a healthy gulp, thinking the situation was getting out of control. "You know he's all bark and no bite. He's never hurt anyone before."

"He bit Kyle's foot yesterday," Ethan said. "Just charged him and took a nip. Drew blood."

She gasped. "What? I can't believe this. Kyle grew up on a farm— animals love him."

"Not Hei Hei," Mia said glumly. "Between the dogs and my crazy chicken, we're having a hard time being in such close quarters—and it's only been four days. I don't think we can continue like this, but I don't want to tell Kyle to leave. This script is so important to him. Plus, Ethan said your mother treated him like family."

The misery in her voice choked Ophelia with guilt.

Oh, this was worse than she'd thought. How could she let Mia continue like this?

She'd just moved in with Ethan a few months ago and they were confronting so many changes together. They didn't need additional stress.

Ethan must have sensed her weakness, because he went straight to begging. "*Please* let Kyle stay with you. He can stay in his room. You'll hardly have to see him. You won't have to cook anything for him or treat him like a guest. Just let him hole up and write for three months. You'll never even know he's there."

Their hopeful gazes caused her steely resolve to tremble. The problem was that *she* would know he was there. His presence would haunt her on a regular basis, mess with her head. She couldn't admit the truth to her brother. Still, Mia was important to her, and this wasn't her problem—even if Ethan had been the one to get them all into this mess.

"I'll check the schedule and see what I can do," she finally said. "I'm completely full this weekend, though. I had two couples already scheduled, and then today I received a call from a group of skiers for a last-minute weekend trip. Great for business, but I'll be slammed for the next few days. Maybe next week I can try to work out an arrangement."

Mia reached across the table and squeezed her hands in gratitude. "That's all we're asking. Maybe he can stay with us if the inn gets over-booked. We can be like a backup."

"Just not a permanent residence," Ethan said.

"I'll check the schedule," she said again. "Maybe next week I can find him a room to write in during the day, and he can stay with you at night."

"That'd be great," Ethan said quickly, putting up his hands. "We decided to head to the city this weekend anyway, so Kyle will have the place to himself until we get back."

"How does Hei Hei feel about that arrangement?" Ophelia asked in amusement.

Mia winced. "He's going to be pissed at me. But I'll have Harper check in to make sure Hei Hei doesn't kill Kyle."

Ophelia laughed, silently cheering on the chicken's bad behavior.

Serves the man right for thinking he could just waltz into her home and declare he wanted to write his screenplay, expecting her to fall in line like she used to. *Hell, no. Not anymore.*

They were finally on her turf and playing by her rules.

She concentrated on her dinner. She figured she'd work something out with her brother when he returned, but no matter how bad she felt for him, Kyle Kimpton would *not* be staying permanently at her inn.

"Stop staring at me. I can't work."

Kyle glared at the chicken currently giving him the evil eye. His clawed foot scratched at the floor and his head feathers crooked to the right, reminding him of a Stephen King–inspired killer fowl.

He'd been trying to work on the script since Ethan and Mia left for the weekend, but between the dogs and crazy chicken and the small space, he couldn't get in the zone.

Muttering a curse, he got up from the too-saggy couch that swallowed his ass and walked to the window. Ethan said he'd talked to Ophelia, who was apparently finally considering his request. Something told him she was harboring a bigger grudge than he'd originally imagined.

It was going to get worse once she heard the news.

He'd been here almost a week already, and she refused to engage with him. The flowers he'd sent were met by a cool "thank you" and a closed door. His phone calls went unanswered.

How was he supposed to move forward with his work and their relationship when she wouldn't even talk to him?

Maybe he needed to woo her a bit. Try to convince her his presence wouldn't threaten her routine. Showing up on her doorstep and announcing he needed to stay for three months to write probably wasn't the best first move.

Decision made, he grabbed his coat and walked up toward the inn. He'd ask her out for lunch, or coffee. He'd be charming and apologize for his intrusion. He'd beg her to give him a few moments to talk.

Ophelia might have a feisty temper, but she also had a soft heart.

It was hard for him to imagine her turning away from a good grovel.

His shoes crunched over the snow, and he breathed in the sharp, clean air.

God, it felt good to be home.

His gaze swept over the thick woods and curving path that led to the horse barns and open meadow. Growing up around horses and farming had taught him to appreciate not only the beauty of nature but also the simple pleasures he'd forgotten in California. The satisfaction of cooking meals with fresh vegetables from the garden and eggs gathered from the chickens. The sense of freedom you get from galloping on a horse as the flash of green grass whipped underfoot. The pride of strained muscles and sweat-soaked skin after a hard day's work that was measured not by a pile of papers or a successful negotiation but hands-on effort. He'd run away from it all for the lure of something greater.

Funny. Now he wondered if he'd had the true prize all along.

Pushing the disturbing thought away, he climbed the porch steps and rang the bell. Squared his shoulders. Recited his speech in his mind.

It all went to hell once she opened the door.

"What do you want?" she asked with a fierce frown, lips pursed as if she'd tasted something bad. But the intimidating effect was completely ruined by the series of racking coughs that came right after. She covered her mouth with her arm. When she managed to lift her head again and try to glare at him, he caught the glassy look in her blue eyes and the stark paleness of her skin.

"You're sick," he said, immediately stepping past her and shutting the door behind him. He laid his hand on her forehead before she could jerk away. "And you have a fever."

"I'm fine. I took some cold meds."

He studied the slight shaking of her shoulders under the thick cardigan wrapped around her. "Baby, you may have the flu. You have to get to bed." The familiar endearment spilled from his lips before he could think.

"Don't call me that." But her voice came out weak, and was followed by another series of coughs. "I can rest later. I have a full house today and a million things to do. There's no time for me to be sick." She spun around as if trying to show him she had everything under control, then wobbled, her hands grasping for the wall as she scrambled for balance.

He caught her before she tumbled, his heart stopping at the lack of color in her cheeks and the burn of her overheated skin. With a growl, he scooped her up into his arms and marched down the hallway. "Where's your bedroom?"

"I don't need—"

"Bedroom," he commanded.

She gave a small humph and pointed to the last door on the right.

He walked in, quickly surveying the feminine space decorated in her favorite colors of powder blue and lemon yellow. It smelled of honey and lavender. He laid her down on the four-poster bed, ignoring her protests. "You can't take care of guests with a fever," he pointed out.

"You'll get them sick, plus spread germs everywhere. Is there someone I can call to help out?"

She blinked as if her vision were blurred, then shook her head. "No. I can get Aubrey to do the cleaning and laundry service, but usually Ethan or Mia or Harper would step in for the main functions like check-in, setting up guests' schedules, or cooking breakfast."

"Okay. I know Ethan and Mia are in the city. I'll call Harper."

"She's not here, either," she said. "She got an emergency call to pick up a rescue horse and won't be back till tomorrow." More coughs choked her throat. "It's okay. I'll put on a mask. Maybe Aubrey can pick up breakfast at the Market Food Pantry so I don't have to cook. I can do this."

Her effort to sit up was so pathetic, his heart squeezed. She'd always been a stubborn, determined creature about whatever task she put her mind to, refusing to admit defeat. It was another reason why he'd been so shocked when she gave up her dreams of singing to run away, bury herself again in the safe world they'd both worked so hard to escape. But that was a discussion for later.

Right now, she needed his help.

"You're going to stay in bed and get better," he said, tugging back the quilt and adjusting the pillow. "I've got this. I'll take care of the guests and whatever else is needed."

Shock widened her eyes. "What? You can't run an inn. I'm expecting a group of ten skiers today, and I already have two couples staying here. You'd need to do check-ins, make dinner reservations, cook breakfast, put out afternoon snacks, do turn-down service . . . No, you can't. I'm fine."

"You're not fine, and I can handle it." She was so weak, he was able to easily shift her under the blankets and tug them over her. "If you allow yourself to burn off the fever and get some sleep, you'll probably be back in full force tomorrow. I grew up watching your mother, remember? The tasks are simple enough as long as I'm organized. I can handle it."

She snorted. "You have no clue," she muttered under her breath. "Mom made it look easy."

"Ophelia, if you don't rest, you're going to end up in the hospital. Can you afford to be out for a whole week?"

"No!"

"Then let me do this for you. Please."

A glimmer of raw emotion flickered in her eyes, but she quickly broke her gaze and turned her head away in retreat.

After a few moments, she turned back, her tone all business. "In the top drawer, you'll find a piece of paper with all the tasks for check-in listed. I have everything saved in Excel with the guest information, credit card numbers, assigned rooms, and personal preferences—including any food allergies. All restaurant and activity reservations should also be included. Tea and cookies go out in the main parlor at three p.m. It's Amanda and Michael's anniversary, so I ordered flowers and chocolate-covered strawberries to be delivered. You need to set up the dining room at five p.m. with a bottle of champagne and the crystal flutes. I've got some frozen scones prepared, so if you're able to pair them with bacon and eggs in the morning, I think we can get away with a basic breakfast. Although it might be nice to have fresh fruit, and Michael specifically requested bagels, so you'll need to pick that up from the Market at six a.m. Kyle?"

His head spun from the list of instructions, but he schooled his expression and nodded with confidence. "Yes?"

"I'm going to throw up now."

He jumped into action. Guiding her quickly out of bed, he got her to the bathroom and held back her tangled hair as she got sick, even as she desperately tried to wave him off. By the time she was back in bed, he'd retrieved a glass of lemon water, another round of meds, and a cool washcloth. He placed a bucket by her side.

She rolled her head on the pillow and groaned. "First you see me in yoga pants with messy hair. Now I'm sick and disgusting. Fate sucks."

He laughed, thinking she wouldn't be so open if it weren't for her fever. He smoothed the cloth over her damp forehead and tucked a wayward curl behind her ear. The years fell away, bringing him back to a nest of memories: the time she drank too much champagne at their very first Hollywood party and he took care of her during the awful night of bed spins; when she twisted her ankle wearing new designer heels and he carried her twenty blocks to the ER because he couldn't get a cab; the time she cried after speaking with her mom and got homesick so he cuddled her in bed while feeding her Hershey's Kisses. The way she'd leaned on him gave him a sense of purpose he'd never been able to duplicate. She was the only woman who made him want to be his best and feel whole.

God knows, he'd forgotten how that felt after so many years.

He decided to take advantage of her honesty while he had the chance. Keeping his tone light, he said, "Those yoga pants were sexier than a tight miniskirt. And you were always the most beautiful without any type of makeup or fancy clothes."

She made a face. "Ugh, you are so lying to me. You're used to those Hollywood chicks now."

He cupped his hand to her hot cheek, his voice husky with emotion. "I don't lie. One of the things I loved most was your vulnerability. The way you opened up only to me. It was a gift that meant everything, and there hasn't been another woman I've even wanted to be as close to as I was with you."

The power of his confession broke through, surprising both of them with its raw force. A soft gasp escaped her bee-stung lips. Her eyes softened and, for one perfect moment, it was like nothing had changed since they first looked at one another and realized they'd become much more than friends.

She opened her mouth . . . and fell into a coughing fit.

His hand dropped from her cheek and he eased back, giving them both space. "I'll come back and check on you soon. Try to rest."

He left her, his chest tight with too many emotions he didn't have the time to examine.

He had an inn to run.

Chapter Five

Within fifteen minutes of the ski guests arriving, Kyle realized he was fucked.

He'd headed back to the bungalow to grab his laptop, figuring he'd have plenty of time to work before check-in. When he'd returned, he'd spent some time familiarizing himself with the computer programs and customer requests. Aubrey had thankfully swept in and made the beds, taken care of the laundry and bathrooms, and prepped the rooms. Ophelia was resting after the second dose of meds. He'd felt ready for the new guests' arrival, even acknowledging a touch of ego regarding how easily he had taken charge.

Running an inn truly wasn't that difficult.

Then four p.m. happened.

The skiers swarmed the place with pumped-up testosterone and male juvenile humor that Kyle would have appreciated if he wasn't the innkeeper. They stomped in with giant dripping-wet boots and cases of beer, jostling each other and collapsing immediately in the common area in front of the fireplace. He pegged them as being in their early twenties and longtime friends. They were respectful—but loud. He was barely able to get them all registered since they had little interest in paying attention to his requests, and by the time he'd organized all their luggage into their respective rooms, they'd begun clamoring for snacks.

At least they were polite. He didn't know how he'd fare with a bunch of jerks, so he was sure he'd be able to handle them with some good old-fashioned assertiveness and organization.

He worked in the kitchen for a while, getting bottles of soda and a small variety of snacks together, including nachos and a decent-size appetizer plate filled with crackers, cheese, and prosciutto. Ophelia definitely had a fully stocked refrigerator, which made prep a lot easier.

The loud roar of approval when he entered the room made him grin. He set up the table, pouring drinks and chatting about the ski conditions on the mountains. He left them relaxing with the television on while he went to clean up.

Five minutes later, one of the guys popped his head in. "Hey, man, you think we can have more snacks?"

Kyle stared at him. "You guys finished them already?"

"Yeah, they were good." He grinned, his surfer hair flipping into his eyes. "We'll take anything you got."

He hesitated. "Well, we provide snacks like tea and cookies, but for dinner you're on your own. How about I get you some takeout menus? We can get some platters or pizza delivered."

The guy's eyes lit up. "Yeah, man, that's perfect. You got a hot tub here?"

"Sorry, no gym or hot tub."

"No prob. This is still way more rad than some rank hotel room, and it was way too pricey to stay at the main lodge."

"We're glad to have you all here."

Kyle got the menus and set them up, gathered all the empty dishes, then went back to the kitchen.

"Oh, hello? Can you tell me where Ophelia is?" a kind voice echoed from the hallway.

He dried his hands and walked out, finding an older couple looking at the rowdy group taking up the main room. One glance pegged them as the Rileys.

He motioned them to the back, where it was quieter. "I'm sorry, Mrs. Riley, but she got sick. Think it's the flu. My name is Kyle, and I'm a good friend of Ophelia's. I'll be helping her out until she's a bit better."

"Oh, that poor thing! Such a wicked flu season this year," she clucked, her eyes peering over her silver glasses. "It's just that we were going to go to dinner tomorrow night at Crystal's, and Ophelia was kind enough to make us the reservation, but we'd like to switch it to tonight and do Galveston's tomorrow. Can you make those arrangements for us?"

He blinked. Ophelia did stuff like that, too? "Um, sure. What time works?"

"Six is perfect. Thank you, dear. We'll be napping for a while. Can you make sure the boys keep it down?"

"Yes, not a problem."

Her husband gave an approving nod and guided his wife back upstairs.

A roar from the main room hurt his ears, so he attacked that problem first. "Hey, guys, you gotta keep it down for the other guests," he said loudly, trying to shout over the blasting game. "And lower that a bit. Sorry, but we have to respect the other people staying here."

"Sure, dude! No worries!" One of the guys cranked the TV volume lower, then handed Kyle the takeout menus. "We marked our orders down. Can you just charge everything to the room? Oh, and make sure they give us extra sauce—they always skimp on the sauce."

The whoop of approval from the guys cut off his initial reaction to balk at having to handle their food orders. He bit back his annoyance, trying to make sure he gave extraordinary customer service, and walked back into the kitchen.

Oh, right, reservation changes.

He made the calls, but Crystal's couldn't change the reservation and asked him a bunch of questions he didn't know how to answer. He told them he'd call them back, then walked up the stairs to knock on the couple's door and ask them if seven p.m. was acceptable.

His hand paused on the door. He was hoping he wouldn't wake them up from their nap. Then he heard it.

Low moaning. A groan.

"Yes, like that. Yes!"

Backing up and shaking his head to get the image out of his brain, he realized the nice older couple wasn't napping, but having wild sex.

Holy crap. This was a bleachable moment.

Shuddering, he went back downstairs and made the food delivery order, grabbing one of the credit cards on file to pay. Then he called Crystal's and booked the reservation for seven p.m., figuring he'd tell the Rileys later. When it was safe.

"Oh, hi. Can I talk to Ophelia?"

He bit back a sigh and smiled at the Porcinis—a younger, hip couple addicted to winter activities in the Hudson Valley. They were regular customers, and he knew Ophelia treated them like royalty from the detailed notes stored on her computer. "I'm sorry, Ophelia is sick. My name is Kyle. I'll be happy to help you with anything you need until she's better."

"Oh, I hope it's not the flu." The fit, attractive brunette frowned with worry along with her husband. "I'm so sorry, we don't want to bother you."

"Not a bother. What can I do?"

The husband—Ted—spoke up. "Ophelia set us up with a snow-mobiling tour tomorrow. She said she'd pack us a special lunch for the day—I already told her to put it on our bill—but we'd like to go up early to the mountain to catch the sunrise. We wondered if we could have breakfast served a bit earlier than usual."

A bad feeling came over him. "How early?"

"Five a.m. But if that's an issue, we can skip it. We don't want to stress her out if she's sick."

Holy hell, how many personal requests did Ophelia take care of on a regular basis? No wonder she had so many repeat customers.

She made everyone feel special, no matter who they were or what made them happy. Not many people had the type of gifts it takes to run a successful bed-and-breakfast.

He needed to keep her high standards of service while she was out sick, so he manned up and swore he'd make it work. "No problem. I can have your breakfast ready early, and a lunch packed to go."

Ted shook his hand. "Thanks so much. I can't tell you how much we appreciate it."

He watched the couple disappear, wincing at the still-too-loud men cheering in the main room. He realized it was going to be a long night.

A very long night.

He got back to work.

On Sunday morning, Kyle looked at the kitchen. It looked like there had been an explosion in there. Pots and pans lined the sink, the dishwasher was already packed, and there were stacks of Tupperware half-filled with leftovers that needed to be sorted. Dirty silverware littered the counters. In the formal dining room, food was stuck on the carpets and empty cups were all over. Muddy footprints trekked through the hallways.

Fuck, he was exhausted.

He refilled his coffee and tried to rally. The guests were out for the day, so he just had to clean the kitchen. And the bedrooms. And the bathrooms. Aubrey planned to come back tomorrow.

He just had to get through today. Maybe he'd even have time to take a quick nap.

He'd slept in the chair in Ophelia's room, and they'd both had a rough night. She'd gotten up a few times to be sick but finally fell into a deep sleep. He hoped the bad stuff was behind her. Of course, he'd been up before dawn to take care of the special breakfast and lunch he'd promised Ted. By the time that was done, some of the guys had drifted downstairs, sniffing around for food and coffee, and it was game on.

It'd only been twenty-four hours, but he felt like he'd been working a week.

This job was no joke. There was no way he'd be getting any writing done this weekend.

He glanced at the clock. Time to give Ophelia the next round of meds. He heated up the kettle and fixed a cup of tea, another glass of water with lemon, and some dry toast. Rummaging through the cabinets, he found a tray and loaded it all up.

Easing into Ophelia's bedroom, he set the tray on the bureau, tiptoed to the bed, and leaned over.

"Holy shit!" She jerked up in surprise.

He jolted back, almost falling on his ass.

Hair a mess of tangles sticking up around her head, skin still damp and flushed from the fever, a dirty T-shirt hanging off one shoulder, she blinked wildly like a night creature awakened by a predator. "You scared me," she croaked out.

"I think you scared me more."

She groaned and flopped back on the pillow. "Sorry, I was having some type of crazy dream. I got stuck in the Willy Wonka factory, and they were putting me through the taffy machine."

His lips twitched. "At least it's better than the one you used to have."

A pained laugh escaped. "The one where I'm a female Ben Stiller in *Zoolander* and the only way to save the world is to walk the runway like a badass, but I trip and fall and rip my skirt and everyone sees me half-naked? Still have that one, too."

"Always wondered why you never wore underwear on the runway."

"I was a slut."

He laughed. "Every time you got stressed you'd wake up screaming from that dream."

"I'd rather be in a taffy machine than naked in front of a judging crowd." Her smile was quickly wiped out by a fit of coughing.

He moved toward the bed and laid a hand on her forehead. "Still warm. We should get you into some dry clothes. These are damp."

"Forget it. I know it's just a plan to seduce me."

His lips twitched in a smile. "Baby, as much as I want to see you naked again, you're too sick for even me to get excited. I'll help get you into clean pj's, and then you can try and eat some toast."

"I already told you not to call me that, and I can do it myself. I have to get back to work anyway." She pointed to the bottom drawer. "Can you just grab me some sweats and a T-shirt?"

He pulled out a cozy fleece set and watched her ease to the side of the bed, brows knit with determination. He tamped back a frustrated sigh. She was never one to surrender gracefully. The woman would fight with spit and sass till her dying breath.

She slowly stood up, took a few steps, and floundered.

"That's it." He swept her up into his arms, carried her to the bathroom, and set her gently back on her feet. "Turn around. I promise I won't look."

The pallor of her skin and the glassiness of her eyes softened her mulish expression. "I'm fine."

"You're not fine."

She fell into another coughing fit, and he gently moved her so her back faced him. With quick, methodical motions, he lifted her shirt over her head and replaced it within seconds. Before she had time to protest, he'd already tugged her sweats over her hips, leaning down to gently untangle the fabric from her legs and replace them with the new pair. He made sure to keep his gaze firmly averted from the tiny scrap of black lace that covered her. Soon, she was fully dressed.

He turned her back around. "See? That wasn't so bad, right? Let's get you back to bed."

He carried her back and propped her up on a few pillows. Then he sat on the edge of the bed and brought the mug of tea to her lips. She took a sip, closing her eyes with pleasure. "Thank you. That's good."

"Welcome. Listen, you need to rest again today. You can't work with a fever."

"How bad is it out there?" she asked, biting down on her lip. "Are the skiers a lot to handle? Is Aubrey coming back?"

"The skiers are fine—nice guys. Aubrey's coming tomorrow morning."

Her eyes widened with panic. "Oh my God, I have to clean ten rooms! I forgot she couldn't make it today."

"I'll do it. Here, drink more and take a few bites. Let's see if this stays down."

She moaned through the motions of eating and drinking her tea. "This is a nightmare—do you know how to prep a room properly?"

He shrugged. "Sure. Clean it up and make the bed."

"Yes, but make sure everything is organized, and the bathroom is spotless, and the toilet paper and tissues are refilled. Use that vanilla-coconut scented spray if it's a bit funky, and make sure you vacuum."

"Got it. Take more meds so you can get some sleep."

She swallowed her pill and coughed. Kyle could tell she had no energy. She lay limply back, barely able to keep her eyes open. "I'm so sorry," she said. "I never meant for you to get stuck with all this."

He stroked her hair back from her forehead and dabbed some lingering crumbs from her lips with the napkin. "I could never be stuck with you," he said quietly. "I like taking care of you."

"Don't be nice to me," she murmured. Her head lolled drunkenly as exhaustion overtook her.

He pulled the covers up to her chin and edged the extra pillow to the side so she'd be more comfortable to sleep.

"Why?"

Her soft voice drifted to his ears in a caress. "Because I can't fall for you again."

Then she closed her eyes and slept.

Kyle stared at her for a long time, his heart squeezing in agony. God, he'd never wanted to hurt her. He wanted a second chance to heal her pain and prove she could trust him. It would be a long road ahead, but being able to help her this weekend was a first step.

He pressed a kiss to her forehead and headed back to work.

Five hours later, he collapsed on the couch. His muscles ached from bending over and scrubbing toilets, and the damn vacuum cleaner had gotten jammed up, so that took him over an hour to fix. The skiers were a bunch of slobs, and cleaning up their crap was a nightmare.

But the inn was finally tidy and polished. The beds were all made. The kitchen was spotless. He'd booked a few reservations, updated the schedule, and baked some cookies for the afternoon snack.

Thank God the evening would be clear.

The guys would probably stay late at the lodge for dinner and drinks, and he'd confirmed the Rileys' and Porcinis' dinner reservations in town.

Maybe he could sneak in an hour or two of writing before checking back on Ophelia. Or hell, maybe he should nap.

He'd just set his computer up and opened his document when the front door flung open. Ten guys stomped in with their equipment and muddy boots, laughing and talking loudly.

No.

No, no, no . . .

"Hey, dude! The mountain is shit—a bunch of ice. We spent all afternoon partying at the bar. We just want to hang the rest of the night."

"Let's put on the game and chill. Should we order pizza?"

"Nah, how about Mexican? Kyle, my man, can you help set us up?"

"What's that smell? Damn, are those cookies?"

"I love cookies! Can we have them now, with some coffee? This place is the bomb!"

All ten guys stared at him like puppy dogs, eager for the fun to begin.

Son of a bitch. How had Ophelia and her mother made this job look so damn easy?

Kyle stifled a groan and shut his laptop. He forced his lips into a happy innkeeper smile. "Sure. No problem. I'll take care of everything."

Chapter Six

Ophelia sat on the edge of her bed and moaned.

What had she done?

Opened her door to the enemy and allowed him full reign. After boldly claiming he'd never be welcome to stay, she had let Kyle take over the inn, tuck her in, give her meds, and wipe her brow. He'd slept in the chair the last two nights, refusing to leave in case she needed something, just like a caring husband.

Ex-husband, she reminded herself. What a mess. Why couldn't he have been a jerk?

She'd expected him to be judgmental about her decision to take over her mother's inn. God knows, for years he'd told her staying in their small town was a trap. He'd spun dreams of Hollywood fame and glory as the only route to true freedom.

But not once had he said anything derogatory. Obviously, he cared about doing a good job, which was way more than she ever expected.

"How are you feeling?"

She looked up. He wore dark-wash jeans and a Tommy Hilfiger red plaid shirt with the sleeves rolled up. His golden hair was tousled. The scruff hugging his mouth and jaw was a bit rough and piratelike, giving him a sexy, dangerous look.

His deep-green eyes met her gaze and pulled her in; his lush lashes only added to the shocking intensity of contrasting color. He leaned against the doorframe, the denim stretching tight over his powerful thighs, arms crossed over his broad chest. He simmered with masculine energy and a delicious potency that made her glad she was sitting down. Her body zinged to life after a long starvation period. She tried to beat it back into complacency and cleared her throat.

"Much better."

He strode in with a panther's grace and rested the back of his palm on her cheek. "Fever broke," he murmured, his gaze sweeping over her disheveled appearance. "Still holding down the tea and toast?"

"Yes. I think I'm past the worst of it. I took a shower, and I'm ready to get back to work. I can't believe it's Monday. I missed the whole weekend."

His golden brows slammed together. "Don't push too hard. I've already handled breakfast, checked out the Rileys and Porcinis, and confirmed what time Aubrey is coming to prep rooms. It looks like your next guests arrive tomorrow, so you should be able to have a light day."

She blinked, trying to gather her composure. "You did all that already?"

"Yes, and I've got a new appreciation for your job. I had no idea guests could be so demanding."

His rough admission softened her resolve to be distant. "Still no issues with the skiers?"

"Like guys at a frat house on vacation. Good guys, though—just needed to keep on top of them. They almost broke that antique lamp thing in the dining room. Guess they thought it was a good idea to test their strength by body-slamming one another. Or maybe it was just the beer."

"Yeah, I've gotten a lot of practice at being a den mother plus hostess plus substitute mom."

She moved to the edge of the bed, but he suddenly kneeled in front of her.

"I don't want you to overdo it. You don't handle being sick well," he said.

A ghost of a smile touched her lips. "Hey, I'm nothing compared to you. Remember the 'man cold' incident?"

He winced. "It wasn't just a cold. It was the swine flu. I could have died."

Her smile widened. "You stayed in bed for three days and never had a fever or a sniffle."

"Your memory is selective. I threw up."

A giggle burst from her throat. "You gagged twice and proclaimed yourself deathly ill. You made me give you a bell!"

He looked affronted. "It was the only way I could be sure you knew if I needed something."

"Oh, I knew all right. You rang that damn thing a million times, asking for water, the remote, an extra pillow, fluffier blankets, tissues—"

"Worked fine until you broke it," he grumbled.

"You mean when I threw it against the wall and declared your sick days over? Best decision I ever made."

"Some caretaker you were."

They grinned at each other. He reached out and touched her cheek, but this time it wasn't to test her temperature. "God, I've missed your smile."

Her breath strangled in her chest. She tried to rally her defenses and stiffened, pulling back.

His hand dropped, and he stood back up.

Why did he look so regretful and pained? He had no right. No right to make her feel such things after she'd locked them tightly away and thrown away the key.

She forced herself to meet his gaze and say the words. "Well, thank you for helping me. I don't know what I would have done."

"Thank you for letting me."

She eased to her feet, relieved her legs held well. "I'm sure you have a lot of writing to catch up on, and you probably haven't slept well. I'll text Ethan and let him know you're on your way back and—"

"Ophelia, let me stay."

She froze. The soft words wrapped around her like a cocoon, squeezing away her resistance.

He stepped in front of her, hands raised in surrender. "I know you don't want me here, but I'm asking again. I promise you can set the rules, and I'll respect your privacy." A touch of misery wound through his voice. "I feel bad about Hei Hei hating me, and Mia seeing me naked, and not being able to work. If I can just get one room, I'll write my script and stay out of your hair. I swear."

Dammit.

Ethan's and Mia's pleas from last week mingled with Kyle's in her mind. She closed her eyes, trying to think.

How could she keep saying no? Even though Ethan was at fault for lying, she couldn't let them go on like this. Plus, he'd taken care of her.

The memory hit hard: him tucking her in, feeding her toast, smoothing her brow, changing her clothes. He'd treated her with a tenderness and care that couldn't be faked.

God knows, it brought up an array of emotions she didn't want to explore. Plus, he'd taken care of the inn with respect and proficiency—giving up his own time to write. Three months. One room.

She could structure a daily agenda to make sure she stayed away from him, especially if he was writing all the time. He tended to immerse himself in a project and disappear. If that still held true, the weeks could fly by painlessly. He'd spend time with Ethan, and she had guests to be her buffer in case her body did something stupid like get all melty and hot for some good old-fashioned, ex-lover sex.

Three months. One room. Then he'd be officially out of her life.

She prayed she wasn't making a huge mistake.

"Fine. You can stay."

"Thank you."

His sweet smile made her breath hitch. She'd always loved his smile. With his dimple, burnished hair tumbling over his forehead, and vivid green eyes, he reminded her of a fallen angel. Too bad she knew he was really the devil.

She reminded herself she had to stay strong or he'd find a secret tunnel and slink under the solid wall she'd built around her heart. "But there are rules. If you break them, you're out of here."

"Got it. I'm listening."

"Do you want to go grab your stuff first, before you get settled?"

He shot her a sheepish grin. "Ethan already dropped my luggage off. I'd texted to let him know you were better, and he packed up my shit. He must have figured you were going to let me move in. Guess he was a bit overeager."

She bit her lip and tried not to be amused. "Fine. Let's head to the kitchen."

She marched through the casual dining room, where she cooked for her family, and into the sunny yellow kitchen, hoping she didn't wobble. The place was outfitted with professional-grade appliances so she could bake and cook for a large crew, and she'd installed large granite countertops, but the cheerful daffodil curtains, oak flooring, and endless knickknacks lining the counters and the top of the stained-pine cabinets gave off a cozy air.

Immediately, she noticed a full pot of fresh coffee, a clean counter, and no dishes lying in the sink. Her heart gave a twerk, but she refused to let it go full Miley Cyrus. She told herself it wasn't a big deal that he'd cleaned the entire kitchen.

She went to the pine wall hatch, unlocked it, and took out a brass key ring. "I'll give you the Windsor Room since it has a large desk and work area. There's a refrigerator and mini microwave for your convenience. Fran's new Market is great for fresh food, and there's always pizza or Mexican delivery if you want to eat here."

"Yeah, I stopped by the Market and talked to Fran. She wanted to come check on you, but I told her to give you some time to get back on your feet. She's sending over a tray of lasagna tomorrow in case you're not able to cook. Also said she'd be happy to send me dinner any night if I'm on deadline."

"Oh. Great." She tried not to dwell on the way he'd gotten himself situated in town so quickly. "Aubrey regularly comes on Mondays. You're welcome to use the washer and dryer in the basement any other day."

"Oh, Aubrey said she'd do my stuff on Mondays."

Ophelia blinked. "What?"

"Yeah, she was really sweet when we spoke on the phone. She said it wasn't a problem to do my laundry with the regular stuff. Did you know her mother is a huge fan of my movies?"

She gritted her teeth and hung on to her patience. Another woman he was able to charm immediately—and this one did laundry. "How fortunate for you."

"Isn't it?"

He had no idea she was being sarcastic. By this point, she was losing her edge. She handed him the key and crossed her arms in front of her chest. "Here are the rules. Number one: You're out on April first. That's when my spring season begins, and I'll need every spare room."

"Fine."

"Number two: You get breakfast every morning, but you're on your own the rest of the day. Don't come sniffing around expecting me to cook dinner or cater to you on the days I have off. I also don't want you wandering around at all hours making yourself at home in my kitchen and private rooms. That means no midnight snacks. You stay in your room, in the public dining room, or on the porch."

"Of course. Would you let me take you out to dinner now and then?"

"No. I also don't want you mixing socially with any of my guests."

He cocked his head to study her. "Why? I've already met and taken care of a bunch."

Because she needed to keep her distance, and any contact with her guests might make them seem like a couple. Because deep inside, she still craved him.

But she couldn't admit to her weakness for him, so she kept her answer short. "'Cause I said so."

His lips twitched. "Got it. Anything else?"

"Yes." She regarded him intently. "Rule number three: I need you to keep away from me. No touching. No flirting. No trying to seduce me."

His eyes flared with heat. The energy in the room tightened. An excruciating awareness pulsed between them. "What if you'd like it?" he asked softly.

"I won't."

His voice dropped to a sexy growl. "That was a challenge if I ever heard one. You always liked when I touched you. In fact, you craved it. Used to purr like a kitten when I'd stroke your hair or your back. Remember?"

Yes.

She remembered every detail. The way his hot, rough palm would slide over her skin to trace her freckles, his tongue following in a sexy game of connect the dots. The way he'd push her hair back to bare her nape, sink his teeth into the vulnerable curve where her neck met shoulder, and hold her when she shivered uncontrollably.

Oh, she already knew she'd like it. Would like everything he wanted to do to her. But her goal was simple: get through the next three months unscathed.

That would mean no *anything*.

"That was a long time ago," she said stiffly. "There have been others in between to take your place . . . and the memories."

Temper ignited his face, and a raw possessiveness flamed from him. "Are you seeing someone right now?" he asked, his features tight.

Oh, how she wanted to lie—but she never could.

"Not right now," she said. "Still, my rules are nonnegotiable. I'm not looking to ignite something that's better left alone. You may not believe it, but I happen to love the way my life is right now. I have no intention of changing anything."

He regarded her with intensity. He'd always had a unique ability to dive deep inside a person and linger. Maybe it was the creative soul within, but he used to enjoy getting to know a person beneath the surface, to learn their quirks and tendencies, their dreams and fears. He'd always been a better listener than talker. It had been another thing the show business industry had managed to change in him. Every time she'd desperately begged him to listen, he'd talk over her, tell her how great everything was, leave her with a kiss on the forehead and alone in a room with an aching emptiness. He'd learned how to skate on the surface and pretend things would be okay, just like Hollywood taught him.

But right now, the old Kyle was back. He seemed to be content to study her body language and linger before speaking. "You don't miss singing?" he asked.

"Not like you think. And I do sing."

"When you're alone. With no one around. I asked Ethan about it, you know."

"Asked him what?"

"If you performed locally anywhere or had created a demo. Hell, nowadays you could post something on YouTube, and it may go viral. You have a gift. But Ethan said he hasn't heard you sing since he's been back."

"I don't need to make money from my gift like you do."

Slowly, he nodded, but she sensed it was already too late. He'd looked deep enough to spot the shred of regret that still lingered.

"Fair enough. I'll agree to your rules. I won't touch or seduce you—unwillingly."

She glared at that clever twist of words but took it. She'd never ask for anything from him anyway. "Then I guess you've scored yourself a room of one's own. Here's hoping we won't see much of each other—unwillingly. It's the last door on the right."

His grin was totally masculine and devastatingly handsome. "Yeah, you're definitely feeling better. I always enjoyed your sarcasm—it's a lost art form."

He sauntered out of the kitchen like he'd won the round and he was just allowing her to believe she was in control.

Damn him.

Ophelia leaned against the wall and tried to catch her breath. Her illness had made her vulnerable, allowed him to touch her and take care of her, but it wouldn't happen again.

She had to make sure she was focused. Cool. Calm. Distant. She'd put up a wall of ice so thick and so deep, not even a *Game of Thrones* dragon could destroy it.

No problem.

Chapter Seven

Kyle stared at the blank page before him on his screen.

His notes surrounded him in a state of organized chaos. He had his favorite Mets baseball hat on backward, and his crappy sweats that were too soft and comfortable to ever be thrown out. His thermos was filled with piping-hot coffee. The wind whistled through the thick panes of glass in an attempt to batter its way in, and outside, a covering of pure white glistened, untouched and unspoiled, over the earth.

The room Ophelia had set him up in was perfect. The décor was a little less feminine than some of the other rooms, with rich golds and navy accents. The writing desk had plenty of room for his laptop and papers and was set against the window so he had a nice view. The mahogany bed was massive, and the attached bath was modern and pleasing in clean white and blue. A small brick fireplace set the mood, paired with a chaise lounge in deep velvet. It was everything he'd hoped his home for the next three months could be.

Dragging in a breath, he refocused his attention on his script. After days of building character backgrounds, playing with plot, and writing a few scenes, he'd taken a look and realized it sucked.

All of it. Well, most of it.

He'd been forced to save everything in a new folder called "Crappy Deleted Stuff" and start all over.

He took a sip of coffee and regarded the page.

Why was writing still so fucking hard?

He'd been a word scribbler since the moment he discovered books, and he'd known early on he was meant to be a storyteller. He'd read voraciously, but there was something about movies that always got to him. When he figured out there was a job called a screenwriter, and that those people actually created the stories on the big screen, his gut had stirred with purpose. That was going to be him.

Fast forward almost fifteen years later, and he was terrified his career was over—especially after this last year, when all the good words seemed to have dried up.

He should have this shit down by now. Be able to whip up a story— taking all the magic and perfection from the thoughts in his head and get them on the page.

Instead, it felt like it was his first script every time he sat his ass down in the chair.

It was a stupid career. He'd counsel people to stay far away. It made you into a muttering maniac, messed with your sleep, forced you to binge on junk food and caffeine, and drove you stark raving mad. His only purpose was to create imaginary people with the goal of manipulating moviegoers into believing they were real.

God, who was he kidding? He fucking loved his job.

He pecked out the first line of the script.

It was a dark and stormy night . . .

Good ol' Snoopy.

He rubbed his head and tried to get in the zone. The beginning was always the hardest for him. And sometimes that damn saggy middle. But once he got 80 percent in, writing was a piece of cake.

The cursor remained still in a quiet taunt.

Fuck you.

The hook was everything. It needed to enrapture a producer and audience. Set up an interesting premise. But did he begin at the beginning, or the end? Sometimes a tease was better—a bit of a spoiler. Sometimes it was better to hammer the audience over the head right away.

He deleted the first line, then tapped his fingers against the desk. After penning endless action movies filled with spectacular car crashes and bromances that rivaled some classics, he'd finally made a name for himself. Critics liked his sharp dialogue and banter, and he'd forged solid connections with a bunch of high-powered executives, producers, and directors in Hollywood.

But his muse was done with the blockbuster action adventures. Had been done for a while now, he'd just been fighting the inevitable. There was another story that needed to be told by his muse: a story with an ending he craved to find out for himself. But he hadn't been brave—or stupid—enough to take the leap.

A love story. One based on childhood friendship and first love. A story that spanned the distance between a small upstate farm and the glitzy land of dreams in Hollywood. It would bring the audience on a journey of hopeful promises, blinding fame, broken hearts, and aching loss.

He just didn't know how it ended. Yet.

An image of Ophelia drifted before him.

Why had taking care of her last weekend felt so right? How had the years and space between them drifted away to nothing, leaving him with an aching heart and sense of loss?

He'd watched over her as she slept, tormented by the past and what he'd left behind.

He knew the connection between them still burned. She'd definitely reacted when he mentioned their past physical intimacy. But it had been that vulnerable flash in her baby blues that convinced him she still had feelings for him, deeper than the physical. He wanted to remind her of how good they'd been together. Every day, he would have a chance to stir up a memory. Every day, he'd be able to learn all the ways she'd changed.

He'd fight to get her back.

Except, the past few days, she'd stuck to her word and barely acknowledged his presence. If they passed each other on the way in or out, she nodded and kept walking. He'd tried several times to talk to her, but her gaze inspected him as if he was a bug under a microscope instead of the man who used to make her shatter and scream. Then she'd coldly dismiss him. He heard her consistently clattering around downstairs, always involved in some type of project. Every time he begged her to give him a few minutes to discuss something important, she shut him down, saying she was busy.

It was humiliating.

And he still hadn't told her the truth.

Guilt stirred. Somehow, he had to force her to listen. Maybe everything would change once he revealed his discovery. To him, the whole thing was a sign that they had a shot at a second chance.

But first, he needed to concentrate on the mess in front of him.

The blank page.

Kyle shifted in the chair, closed his eyes, and sought his muse. He'd learned through years of hard work the temptress sometimes decided not to show. When that happened, he would write anyway, vomiting garbage on the page until something worth saving appeared. Usually, she got annoyed that he was doing it alone and nosily inserted herself into the process to help him come up with something decent. Eventually, something good. And finally, something great.

The fucked-up, glamorous life of a writer.

After waiting the proper amount of time and realizing she was taking a winter nap, he opened his eyes and let his instincts take over.

This story began with a young girl and boy in love.

They were running away from home, toward fame and fortune.

They lay back on the soft carpet of green grass and stared up at the stars. He didn't care about the occasional crawly bug on his body, or the swarm of gnats above them, or the threat of ticks feasting on his skin. His focus had narrowed to the girl pressed against him. Her red-gold hair spilling over his chest and her fingers entwined with his drove such earthly irritations away. She smelled of lavender and honey, a mixture of the ingredients she mixed for the body cream she sold at the farmers' market. He wondered if any expensive perfume could make him as crazed, like a horse ready to breed.

How many years had she annoyed the shit out of him? Sure, they were friends, but she was a girl and always busting in on the cool stuff he was doing with her brother, who was his best friend. Everything they did she insisted she could do just as well, until she was more tomboy than girl. By the time he'd reached adolescence, she was just part of the fabric of his life.

Was she sixteen when he finally realized she was beautiful? Her lips always looked like they'd been stung by a bee, and those jeans and T-shirts she wore seemed so much tighter, emphasizing sudden ripe curves that kept seizing his gaze. Suddenly, those fiery blue eyes held a different heat—one he wanted to delve into and explore. Her brother didn't seem to notice the strange new vibe in the air when they squeezed into the cracked vinyl booth at the diner in town or worked side by side in the barn, sweat sticking to their clothes and the scent of horses, hay, and hormones hanging thickly in the air.

He wondered what she'd taste like. He wondered how smooth her pale skin would be under his hand. He wondered if she thought of him in the same way, or if he was just being a sick, horny bastard—he was like another brother to her.

Shame and fear kept him from doing anything. He'd tried kissing another girl, but her face swarmed his vision. He backed away, because it felt like a betrayal. He'd never tried to kiss someone else again.

When she was seventeen, they went for a ride in the field and she challenged him to a race. Hooves thundering, he chased her through the woods, obsessed with the way her long hair caught the wind and the perfect curve of her ass as she rose in the saddle and expertly urged her mare to go faster.

The crash of deer in the woods had startled the horses. He'd reined in his mount at the same time he watched in horror as she tumbled off her seat and lay motionless in the grass.

Choking fear vaulted him to her side in seconds. He ran his trembling hands over her body, checking for breaks, cupping her face and whispering her name like a prayer, over and over, until she opened her eyes.

Their gazes locked. The air warmed, hanging heavy and stagnant. The sun burned. A bird screeched in the trees. The snort of horses' breath echoed behind them.

"Are you hurt? Baby, please talk to me."

A small smile rested on her lips. "I'm fine. Just got winded. I still won."

He cursed and pressed his forehead to hers in sheer relief. "I'm going to kill you. You scared the shit out of me. I told you not to go toward the creek path, but you never listen. Why are you always trying to prove you're better?"

Her arms lifted, and her fingers rested in his hair. "Don't be mad," she whispered. Her bright-blue eyes flared with a mix of raw emotions. Heat. Want. Need. "Maybe I just wanted to get your attention."

The energy shifted. Suddenly, he realized his hands hadn't moved and his thumbs were stroking the edges of her mouth, his lips inches from hers. Her sweet breath rushed over him, and suddenly he was hard, aching, and insane to touch her, kiss her . . .

So he did.

It was a kiss that had built for a year in his memory, and maybe more in his dreams. With a breathy sigh, her arms tightened around him, and then she was kissing him back. The pleasure was so intense, the ground shifted beneath him.

They kissed each other in the long grass under the stinging sun for endless, stunning moments. He tasted her with his tongue, stroked her hair, and drank in her scent. He was changed forever because he knew he loved her more than anything, this girl who knew every one of his secrets. There was nothing to hide from her, which made the kiss the purest of all—a kiss of innocence, openness, and giving over everything he was for safekeeping.

When he finally lifted his head, they smiled at each other. He pulled her up, took her hand, and walked back to the stables, guiding the horses. There was never any explanation or discussion or questioning about the turn of events. No drama or pain or teen angst that could rip and shred the heart and soul.

After that kiss, everything had changed.

They were just . . . together.

Kyle emerged from the fog. He stretched and read over the words, excitement stirring in his gut.

Yes. This was what he needed. He'd been wrong to try and write it as a script. This particular story needed to be written as a book first, evolving from his memory. Once the images and emotions took hold, he'd be able to structure the script from the novel, swapping out narrative and thought for dialogue and action.

He went back to work.

Outside his door, Ophelia cocked her head and listened to the frantic tapping of the keys. He'd been completely engrossed for the last three days. Occasionally, he stumbled out, looking a bit confused, and left the inn. He would return an hour later with a variety of food and drink—especially coffee—and disappear back into the room.

Oh yeah, he was in the zone.

She remembered the same exact look years ago, except back then when he emerged it was always to drag her into bed. He'd silence her pleas to talk with his wicked lips and talented tongue until orgasms became more important than speech.

She steeled her shoulders and walked down the stairs. Distance was crucial. At least he'd stopped testing their agreement by constantly asking to talk, citing an important thing he desperately needed to tell her. Each time, she'd blasted him with an icy stare and walked away.

Damned if she was going to give him an opportunity to try and bond with her.

Of course, his hurt expression only made her more pissed.

Why did she care about his feelings? He was the one who forced his presence back into her life. Hell, she was glad he was back to his old workaholic routine, isolating himself and refusing to engage with anything that didn't have to do with his career.

Or anyone.

Cursing softly under her breath, she swore it didn't matter any longer.

It was good to be reminded of how he truly was. She was determined to treat him like a guest who'd requested complete privacy and no interruptions to his vacation.

But he's not any guest, her inner voice whispered. *He still affects you. Crack open the door, and he'll push right through.*

"Nope, not this time," she shot back.

Liar. His presence alone is beginning to change you. You think about him all the time. You haven't slept since he arrived.

"Shush. I have no time for you."

God, her habit of talking to herself had to stop.

The doorbell interrupted her crazed, one-sided conversation. She assumed it was probably FedEx with the cleaning supply delivery. She went through so much she bought in bulk.

She yanked the door open and stared in shock at the person on her doorstep.

"Hello, Ophelia."

He was old. Battered-looking. Years of hard drinking and hate had done their job well. His decline was evident in the harsh lines of his face, slightly bloated cheeks, and stooped posture. His gray hair was much thinner, but still present. But within those familiar forest-green eyes a light gleamed—one she'd never glimpsed from the angry man who'd raised the man she'd loved.

How long had it been since she'd seen Kyle's father? Over a year?

He lived down the road, but other than the occasional run to one of the local stores, he kept to himself. His once-productive farm had fallen into disarray after Kyle left. Just another thing Patrick Kimpton could hate his son for.

"Patrick. This is a surprise." She hesitated, caught between her good manners and the instinct to send him away. Manners won. "Umm, do you want to come in?"

"Thanks." He moved slowly, reaching out to grip the railing and guide himself inside.

She'd remembered him as much taller and more intimidating, with a deep, angry voice and a whipcord strength that came from working the land. Now, he seemed almost frail.

"Would you like a cup of coffee?"

"That'd be good."

"Black?"

"No other way."

"Have a seat."

He followed her into the kitchen and waited while she poured the coffee. When she leaned over to give him the mug, she noticed there was no stink of alcohol on his breath or tremble in his hand.

Good. She really didn't need him drunk when Kyle was upstairs.

She settled in the chair next to him. "So what can I do for you?"

"I'd like to see my son."

She blinked, studying him closely. As far as she knew, Kyle hadn't seen him since he'd left for California a decade ago. His father had made no attempt to ever get in touch with him. Their father-son relationship was so damaged and broken, even Ophelia had finally given up trying to get them to communicate.

When she got back home years ago, she'd tried to check in on Patrick regularly—along with her mother, who'd show up with dinner—and had offered to help on the farm. Ophelia had been afraid that, with Kyle permanently gone, something bad would happen to Patrick.

And something did.

He refused to let them help him, becoming a recluse with a goal of drinking himself to death. Ethan had tried contacting AA and Al-Anon, but there was one message that came back every time: Patrick had to *want* to get better to stop drinking.

He'd made it clear he didn't. Eventually, Ophelia and her mom stopped checking on him. She and Harper had rescued the leftover horses, chickens, and other animals from his farm. In the end there was only empty, endless acreage, ghostly barns, and a terrible silence.

Now that Patrick was sitting in her kitchen, looking and sounding nothing like she remembered, a surge of sympathy overtook her. She'd burned with rage toward Kyle's father and the way he treated his son, but blood was blood, and her Irish genes kept her stubbornly hoping they'd be able to salvage some sort of relationship. That one day Patrick would see his mistakes and offer to make things right. But Kyle swore he'd never talk to his father again.

"Has Kyle contacted you?" she asked gently.

He gave a quick shake of his head. "Didn't expect it. I know he hates me. Just want to look him in the eye and say a few things that are overdue."

"I'll go ask him, but I'm not sure he'll want to talk, Patrick. Maybe with some time? He just got into town a couple of weeks ago."

"How long will he be here?"

"Three months." She studied him. He wore an old mustard sweatshirt and faded jeans. His usually stocky body looked thin. The way he cupped his mug and tended to shake his right foot was so similar to Kyle's own mannerisms. "How are you doing?"

She expected his gaze to drop, or for him to change the subject. Instead, he lifted his head and looked her straight in the eye. "Better. Not gonna give you a bunch of bull about how getting sober has changed my life. Don't expect forgiveness, either, but I'm here to ask for it."

"Did you go to rehab?"

He nodded. "Been clean almost a year and got a part-time job helping over at the Nelsons' farm. Been working on making my amends, but Kyle hasn't taken my calls. I just heard today he was in town, so I drove right over."

Yes, gossip would fly fast in Gardiner, as in any small town. Like Ethan, Kyle was the prodigal son who left to do big things. In fact, she was surprised there hadn't been a long line of visitors pretending to check in with her this week, simply eager to see Kyle.

"Does he know you went to rehab?"

"Nah. I left a few messages, but I knew he wouldn't listen to them. Don't blame him. Thought about going out to California, but I don't have the money yet. I'm saving."

Her heart suddenly ached for what could have been. Even though Patrick had caused so much pain, she hoped Kyle would at least hear him out.

"He's in his room, writing. I'll go get him."

She climbed the stairs and stood at his door, her nerves tightening. Dragging in a breath, she knocked.

Nothing. The mad clack of the keyboard was the only sound.

She pounded harder. "Kyle? Open the door. It's important."

A low mutter. The clatter of a chair. Then the door swung open. His beard was scruffier, his hair crazily mussed, and his eyes had that sheen that hinted at a bit of madness.

"Sorry. Are you okay?"

She stepped in closer and kept her voice soft. "There's someone here to see you."

"Oh. Can you tell them to go away till later?"

"It's your father."

His stunned expression ripped at her heart. For just a second, he reminded her of the young boy who had been desperate and happy to take any attention his father would give. It was only later, after being rejected cruelly too many times, that there had been nothing but emptiness when he spoke about Patrick. The rage and pain had numbed over to ice, and Ophelia always believed that was so much worse.

His lips twisted. "Are you fucking kidding me? What does he want? Money?"

"No. Just to talk."

A vicious curse blistered her ears.

"I cannot believe he actually came here. Damn town gossip must've let him know I'm back." His face hardened with resolution. "I'm going to take care of this once and for all."

He'd shared his stories with her, and she'd shared his pain. It was as if Patrick's acts had affected both of them, especially when they ended up falling in love. "Do you want me to go with you?"

He shook his head but reached out to touch her shoulder. "No, I have to handle this myself. But thank you."

Her heart ached to help him, but she remained quiet. Ophelia watched him stalk down the stairs. She drew a shaky breath. She'd stay right here, out of the line of fire, but close enough . . . just in case.

Maybe he'd glimpse what she just had. Patrick clearly seemed different. He'd stopped drinking. He wanted to make amends. It was a step. Wasn't the first step always the hardest?

She gripped the banister as their voices drifted upward. No yelling. Just low, murmured conversation. Maybe enough time had passed to scab over some raw wounds so they could communicate for the first time.

Time blurred, but it seemed like a good sign that she still hadn't heard the door slam. Finally, she heard the shuffle of footsteps down the hall. A click. Then quiet.

She waited for a bit. When Kyle didn't appear, she made her way down the stairs. He was leaning against the antique writing desk, staring out the window. He shook himself out of his trance when she got closer.

"Hey, sorry. He's gone."

She hesitated, studying his face for clues. For a moment, she swore there was a flash of regret in those green eyes, but it was quickly replaced with nothing. "Did you talk to him?"

His features hardened. "Not really. I explained that it was best he stayed away. I told him I had nothing to say to him, and that there was nothing he could say that I'd want to listen to."

She nodded, but her heart ached. "He looked different. Like he had stopped drinking."

Kyle lifted a shoulder in a half shrug. "Maybe. It doesn't matter any longer, though."

She took a step forward, wanting to reach out and touch him, then quickly drew back. Pain reverberated in waves around him, urging her to wrap him in her arms and soothe it away with her touch and her kiss and her words—like she had so many times before. Instead, she swallowed back the lump in her throat and forced her feet to turn away.

"Ophelia."

"Yeah?"

"Want to sit down with me for a bit? I can grab us some lunch in town. We need to talk."

An impatient sigh escaped her lips. "Look, I can understand if you want to talk about your dad—"

"I don't want to discuss Patrick." Ice flecked his tone. "That subject is dead. What I want is for you to give me a few minutes to have a real conversation about something important. It's about us, Ophelia. You need to hear it."

Her emotions roiled close to the surface.

Wasn't letting him live here for three months enough? Couldn't he just leave the past and their relationship alone in the locked box she'd safely stored them in? God, any moment she softened he tried to take advantage of her.

Twice now she'd gotten flashes of the man she'd fallen in love with. The one who'd taken comfort in her presence and shared his pain about his dad. The one who'd stepped in to take care of her and the inn without hesitation.

But it wasn't real.

She couldn't be misdirected by lingering emotions for a relationship that was over. The man she'd once loved had changed, and he was never coming back. She had to stop letting him sneak past her defenses.

Angry at her own weakness, she clenched her fists with frustration. "No. I don't need to hear it. I need you to follow the terms of our damn agreement and leave me alone!"

His jaw clenched. He studied her defensive stance, then muttered a soft curse. "Do you hate me that much?"

She jerked. She didn't want to do this. Once, he'd been her everything, but examining the past too intensely would only lead to more pain.

"No. I could never hate you—it would be like hating part of myself. But I don't want to talk about *us* ever again."

His gaze delved deep. "We may have a problem, then."

Her nerves tingled in warning. Immediately, she sensed everything was about to change. The trembling began deep and broke slowly apart; the words hovered on his carved lips, and she knew she had to stop him. In sheer panic, she lifted her hands up and shook her head hard.

"I don't want to know. Keep your truth to yourself, and let's leave the past where it is—behind us. I have to go. I have a million things to do."

"Ophelia."

"Let's just stick to the plan and move forward. I mean it. I've had enough."

"Dammit, I have to—"

"I'm not listening," she sang loudly as she whirled around and took off down the hall, focused on reaching the safety of her bedroom. She knew she should be humiliated by her ridiculous urge to run and hide, but she didn't want to have a deep discussion about the many events that had ripped them apart and broken her heart.

A few steps from her room, she heard his voice bellow through the air and vibrate in an explosion of sound that froze her midmotion.

"For God's sake, woman! We're still married!"

She'd been right.

His words had changed everything.

Chapter Eight

Ophelia stared at him from across the dining room table.

Her vision was still a bit shaky, as if the world had tilted. Which it had. At first, she'd attempted to deny his declaration a hundred different ways. He quietly told her to take a breath, then guided her into a chair while he got some papers.

Still half in shock, she accepted the glass of water he brought her and gulped the liquid down in a few swallows. She was sure once she saw the papers, she'd spot an error.

Then they could have a big laugh and get back to ignoring each other.

After all, this was impossible. They were divorced. She'd signed the paperwork, and so had he.

"You must be wrong," she forced out after her voice began working again. "We have copies from the lawyer."

He pushed a fat folder in front of her. "Those are my copies of what we signed and gave the lawyer. But did you ever get an official dissolution of marriage form in the mail? Legal documents stating the divorce was final?"

She desperately rifled through the papers and tried to think. "No. I assumed they were mailed to our address in California and you just never sent me a copy. I never needed it. I never thought about it."

He nodded. "Neither did I. In my mind, we had done the hard stuff. We paid the lawyer and signed paperwork. But recently, I found out the lawyer we used was a fake. He was taking money from clients without ever filing the official documents. It was just a big scam. When the story broke and I realized it was him, I dug a bit deeper and confirmed with the court that we were still legally married."

"This can't be," she whispered. "Isn't there a recourse for the people he scammed?"

"Unfortunately not. He'll go to jail or claim bankruptcy and keep our money. If we want to go through with this divorce, we have to start over. Because right now, I'm legally your husband."

Her lungs seized, and she scrambled desperately for calm. The way he said *husband* pummeled her back into the past, swirling with memories of raw intimacy, giddy highs, searing pain, and her broken heart that had never fully healed. Her belly tumbled when she thought of still belonging to him, but her traitorous body lit up with anticipation.

Focus. She had to focus on the problem at hand, solve it, and move on. It was the only way to deal with the fallout.

"Okay, so we need to fix this. Fast. Discreetly. No need to panic."

"I'm not panicking."

Ophelia frowned, taking in his calm demeanor. He looked almost . . . glad.

Was it because he'd had more time to deal with the shock? Or was he up to something more sinister?

"Good, then we're in agreement to move forward. Do you have a lawyer you want to use? I'm figuring we have to file again in California, right? I wonder if we have to start the whole thing over, or if we can just refile our papers."

"It's been too long, so we start at the beginning. We have a fresh slate." He was staring at her with a strange intensity.

Why did his words sound like they held a hidden meaning?

There was a predatory aura pulsing around him.

"Why are you looking at me like that?" she asked, gaze narrowed in suspicion. "Is there something else you haven't told me?"

"I think this was a sign, Ophelia. The story broke the same time I planned to come back home and see you. The script isn't the only reason I wanted to stay here. Didn't you ever wonder about us? If we were too young to really understand what we needed from each other? We've both grown up and changed. We know who we really are now. And no matter how hard I've tried, I haven't been able to forget you."

"Don't." Her voice broke, but then the anger hit and strength flooded back. "Don't play games with me. You can't waltz back to your first girlfriend almost a decade later and decide to try things out again just for the hell of it."

"Wife. You're my *wife*," he said forcefully. "So yeah. I've been think-ing about second chances. We spent our childhood together. Fell in love, got married, and tried to build a life. We were each other's safe place. You want to throw away all of that just because it makes you uncomfortable thinking about what went wrong?"

She gripped the file and practically hissed back, "Are you forgetting how you locked yourself away for days on end, only emerging to kiss your so-called friends' asses?"

"I had the opportunity to work on a script that became a hit and changed my life. You didn't give it time. You didn't give *me* a chance, or the lifestyle, or your own career. And I think that's what you're really mad about, Ophelia. You gave up your singing—your one true dream. Why? What really made you run away?"

Emotion choked her. She never let herself remember. Only in short glimpses. Sharp, rapid scenes that played behind her closed lids late at night, forcing her back. It had been so classic. They had been the perfect trope: young lovers who eloped and tried to conquer fame and fortune, only to be torn apart by the cruel world around them. Except she'd figured out something that could never be fixed—no matter how hard they tried.

The man she loved had blossomed in the land of dreams, but meanwhile, she had crashed into a million pieces. When she looked over, she'd realized he wasn't around to pick her back up. He'd already checked out long ago, confident they still wanted the same things.

So she'd acted on her only option.

She'd come home.

When she answered, it was with the desolation of knowing how high they'd climbed together, and how completely their relationship had shattered—and way too soon.

"I didn't run. I finally saw the truth right in front of me. But you still don't see it, Kyle. You never did. And that's why it will never work between us."

Frustration carved out his features. "You're talking in riddles. The only thing you ever wanted was to be a singer. You were offered that reality-show spot where you could reach millions. The producers and judges loved you! There was buzz at *Entertainment Tonight* that you were the one to beat. You had it all at your fingertips, but you turned it down because you were scared. Your fear destroyed us."

Grief pounded at her like violent waves attacking a pier in a storm.

How could she explain how her path had played out, allowing her to clearly see where she was headed? How many times had she tried to talk to him, but he was caught up in his own world, until there was only silence left between them? She'd felt so alone and confused, but he'd refused to see, assuming it was nerves or fear of failure.

It had been so much more.

The fight faded from her body.

He'd never believe the truth. He was still stuck on his side of events and refused to alter his viewpoint. After all this time, why try to convince him otherwise? No, this was a reminder that they could never heal the broken rift between them.

"Believe what you want. It doesn't change the outcome anymore."

He flinched, but his lips set in that stubborn line she knew so well, even after all this time. He tilted his head, studying her. "How do you know? It's still there."

She stiffened. "What?"

His voice dropped to a low, velvety growl. "Our connection. My body remembers yours. Every inch of your skin is ingrained in my memory. The scent of that lavender-and-honey lotion you wore, and the way your eyes turn to blue fire when you're mad, and how your smile can make a whole room hold its breath."

He was killing her, and she was allowing it to happen. Each word was like a knife slicing another cut into her flesh.

He leaned forward, his hands lifted in supplication to drive his point home. "When you got sick and I took care of you, I remembered how we were part of each other. It hasn't changed for me. Yes, it all fell apart, but we had so much going against us. We ran away and cut our friends and family off, thinking we could do it all alone. We didn't know what the world would be like, or who to trust, or how to balance our relationship with the need to make a mark. Don't you think we owe it to ourselves to begin anew? We're adults now, and we're *married*. I'm asking for a chance, Ophelia. As I write my script, I want to get to know you again."

Hysterics bubbled up from her throat.

This whole conversation felt like *Twilight Zone* material. Why would she open herself up to more heartache when she already knew the ending?

She shook her head, trying to clear it. "I'm sorry, Kyle. I can't go down this road again. It's too . . . much."

She rose from the chair with the folder clenched in her fingers. "I'll go over these and do some research so we can come up with a plan of action to move forward with the divorce. For now, I think it's best if you concentrate on the script."

A Brand New Ending

This time, he allowed her to leave and lock herself into the safety of her room.

Ophelia closed her eyes and slumped against the door.

How was she going to get through the next few months now that everything had changed?

It was more than the divorce papers. It was the look of determination glinting in his green-mountain eyes, the set of his square jaw, the hardened features of his face. He was curious enough to poke at the bee's nest to see if he'd gain honey.

Too bad. She could've told him it would only wreak stinging pain and little sweetness.

Chapter Nine

Kyle sat in the lingering silence and fought the impulse to follow her. The pain in her face almost drove him to his knees.

God knows, he didn't want to hurt her.

He cursed under his breath and headed up to his room.

Better to give her some space. He'd try again later with a gentler approach. He'd really fucked things up by yelling the truth at her, but he'd been so frustrated by her refusal to even talk with him after the strain of seeing his father.

The image of his father trying to apologize stirred up a black cauldron of junk he didn't want to investigate. He'd been sober, at least, but that didn't count for much. It was the way Patrick had talked to him that really cut deep.

Gently. As if he actually gave a fuck. What a concept.

Memories assaulted him like a bunch of gleeful gremlins bent on torture: the little boy dying for one approving glance, one kind word, one decent gesture to remind him he had some worth to Patrick Kimpton. Instead, he got slurred insults muttered between sips of Clan MacGregor Scotch. He got emotionless grunts and blistering accusations. He got an occasional punch to keep him in line.

But it was what his father lacked that gave him the most trouble.

Kyle could've taken the abuse if he hadn't had the shroud of guilt hanging over him. He'd been pretty tough, and his consistent escape into his writing helped soften the hard edges of his existence. So had the Bishops' farm, where there was always a hot meal, a warm hug, or a good conversation to be had with guests or family.

No, he would've managed if there'd been no real reason his father hated him.

Books had taught him young that the world wasn't fair, and that plenty of bad things happened to good people. Pick up Dickens or Hemingway to get a peek at the truth. It had actually helped. If you had no expectations, the good stuff was savored and held tight with gratitude. It built character, persistence, and fortitude. Not a bad bargain. He'd never been afraid of patience or hard work since it got him all the way to the heights of success.

But now he was here to look back. Unfortunately, his father was part of the story whether he liked it or not.

Kyle stumbled to the keyboard.

He came in from the barns, sticky with sweat and smelling of manure. Worry twisted in his gut, but he couldn't show it. He had to talk to his father, and Kyle had no idea if he was passed out yet with an empty bottle at his feet, or if he had managed to stay sober and actually do some work that day.

Kyle dragged his arm across his forehead to clear his vision. He began searching the house. "Dad? I need to talk to you," he called out, ignoring his pounding heart. Usually, he wouldn't care what type of mood Patrick was in—they all tended to be crappy—but this time he needed something. Something important.

He heard a grunt from the office.

Good. If he was doing paperwork, maybe he was in a decent enough space to just give Kyle what he wanted.

"What is it?" Patrick was at his desk, but instead of focusing on the screen, he was slumped in the chair, staring out the window. Definitely not a good sign. Shit.

Kyle stepped in. "Got a problem with Lucy."

"Did you make all the deliveries this morning before you decided to play? 'Cause that's what's keeping a roof over our heads now—not your pretty horses."

"I did them all and even managed to score another account. Tantillo Farms wants to switch to us since they've been having problems with their produce. We start delivering next week."

His father grunted again, swiveling around to look at him. His hard gaze flicked over Kyle's mud-encrusted body.

"They can promise anything to you, but without a contract—"

"Got one signed. Along with a deposit."

He waited, but his father just nodded. "Make sure the booth will be ready for the Strawberry Festival in Beacon," he said. "I'm getting killed here with bills. We need all the help we can get."

"I'll take care of it."

"Good. We don't need any more problems on this damn farm."

He threw out the words before he chickened out. "There's a problem with Lucy's leg."

His father flinched.

Lucy was strictly Kyle's horse, since his father avoided her at all costs. The sweet mare was the offspring of Kyle's mother's horse—Sunny—who had died years ago. Patrick had been ripped apart when Sunny died, as if reliving his wife's death all over again. He'd refused to have anything to do with Lucy. Kyle had fallen in love with the foal immediately, sensing a kindred spirit. He'd named her with his mother's middle name and had been her primary caretaker for years. Funny, when he thought of leaving home, he knew it was Lucy he'd miss the most.

"Why are you telling me this? It's your horse. Deal with it."

Kyle swallowed and tamped down his worry. He had to present the scenario in the best way possible. "The vet examined her and said she needs extra care to heal the fracture. I'll need to set her up in the other barn and keep a close watch on her."

Patrick frowned. "Wait—she fractured her leg? What was the diagnosis from the vet?"

He shifted his weight. "Officially, she's lame. But he told me if I get her off her feet and do a strict regimen of care, she could pull through." Actually, the horse's leg would require round-the-clock tending, but Kyle didn't care. He'd slept in the barn before and had no issue bunking down with Lucy for the next few months—especially if he could save her. Unfortunately, that meant he had to let his father know what was going on, though he'd prefer to keep it a secret. Kyle was usually in charge of the horses, but occasionally his father would storm the barn to check up on him and make sure things were running the way he expected.

"Boy, I'm not paying a huge vet bill to save a horse that doesn't matter to this farm. If she's lame, we'll put her down."

"I paid the bill already, and I'm the one doing the care. I'm just letting you know."

Patrick muttered a curse and glared. "This isn't your farm yet. I'm the one who says what goes. We're not emptying out the other barn to care for an old, lame horse. The only reason you kept her around was to ride her, and now she ain't going to be doing no riding. We're putting her down."

Kyle snapped. "You're not touching my horse."

His father regarded him with distaste. "You don't order me around, boy. Now, either you can call the vet down so it's done humanely, or I can take care of it myself."

The years of frustration and pain twisted tight in his gut and spilled out the poison that had been trapped for too long. "Old man, if you dare to lay a finger on Lucy, I swear to God, I'll kill you. Don't you care about anything? I have to try and save her. Can't you give me this one thing?"

Patrick lurched from the chair. An empty bottle of Scotch dropped and rolled from his grip, and he stumbled forward. His green eyes misted with familiar rage. "How dare you question me? I gave you a roof over your head and food in your stomach. I wiped your ass when you were young, took care of your needs, and was forced to look at you every damn day and remember how you killed her. I chose her, but she chose you and gave you life. And shit like this proves she made the wrong choice."

The venom shot across the room and buckled his knees.

He'd always known the story, of course. Instead of hearing about fairy tales with princes and knights slaying dragons, he'd learned about how his mother chose to save her baby rather than her own life during childbirth. His father had begged the doctors to save his wife and let the baby go, but his mother refused. Even then, she'd loved him.

But that meant he'd been the cause of her death—his father never forgave him. Kyle's face was a constant reminder of the loss, driving Patrick to the bottle to forget.

His entire childhood consisted of being silently resented. He'd always carried a grim sense of duty. There'd been no love. He'd found that down the road—first with the horses, then Ophelia. He'd found it in books and music and movies. He'd hung on with the determination to finally escape his hellhole of an existence and lead a big life—a life of luxury and adoration and purpose. But right now, with his father's words echoing in his ears, the realization of his pathetic existence slammed through him and exploded like bullet fragments, tearing away the last of his heart.

He straightened to his full height and looked his father dead in the eye. "I'd rather she was dead than alive to see what you've turned into."

His father's eyes widened in shock. Then he drew his arm back and slammed his fist into Kyle's cheek.

He staggered back, falling to his knees, pain blossoming in his face. Blinking furiously, he gathered every last bit of strength and managed to stand back up. For one brief moment, he recognized the grief and regret glinting from his father's green eyes, but it was already too late. For either of them. "If you touch Lucy, I'll make you regret it. Just leave us both alone."

Kyle walked out slowly, with dignity, and kept going. The sun was sinking below the horizon, throwing the valley into a shimmering rainbow of earth tones. His feet measured every step on the path that he could have walked blindfolded, until the clean white-and-blue Victorian farmhouse hovered like a queen on its throne before him.

He went to the door, knocked, and prayed she was there. His insides were shifting and breaking apart, and he didn't know how much time he had left before he allowed the wound to bleed.

She opened the door. "Hey, I wasn't expecting you—Kyle? Oh my God, what happened?"

He lifted his hand to his cheek and stared at the blood pooling over his fingers. He blinked. Tried to speak. The words were stuck, along with the festering pain tearing him apart. His body shook.

"Ophelia." Her name broke from his lips.

She opened the door and gathered him in her arms. Slowly, she led him inside. The scents of freshly baked bread and lemon sun tea wafted in the air, guiding him down the hall to her room. She grabbed a damp towel from the bathroom and pressed it to the wound, guiding him down on the bed to cradle him in her lap. She stroked his hair, kissed his head, and murmured nothings in his ear in her beautiful, musical voice that reached deep inside his empty spaces and began to fill them.

And Kyle cried for the first time with the woman he loved for everything that was lost.

He blinked, and suddenly he was back in his room, staring at the words on the screen. Amid every painful event he'd experienced, there was one person who he could trust. One person who was his own personal sanctuary in a world that cared little for the broken and lost. One person he'd loved with every bit of his heart and soul.

Ophelia.

Seeing his father made him realize he couldn't lose her again. He had to find a way to convince her to give him a second chance.

He had to find a way to make her love him again.

Chapter Ten

Ophelia propped her arms on top of the stable and peered down at her sister, who was working on Flower's horseshoe. As usual, Harper was in the zone with her work, her fingers deftly scraping some junk from the sweet mare's foot, occasionally swatting away the horse's nibbling teeth as Flower showed her affection.

"Hey, Harp."

Her sister looked up, startled. "Hey, what are you doing out here?"

"Just taking a walk. Figured I'd check up on you and see what's going on in the barn. Where's Ethan?"

"He went with Mia to the city—they'll be back later. Are we still having dinner tonight?"

"Yes, I have a great meal planned," she said with a grin. They all looked forward to her big dinners, which happened on most Sundays—not least because they provided them all with leftover food for the week. Neither Ethan nor Harper had inherited her love for cooking, but she never minded. Ophelia loved their time together, when everyone got caught up and properly nourished. "Whatcha doing?"

"Some odds and ends. Miss Flower has delicate feet, so winter is definitely not her favorite season." The pretty mare whinnied, then nipped again at Harper's hair in affection. "I also need to work out Phoenix, but he seems to be a fair-weather type of horse, too." A smile curved her lips. "He throws a bit of a temper tantrum if I try to exercise him when it's too cold."

Ophelia laughed. "Now that's a big turnaround. I can't believe a few months ago he wouldn't even let anyone ride him. You really have made progress."

Her sister's eyes lit up with excitement. "Ethan did the healing work, and now I'm taking over his training. There's something different about that horse. He's got a fire and heart I've rarely seen. I think he's a winner."

"Derby possibility?"

Her sister brushed mud from her jeans. "Not sure. We'll see." She sighed. "I'm just happy things around here have been relatively quiet. I need a break before we hit the spring season and everything explodes."

"Same here."

Ophelia studied her sister's calm aura and steady hands. Harper had always been different. She was the only one in the family with the Black Irish gene, which skipped the pale skin, red hair, and endless freckles. Her dark hair was kept short, curving sleekly under her chin for minimum effort, and her eyes were a stunning sea green. With her olive skin tone and staggering height at over six feet, she was beautiful, but with a quiet presence that sometimes got ignored.

She was only two years younger than Ophelia. She had always been more comfortable around animals than people, preferring to stay away from social groups and to bury her nose in a book in the barn. Sometimes, Ophelia felt like they worked in two different worlds since she rarely came into the barns and Harper only visited the inn when there was a family meal.

"How's it going with Kyle?" Harper asked curiously.

She shifted her weight. The real reason she'd sought out a brisk walk was to clear her head. Since discovering she was still married, she'd thrown herself into research the past twenty-four hours, trying to find the easiest, most organized way to fix the mess. Unfortunately, she'd ended up with a slight headache from looking at all the divorce and court sites.

Harper knew she'd run off to California with Kyle, but she believed it was more about pursuing their careers than a love affair. When she'd moved back home, Ophelia told her they'd had an epic fight that hadn't been settled, and Harper didn't ask any questions. Harper had mastered the art of simplicity and one-word answers and avoided long, rambling confessions of emotion like the plague. Ophelia always wondered how that'd work if one day her sister wanted to have a love affair of her own. Harper tended to stay close to home and didn't date much.

Ophelia kept her response neutral. Ethan had always been her confidant, and she rarely ran to her sister with her troubles. "Fine. He's working on a new screenplay."

"Cool. I'll ask him more about it at dinner."

Ophelia jerked. "He's not joining us for dinner."

Her sister frowned. "Why not?"

Panic nipped at her nerve endings. "Well, he'll be working. Or busy. I'd rather it be just us."

Usually, Harper would nod and stay out of it, but her frown deepened. "That's messed up. He was practically part of the family, and now he's staying at the inn. Why wouldn't you invite him to dinner?"

She tried not to sound desperate. "Just because he has a room doesn't mean he should automatically come to every family gathering."

Suspicion glinted in her sister's eyes. "What type of falling out did you guys have, anyway? Seems a bit extreme to me—especially since you're the forgiving type."

Ah, crap. How was she going to explain her way out of this one? Damn him. His presence was screwing up everything.

"It's complicated," she finally said. "There's more history than I let on between us."

"Ah. I always figured you guys were banging when you ran away together. Still hot for him, huh?"

Her mouth fell open. "No! I don't want to talk about it. I just . . . I don't like him anymore, that's all."

Harper laughed and rose from the stool, giving Flower a pat. "Sounds like Ethan and Mia. They bantered all summer and swore they didn't like each other, but I knew they just wanted to rip each other's clothes off."

"It's not like that with Kyle," she insisted. "Yes, we had an affair when we were young, but things changed."

"You were so different when you got back from California," Harper said. "Mom always said a broken heart causes more character growth than a Disney movie."

Ophelia shook her head, laughing. "Mom was always right." She paused, but in that fleeting moment, she wanted to share more with her sister. "He hurt me. I guess I still haven't gotten past it."

Harper nodded. "I get it. Makes sense now that you didn't want him staying the winter. But maybe it's a sign."

The words gave Ophelia an eerie sense of déjà vu.

Hadn't Kyle said the same thing?

"What do you mean?"

"You can't run away from the past forever. Maybe he's back because you need closure." Her sister gave her a meaningful look. "Or not."

Ophelia opened her mouth to protest, but Harper just waved her hand in the air and cut her off. "I'm on your side either way. Invite him or not. Just saying it may be a bit strange to have a family dinner while he's holed up alone in his room."

Ugh. Her sister was right. How could she possibly tell him he couldn't join them?

"I'll think about it," she said. "Thanks for the chat. I better get back."

"Sure. See ya later." Harper left the stall, locking it behind her, and headed toward the field.

Ophelia retraced her steps on the path to the inn. The sharp air stole her breath and reddened her cheeks, but she loved the surge of adrenaline that shot through her. A distant bark warned her that Wheezy and Bolt were on their way. When they spotted her through the bare trees, they made a mad dash, sprinted full speed ahead, and knocked into her legs, making her laugh.

She walked with the two furballs bouncing at her heels, drinking in the magnificent view of ice-crusted branches, blue sky, and the snow-topped peaks of the Gunks shimmering in the distance. Deep inside, peace settled over her with the reminder she'd made the right choice. This was her home, where she belonged. As badly as she had wanted to love her time in California, she always felt displaced, as if something in her soul was off. She'd run across the country to find something that had been at home all along.

But Kyle had been lost in the process.

She sighed, lingering on the memories, and decided to invite him to dinner. If she was clear and forceful enough to explain it was only for appearances, maybe he'd understand she wasn't weakening or giving him an opening. Between Ethan and Mia and Harper, she wouldn't have to say a word to him, and afterward he'd disappear back into his room.

It'd be safe enough.

Decision made, she finished her walk and began planning the menu.

"What are you doing here?"

Ophelia stared at Kyle, framed in the kitchen doorway. Clad in black pants and a snug charcoal Henley emphasizing his impressive pecs and broad shoulders, he emanated masculine yumminess.

Irritation coursed through her.

He was a writer, dammit. He shouldn't be so fit, considering his profession judged success by how many hours his ass was in a chair. Was he still doing that crazy core workout?

After long writing sessions, he'd complete his own gym circuit consisting of push-ups, sit-ups, pull-ups, and a variety of creative Pilates moves that pit his own body weight against him. She used to make him do his routine shirtless so she could sit back, watch, and drool. Most of the sessions had ended with them both naked in bed.

"Helping you cook, of course. Got any extra aprons?"

Her eyes widened. "No, and I don't need any help. I'll call you when Ethan gets here. Just go back to your room."

His lips quirked. He ignored her, prowling around the kitchen with curiosity. "Absolutely not. Besides, we always cooked together."

The memory slammed into her and stole her breath. In the beginning of their marriage, they'd spent endless hours exploring various ingredients available in California and experimenting with recipes. Cramped in their one-bedroom studio, with no counter space and a small oven, they'd squeeze together, drink cheap wine, and feed each other morsels of food. She'd learned how to cook well from her mother, and Kyle had been forced to learn early since his father barely knew how to boil water.

Cooking together gradually became less frequent as he spent more time at the production company's offices.

How many nights had she stared at a perfectly prepared meal while she ate alone? Too many to count.

She kept her voice firm. "Things are different here. I have a strict organizational plan and have to cook alone. I need plenty of space. You'll only mess things up." Serving guests required following a routine to make sure she got all the food on the table at once and was able to quickly reproduce dishes on demand. Once, preparing a meal had been a choreographed dance between partners. Now, after so many years apart, it'd become a solo effort—and she was stingy with her spotlight.

He unsnagged an apron from one of the kitchen hooks and tied it around his waist. The Tuscan flowers should've made him look ridiculous, but he exuded such masculinity and confidence it only made him look hotter.

"You can lead. I'll take direction."

She glowered. "You always sucked at that role."

He shot her a heated glance. "You never complained about it before."

Heat soaked her cheeks.

Damn him. He'd always been demanding in bed, and she'd been thrilled to surrender to every delicious command.

She grabbed at her composure. "Stop. If you're going to keep bringing up our past, you can't stay for dinner."

He tried to look apologetic, but his eyes danced with mischief. "Sorry. I'll be good. Let me help, Ophelia. I've missed cooking. It's been too long since I helped prepare a meal."

Her brow lifted. "Takeout? Or fancy in-house chef?"

"Both."

She rolled her eyes and sighed. She was such a sucker. "A pity you've gotten lazy on me. All those millions make you soft, Kimpton?"

He cocked his hip and regarded her in an obvious challenge. "My skills may be rusty, but they're still badass. What've you got for me?"

She turned so he couldn't spot her grin. "Pork loin roast. Rosemary-herbed potatoes. Butternut squash quiche. Biscuits."

"I'm assuming not Pillsbury."

She snorted. "Don't curse in my kitchen. Pick."

He regarded the various stations and ingredients like he was entering an *Iron Chef* competition. "Meat and potatoes."

"A bit ambitious, don't you think?"

He leaned toward her and whispered in her ear, "Always aim high."

Her belly rolled and tumbled. She remembered the night he was referencing like yesterday. His arrogant assumption that he could break his record and give her a dozen orgasms before dawn. The patient, intense way he'd coaxed her body through the endless hours, wringing out pleasure after pleasure.

He'd not only met his goal, he exceeded it.

She shifted, growing wet and achy between her thighs. Those dark-green eyes lit with recognition, but he didn't push—likely sensing she was on the edge of throwing him out.

Grabbing a bottle of wine from the refrigerator, she filled them both glasses of Chardonnay. "Oh, the spice rack is over there. Sauces to the left. Herbs in the till."

"Got it."

She nodded and commanded her Amazon Echo to play her cooking music list.

"Not the Broadway musicals," he groaned, clearing out a work area at the end of the countertop. "I'll fall asleep and chop my finger off."

She made a face. "My kitchen, my songs. Don't tell me you still enjoy that alternative stuff Ethan likes? The bands with the crazy names that make no sense?"

"Yes. Don't even think of making fun of Radiohead or Nirvana. They're like the Sinatra and Martin of our day."

"Not with names like Cage the Elephant and the Arctic Monkeys."

"At least the sound is sick. Those musicals are ridiculous. You get to the good part between the hero and heroine, and then they break into song and ruin the whole dramatic moment. True artists know that music needs to be listened to in its purest state—alone. Not as part of a musical."

"Tell that to Meryl Streep, who starred in *Mamma Mia!* and gave ABBA a whole new resurgence of fans."

He didn't deign to answer, just shot her a look and got to chopping the garlic.

The strains of "City of Stars" from *La La Land* caressed her ears. The scent of a limoncello candle burned bright and soaked the air with fragrance.

Singing softly under her breath, she attacked the dough for the quiche crust with flour and a rolling pin. With each motion her body relaxed, her mind cleared, and she gave herself to the experience of preparing food for loved ones to eat.

"I like Mia," he announced. "It's good to see Ethan happy and settled here. Sometimes I can't believe he actually lived in Hollywood." In between Special Forces assignments, Ethan was a bodyguard to a famous actress. He had settled into the glitz and glamour before returning home wounded from a mission.

"Me, too. I'm glad home was not only able to heal him, but find him love. It was a hell of a summer watching those two dance around each other."

"I bet—Mia's a pistol."

"I never knew much about his life in California. How often did you get to see him?"

He began prepping the marinade for the meat. "Not much. He had a crazy schedule as a bodyguard, and he was flying out on missions where he'd be gone for a while. He came to some of my big screenings, though, and I always knew he was there if I needed him." A smile curved his lips. "He's my brother," Kyle said simply.

Her chest tightened. Yes, they were brothers—in the way that mattered. Which only made keeping Kyle distant from her family even harder, since he was truly one of them.

They fell into a companionable silence. He seemed busy with his own thoughts as they worked. "Other than Aubrey, do you have any help with running the inn? I know winter is a slower time, so I wondered how you handled the busier seasons."

She shrugged. "I'm ruthlessly organized, so I don't need much extra help. I have a savvy accountant, and Mia's been incredible at instituting some marketing techniques to increase our bottom line. It all revolves around packing in high turnover for the tourist seasons and coming up with ways to get people to stay in the winter. Next year, I'm going to work with one of the parks that sponsor the Winter Festival and offer discounted rates on rooms."

"Smart." He looked up from his chopping to study her curiously. "Do you ever get bored doing the same thing day after day? Or lonely? It can get pretty isolated here in the winter, and then in the summer, you're surrounded by strangers. You used to tell me this would be your nightmare job. In fact, it's one of the reasons we moved away together— so we wouldn't have to live a life like our parents'."

His question hit her like a fist in the gut. Her fingers squeezed the dough, and she was confronted by the depth of her lie—to both him and herself. Although *lie* seemed a bit too stark, colored in black and white. Hers was more of an untruth, in muted gray, that she didn't even realize until it was too late.

God, she didn't have the strength to tackle the true answer to his inquiry. Not now, when they were deep in the intimacy of cooking a meal for her family.

She struggled to give him just enough to satisfy—and defend—the career she loved. "Yes, sometimes it's hard. Even though my family's here, I'm the one responsible for the inn. It took me a while to find what works best for me, rather than what worked for my mom. But I love meeting new people. For a little while, I get to share part of their lives and give them a beautiful memory."

"Your mom used to say that—her real job was to give people a beautiful memory."

She smiled with pleasure. "Yes. When the porch is full, and I hear laughter and chatter drift through the window, I realize how much I love my life. I love when they praise my food and leave reviews about their experiences. And I get postcards from onetime strangers who start to see me as a friend." She motioned to the board by the refrigerator filled with various notes and cards. "Last summer, I hosted a group of six senior citizens—they were the most fun. They did horseback riding, skydiving, poker, you name it. They send me letters now, telling me what they're doing and checking up on Mia and Ethan and the horses. They can't wait to come back this year, and they've already rebooked. And a past guest told me her baby was conceived in this inn last year. Isn't that cool?"

He cocked his head and regarded her intently. "Very cool."

Feeling like she was safely past the danger zone, her muscles relaxed. She formed the crust in the pan, pinching her fingers along the rim. "I may not be a big star making a splash in the world, but I'm pretty damn satisfied knowing I've made a few people happy along the way. I like being reminded how simple kindness can be completely underrated, yet change so much."

She glanced over at him—and froze.

He was staring at her with such hungry intensity, her nipples tightened in awareness and her blood began to heat. As if he'd finally heard her words and understood. He'd always been able to read her—to delve beyond the surface of fake civilities and barriers and fears to the truth hidden deep. What shattered her was how, after finding her truth, he'd loved her anyway. Loved her so hard and completely, she'd have willingly given him anything he asked.

And she had. Oh, how she had.

Until he changed and let her walk away without a fight.

But right now, he reminded her of the old Kyle.

If he asked again, would she be able to fight him? Maybe not. Because nothing had ever been as good as being loved by Kyle Kimpton.

He seemed to sense her struggle and allowed her to retreat. The knife flashed as he expertly attacked the potatoes. "I never looked at it like that. Age changes our perspective. The things we imagined we hated are the same ones to fulfill us now. Quite a conundrum."

"Ah. Pulling out the big writer words, huh?" she teased.

"Just making sure you haven't gotten lazy with your vocabulary," he said.

"Smart ass."

He grinned and placed the meat into the marinade to season. "What time do the troops come?"

"An hour. They like to have a cocktail and pick on cheese and crackers before we serve." He started laughing, and she glanced up in puzzlement. "What's so funny?"

"Remember that big party we went to at that producer's house?"

"We attended too many; they all blur together," she said.

"No, the very first one. The producer with the fetish for naked Greek statues—remember they were all over his property? He said he wanted me to write for him, and we had to meet the team."

She gasped. "The party with all the cheese!"

He broke into more laughter. "Yes—the cheese. We were so excited—thought we'd be feasting on caviar and crab cakes and champagne—"

"And we were starved because we'd skipped dinner."

"We started looking around frantically for the cocktail servers, but there was only drinks and a table filled with cheese," he said.

"And crackers! I thought Hollywood despised carbs, but there must've been a hundred different crackers and cheeses laid out—and nothing else." She shook her head.

God, they'd been so young.

"I can't believe we drank all that champagne on an empty stomach."

"Well, no one was eating the cheese! We would've looked gauche if we began tearing into the stuff. It was only there for show."

"And then I got sick." She groaned at the memory. "The bathroom was so nice, too. Chandeliers and carpeting and pure marble counters. But all I saw was the fancy toilet."

"I felt terrible. I should've demanded a PB and J for you."

His serious tone made her laugh harder. "I felt terrible for *you*. Besides holding my hair back as I puked, we had to leave early. You missed the opportunity to schmooze with the team." She'd been racked with guilt when he hadn't gotten that job, always believing she was at fault.

His voice was whisper soft. "I didn't care. I had everything that mattered." He paused. "I had you."

The breath stuck in her lungs. On cue, the air tightened and hummed with a wicked surge of electricity and awareness. Her entire being ached to cross the kitchen and walk into his arms. It would be like going home again.

Would he still taste like coffee and peppermint? Would his body still fit against hers in perfect symmetry? Would his lips and tongue still plunder her mouth with the same passion and intimacy, building her up toward a shattering release?

Yes.

But it was too late. She had to keep reminding herself that their time had passed and that, sometimes, there was no going back. If she tried, she might get stuck again—and she'd never be able to survive a second heartbreak.

Ripping her gaze away, she concentrated on mixing the eggs and butternut squash with the flour mixture, carefully blending wet into dry.

"I found two lawyers that may work for the divorce," she said, keeping her tone light. "I'll send them over. I left messages for them to call me back Monday."

"Are they in California?"

"Yes. My research shows we can do most of it through the mail, with some conference calls."

He didn't answer, just spent long moments concentrating on his task.

She shifted her weight and spoke again. "I know you're working on the screenplay, but this is important. We need to have things in motion before you leave. So if you don't pick a lawyer quickly, I will."

He grunted. "I don't know what the rush is. Not like we're looking to marry someone else. Right?"

She ignored the warning in his voice. "This time I want the official papers in hand. As long as we both work together, there shouldn't be any reason the process won't go smoothly. I mean, for all intents and purposes, we're divorced. We just need to file the paperwork and make it legal."

"Is that how you look at it?" He regarded her intently, hip cocked, his shirt emphasizing the carved muscles of his chest. One stray golden lock fell stubbornly past his eyebrow. Those lips tightened in irritation.

She ignored his body language and plunged ahead. "Of course. I'm viewing it like a bankruptcy."

"Excuse me?"

"A bankruptcy. Let's say you lose all your money and become destitute. Your credit is wiped out, and you have to deal with the emotional fallout of shame, devastation, and wondering what you could have done differently. You go to court, file the papers, go home, and move forward. After a few years, you rebuild your credit and become financially stable again. If you're contacted by a lawyer and told the actual bankruptcy papers never went through so, legally, there was no bankruptcy, does that change the outcome? No, because you've already gotten past the hard stuff. You've already grieved over having no money and left it behind. It's just paperwork that wasn't filed correctly. Emotionally, it means nothing. Get it?"

Her eyes widened when he carefully placed the pan down and stalked across the room. She had no time to retreat, no time to emotionally prepare. Within seconds, he was just there, towering over her, pinning her hips against the countertop, raking his gaze over her face as if memorizing every one of her features for his dreams tonight.

"Wanna know how I see it?" he drawled.

She cleared her throat and frowned. "No. Why are you so close? Go back over there."

"See, I may have gone through all the emotion of losing my money, but somehow, deep inside, I still hoped the whole thing was one big mistake. I still dreamed I'd get a second chance at getting it right." His hand lifted as if to stroke her hair, then fell back to his side. Sexy scruff clung to his jaw and outlined his lips like a frame for an erotic picture. "So when I get that call that there was no bankruptcy, my ass is going out to purchase one sweet red sports car."

She tried to pretend his close presence wasn't bothering her. "That's not a good idea. It's the type of action that got you in trouble in the first place!"

His lower lip quirked. "Yeah, but now I know exactly how to drive it. Now I know how to pay for it." His breath whispered against her lips, and her body shuddered with want. "I learned my lessons. It's not about want or greed or impulsiveness." She stared in total fascination, transfixed by those simmering green eyes. "It's about care. Love. Patience. This time, I can get it right."

The ground tilted under her feet. Helplessly caught in a spell, her body craved closer contact, ached for his touch—just one time. She moved an inch closer, her arms lifting to grip his biceps for balance. He muttered something under his breath, then lowered his head and—

"We're here!" a voice shouted from the other room. "We're early, but we figured we'd come help you. No arguments this time!"

Kyle stepped back. Ophelia's arms fell to her sides.

"Are you in the kitchen?" Mia called out again. "I brought some cream puffs from the Market so you don't have to make dessert and—oh, Kyle. Hi! I'm sorry, I didn't realize you already have help." Mia swung her gaze back and forth, as if sensing the tension in the room.

Kyle had retreated. He didn't fully turn to face her, just called out a hello from behind the counter.

Ophelia suspected why.

Pasting on a smile, she gave Mia a hug. "You didn't have to bring dessert—I was going to bake that apple crumble you like."

"And you have a weakness for cream puffs, and I wanted to bring something you love today. Kyle, were you recruited to help, or did you volunteer?"

"Volunteered all the way. A real man knows his way around a kitchen. Too bad you got stuck with Ethan."

"I do other things that are more fun," Ethan shot back from behind Mia. "You probably just peeled potatoes anyway—or did you actually prepare something?"

Kyle grunted. "Wait till you see my meat. I'll hear your apology then."

"Your meat never impressed me, dude."

Mia burst into laughter. "Do you always descend into adolescence when you get together?"

"It's Kyle's fault. Ugh, why are you listening to Broadway crap? Alexa, play Radiohead."

Her Echo halted the stirring ballad of "All I Ask of You" from *Phantom of the Opera* and began belting out loud guitars and low, whiny song lyrics. Kyle began banging his head as he finished up the potatoes, and Ethan dove into a disturbing imitation of *Guitar Hero* moves.

Mia gave a long-suffering sigh. "I'll set the table while you finish up. Harper's on her way."

"We're starving," Ethan yelled above the music. "Harper better get here fast—we had no time for lunch driving back from Manhattan. I hope you have a ton of cheese."

Ophelia pressed her lips together and met Kyle's glance across the room.

Then they both burst into laughter.

In under an hour, they were seated at the carved pine table, passing around steaming platters, bread baskets, and wine. Mia forked up a piece of buttery quiche and let out an appreciative moan. "Superb," she announced.

Kyle gave a snort. "Still not going to beat my meat and potatoes. I'll take a poll of everyone's favorite dish after dinner to see who wins."

Ophelia shook her head. "Just as competitive as ever. Do you still throw a tantrum when you lose?"

Ethan laughed. "She's got you there, man. You didn't talk to me for three days after I kicked your ass in that 3K race."

"And you accused me of hiding tiles when I won our Scrabble tournament," she pointed out. "Mom used to say—"

"'Take a breath and take it outside if you're gonna be a sore loser,'" Harper cut in, grinning. "Remember when Kyle insisted I screwed up the envelope in Clue when he announced Colonel Mustard did it, but he was wrong and got eliminated?"

Kyle groaned. "Really? My first family dinner back in a decade and you're giving me shit over some dumb games?"

"Got a lot to make up for," Ethan said, sliding a piece of pork onto his plate. "Do you pout when your characters don't do what you want?"

Kyle gave him the middle finger, and they all laughed.

"How's the writing going?" Mia asked.

"It was slow at first, but I'm starting to break through. It takes me a while to really get into the guts of the story, then it's easier to tweak and revise."

"What is it about?" Harper asked.

The words popped out of Ophelia's mouth automatically. "Kyle never shares the details of the story until the first draft is done."

"How come?" Mia asked.

"This may sound weird, but if I talk it out too much, the story loses its mystery and I stop wanting to write it. Made that mistake with a few ideas that died on the vine. My muse probably strangled them to death—she's a demanding mistress. Doesn't like me to tip our hand too soon."

"Remember when you told me that amazing conspiracy plot where the best friend's lover—"

"Was the killer?" Kyle finished. "Holy crap, that would've won me an Academy Award. But I told Ophelia the whole thing and then, no matter how hard I tried to write it, nothing came. I worked on that thing for six months and couldn't dredge up a decent scene."

Mia leaned forward in obvious curiosity. "So you've been writing since you were very young?"

"Yeah, sometimes I feel like I was born with a pen in my hand. Been writing as long as I could remember."

"Figured he'd make it big," Ethan said, pride carved on his face. "He won a national writing award in high school, and always had his sights on the movies. Mr. Fancy Pants."

"Fancy, huh? I remember you showing up for some of those parties dressed in your sparkling duds, too. You were quite the beefcake in Tinseltown."

"You did not just call me a beefcake."

Mia grinned. "Oh yes, he did. You don't happen to have any pics of Ethan in his Hollywood finery, do you, Kyle?"

Ethan shot him a warning glare. "No, he does not."

"As a matter of fact, I do." He whipped out his phone, scrolled through a few screens, then passed it around the table, ignoring Ethan's murderous glance.

Mia clapped a hand over her mouth. "Are you wearing a white tux, babe?" she murmured. "You look so . . . Redford."

Harper hooted with laughter. "He looks like he's going to prom!"

Ethan muttered a curse and ripped open a biscuit with leashed savagery. "Oh, you just wait, Kimpton. I got some stuff to show on you—and all bets are off."

"Now who's being a sore loser?"

Mia gave the phone back and stroked his shoulder, soothing her beast. "I think you looked hot."

"Really?"

"I'll show you later how much," she whispered, causing a chorus of groans around the table.

Ethan grinned and relaxed back in his chair, shooting Kyle a sympathetic look.

"Can you at least tell us the genre?" Harper asked. "'Cause I love the twisty stuff you write, plus the car crashes. They're spectacular."

"Thanks! This one is a bit more mainstream than my other stuff," he said. "I'm trying something different."

"Psychological thriller? Sci-fi?" Harper asked.

His aura screamed unease, making Ophelia even more curious about the real subject of his screenplay.

"It's a love story," he finally said.

"Oh, like a funny chick flick?" Mia asked.

He looked up from his plate, his jaw clenched with resolution. "No, much deeper. Bigger."

Harper nodded. "Like Nicholas Sparks? Where someone dies, or a great love is lost, and the audience files out in hysterics?"

"Sort of. But no one will die."

"Good. I hate sad endings," Harper said. "Will there be a dog or a horse in it as a best friend? Putting a rescue animal in a movie could be huge for the publicity of shelters."

"I'll think about it," Kyle said with a smile.

"Why do you want to change genres?" Mia asked. "Do you feel like you need to do something different? Or is there a reason why you want to tell this particular story?"

Suddenly, his gaze swiveled and crashed into Ophelia's. Heat blasted her veins, and her family faded to the background under the sheer intensity emanating from him.

His voice was a deep rumble of sound, but even as he answered Mia's question, Ophelia knew the words were meant for her. "I've been dead blocked for almost a year. Each time I tried to write a new screenplay, I couldn't deliver. I was unable to write anything until I sat up in bed one night and knew I had to write this particular story—a story stripped down to the bone. No villains or car crashes or plot twists. Just a movie about two people falling in love and losing each other, and how that type of loss can affect a person's entire life."

"Will they get together in the end?" Mia asked.

Kyle paused. "I don't know yet. I have to follow the story to figure out the ending."

Mia nodded. "Well, don't forget one important thing that too many people overlook, especially with second chances."

"What?" Kyle asked.

Mia gave them both a pointed look. "Forgiveness. Nothing can be truly resolved without it."

Silence fell.

Ophelia tried to hide her shaky fingers by fiddling with her napkin.

Was Kyle writing a story about them? And how did she feel about him penning that particular tale from his own viewpoint?

Questions whirled in her mind, but she forced herself to pin a smile on her face and redirect the conversation.

"Well, that sounds interesting. Harper, how was the auction? Did you pick up any new horses?"

"No, thank God. All the horses got picked up and went to good owners. Anyone know when Chloe is coming for a visit? Chloe's Pride misses her."

"Who's Chloe?" Kyle asked, adding a generous portion of seconds to his plate.

Mia broke into a joyous smile. "She's the New York City mayor's daughter. I was his PR representative. Over the summer, Chloe stayed here at the inn and helped with the horses. She'd gotten into some trouble at college and was mandated community service on the horse farm. I was her guardian."

"That's how Mia and I met," Ethan said, giving her a wink. "She came to Gardiner in these sexy heels and stole my heart."

Mia punched his arm. "Liar! He thought I was a spoiled, silly city girl who couldn't cut it on the farm. Of course, I didn't think very highly of him, either, so it was an epic battle."

"But you fell in love with me, and we both won," Ethan said.

Kyle made gagging noises. Harper cracked up.

Mia rolled her eyes. "Anyway, Chloe will be here in a few weeks. She can stay the night and have dinner with us on Sunday."

"That'd be nice," Ethan said. "She already texted me about her new boyfriend. Did you see his pic on Instagram? I want to meet him."

Mia gasped. "I didn't see it yet! I can't believe she shared that with you first!"

Ethan shrugged. "We're tight. Alternative music lovers unite."

Kyle shook his head and leaned back in his chair. "Damn, dude, you've changed. Thank God it's all for the good. Now, are we going to vote or not? What was your favorite dish?"

Ophelia groaned. "Is this really necessary?"

"You're just afraid of losing."

"Oh yeah? And what do I get if I win?"

He seemed to ponder her question with seriousness. "If you win, I'll do all the cleanup tonight."

"Good. I need a break."

"But if I win, you take me to dinner this week. And no takeout, either. I want real napkins and fine china."

Ethan whistled. "Be careful, Tink. Last time he made me pick up the bill, he ordered two bottles of pricey wine I couldn't even pronounce. He's gotten a bit pretentious."

Kyle ignored him, his eyes probing hers. "Deal?"

She pursed her lips, refusing to back down even though she knew it was a trick. He thought he'd win and force her to spend time with him. But the odds were stacked against him. Her family went nuts over her cooking. It was an easy victory.

"Deal."

"Harper, what dish did you like the most?" he asked.

Her sister didn't even look sympathetic. "Potatoes. They rocked."

Kyle smiled smugly. "One point for me. Mia?"

"The quiche. Simple perfection."

"And that's a point for me," Ophelia said. "Ethan?"

Everyone stared at her brother. He surveyed the cluttered table. She sat back, relaxed. It'd be the biscuits. He had a weakness for her baked goods and any type of bread.

Thank God she wouldn't have any cleanup and could retire early tonight.

"This is hard, but I have to be honest." He shot Kyle a regretful look. "Sorry I have to say this, Kyle. It's kind of embarrassing, but—"

"I guess I win," she cut in.

"I love your meat."

Her jaw dropped. Kyle gave a shout and did some type of high five with Ethan across the table. Mia murmured her condolences and swore she'd help her do the dishes. Ophelia burst into laughter at the whole ridiculous situation.

God, why did it feel so good to have him back?

And what the hell was she going to do about it?

Chapter Eleven

Ophelia finished piling in the groceries and shut the trunk of her lemon-colored SUV. Her guests were arriving tomorrow morning. By next weekend, she'd be at half capacity. She had a million things to do and needed to focus on work.

An image of last night's dinner flashed in her mind. It was almost as if Kyle had slipped back into the family fold without a bump, even after all this time. He radiated a warm glow of ease and belonging that made her heart sigh. And after he'd won the silly contest, the promise of their dinner date hung heavily between them, causing her to shiver and stumble like a schoolgirl.

It was like she was becoming smitten with him all over again.

Ophelia groaned and headed back to the inn. She had to keep reminding herself that these next few months would be like a dream that would quickly end. They could all pretend they were united again as a family, but on April 1, Kyle intended to return to his real life. He would forget them like a blip on a screen. He'd spent too long carving out the career of his dreams to give it up. He lived in a fancy house with chefs and cleaners and had beautiful women hanging on him. He'd probably had dozens of lovers since her. Hundreds, maybe. The thought made her stomach twist with nausea, but she had to deal with the truth.

When he spoke of a second chance, he meant temporarily. Maybe he wanted her back in his bed. To relive the raw intimacy they'd shared that only the very young and very in love could experience. Maybe it was even all for this screenplay he was writing, in order to steep himself in the emotions of the past. Once he was satisfied and the screenplay was complete, he'd move on.

He'd agree to the divorce and never look back.

And she'd be left alone with a broken heart. God knew she'd barely survived the first time. It was as if a piece of her had been ripped away. She'd been forced to live without him and carve out her own path. Yes, she'd discovered her strength and eventually became happy.

But to put herself through such agony again? To watch him pick his career over her?

She may not survive.

She needed to keep herself emotionally distant and safe until then.

On her drive home, she passed the road to Patrick's house and spotted flashing lights glimmering from the thicket of bare trees. Frowning, she made a quick right turn and followed the path to the farmhouse.

An ambulance was parked in his driveway.

She jumped from the car and raced toward the door, pausing at the scene in front of her.

"I told you to go away!" Patrick bellowed, waving the two medics away. He was seated in a battered mud-brown chair, a blood pressure cuff wrapped around his upper arm. "I told you it was a mistake!"

They exchanged glances. The younger man held a stethoscope, and it seemed like they'd been there for a while, trying to cajole him. "You called 911, sir. Your blood pressure is definitely low. We'd like to get you in for a quick check."

"I'm fine. Now you're wasting valuable time when you could be helping people who really need you. Get this thing off me."

"Patrick? Are you okay?"

Three glances swiveled toward the door. The medics looked relieved. "Ma'am, are you a family member?"

The ridiculous thought that he was technically her father-in-law floated by, but she pushed it away. "No, I'm his neighbor. Is there something I can do?"

"Yeah, get them the hell out of here," Patrick grunted, ripping at the cuff. "I felt faint so I called 911, but now I'm fine. They keep pressuring me to go to the hospital. I don't need it."

"Technically, we can't make you go, sir. But your pressure is low, and with your prior heart attack, I'd recommend some extra tests. We can do an EKG right now."

"Heart attack?" she asked in a high voice. "I didn't know about that."

Patrick grunted again. "Happened years ago. Don't need no EKG. I'll rest and drink water, okay? I'd appreciate it if you'd go now."

The medics exchanged a few words, and then the younger one nodded. "You'll have to sign a waiver for me. There may be charges for coming out for a false alarm."

"Yeah, yeah, give me a pen."

They gave him the waiver, he signed it, and they packed up and left. Ophelia drifted into the house and sat beside him.

"You never said you'd been ill," she said quietly. "I didn't even hear about it in town."

"'Cause I know how to keep a secret. Been practicing my whole life." He leaned back his head in the chair and groaned. "I'm just tired. Pushed myself today and paid." He shot her a suspicious look. "What are you doing here?"

"I was passing by and saw the ambulance. I got worried."

"False alarm."

Ophelia surveyed the room. She hadn't been in Kyle's house for nearly eight years, but what she remembered still looked the same. Basic furniture, scarred wood floors, spartan décor, and the usual quirky characteristics of an old farmhouse. The walls were thick with various built-ins, a Dutch door led to the kitchen, and the drafty, high ceilings echoed their voices. Her practiced eye also surmised Patrick hadn't cleaned in weeks—it was obvious from the dust and clutter. Empty boxes of prepared foods littered the kitchen counters, and dirty mugs stuffed the sink that she could see.

"Ever think of bringing in some help?" she asked, trying to sound casual. She steeled herself for an angry outburst and swore she'd leave if he lost his temper. She'd done her Good Samaritan thing. Kyle's father didn't need anything else from her.

Instead, he nodded. "I did. Hired a local girl for a while to do light cleanup, but most of the time she didn't show. College students aren't the most dependable."

"What about meals? Are you eating?"

"Sure. Got my freezer stocked full of meals, even veggies."

She winced. His diet was packed with sodium and preservatives. Definitely not heart healthy.

Not her problem.

"Okay, as long as you have what you need. I better get back to the inn. You should rest today."

"I will."

Uneasy just leaving him, she scooted toward the door and tried to tell herself he'd be fine.

Why did the silence sound so lonely? Did he have anyone who cared enough to check in on him?

"Listen, if you need anything, give me a call. I'm right down the road."

"Okay."

She stepped outside the door and glanced back. Head tipped back, eyes nearly closed, his body seemed half the size she remembered when she was young. He was no longer a fierce monster who consistently hurt Kyle and refused to be social with her family. Suddenly, he was just an old man alone in a house with no one. His choices had finally caught up with him.

She waited for the surge of emotion that would tell her he was getting justice, but it was eerily absent as she got to her car. She slid into the driver's seat, trying to push the image of Patrick's face out of her mind.

She was avoiding him.

Kyle cracked his knuckles and stretched his neck side to side. Dinner had been perfect. Reconnecting with Ethan and Harper was special, and Mia was now part of their inner circle. And cooking with Ophelia made him realize how much he'd missed her.

He figured he'd collect on his dinner date debt and keep things moving forward. He already knew he wanted to go to Crystal's—a fabulous steakhouse with intimate décor. Unfortunately, he'd already mentioned the date twice and she'd waved him off, citing her calendar as too busy.

He rubbed his head and pondered his next move. He'd tried to talk to her various times, but she was back to her chilly, distant self. She just kept asking him about the damn lawyers and if he'd made a choice.

Yeah, he had.

He chose neither.

No lawyers. No papers. No divorce. But he needed to ease her into the idea.

Maybe he could use the whole divorce mess to arrange more time with her. It might be the only excuse that would get her to sit down and talk. An evil plan, yes. But necessary?

Yes.

He looked back at the last chapter and did a quick read-through. The shiver that raced down his spine told him the truth.

It was good. Really good.

Once he'd given up on writing it as a screenplay, the story had begun to flow. He'd never reached a level of raw emotion in his work like this. It was as if he were reaching deeper, fleshing out characters instead of moving them frantically forward to deliver a stunning plot.

The characters were the plot, along with their emotions. He was showing how they affect everyone and drive decisions that could end up haunting you forever.

Especially love.

He took a sip of lukewarm coffee, squinted at the screen, and wrote.

"I think we should leave." He'd been thinking about it for a long time but was finally ready to bring it up.

She sat between his legs on the high hill by the barns. The sun was a circle of fiery orange, suspended high in the sky, brushing the tips of the jagged mountain peaks. Fingers entwined, her head leaned back against his chest. His lips brushed her cheek.

"Where would we go?" she asked, sounding more curious than shocked. She'd known his frustration with his father had reached an epic level. He was trapped, and the only way to freedom was to blow everything up that kept him tied down.

Everything but Ophelia.

She was his everything. If she decided to stay, he'd stay with her, but he hoped to hell he could communicate his vision for their future.

"California," he answered. "It's the best place for us. Besides having great weather, that's where the jobs are. I want to write screenplays. You want to sing. We can both follow our dreams there."

"What about college? I thought we were going to the community college in the fall together?"

He stroked her hair away from her nape, kissing her sensitive skin and reveling in her shivers. "What is college going to do for us other than delay our dreams? We already have talent. I won that writing contest, and

I've clocked in endless hours studying books on how to write screenplays. I already have two ready to go."

"And they're good," she added.

He smiled. "Your voice is everything, baby. When you sing, people stop to listen. Everyone talked about your solo in Grease *for weeks. You could probably stand on a street corner and get your bucket filled up in a few hours."*

She chuckled and stretched out her legs. The heavy weight of her breast pressed into the back of his hand. He ran his knuckles over the sweet curves, his erection pressing with demand against her ass. He ignored it, used to the condition whenever he was around Ophelia.

"I don't know how to do big auditions and stuff," she said worriedly. "I've never been out of New York."

"Neither have I, but we could do it together." His voice filled with intensity. The vision shimmered before him in all its glory—sharing an apartment, working to follow their dreams, sleeping with her every night. Away from the farm and the suffocation of daily existence. Ethan already planned to go into the military. How could they just go to the local college and believe anything would change?

He grasped her shoulders and turned her around. Looking into her beautiful face, he tried to make her see. "Do you want to spend your life serving guests and being a glorified housekeeper? I sure as hell can't keep living with my father and taking care of his farm. We were meant for more than this. We're special. We were blessed with talents, and it wouldn't be right not to go out and try to use them."

Excitement glittered in her sky-blue eyes. She chewed her lip, obviously thinking over the possibility. "We don't know anyone out there. How would we get a job? An apartment?"

"I contacted my uncle, and he said he could set us up with a small place. I already have enough money saved to get us started." He'd been saving every dime for years now, just for this moment. "My uncle said he knows some people in the entertainment industry and will introduce us."

"Your uncle Tony?" she asked. "Won't he tell your dad?"

"They're not close—they barely talk. He said he's willing to help us. I have my car. We'll drive out to California and finally get to be together."

A nervous laugh broke from her lips. "Oh my God, my mother will kill me. So will Ethan."

"We don't have to tell them until we go. It may be easier that way. But I don't want to do this unless you want it, too, Ophelia. Leaving would mean nothing without you."

Her eyes softened. She stroked his cheek, and he kissed her, plunging his tongue deep into her honeyed mouth, gathering her taste and falling into her with everything he was.

He still hadn't made love to her. He was waiting for the perfect time, and it was hard to get her alone for a night with Ethan and her family constantly around. He refused to rush. He wanted a full night of her stretched out in his bed—not a literal roll in the hay.

"Do you think we can do it?"

He smiled, clutching her tighter, willing her to believe what he already knew. "Yes. California will be magical. And warm. And exciting—the perfect place to start our lives together." He couldn't stand seeing doubt in her eyes, so he gave her the truth, not wanting to wait any longer. "I don't just want to live with you, baby. I want us to get married."

Her eyes widened. He held his breath and waited, but only caught joy and want in her face. "You want to get married?" she repeated, her voice a breathy wisp of sound. "Kyle, are you serious? You don't need to promise me marriage for me to go with you. I don't need that." She tilted her chin up. "And I don't need a wedding to sleep with you. I'm tired of waiting. I want you. It's starting to drive me a bit crazy."

"Me, too, baby. But maybe I'm the one who needs the wedding." He pulled her tight and kissed her. "Maybe I need reassurance that you're not just using me for my hot bod."

She giggled against his mouth—a sweet, feminine sound he adored—and ran her hands over his back. "How'd you find out my evil plan?"

"You undress me with your eyes. I have to prove I have more to offer you than sex."

Her face grew serious. She tipped her forehead to his. "All I want is you, Kyle. Always. Forever. Just us."

"Just us. So we're going to do this?"

Her smile was slow and sweet and perfect. "Yes. Let's go to California and get married and become famous."

He laughed and tumbled her to the ground, tucking her tight against his body. The sun sunk and bled out muted golds and dewy oranges, throwing the valley into shadow. He kissed her and promised her the world. He knew he'd deliver.

There was absolutely nothing to stop them.

Chapter Twelve

"We have reservations at Crystal's tonight. Seven p.m."

Ophelia froze midstep. She'd been completely focused on trying to run away when she heard his footsteps on the stairs, but Kyle's commanding voice stalled her retreat. She swiveled back around and stared at him.

"I can't go out tonight. I'm busy!"

He climbed down the last few steps and crowded her space, his lean build practically vibrating with masculine body heat. He smelled like chocolate chip cookies and coffee and washed cotton. She dug her nails into her palms and tried to look calm, to pretend she had no interest in those delicious, sulky lips and their immense talent.

"It's Thursday night. I double-checked your schedule. Your guests arrive tomorrow, but you have time to have dinner with me tonight."

"You spied on my calendar!"

His lip twitched. "Yeah. I learned your programs when you were sick, remember? Why? Is your calendar like your diary or something? Are there little scribbled hearts with my name scrawled in them that you didn't want me to see?"

Her cheeks grew hot, which made her even madder. "Don't be ridiculous. I just don't like you sneaking around and trying to manage my time."

"You lost the bet. Are you going to welch?"

His direct question got her ire up. She stood on tiptoes and jabbed a finger in the air. "I'm not a welcher! Fine, let's get this whole thing over with. We'll talk about the divorce and finally get things moving."

"I don't think that's a good idea. We don't want anyone overhearing our private business and figuring out we're married. Crystal's is packed with locals."

She glared.

Damn, he was right—even though his innocent look was anything but. How was she going to get through the evening without falling into bad habits? Without her weak body betraying her mind?

She steeled her shoulders like she was going into battle. "Oh, you're good," she drawled. "But don't think you'll be able to tempt me by taking a walk down memory lane. I said I'd buy you dinner, but I never promised you conversation. See you at seven."

She ignored his arrogant grin and spun on her heel, marching away. He had her trapped. The sooner she got this dinner over with, the sooner she could continue ignoring him. She had to make sure she wore pants, and a thick sweater, and definitely thermal underwear. Maybe her tucked-in-the-back-of-the-drawer granny panties, too. Just in case he spiked her drink and she got all hot and tried to have sex with him. The thought of what lay underneath would be enough to sober her up.

Hours later, she was seated across from him at a small table, frantically questioning her sanity.

She'd forgotten how devastatingly handsome he was dressed up. He wore black pants; fancy, low-heeled black leather boots; a green button-down Robert Graham shirt with the cuffs turned up; and a sleek black leather jacket that gave him the perfect air of bad-boyness. He smelled of pine and spice. She'd barely been able to control herself in the car, fighting the impulse to lean close and take a whiff in the curve of his neck. He looked dashing and graceful—the darling of Hollywood.

Ophelia studied the menu and tried to keep an icy distance. Even the surroundings of Crystal's were working against her. The sultry tones of Etta James spilled from the speakers. The tables were scattered around the room with enough distance to give off a romantic vibe. Endless candles flickered in the dim light amid fine crystal and classic china. The ornate chandelier rivaled Cinderella's castle, accented by the warm touches of dark wood and burgundy.

She ordered a martini, and Kyle ordered a glass of pinot noir, his favorite red. He rarely drank more than two beverages in an evening, choosing to switch to seltzer after his two-drink maximum. Alcoholism ran in the family, easily passed on to the next generation, and he'd been ruthlessly determined to never fall into the trap like his father.

The thought of Patrick gave her a buzz of guilt.

Should she tell Kyle about the ambulance? Or would the information only cause him pain?

"I missed this," he said, closing his menu with a smile. "When I left town, there was only Galveston's and Lombardi's if you wanted a fancy place to eat. When did this open?"

"Five years ago. The owner's name is Albert. He lost his wife and opened this place up in her honor."

His eyes flickered with sympathy. "Can't imagine that type of loss. I'd like to meet him."

"I'm sure he'll want to meet you. You have many fans here." They'd already been stopped twice on the way to their table, and Ophelia caught Maureen Garry craning her neck around, furiously whispering to her husband. Kyle had always been well liked in town, despite his father's drinking problem. Now that he'd returned as a star, the town was buzzing. It reminded her of when Ethan came back, except he'd hidden himself away from the world for a while to heal. Kyle had an easygoing charm that made people feel comfortable approaching him.

"Only interested in one woman's approval and adoration. Unfortunately, she doesn't even want to talk to me."

A reluctant smile tugged at her lips. "Women always fell over you wherever we went," she pointed out. "It was exhausting. I'd overhear conversations in the ladies' room about how hot you were and how they intended to replace me."

He pinned her with his gaze. "I never really noticed. When you walked into a room, the world came alive. No one else meant anything to me."

She shifted in her seat, trying to hide how much his words stirred her.

A frown creased his brow. "Is that why you ran away? Because you thought I was interested in other women? Did you think I was at those parties flirting and looking to replace you?"

She shook her head. "No, I trusted you completely."

"Yet you fled without a goodbye. Or a warning. I came home a bit late one night, and you were gone."

She stiffened and narrowed her gaze. "Funny how those same events played out differently in my recollection. But it doesn't matter anymore."

"Yes, it matters," he said strongly, leaning across the table. The candlelight turned his hair to white-blond and emphasized the intense glint in his eyes that screamed of a goal she only wanted to avoid. "I came back not only for a second chance, but to figure out what went so wrong. I need to know."

"For us? Or for your script?"

He flinched.

Just as he opened his mouth to respond, he was interrupted by the waiter stopping by the table to recite the specials and take their order. By the time he glided away, she had taken a few sips of her martini, and the moment had passed.

He surveyed her moody silence and rubbed his head. "I'm screwing up again, aren't I?"

She arched a brow.

"I wanted to remind you how much fun we have together, but I'm digging myself into a literal hole. And God, I just uttered a terrible cliché."

"It's okay."

"No, if you're buying dinner, I can at least dazzle you with conversation without pissing you off. I know—let's play a game. Truth or dare?"

She tilted her head. "Are you kidding me?"

"No. We used to play when we got bored waiting in line for the buffet, remember? Go ahead, truth or dare?"

"This is ridiculous. We're too old for such a game."

"What are you scared of? I'll go easy on you, I swear. Truth or dare?"

She let out a breath. "Fine. Truth. But I'm not answering if I don't like the question."

"You can't pick and choose, or you lose." He tapped his chin as if thinking hard. "What's the worst thing you ever did to a guest you didn't like?"

The memory caught her by surprise and made her laugh. "Well, I had this really cranky elderly woman who insulted me all weekend. She was just horrible. I tried everything, but I couldn't please her. When she checked out, she said she intended to write a bad review, but I told her she'd been so unreasonable that I was going to write a bad review about *her*, and she'd never find another hotel or inn who'd take her."

He blinked. "I don't get it. Is there a site like that?"

She gave an evil grin. "No, I made the whole thing up. But she had no clue. She got all flustered, thinking I was going to put her name out there to be blacklisted from vacation spots, and she apologized! It was awesome."

He laughed, slathering butter generously on his roll. "I never would've thought of that. Kind of brilliant. Much more creative than messing with their toothbrush or food."

"I have standards, and messing with guests' personal hygiene or diet is something I'd never do."

"Good to know. I was getting worried about who was cleaning my bathroom." He flashed her a mischievous smile, and she laughed. "Your turn."

She grabbed a roll. "Truth or dare?"

"Truth."

"What's the craziest thing you've had to do to promote a movie?"

His adorable face crinkled up as he thought hard. "Hmm, I'd say the premiere for my third movie, *Conspiracy*. The marketing department came up with this crazy-ass plan to involve the audience in a fake conspiracy game, and they forced me to play a part. You know how nerve-racking those things are without additional responsibilities? Instead of worrying about the reaction to the movie, I was running around and interrogating a bunch of strangers, asking them if they had these little pieces of paper that said a code word on them. I had to find a fucking spy at my own damn premiere. Needless to say, it was a disaster. I never found the spy, the marketing department got pissed and blamed me for not being a team player, and the audience surveys said the movie sucked. Hell, at least the movie made a crapload of money and was still considered a success."

His laugh held a hint of self-mockery, and her gut twisted. She fought the need to reach across the table and touch him—to smooth his hair back from his brow, to kiss his smiling mouth and lose herself in the searing, deep connection that had always burned between them. Instead, she smiled back and kept her distance.

They ate their filets with shared gusto and fell into lighter chatter. She caught him up on the town gossip, and he entertained her with funny stories about celebrities. Soon she was relaxed, glowing from an abundance of good alcohol and rare meat.

"Kyle Kimpton!"

Ophelia smiled at the starstruck-looking couple. She'd known it was only a matter of time before Maureen interrupted them, but she understood. Maureen and her husband, Jack, ran the local movie theater and had watched them grow up. Kyle stood to greet them with genuine warmth.

"My goodness, you look wonderful," Maureen squealed, her brown hair now peppered with gray, and her trim figure a bit more rounded from the generosity of age. "I cannot believe I'm screening your movies now! Remember when you both used to request a giant tub of popcorn with extra butter and then add snowcaps?"

They laughed. Jack clapped Kyle on the shoulder. "We're really proud of you, son. Knew you'd be a big hit in Hollywood. You were always our first customer when a new movie came to the theater. Glad to see you got Ophelia out for a date night. She needs a break from the inn."

Maureen practically glowed with triumph. "I always thought you'd make a cute couple."

Warmth flushed her cheeks.

God, did the whole town assume they were together?

She opened her mouth to tell them he was only staying temporarily, but Kyle smoothly cut in. "Ophelia does work way too hard. I need to remind her how to play." He gave her a wink, and she tried not to glare.

Maureen sighed. "Well, she's just like her mom. She runs the best bed-and-breakfast in town. It's too bad that the singing didn't work out, though. You were so talented, dear, but I know Hollywood is brutal. At least Kyle made it. I'm sure you're happy to have a quieter, more stable life."

Jack nodded. "We're just grateful to have you back. Maybe you can stop by the theater sometime and do a talk for the college students? They'd love it. We can screen one of your movies."

Ophelia noticed Kyle sending a worried glance toward her, as if shocked at Maureen's raw words, but he managed to smile and agree and end the conversation gracefully.

As the waiter cleared the table and handed them the dessert menus, an uncomfortable silence fell between them.

"I can't believe she said that to you," he muttered, temper carving out the lines of his face. "I'm sorry, Ophelia. I should've said something."

She shrugged, regarding him openly. "Why? She's right, and I don't disagree with anything she said."

"Really? Well, I don't agree. I know if you would've stayed on that show, you would've become a huge star. And though you say you're happy at the inn, I know how often you must think about what could have been if you stayed. I remember how badly you wanted a career different from your mom's. I just want you to know I understand." He paused, as if reaching deep inside himself and connecting with his emotions. "I also want to tell you I forgive you for running away. We were young, and we made a lot of mistakes. I'm sorry for everything I did that contributed to the breakup, but let's both move forward and start fresh. What do you think?"

The world shifted. A deep, uncurling anger began in her belly and flowed outward, heating her blood. She stared into his familiar face, now carved out in sympathy, and began to shake with the need to yell, scream, throw, hit. The years of silence and buried resentment sprang up with vicious glee, until her vision blurred with the need to make him finally understand the truth.

"I'm glad you forgive me, Kyle," she said quietly, her voice so sharp he watched her with a wary glint in his eye. "Unfortunately, I don't forgive *you*."

He blinked. "I don't understand."

"You never did. I don't think you ever really wanted to." She closed her menu, retrieved her purse, and pushed her chair back. "I'm going to pay the bill. I'll meet you in the car."

"Ophelia—"

"Not another word. I'm not about to lose it in front of your fan club."

"But—"

She stood and walked away with her chin high and her emotions roiling like a witch's cauldron.

What the hell had just happened?

Kyle drove back to the inn, going over the evening. Yes, it had started rough, but eventually, he'd sensed her walls lowering. The hum of attraction had deepened into that comforting familiarity he always loved about being around her, as if there was a piece missing inside him that only she was able to fill.

He thought offering his forgiveness and understanding for her abandonment had been a good thing. A grown-up, healthy way to heal the wounds of the past. Instead, she'd stormed out and now maintained an icy silence he hadn't been able to break.

He needed to find out exactly what had pissed her off.

"Not talking to me isn't going to solve the problem," he reminded her. "I'm on your side, remember? I apologized. I offered forgiveness. I told you I understood how hard it must be when you think about your singing."

"You have no idea how I feel, because you never stopped long enough to talk to me."

Her profile was edged in ice, and suddenly his own temper surged, mixed with confusion. "Then for God's sake, why don't you end the mystery and tell me! What did I say back there that was so wrong?"

He pulled into the parking lot and cut the engine.

She gnashed her teeth, jerked around, and lit into him. "Let's start with your arrogance. You forgive *me* for running away, Kyle? How generous of you—to try and understand how I could leave after you broke your final promise to me. I begged you for weeks to talk with me. I told you I was confused and not happy, and you ignored me. You'd kiss me and run off to work—sometimes for days. And even when you were home, you were in this fog, refusing to engage. At night you'd fuck me, roll over, and fall asleep. I watched you slip away day by day. I fought with everything I had, but do you remember what you'd say?"

A flare of guilt ignited deep. He didn't like to think about the way he may have treated her during his intense work sessions. He'd tried to explain how important it was that he be on call and throw himself into his career, assured her that it would eventually calm down. That he'd finally give her time.

Had he, though?

"What did I say?"

"You said I wasn't supportive. That I was being selfish by nagging you, and that we'd made an agreement to support one another in our quest for success." Her laugh was bitter. "God, I begged you for time. I told you I couldn't take any more, and you promised to come back that night to talk. I waited for you all night, but you didn't even call. You didn't text. You did nothing. Because I had become unimportant."

"I tried to explain how crazy things got," he said stiffly. "I brought home roses. I swore I'd take you away for a quiet weekend, but when I got home, you weren't there."

"I didn't need roses or a fancy getaway. I just wanted you to look into my eyes and see me again. I was so lonely."

His heart shattered. The silence settled around them, throbbing with memories and regrets. "I was wrapped up in my own head," he finally said. "I didn't realize how far I'd drifted away, or that I took you for granted. I wanted so badly for us to succeed together—I thought that was the reason we left for California. I wanted you to have it all."

When she looked at him, he sucked in his breath. The truth in her eyes slammed through him and tore apart every last shred of belief he had regarding their relationship. He realized maybe he hadn't known the woman he loved after all.

"I already had it all," she said quietly. "I didn't leave with you to be a famous singer. Oh sure, I intended to try, but it was never my focus." Her voice broke. "Singing wasn't the only thing I wanted. It was just you."

He jerked at the raw admission, shaking his head as if to deny the pain. "No, we both wanted different lives. Neither of us wanted to end up like our parents—stuck in a small town in a small job. We wanted more."

"No, *you* wanted more. Remember what you asked me that day in the fields? The day you said you wanted to marry me?"

The breath stuck in his lungs. "What?"

"You asked if I wanted to spend my life as a glorified housekeeper. Like my mom. And I knew right then and there that I wanted you more than anything in the world. I loved you with my heart and soul, and that I needed to be the type of woman you'd admire. A woman who went for the brass ring and was bigger than life. A star, like you."

He stared at her, his heart squeezing with tension. Somehow, he sensed her next words would change things.

She shook her head. "Yes, I wanted to sing, but I didn't look at my mom the way you did. I saw her happy and fulfilled. I saw her laugh and chat with guests and learn about the world through other people. I watched her serve with a giving heart. I thought it was a good life— until you convinced me it would be too limited. Too boring. How could I have expressed that I didn't mind spending my life in Gardiner, taking care of people like my mom? You would've left me. So I tried to change and focus on my singing as wholeheartedly as you focused on writing. It just wasn't me. I loved singing, but I despised every other part of that world—your world. The world you loved and became a part of."

She leaned over and touched his cheek. Her eyes glinted in the shards of moonlight spilling into the car. Her musical voice seethed with sadness.

"I only wanted you, and when I realized you needed so much more than just me, I knew I had to leave. Before we completely destroyed each other, worse than we already had. I didn't run away as much as I returned home to be who I wanted. And I'm not ashamed to say this is who I am. I'm proud of my life. I'm happy running the inn."

He blinked, trying desperately to fight for clarity as his head spun. She'd never craved success the way he had?

The truth she'd never truly wanted to leave her home was like a fist in his gut.

Her hand dropped, and she moved back. "So there you have it. The real truth. I don't blame you for going after success. I only blamed you for not listening when I finally tried to tell you the truth."

"You were just as important to me as my writing. I would have understood."

Her soft laugh held a touch of bitterness. "I wish that were true. You told me in the kitchen on Sunday that I was everything that mattered to you. But you never chose me, Kyle. Not once." She shook her head and turned. "I have to go in."

His head spun, trying to sift through the words that pounded at him like nails. Her pain was unbearable, and he ached to soothe it away, to convince her she meant everything to him.

"Ophelia—"

"Don't," she said softly. "I feel too raw right now. I just need to go inside and be alone, okay?" A tiny laugh escaped her lips. "Maybe it was just too much truth for one night. For both of us."

She slipped out the door and disappeared inside.

Kyle stayed in the cold, silent car, thinking about what she'd said.

Dear God, what had he done? All this time, he'd believed she hated her life in Gardiner the way he had. But then again, had he ever truly asked her? Or had he just assumed she wanted exactly what he did? Had he been wrong this entire time about how their story had played out?

And if so, was there any way he could make it right to give them a second chance?

He didn't know.

Nausea churned his gut. Everything he'd once believed was tilted on its axis, challenging him to see things in a new light. The woman Ophelia had become was so much bigger than the girl he remembered. Tonight had only proved it.

This time, he'd make sure to listen to her and be what she needed.

This time, he intended on writing his own ending.

Chapter Thirteen

Ophelia dropped a platter of steaming bacon on the table and refilled her guests' half-empty coffee mugs. "How are the omelets?" she asked brightly.

The older couple sighed in unison. "Delicious," Marian said. "I had no idea fresh herbs could make such a difference in eggs!"

Her husband, Carl, forked up another piece of pork sausage and patted his belly. "Haven't had a meal like this in a while. Ever think of visiting Boston and staying with us, Ophelia? You can have a free tourist weekend if you just cook us breakfast."

She laughed, charmed by their easy demeanor. They were visiting their son, who'd just had a new baby, but his house was too small to accommodate the new grandparents. She'd already been treated to dozens of pictures proudly showing the wrapped-up-in-a-blanket beauty, but Ophelia didn't mind.

"I'll keep it in mind," she said, deftly clearing empty plates. "Would you like me to make any reservations for dinner? Or are you eating with your son tonight?"

"Actually, we're babysitting and letting them get out. We'd love to get them a table at Galveston's, but it's probably booked up."

"I know the owner. I'd be happy to call and tell him it's a special occasion. I can even arrange for some flowers on the table and the crème brûlée, which has to be ordered ahead of time."

Marian clapped her hands. "That would be wonderful! Thank you so much, Ophelia. You're a dream."

"We'll make sure we leave a very high review on Yelp and TripAdvisor," Carl said seriously.

"It's my pleasure. Seven p.m. okay?"

"Perfect."

"Good. I'll leave the coffee out. Let me know if you need anything else."

She headed back to the kitchen for cleanup, adding the call to the restaurant on her to-do list. Two more guests were checking in later today, and she wanted to have tea, hot cocoa, and cookies ready when they arrived. The rooms were made up and laundry was finished, but she needed to freshen up the main area near the fireplace. It would be nice to offer the guests s'mores tonight in front of the fire, and set up a cozy area to play board games or watch some movies on the new flat-screen TV she'd just invested in. She scribbled it on her growing list and began the cleanup.

The phone rang, and she carefully hit the speaker button with her soapy hands. "Hello?"

"Hey, it's Mia. Whatcha doing?"

"Dishes."

"Ugh. I hate dishes." Ophelia practically heard her shudder. "And cooking. I kind of hate all types of domestic duties."

"Then it's a good thing you don't own an inn," she teased. "What's up?"

"I want to go out."

"I can't right now. I'm slammed with work."

"No, at night. Like grown-ups. It's been snowing here for almost three straight weeks, and all I've worn is practical snow boots and shape-less sweaters. I love our bungalow, but there's only three rooms to see, and Hei Hei is driving me crazy. I want a girls' night out."

"I can't leave tonight. Too much going on," she said.

Mia did something Ophelia had never witnessed before.

She whined.

"Oh please? Don't say no. I want to go dancing and have pretty pink cocktails and wear my Louboutins. I want to talk about boys and trashy television and fashion. I'm going mad. I think I have that winter disease that makes people do bad things. Didn't Jack Nicholson have that in the movie *The Shining*?"

"No, it was the hotel ghosts haunting him. You're probably lacking vitamin E and D. I'll bring some over for you today."

"Harper already said she'd go with us," Mia said.

"Really?" Her sister rarely left her home or the barn in the winter. "Boy, that's proof you *are* good at your job." Persuasion was a key trait in the world of public relations, and Mia was a savvy, talented CEO of her own successful company. "How about tomorrow night? I can get ahead of schedule today and be free then?"

Mia squealed—another thing she rarely did. "Perfect! I've already done some research and know exactly where we should go. I'll tell Ethan we'll be out the entire night and home very late."

"Not too late," she said.

"Very late," Mia insisted. "I have to pick out my outfit. Do you have something to wear, or do you need to go shopping?"

Ophelia laughed.

God, she loved Mia and her love of a good designer. It was such a breath of fresh air.

"I'm sure I have something appropriately slutty to put on."

"Excellent! I'll make all the arrangements and see you tomorrow night!"

She said goodbye and hit the button.

"Where are you going in slutty clothes?"

Ophelia jumped, turning half around. Kyle was stretched in the doorway. From the looks of his mussed hair, sweatpants, old shirt, and socks without shoes, he had been in a deep writing mode.

Had he slept as poorly as she had? Her mind kept replaying their conversation, going over every detail. Had her confession allowed him to view their past differently? Last night had been intense, but she felt free for finally telling him the truth.

The only problem was it hadn't dulled her attraction—or intense need—for him.

Her fingers itched to bury themselves in his hair and comb through the silky strands. She ached to kiss those full lips and have him lift her high to take the embrace deeper, lay her out on the counter, tug off her clothes, and feast on every naked inch of her body before he—

"Ophelia?"

The plate she'd been washing almost slid out of her grasp and crashed. She caught it at the last second and winced. "Sorry, I was thinking about my to-do list. Umm, Mia wants to go out tomorrow for a night of debauchery. She's used to living in Manhattan, so this is her first winter snowbound in the mountains. She's going a bit mad."

"Aren't we all?" he murmured, his gaze snagging hers. "Need any help?"

"No, thanks. How's the writing going?"

"Good." His eyes lit with excitement, a sign he liked what he was creating. "The story is moving slow, but there's potential. Wanted to see if we could have lunch. Talk. We can go down the road to the diner. I've been thinking about our conversation last night."

She turned back to the sink and steeled her shoulders. This was exactly what she'd been trying to avoid—this forced intimacy that only reminded her of their past and how she still ached for him. Their last family dinner had proved she was still vulnerable with him.

My God, she'd almost kissed him in the middle of cooking! She had to stick to her original rules—no interaction while he stayed here.

"Sorry, I'm busy all day. Lots of work to do."

"What if I get us sandwiches and we eat here?"

"I had a late breakfast, so I'm skipping lunch. Maybe you can eat with Mia. She could use the company."

Though she had her back turned and couldn't see his expression, she sensed his frustration in the air. Prepared for another invitation, she got ready to give another excuse.

"What if I promised not to bring up last night at all? We can go over my pick for lawyers. I've narrowed it down to two, but I need help deciding who to book."

She switched off the water, dried her hands, and faced him with pure suspicion. "You looked at my email?" He'd rejected the first two lawyers she suggested, so she'd sent him a more comprehensive list with contact and background information. So far, he'd been unresponsive.

"Of course. I wanted to see if we could make a list of the things we need to complete to get organized. But if you're busy . . ." He trailed off, shrugging as if it wouldn't be his fault if their divorce took years to settle. "I'm in no rush."

Dammit. She needed that divorce ASAP.

She knew he was using it as blackmail to get her to spend time with him, but at this point she didn't care. It was a means to the end she needed. "Fine. I can squeeze in half an hour."

His smile lit up his face, and her heart tripped. He was so beautiful. He could've easily been the one in front of the camera. She bet he was highly sought-after by many beautiful, famous women. Hurt cut through her at the thought, but she knew she had no right to be jealous.

"Great. I'll pick you up a tuna wrap and meet you downstairs at one," he said. "If you need me, I'll be working."

"I'll bring the printouts and research," she said. "We can make some calls."

He didn't answer, just nodded. With one last long look, he headed back to his room.

Ophelia spent the rest of the morning making sure the inn was running smoothly, baking her chocolate chip cookies that were always nut free, and pulling out a variety of crocheted afghans to place around the rooms. She still had a few hours of work on the computer, but she'd have plenty of time for that this afternoon.

Kyle had just walked in the door when she bumped into him in the hallway.

"Perfect timing," he said. "Want to eat on the porch and get some air? It's pretty mild."

"Wow, a whole twenty degrees? I could wear my bikini."

"Thirty. And yes, please do."

She laughed at his wolfish leer. "Sounds good. I'll get the papers and some plates if you set up the heater."

"Why don't we eat first, then move on to work? I need to decompress a bit."

She studied him, but he looked innocent enough. "Okay." She grabbed place settings, two bottles of sparkling water, and one of the giant afghans in post-Christmas red, then stepped outside.

He'd positioned the table and chairs in front of the heater and begun to set out the lunch. They took a seat on the matching rockers, and Ophelia shook out the blanket to cover their legs for extra warmth. Then they ate.

The afternoon was cold, crisp, and clear. The heater crackled and spit warmth. Pure white covered the ground, and the mountains peeked through the clusters of bare trees. Woodsy paths led off in various directions toward a winter forest that seemed enclosed and embraced with magic.

A smile rested on her lips as she looked at the beloved land that her family had tended with hard work, sweat, and dreams. Besides welcoming and serving guests, they'd rescued hundreds of animals over the years, placing them in good homes and saving them from abusive situations.

"I missed this," Kyle murmured in the winter hush. "The quiet. The beauty. I finally feel like I can take a deep breath and just be."

Curiosity struck her harder than the need to keep her distance. "What is your life like now in California?" she asked. "Is it what I remember?"

A sadness clung to his aura. He took a bite of his fries. "Yes and no. The social obligations are still insane. But back then, it was new to me, and exciting. I was beginning to carve out a name for myself, and producers and agents were taking notice. As I began getting the bigger projects, I started to notice how many new friends I'd collected. For someone who reveres being alone in order to create, I found myself surrounded by endless noise and demands."

He stared at the landscape, seemingly lost in his thoughts. "My work kept getting diluted. I was told to chip away at some of the emotion I built into the characters, and to focus more on plot. More action and violence and excitement. I figured after I had some big movies on my résumé I'd get to pick my projects, but it didn't work like that. I was churning out scripts that began to look all the same."

"That end-of-the-world movie made tons of money," she commented. "It opened Memorial Day and broke records."

Suddenly, his gaze swung to hers. Intensity vibrated from his figure. "Did you ever watch it?"

She shifted her weight. "Of course."

"What'd you think?"

Startled, she searched for the right words. Watching his work unfold on-screen had been surprisingly difficult. Knowing she couldn't be with him during such an important part of his life had ripped at her heart. "It was very exciting."

His lip twitched. "And shallow, right? No characterization or bigger goal to really save the world. No true-love story to glue it together. It had two big stars, a lot of buildings blown up, monsters attacking. It was a huge box office success and should've made me proud. Instead, I felt like the biggest failure. I refused to attend celebration parties. I became a hermit for a while, delayed my next project because I felt emptier than I ever had."

She'd seen the seeds of that type of compromise in the beginning, but he hadn't wanted to listen. Frustration seethed in her tone when she spoke next. "Then why did you keep doing it? If you knew your creative soul was slowly dying, why did you keep selling out? For money? Fancy cars and houses and clothes? Did you like the women? The attention? What was it, Kyle?"

He jerked back at the rapid-fire questions. His face hardened, and a wall slammed down for a moment, barring her entry. This was one of the reasons she hadn't wanted to spend time with him. The endless questions still haunted her, echoing in her mind, over and over.

Why had he chosen his career over their marriage?

Why had he agreed to become hostage to everyone else's vision of his future?

And why had he allowed her to leave without a fight?

"There was a lot to consider," he said stiffly. "I wasn't a kid any longer. I had responsibilities."

Her shoulders sagged. There were no answers here. And maybe she had no right to judge. He was the one who'd made his Hollywood dreams come true. She'd been the one to give up and go home to run the family inn.

Yet it had been the only decision left.

"Why are you really back here? You could've locked yourself up in some exclusive resort and gotten the quiet you needed to write. Why do you need to remember your past to write this story?"

He shifted in his chair and avoided her gaze. "I need to connect with my old self to get past the barriers I've built," he said. "I've been dead for a year, and I've finally broken through. Being back here is the key."

"Okay, but I still feel like I'm missing something. Why do you need to write this particular love story here?"

He paused, as if assessing whether he should tell her the truth or duck the question with further excuses. Frustration simmered. She crossed her arms in front of her chest and kept her gaze trained on him, willing him to answer. Finally, he dragged in a breath and met her stare head-on.

"The story is about us."

She blinked. "What? You're writing a story about what happened between us?"

He nodded. "Yes. The story has haunted me. You've haunted me. I've felt as if I need to write and explore what happened between us. I wanted to come home in order to do the story justice."

Her throat tightened. Pain cut through her, sharp and relentless. "Is that why you wanted to connect with me again? So I can help you write your big movie and have it feel realistic? Am I just another tool to get you to the next rung of success?"

He sucked in his breath and leaned toward her with a fierce urgency. "No, Ophelia. I swear it on my life. This story has been inside me for a long time, and I finally found the courage to write it. The only reason I want you back is because I've never gotten over you. It's completely separate from the screenplay. You have to believe that."

She searched his face.

God, she wanted to believe him. The truth seemed woven into his words, but she didn't trust herself anymore. Her defenses were shaky, and he'd hurt her before.

Another question tumbled from her lips before she could stop it. "Have you loved anyone after me?"

He didn't hesitate. His answer came as quickly as her question. "No. My relationships have been brief, and empty. Work took your place."

She nodded. "And now that work no longer does the trick, you've come back here." Anger simmered within.

How could she possibly trust him when he was so desperate to write the perfect screenplay? His work would always come first.

"I won't go back on our agreement for you to stay, but I also won't let you use me as part of your research."

"You're more than that. Every day I spend here, every moment I get to hear your voice or study your face, I'm reminded that you were the only woman I've ever wanted." His gaze caught hers. "I'm reminded of how you were the only woman I've ever loved."

She ignored his stirring words and put her plate on the table, desperate to change the subject. Hearing about his screenplay made a whole bunch of messy emotions roil up inside of her.

"We need to focus. I'll get the paperwork."

His hand shot out and clasped around her arm. The shocking warmth of his skin sent heat rippling down her spine. "Why haven't you remarried or settled into a relationship with a man who can give you everything I couldn't?"

"It doesn't matter."

"It matters to me."

She gritted her teeth and tried to pretend his touch wasn't burning into her flesh, her heart, her soul. "Work replaced you, too," she said.

"So you haven't dated anyone since returning home?" he asked, his voice insistent.

"My affairs have been short, sweet, and with a timed ending. But that had nothing to do with you."

He leaned in. Moss-green eyes seethed with intensity. "Bullshit. You can't get over me just like I can't get over you. We're still married. We're together in the place we first fell in love. What are you fighting so hard to protect? Why can't you take a chance with me when you have nothing to lose?"

If she moved one more inch, his lips would be on hers.

If she moved one more inch, he'd kiss her and touch her and drag her into bed, where they could both finally forget.

If she moved one more inch, she'd get a second chance.

Trembling, she managed to pull back and stand up.

"I have everything to lose," she said simply. "I'll get the papers."

"The first one."

She paused. "What?"

Masculine frustration pumped around his figure, then he let out a breath like a sigh from the soul. "The first lawyer. Collins. We can use him."

"Fine. I'll give him a call and let you know."

"I'll clean up."

Ophelia nodded and walked back inside. But for the rest of the day, his words echoed in her head with haunting insistence.

He was such an ass.

Kyle sat in the chair and stared at the fire. His plan had been so fucking simple. After the intensity of last night, he figured he'd back off a bit and keep things light. Chat her up. Flirt. Make her laugh. Remind her of how good they were together, whether it was in the kitchen or just hanging on the porch talking. By the time they were done, she would've forgotten about the stupid lawyer and felt a bit safer in his company. He'd meant to play the charmer, soften her up, and make his move in the next few days, when it was harder for her to remember what she was fighting him for.

Yeah, goodbye to that big plan.

First he'd told her about the damn story line. Then he'd gotten broody about the past and spooked her all over again.

No wonder she freaked out.

He had to back off no matter how hard it was.

The work was bringing up emotions he hadn't counted on.

How could he have forgotten the easy way they'd been together—both mind and body?

Nearly a decade of chasing the ghost of what Ophelia had made him feel had eventually turned him numb. Finally, he was waking up. His muse, his heart, his hunger for something more than he'd settled for after she'd left him.

His thoughts crashed together in a tsunami, giving him a slight headache. *Go slow*, his inner voice warned again. *Let her catch up.*

He needed to show her it wasn't too late. The longer he stayed here, the more he realized their story wasn't finished. And at the end of his three months, he had no intention of leaving her behind.

Not this time.

The buzz of his phone interrupted his thoughts. He glanced down and swiped the screen. "Robbie. Good to hear from you."

"Been waiting for you to check in. You've gone dark on me, man. We've got some stuff to discuss."

He settled back in the chair. "Can't do much until I'm done with this script. Told you that before I left."

His agent snorted. "Yeah, yeah. The secret project you're all pumped about. That's great, but I need you to fly back this weekend. Something big is going down, and you need to be here."

He frowned. "What is it?"

"Cal Jenkins wants to talk to you about writing the screenplay for his next movie. We have a small window of opportunity this upcoming weekend to schmooze him. So get your ass on a plane, and let's lock this fucker up."

Kyle closed his eyes. *Dammit.*

Jenkins was one of the most successful directors of action films. His work was brilliant, sharp, and full of violence. The idea of cementing a relationship with Jenkins would put him at the top of the Hollywood food chain.

"You're kidding me. He actually asked to speak to me about it?"

"Just got off the phone with his agent. The party is at his mansion, but it's a small crowd, so we can talk work. When can you get here?"

His thoughts whirled. His immediate reaction was to tell his agent *Hell yes!* and book the next flight out. But as he thought about the bigger picture, he realized he couldn't leave. Not now.

He'd reached a turning point in his book—and with Ophelia. After telling her he'd changed, how could he casually fly off and interrupt their time together? Also, as brilliant as Jenkins was, his movies were not Kyle's preferred genre. He needed to move away from being typecast, and the story he was writing was his opportunity.

He couldn't fuck this up.

"I'm sorry, Robbie, but I'm gonna have to pass."

A shocked silence buzzed over the line. His agent's voice came out squeaky. "Tell me I didn't hear that correctly. Tell me I need some goddamn hearing aids, Kimpton. Tell me!"

He gritted his teeth and hung on to his resolution. "I can't walk away from this project right now, and I have stuff going on here. Plus, Jenkins isn't my goal. I've told you that before."

"You can get to your goal after you accept your Academy Award next year!" Robbie yelled. "Get your ass on a plane, man. Please. I'm begging you."

"Sorry, I can't. Give him my apologies and make sure he knows I'm grateful he thought of me. Do your job. I gotta go. I'll check in with you later."

He clicked off before his agent had a meltdown, then buried his face in his hands.

Who would've thought he'd be turning down a Willy Wonka golden ticket? A few years ago, he would've sold his soul for such an opportunity. But now, everything seemed . . . different. Chasing after directors and new ways to achieve fame didn't seem as important any longer.

He had to keep his gaze on the prize. The real prize.

Ophelia.

The book.

His future.

Ophelia stared at the second cooling pecan pie and wondered if she was losing her mind. She'd been so upset after the whole encounter with Kyle, she'd retreated to her safe place.

The kitchen.

Wrapped in the warm glow of flour, sugar, and chocolate, she'd pounded out her frustration on the dough and wielded her mixer like a weapon. By the time the two pies slid out of the oven, she'd felt as if she'd completed a workout at the gym.

She let them cool on the counter. It was always a good idea to have some desserts in the freezer for emergencies, especially for impromptu celebrations or sick calls.

Her mind flashed to Patrick and how he'd looked arguing with the EMTs. She'd tried to call him yesterday, but there'd been no answer. The man's image had been haunting her lately, and though she wanted to tell Kyle about his dad's health scare, she knew it wouldn't matter. An apology and time still couldn't take away the memories of the anguish he'd wreaked on his only son.

Still, as much as she was on Kyle's side, she was worried about Patrick. For her own peace, she decided to check on him and make sure he was okay.

She packed up the pie before she could change her mind and drove out to his house. She pulled up behind his battered Subaru, grabbed the pie box, and knocked on his door.

It was a while before he answered. His green eyes widened in surprise when he saw her, and he immediately succumbed to a wicked series of coughs.

She frowned and stepped into the hallway, taking in the thick sweatshirt, jeans, and fleece robe wrapped around him. "Are you sick?" she asked.

"Just a cold. What are you doing here?"

She put the pie on the table and studied his face. Definitely gaunt, with red-rimmed eyes and a swollen nose. "I brought you a pecan pie, fresh from the oven."

He squinted in suspicion. "Why?"

She laughed and took off her coat. "I don't know," she said honestly. "I have no idea why I'm here."

He snorted, but a tiny smile quirked his lip. The expression was a duplicate of his son's. "Good. I'd rather you be honest." He gave another series of coughs and grabbed a tissue. "Nice to know if I croak someone will find my body before next Christmas."

"Don't say stuff like that. What have you eaten today?"

"A Hot Pocket."

She winced. "That won't help. Do you have any chicken broth? Soup?"

He waved a hand in the air. "Nah, I don't shop much. I'll be fine, especially with a fresh-baked pie."

She tapped her foot, half-torn about whether she should just let him be. The pie was enough of a gesture. She'd hated this man as much as Kyle, yet she couldn't leave him like this. Not if he was sick and had no one to help.

Lord knows he would never go to the hospital or call 911 again after the ambulance debacle. Aw, hell.

"No pie," she announced, scooping up the box and walking back into the kitchen. "Not until you have something healthy."

"Hey, you're the one who brought the pie! Now I can't have it?"

"Not yet. God, this kitchen is a mess. How do you even find anything in here?"

He followed her in, his slippers slapping against the wood floor. "Don't need to find much but the toaster oven and microwave. I do the dishes every couple of days."

She noted the half-full sink, the crumbs littering the counters, and the long row of empty coffee mugs. It took her only a few minutes to pull open his cabinets and refrigerator and find absolutely nothing that would help his cold. "You live like a twenty-something bachelor," she scolded. "You're only going to get worse if you don't do anything to help your body."

"I gave up alcohol. I stopped smoking. I got nothing left to give up, and I'm too damn tired to learn how to cook and have healthy habits at age seventy-one." He blew his nose and glared. "If you came to give lectures, leave the pie and go. I'm fine."

"Don't be grouchy, or I'll take my pie with me, Patrick."

He grunted.

It took her a minute to make the decision. Rifling through her purse, she grabbed a scrap piece of paper, a pen, and scribbled down a list of items. "What are you taking for the cold?" she asked.

"Nothing." His voice came out a bit rebellious. "I can't. Alcohol is in most cough medicines."

She nodded. "I'll be sure to read the ingredients. I'll be back in an hour. Don't touch the pie."

"Where are you going?"

"Grocery shopping."

"But—"

"I have no time for chatting. I'll be back. Go to bed and drink water. You need to flush out the germs."

He glowered. "You're pushy, girl."

"And you're wasting my valuable time."

Ophelia didn't wait to see if he'd obey her orders. She grabbed her purse and her list and headed into town.

It only took her forty minutes to get everything she needed. She let herself back in, and heard snoring from the back room. Using her time wisely while he slept, she unpacked the groceries, donned rubber gloves, and got to work.

Singing softly, she attacked the dishes, sprayed the counters with bleach, then got a broth heated up on the stove. She kept it simple, adding only celery, carrots, spices, and chicken, then let it cook. The cabinets were stuffed with expired boxes that quickly went into the garbage, replaced by new. She sliced up peasant bread and put together a half-ass garlic loaf, sticking that in the oven. She was just finishing up when she heard him shuffle into the kitchen.

"What are you doing?"

She raked her gaze over him. "You look a little better. Sit. I have some soup and bread."

He opened his mouth, and she prepped herself for some nastiness. She'd already expected it and made peace with her intentions to help him anyway. It was more for her at this point than for him. Ophelia just couldn't leave him alone and sick with nothing in the house to eat or drink.

But instead of speaking, his eyes filled with a mix of emotions. He seemed to have trouble swallowing. He nodded and sat down.

She served him a bowl of hot soup and a plate of bread slathered in garlic butter and parmesan. She squeezed lemon slices into a large glass of water, and had already prepared a pot of tea with honey and lemon.

He ate in silence, the hand holding the spoon shaking slightly. She wondered about his sobriety and how he managed, especially alone. But right now didn't feel like a good time for questions. Even with the bad memories, she was glad she could help him.

"I picked you up a holistic cough syrup, lozenges, and Tylenol. There's enough soup in this batch to last a few more days, and the tea I made can also be reheated. There's sliced turkey in the fridge, and I got a ton of fruit—make sure you have an orange for vitamin C. You can't get the same nutrients from juice, but there's a bottle in there to supplement. I bought paper plates, cups, and utensils so you don't have to worry about dishes. I already took out the garbage. The pie is in the fridge for your dessert. Drink tons of water. And next time, please answer the phone if I call, or you'll be opening the door to the ambulance crew again. I gotta go."

She shrugged on her coat, her mind already clicking madly through her to-do list and how she'd make up the time in her busy schedule once she got back to the inn. She was halfway to the door when she heard her name called.

"Yes?"

Patrick's gruff voice broke. "Thank you."

She didn't answer. Didn't want to, still torn by what Kyle would think of her helping out his father. Instead, she left and pushed the whole encounter to the back of her mind.

Chapter Fourteen

"Are you dressed slutty?" Mia demanded over the phone. "'Cause I'll make you change if you're not in a skirt."

Ophelia sighed. "Yes. I may even get arrested on prostitution charges. How does that sound?"

Mia squealed with glee. "Perfect! Pick you up in five. I have the whole night planned."

The click in her ear sealed her fate. She couldn't remember the last time she'd been out to hang with some female friends, and excitement flickered in her gut. For a few hours, she wasn't going to worry about anything but having fun.

She swiveled one last time in the mirror to check her outfit.

Yeah. She looked hot.

She'd gone with a classic black mini, but this skirt had choppy cuts slashed at the hem to give off a serious peek of bare leg. Her boots were leather, over the knee, high-heeled, and badass. The red-and-black polka dot tank was flowy and paired with a tight black jacket. She'd used beach wave spray on her hair, so it was a bit wild with a natural curl. Her makeup was light except for her bright-red lipstick and heavy mascara. She looked like a woman ready for some serious fun and drinking.

Exactly what she wanted from tonight.

Grabbing her clutch bag, she did one last check of the inn to make sure her guests had everything they needed for the evening. Hot cocoa was out with a full-fixings bar. The fire crackled merrily. Already she caught gales of laughter as a group watched one of the new DVDs she'd purchased.

The steady clack of the keyboard drifted faintly in the air. Seemed like Kyle was also set for the night.

Disappointment flared that he hadn't emerged to catch a glimpse of her very sexy outfit, but she smothered it quickly, annoyed she even cared about making an impression.

A beep sounded outside.

She grabbed her coat and skipped out to Mia's car, where blessed heat blasted from the vents.

"You look amazing," Mia announced, her gaze critically taking in her outfit. "Holy God, woman, you are a sexpot."

"Thank you!" Ophelia laughed. Mia was also dressed in black—her signature color. She wore a sleek pencil skirt and peekaboo lace camisole that hugged her sleek figure, along with some platform shoes with gold-block heels that looked like Stuart Weitzman. "You look absolutely gorg."

"Thanks." Mia pulled out of the lot. "I barely got past Ethan without him ravishing me. I had to promise him stuff later."

"TMI."

"Sorry."

Ophelia grinned and relaxed as they drove to pick up Harper. "So where are we going?"

"I have everything planned out perfectly. We're going to grab something to eat at Lemongrass first, then we're hitting the Gardiner Liquid Mercantile, then Joe's, and finally the Depot."

Ophelia stared at her in disbelief. "You're kidding, right? We can't hit four places. We won't get home until two a.m."

Mia grinned proudly. "Exactly. No turning into a pumpkin at midnight, girlfriend. We're doing this right."

"But Joe's is a college bar. We're too old to go there."

"We need some college fun around us. When was the last time you went out?"

She chewed the inside of her cheek, not wanting to answer. "I've been busy."

"I rest my case. You're too young to be locked up at the inn. You need to cut loose."

She didn't get to protest because they'd stopped in front of Harper's apartment.

Her sister jumped in the car with a scowl on her face. "We're not staying out too late, right?" she asked.

Mia groaned. "You both are hopeless."

"We're in for a long night," Ophelia told her sister. "Mia wants to go to Joe's."

"It's a college bar! They do beer funnels!"

Mia laughed with a touch of evil. "Even better than I imagined. Get ready, ladies. Harper, why are you wearing jeans?"

"These are my best pair. Dark wash. They make my butt look good."

Mia studied her critically from the mirror, then nodded. "Yeah, you do have a great ass. But you're losing that baggy jacket. You look amazing in the camisole, and we don't want to hide it."

Ophelia giggled. "She's trying to get us both laid, Harp."

"Hmm, doesn't seem like a bad idea."

They all laughed. A few minutes later, they were pulling up in front of Lemongrass.

"Let's do this, ladies," Mia announced with a smile and a wink. Then she led them inside, and Ophelia already knew it was going to be a great night.

He carried her over the threshold, barely managing not to crash her into the narrow doorframe, and she giggled against his chest, the white veil

scratching his cheek. He kicked the door behind him closed—just like in the movies—and whirled her around so her satin skirt billowed out around them.

"You're my wife," he stated. Satisfaction and a raw tenderness coursed through him as he gazed at her beautiful face. "We did it."

"We did it," she whispered, stroking his clean-shaven jaw. "I can't believe we got married by Elvis."

He groaned and set her gently on her feet. "Baby, I told you we didn't have to go to that chapel."

"I loved it." She slid her hands around his shoulders and kissed him, her lips soft and tasting better than cotton candy. "I loved every tacky, gorgeous moment. Our song is 'A Little Less Conversation.'"

He laughed, tugging off her veil and running his fingers through her hair. "At least we'll never be predictable. I knew you'd never pick 'Love Me Tender.'"

She scrunched up her nose in an adorable face. "Everyone chooses the slow, mushy songs. I wanted something different for us."

He gazed at her for a long time. Her dress was a simple flow of elegance in white satin. Pearls encrusted the low neckline, and the fabric hugged her figure, pooling into a small train behind as she walked. "You're beautiful, Ophelia. When I look at you, everything hurts. I've wanted this for so long, I'm almost afraid to touch you."

She smiled up at him. "If you don't touch me, it'll hurt more." She tugged his head down, arching up to meet him. "I want you to touch me, Kyle. Everywhere. I want everything."

He groaned, picking her up again and carrying her to the bed. Their one-bedroom studio was cramped. They were able to afford a full-size mattress, a couch, a TV, a lamp, and a desk for his laptop. There was one closet. Their pots and pans and mugs came from flea markets and garage sales.

They'd spent the last month finding a place to live, getting menial jobs to pay the rent. She'd scored a secondhand bridal dress from Craigslist. He'd rented a suit and financed the quarter-carat diamond ring on a brand new credit *card that some crazy bank had mistakenly offered him. They'd feasted on a full-course breakfast at the local diner she had scored a part-time job at, changed into their bridal clothes, and made the drive to Vegas. For only $299, they'd gotten married at The Little Vegas Chapel, reciting their vows for Elvis with no family in attendance and a small bouquet of red roses gripped in her hand.*

It was the happiest day of his life.

He undressed her slowly, his gaze devouring her nakedness, a raw hunger in his gut from the endless months of kissing and touching and foreplay. He stroked her naked skin with shaking fingers and a reverence he swore he'd feel for a lifetime. His lips pressed against her neck, then moved down to her breasts, her hips. They slipped lower to kiss between her thighs, and he held her open as she cried and begged. He kissed her while she crashed into an orgasm with open abandonment and couldn't wait until he could do it again . . . and again . . .

He rolled on a condom and kissed his way back up her body, sucking on a nipple before diving his tongue deep into her mouth. He moved between her thighs, pushing with a steady rhythm while she clung hard to him.

He went slow, praying he wouldn't hurt her, easing into her tightness until her body relaxed beneath him. He whispered her name like a prayer and moved in and out, filling her, claiming her, his fingers slipping down to rub her clit with gentle, tender touches until she shattered beneath him. He swallowed her cries and let himself go, his body shuddering helplessly, clinging to her just as fiercely.

He looked deep into her eyes as he came. He studied her beloved face, memorizing every angle and curve, and then he tucked her against him and held her, telling her over and over that he loved her. That he'd love her forever . . .

He had to get the hell out of here.

Kyle looked down at himself. After the disastrous episode with Ophelia yesterday, he'd focused on getting through the next chapter, but he'd fallen into the hole. The hole was wonderful for creativity.

It was not so wonderful for hygiene.

Blinking as if he'd just emerged from a dark cave for months, he stared at the mud of leftover coffee by his elbow. Crumbs from a granola bar littered his lap. The seltzer next to the coffee had long ago gone flat. Then he realized he was still in his clothes from yesterday and that taking a morning shower had slipped past his consciousness. His mouth felt like a big old fuzzpot.

What time was it?

Hell, what day was it?

He peered at his watch and groaned. Seven p.m.

He needed out of this room.

Grabbing his phone, he punched out a text to Ethan.

Wanna grab a beer and some dinner?

He figured his friend would decline going out on a Saturday night when he had a live-in lover, but the three dots suddenly popped up with a GIF of Will Ferrell guzzling beer.

Hell yes. Half hour?

He sent a thumbs-up emoji and grinned. He hadn't been out with just Ethan in a long time, and he was looking forward to hitting their favorite bars in town.

He brushed his teeth, showered, and changed in record time, keeping it simple with jeans, a dark purple Stone Rose shirt, and low black boots. He jumped in the rental and beeped after he pulled up in front of the bungalow. Through the front window, he spotted Ethan trying to back out from the menagerie of dogs and the mean chicken, finally managing to shut the door.

Ethan slid into the front seat.

Kyle lifted a brow. "So how's domesticated life?"

"Fuck you."

He laughed and drove to their favorite Irish pub. They packed themselves into a boisterous drinking crowd currently watching the Syracuse basketball game. Shoved into a table by the bar, they ordered two IPAs and relaxed into the stools.

Kyle munched on peanuts and threw shells on the floor. "Where's Mia?"

Ethan shrugged. "Girls' night out with Ophelia and Harper."

She was on the town with her girls. Kyle remembered them partying together in their youth. That woman had such pure Irish blood, she'd been able to match his and Ethan's pace at any drinking game. He'd always been so damn proud of that ability.

"You know what they were doing?"

"Not sure. Dinner. Movies. Maybe one of those paint-and-sip things that are popular. Girl stuff."

His lip quirked. She was probably drinking wine, eating sushi, and sitting in some bar at a fancy restaurant with a bunch of uptight suits.

The waitress glided over, and they ordered burgers and another round of beers.

"How's the writing going, man?"

He snorted. "Let's just say you're lucky that I showered."

"That means it's good, right?"

"Yeah. It's a sad career when productivity means being fat and unclean."

"You think coming back home made a difference, then?"

"Definitely. I needed a change of scenery. Plus, even though you're a pain in the ass—I missed you."

"Back atcha. What about Ophelia? You two are getting along better now, right? She finally forgive you for whatever fuck-up you did in California?"

Guilt hit him. He tried to keep his answer casual. "Yeah, we're good now."

Ethan nodded. "When I first heard you guys had run off to California while I was deep in basic training, I freaked. I worried about Tink. Worried Hollywood would eat her up and spit her out. But knowing she was with you helped. Even though you had a big fight and she ended up coming home, I knew you'd taken care of her out there. Made sure she wasn't hurt. I never thanked you for that, man."

Kyle's gut roiled. His friend's heartfelt words filled him with stinging shame. Kyle took a swig of beer and wondered if he could tell Ethan the whole damn thing.

It'd be such a relief to talk to him and get his advice. To spill his guts and admit his feelings for Ophelia, and how badly he wanted to reconcile. To confess how he'd fucked it all up and ended up hurting her anyway.

He ached to spill his soul. Though he knew tons of people in Hollywood, no one knew the real him. He'd never been able to make a true bond with someone he'd trust with his hidden secrets. Sure, he was popular on the party circuit, with plenty of people to keep him occupied and entertained. But inside, he was lonely.

Still, Ethan might lose his shit if he found out he and Ophelia were married. He may feel betrayed and blame Kyle, and then he'd lose his best friend.

No, he had to keep his mouth shut—at least until he convinced Ophelia to give him a second chance. Then they could tell Ethan together.

"No worries." He cleared his throat and tried to change the subject. "Hey, remember when we used to party at Joe's? You used to get so drunk and pick fights with bigger guys."

"I had mad fighting skills. It was the only time I got to use them."

Kyle laughed. "Except that time with the Asian guy who kicked your ass and was half your height."

"Fuck you. I remember when you couldn't finish a beer funnel, threw up, and passed out under the bar. We couldn't even find you. You were sleeping in the shit that night."

"Oh yeah! How about when you did those body shots with the blonde, and her boyfriend showed up?"

Ethan snapped his fingers. "Yes! He followed me out to the car where I was making out with her and—"

"Threatened you with a shotgun! Thank God I kept an eye on you."

"Dude, you tackled him. We ran out into the woods—"

"With your bare-naked ass on display." Kyle tipped his beer back and sighed with sheer joy. "Fucking good times, man."

"The best."

Their burgers came and they dug in, talking about their greatest hits. Yeah. It was going to be a great night.

"Drink, drink, drink, drink—YES!"

The guys bellowed and thumped her back as she finished guzzling. Mia and Harper stared at her with matching worried gazes.

She stepped back. Fought the slight nausea. Then let out a long burp.

Another roar echoed in the air, and she gave the crowd a thumbs-up signal. Mia and Harper gave a whoop and stuck out their palms, collecting on the bet wagered by a bunch of frat boys who'd challenged Ophelia to drink from the funnel without vomiting.

Head spinning a tad, she managed to extricate herself from her new friends, who were now pounding down shots. She headed over to their coveted small table at the end of the bar.

"Fifty bucks!" Mia said, shaking the cash in her hand. "Not bad, especially since the drinks have been free all night."

Harper hooked her boot heels on the rung of the stool. "That was impressive. I had no idea you still had mad drinking skills."

Ophelia hiccupped. Then giggled. "Been a long time, so I'm glad I didn't embarrass myself. Did you see the cute blond checking you out, Harp?"

"Oh yeah! He was into you," Mia said. "Why don't you go, talk to him?"

Harper snorted. "'Cause he's barely drinking age, and I'm not a cougar."

"Bet he'd know how to make you roar, though," Mia quipped.

Ophelia laughed. "Oh my God, that's as bad as Ethan and Kyle together. What is it about men? Why does their intelligence factor drop when they're hanging with friends? I never got it."

"I never understood men at all," Harper grumbled, taking a swig of her beer.

"You dating anyone?" Mia asked, propping her hand under her chin and regarding Harper. "You've got that mysterious quality men go crazy over. Plus, you're hot."

"I'm not hot."

Mia gasped. "Yes you are! Holy crap, with your dark hair, green eyes, and lean figure? Add in the way you connect to animals and can banter like a badass—you are a catch."

Harper scoffed and rolled her eyes. Ophelia still couldn't understand why her sister lacked confidence when it came to male attention. She was so sure in all aspects of her life except her sexuality.

Ophelia slid her hand across the table and squeezed her sister's. "Mia's right. I know you're happy with your life, but you should give dating a chance. You may find love."

"I don't know if I believe in love," Harper said. "The few dates I've gone on made me feel lonelier than I did home alone. Does that make sense?"

Mia nodded. "Totally. That's why I stopped dating, too—before I met your brother. And of course, because I got cheated on."

Ophelia winced and grabbed her water to try and hydrate. "Assholes weren't worthy of you."

"Ethan told me the same thing."

"He's right. I'm just so glad you both found each other. I've never seen him so happy," Ophelia said.

Mia smiled. "I feel the same way. So are you and Kyle doing it?"

Ophelia choked and slammed the glass back on the table. "What did you ask?"

"You heard me. What's going on?"

Harper cracked up, practically wiping her eyes in mirth. "Damn, that was good. I'm glad Mia asked, because I've been dying to all evening. I heard he took you to dinner at Crystal's. Maureen said you were looking quite chummy. Are you hooking up again?"

Crap. She had no idea anyone even suspected she still wanted to jump into bed with her ex. Of course, it was pretty hard to keep secrets in this town, and she should've known these two females were too savvy to be fooled.

She frowned, trying to figure out what to say. She'd kept the real story from Harper during their talk in the barn, but the growing need to talk to someone she trusted shook within.

Her feelings for Kyle confused her, and she desperately needed an outlet. Harper and Mia were family.

This time, she didn't try to hold back when the words loosened and flew out of her mouth.

"If I tell you a secret, do you swear not to tell Ethan?"

Mia bit her lip. "Is it a female pact thing? I can't lie to him."

"I'm not asking you to lie . . . just don't say anything."

"I can do that," Mia said. Harper agreed.

Ophelia filled her lungs with air and then let it out. "We got married when we ran off to California together."

"What?" they shouted together. A group to their right shot them a look, and Ophelia leaned in, lowering her voice.

"Yes. We were young and in love, so we eloped, thinking we could do and be anything we wanted to as long as we were together. But after a year and a half, the innocence wore off. We had a huge falling-out, and I came home."

"Holy shit," Harper breathed out. "I didn't see that one coming. Sex, yes. Marriage, no. Why didn't you tell us?"

Guilt hit her. "At first it was like this big, delicious secret—straight out of a romance movie. And I didn't want anyone to talk me out of it by saying we were too young, or to wait longer, or that it wasn't smart. I just wanted to marry the man I loved with no one holding us back. Does that make sense?"

Harper nodded. "Yeah, but how come you didn't tell me later?"

"It became easier keeping it a secret, especially when we decided to divorce. I wanted to move on with my life."

"So you've been divorced for all this time. I get it," Mia said. "No wonder you didn't want him staying with you."

"There's more," she said. Her heart pounded, but the beer funnel helped lower her protective walls. "The divorce never went through. Our lawyer was a scam artist . . . so we're still legally married."

Mia's mouth fell open. Harper stared in shock.

Relief loosened her muscles. Finally, she had shared her secret. She felt like a new person.

"I gotta pee," she announced.

"No!" Mia shouted. "We need more info. I have a billion questions."

"Hold that thought. I'll be right back."

She waited in a long line for the ladies' bathroom while glaring at the nonexistent queue for the men's room, then shuffled crookedly back to the table, trying hard not to stumble. She'd just reached her seat when some of her favorite, iconic music blasted over the speakers and cries of excitement shot in the air.

"'Living on a Prayer'!" she shouted. "Oh my God, I love Bon Jovi. Let's go dance!"

"Now? We need the rest of the story," Mia demanded.

Ophelia grabbed their hands and dragged them onto the over-crowded dance floor. "Not now—it's time to boogie!"

Harper groaned. "You're so trashed."

Mia laughed. "She is, but dancing will help. We still have one more stop before our evening is over, so we'll have time to get the details out of her later. Let's go."

Ophelia agreed and sang the lyrics she knew by heart. The bright flashing lights flooded the floor, and bodies pressed in on her. All joined in the quest to let go for a few moments and let the music take them away.

Ophelia threw her head back and surrendered.

Chapter Fifteen

Kyle stepped into the small dive bar and groaned. It was karaoke night, and it already looked like a fire hazard. "Dude, why don't we go home? It's late."

Ethan's features were set in determination, as if he was embarking on a mission. "It's not even one a.m. I'm not old."

Kyle groaned again and rubbed his head. "Oh hell. Are you actually listening to those bozos? Who cares if we don't hang out at the bars anymore? I'm okay admitting I want to go to sleep."

After burgers and a brownie bomber sundae, they'd run into some guys from high school who were on a serious mission to do some partying damage. They'd played catch-up on who was married, who was divorced, and who worked a job they didn't despise, then made some jabs about Ethan never being seen partying in town. Kyle shrugged it off, but it seemed his friend had something to prove. Ethan insisted they walk down Main Street to the Depot to see what they had going on.

"I'm not getting home before Mia," he announced, deftly maneuvering them through the thick press of bodies and to the bar. "We're having fun, right? We're partying."

Kyle smothered a yawn. "Sure."

Ethan yelled something Kyle didn't catch.

"Huh? I can't hear you." A very bad version of "I Will Survive" assaulted his ears and made him wince. That damn woman-hear-me-roar song gave him goose bumps—it usually was a setup for a dramatic breakup.

"Shots!" Ethan shouted. "Tequila."

"We won't be able to drive home," he pointed out.

"We can walk, or there's Uber."

Kyle rolled his eyes. "You do your shots, and I'll drive your ass home. Just get me a seltzer, okay?"

"Pussy."

Kyle laughed.

Suddenly, a shout rang out and a couple began to argue quite loudly. He turned his head and watched a woman jump from the table and race outside, her girlfriends trailing behind her, shouting her name and insults at the schmuck who was left looking confused.

Yep, that song did it every time.

"Oh good, a table just opened up. I'll grab it." He took the two empty seats with a ruthless efficiency and sipped at his drink. The place was so packed, he could barely see the stage.

Maybe he'd be able to drag Ethan out after his shot.

He sat through a terrible version of Queen's "Another One Bites the Dust," which reminded him why he'd stopped attending local karaoke, and drank his seltzer.

Thankfully, the song eventually ended. He glanced at Ethan. The shot glass was empty, and his friend was blinking way too rapidly, confirming he was officially hammered.

Poor Mia would have to deal with the aftereffects, but—

"Hi, everyone. I'm going to try to do this one justice, but if it sucks, just feel free to throw some peanuts at me." Laughter filled the room along with encouraging applause.

Kyle frowned, the familiar voice ruffling his nerve endings. His gaze snapped to the front of the stage, still halfway blocked by the crowd.

"Do you recognize who's singing?" he asked. "I can't see."

Ethan swiveled around, squinting. "It's Ophelia." A sloppy grin curved his lips. "Hey, Mia's sitting over there." He stood, cupped his hands around his mouth, and began yelling their names.

Kyle grabbed his arm and yanked his ass back in the seat. "They can't hear you—text Mia. Stay here, Party Boy, and I'll be back. I'm going to get closer."

His heart hammered, and every muscle in his body tightened in anticipation. Slowly, as if in a dream, he weaved his way through the crowd until he scored a position to the right of the stage.

The opening strains of Adele's famous song "Hello" belted from the large speaker, and the lyrics lit up on the screen in fluorescent green. But Kyle already knew she wouldn't need to read the words. The song unfolded from her body, the first notes lingering in the air with a teasing promise that stirred the crowd's curiosity. Rooted to the floor, he clenched his fist and prepared himself for what was to come.

Ophelia was going to sing.

His gaze drank her in. Even under the garish lights, she glowed with an inner joy that she always exuded when she sang. Her strawberry-blonde hair tumbled past her shoulders. The black jacket framed the curve of her breasts and hips. The short miniskirt indecently exposed a good portion of thigh, stopped by the edge of the sexiest black motorcycle boots he'd ever seen. Her fingers caressed the microphone, and her mouth hovered inches away, lush red lips damp from her tongue. Her blue eyes turned a smoky hue. She held them half-closed as she gave herself up to the song, practically seducing the audience with sensuality.

Fuck, she was beautiful. But her voice. How long had it been since she was in her element and got to use those gifted pipes?

The first lyrics fell into the air, the rich, husky undertone of her voice just hinting at what she would give them if they only listened. And in that tiny, overcrowded, loud bar, there was a sudden hush as everyone began to recognize that the woman who was singing was different.

The words started low in her belly and grew to a rising, booming entreaty straight from her heart. Threaded with sadness and a longing for a love already gone, she stared out into the crowd and gave it all to them—every emotion sprung open and unleashed—and they took it, reveled, savored.

The music faded until all that remained was the most haunting voice he'd ever heard, the smoky strains interweaved with such richness, it was as if he'd indulged in every vice imaginable: chocolate, champagne, caviar.

His gut twisted and his eyes stung as she moved into the final lines. She reached deep with her voice and let it explode before softly bringing it back down until it was a whisper. He wondered if the entire episode was a dream.

He watched as her head hung down in submission as the final notes lingered and fell silent. No one breathed. No one spoke.

Then she whipped her head back and gave the audience a dazzling smile, lifting up the microphone and doing a small bow.

An aching loss tore at his gut. Once, she'd sung for him, her face joyous, sharing not only her gift but also her full heart. She'd trusted him to take care of both in the vows they'd recited, and the way they'd loved each other.

But he hadn't been there when she needed him the most.

He bent over and grabbed a chair to steady himself. The realization hit him like a freight train, and the ground shifted under his feet.

The words she'd confessed in the car a few nights ago suddenly held new meaning. She hadn't left him because she was afraid of a singing career, or jealous over his success, or that she couldn't handle the intensity of their relationship.

She had left because he'd stopped choosing her.

The cheers of the crowd rose to his ears—not only applause but also catcalls and hushed conversations about who she was. Was she famous, or from *The Voice*? He took it all in but was still unable to move. She'd done it again. She'd wrecked him and left him scattered into a million tiny pieces, wondering how he'd be whole without her.

Somehow, he had to let her know he finally understood.

Kyle stumbled forward in an effort to reach her.

Cheeks flushed, eyes bright, her gaze scanned the crowd, grazed over him, and swung quickly back.

Their eyes locked.

Recognition. Understanding. Remembrance.

Hunger.

Holding her gaze, he walked toward her. She met him halfway, stepping off the stage.

"You're here." It was a statement, holding so much more meaning than those simple two words.

His voice got stuck in his throat and came out hoarse. "Yes." He drank in her face, reaching out to trail a finger down her cheek. "You were extraordinary."

She had no time to respond. Bumped by the crowd, suddenly Mia and Harper and Ethan surrounded them, congratulating her and leading them back to their table. They chattered in excitement. Harper hugged her and Ethan ordered another shot in celebration, but all Kyle could see and hear and smell was her.

He felt drunker than Ethan. All of his senses jammed into high alert. He registered the slightest movement of her fingers, the cock of her hip, the way her lips parted and her tongue touched the very top of her teeth before she spoke. He wanted to soak himself in her essence and flavor.

If he didn't get her out of this club right now, he was going to fracture into insanity.

Ethan hugged his sister and grinned proudly. "I can't believe you did karaoke. You're so cool, Tink."

Mia and Ophelia laughed. "And you're drunk, baby," Mia announced.

"Just abalittle."

"I'm feeling little pain myself," Ophelia admitted. "That's probably the only reason I got up there."

"She guzzled an entire funnel of beer at Joe's," Harper said. "And we won fifty bucks."

"No shit?" Ethan asked. "We had burgers at the Irish pub. I had shots."

Mia stroked his hair back lovingly. "Bunch of rebels, huh? Kyle, do you need me to drive you home too?"

"No, I'm good. Been drinking seltzer the past two hours." He stared at Ophelia, then reached out and touched her upper arm. The muscles stiffened under his touch. Awareness between them flared to life. Her pupils dilated, and she swayed slightly on her feet, leaning toward him. Heat practically burned his hand. "Let me take you home."

His meaning was so much bigger than his words. He waited, knowing if she said no it would rip him to pieces. Her breath came in choppy pants, and her gaze dropped to his lips. In seconds, his dick was rock hard.

Mia cleared her throat. "Umm, Ophelia? Do you want to go home with Kyle? Or we can drop you off . . ."

Both Harper and Mia seemed to wait for her response with a strange intensity. Their gazes bounced back and forth between him and Ophelia with a shrewd knowledge that made Kyle shift his feet uncomfortably.

Why were they looking at him like that? Did they suspect something was going on with him and Ophelia?

"I'll go with Kyle."

His knees weakened in relief. Ignoring the women's narrowed gazes, he secured fast goodbyes, making sure Mia and Harper could handle walking with Ethan to the car. He thumped his friend on the back and escorted Ophelia out of the bar. The cold bite of wind tore at their flesh, so he tucked her against him, shielding her until she was safely inside the vehicle.

He pulled away from the curb, careful not to blast the heat until the car warmed up. The tiny strip of bare flesh between her skirt and boots was peppered with goose bumps.

She shivered. "I must've been crazy to wear a skirt in this weather."

"Can I say how grateful I am for your bravery?"

She turned her head and smiled at him. He was a goner. "I didn't know you were going out tonight. Did you have fun?"

"Yeah, Ethan was on a mission to prove he wasn't old. Let's just say I learned two things tonight."

"What?"

"First, we are definitely too old to party this hard."

She gave a small laugh. The sound ruffled him with pleasure. "And the second?"

He shot her a look filled with intention. "You can still bring me to my knees."

She sucked in a breath. The tension cranked up a few notches. She didn't speak for a while, but he waited her out.

"I haven't allowed myself to sing in public for years," she said softly. "I forgot the pull of an audience. The way the music takes over and you become completely connected. It's the biggest high."

"Then why are you denying yourself such pleasure? You have a gift. Everyone in that bar knew it."

She stared out the window. The edge of loneliness pierced through him, so he reached over and entangled his fingers with hers. She squeezed back.

"Because I remember how it was when I was on the verge of discovery. I remember how I realized it'd be too easy to lose who I really was."

"A singer."

She smiled with a touch of sadness. "Yes, but they didn't want me to sing. They wanted me to perform. To be a star. To change my clothes and my appearance and the way I talk. To be someone I'd never be."

"You could've fought them. Refused to change until they had to listen."

"Like you?"

He jerked. At first, he hadn't been interested in writing action movies. He'd craved a deeper, bigger playground to write and explore stories. But eventually, he had to make a decision to fit into the box that would accept him.

Was that how it had been for Ophelia? The memories were a blur—he'd just been so happy she was going to finally become big enough for everyone to experience her voice. Now he realized he'd been so consumed with his own quest for fame he hadn't really listened.

The thoughts troubled him. It'd been easy blaming her for leaving. But with all the revelations he'd been having lately, the past suddenly seemed a blur of gray rather than the black and white he'd once believed it had been.

He pulled into the inn's driveway and parked the car. The white lights on the building twinkled merrily in the dark and added a welcoming touch. They walked inside, his arm firmly guiding her by the elbow, and shut the door behind them.

The fire had died out. The lingering scent of smoke and wood hung in the air. The lone light from the foyer illuminated the hallway.

"Thanks for driving." She fumbled with the locks and switched off the lamp. He noticed she refused to look him in the eye. "I better get to bed. Good night."

She headed to the safety of her bedroom, her steps a bit awkward—which told him she was definitely still tipsy. The next question his mind posed was more important.

Was she sober enough to know what she was doing?

Her fingers clasped around the knob with a touch of desperation.

He moved and, in seconds, he was behind her.

She stiffened.

"Ophelia?"

Her voice came out ragged. "What?"

"How drunk are you?"

She spun around and tilted her head back. His gaze delved deep and found a cocktail of emotions he had to explore. Those fiery blue eyes shot sparks of rebellion, frustration, and a raw hunger that touched the primitive part of him.

"Not drunk enough to claim I don't know what you're trying to do."

A smile touched his lips. He reached out and stroked her hair back, the silky strands jumping and clinging to his fingers in sensual abandon. "What am I trying to do?"

She pressed her lips together. "Seduce me. Am I right?"

"Oh yes. You are."

She blinked, as if shocked at his honesty. "You can't."

"Why not?"

"We're getting a divorce."

He gave a small laugh and lowered his head, his nose nudging her ear. Her scent made dizzy circles around him—a touch of musky perfume mixed with feminine sweat and an underlying honeyed sweetness from her body cream. "Right now, we're married. And I want to kiss my wife."

The connection between them tightened; desire raged for escape from its prison. She lifted her arms. He waited for her to push him away, but she twined them around his neck and pulled him closer.

This time, his breath collapsed from his lungs, and his dick strained against his jeans. He pressed her against the door and reveled in how every one of her curves cradled against his hard length.

She tried for one last rally. "I don't think this is a good idea," she whispered, already reaching up on tiptoes to bring her mouth next to his.

"I do. Just stop me if you don't want this as badly as I do."

Then his mouth crashed over hers.

♥ ♥ ♥

She was dying.

The shocking warmth of his mouth shook through her body, causing mini convulsions that seized each muscle with bone-melting pleasure. The past and the present collided and shoved her underwater. There was no thought to fight, or reason, or back away.

There was no thought at all—except him.

He devoured her whole, his tongue pressing deep inside to reclaim what had always belonged to him. She hung on, her fingers stabbing through the golden-blond strands of hair. The silky thrust of his tongue paired with the delicious scrape of beard on her jaw. He overtook her completely in that one perfect kiss, consuming her breath and her body.

"You taste so good," he muttered against her lips. He sucked her lower lip and gave it a sexy little nip. "So damn sweet."

She arched up with unspoken demand and bit back. They fell into another deep kiss, and she realized in this moment she had a choice. If she took him to her bed, everything would change.

Unless it was only for tonight . . . Maybe she could handle it.

When her gaze had collided with his after her song, something had shifted and broken inside of her. There seemed to be a new understanding as he looked at her, an intensity that ripped down her barriers and dared her to take what she wanted.

Him. For one night.

God, the high of singing still buzzed through her body.

It had been so long since she'd felt this alive—so long since her body had lit up and wept for a man to touch her.

If she gave herself this one night, maybe she'd be able to let go of some ghosts of the past. It would be like a perfect, bittersweet goodbye to the man she'd once loved.

Her inner voice laughed hysterically at her naïveté and the outright lie. But the needy, lust-filled part of her drove her forward with determination.

She broke the kiss, panting against his carved lips. "Come inside."

He groaned, stroking her bare arms, and nipped at her ear. "I need you to be sure. We can make out right here, for as long as you want, and I'd be happy as hell. I don't want to push you, baby."

She gave a low laugh. "Thought you promised to seduce me, Kimpton. You going back on your word?"

One beat passed. Two. She watched him struggle with his conscience. She could see the naked hunger in his eyes as he stared at her. Then he moved.

With a low growl, he lifted her high, opening her door and stepping into the darkened bedroom. Swiveling on his heel, he pinned her back against the wall so her legs wrapped around his hips and his hard shaft pressed into her inner thigh.

She wriggled to get closer, so that delicious hardness would rub against her sensitive, swollen folds throbbing between her thighs.

God, how bad she wanted him.

Her entire body was on fire and practically weeping for relief.

As if he knew exactly what she craved, he hitched her higher, hiked up her skirt, and ran his palm over the damp black lace of her panties.

She cried out and shuddered, rolling her hips in silent need.

"You're so wet for me," he gritted out. He took her mouth again with a raw hunger, his tongue sinking deep, his fingers coasting over the sheer lace in teasing strokes that drove her mad.

She frantically pulled at the snap of his jeans, yanked the zipper down, and plunged her hands inside his pants.

He groaned her name, moved her underwear to the side, and dipped a finger into her dripping channel.

She clenched around him in greed. "More," she gasped.

"Baby, it's too fast. You're too drunk."

She squeezed his throbbing dick in her hands in punishment. "Not drunk. Just want you. Get naked."

He gave a tortured laugh, jerking helplessly in her grip. "I don't want you to have regrets in the morning."

Mad with lust, she fisted him tight and growled against his full lips. "I dare you to make me come, Kyle. And if you can't, you can leave right now."

"Brat." He sunk his teeth in the vulnerable curve of her neck and plunged two fingers into her pussy. She shuddered, helpless under his command. "This what you want?" His thumb rubbed her swollen clit while his fingers played, stretching and finding that magical place that made her head spin and her belly clench and her hips twist for more. "Right there?"

"Yes! Oh God, yes."

He took her mouth again, swallowing her cries as he pushed her to the edge and held her there ruthlessly, teasing the swollen bud with tiny flicks of his thumb, forcing her to beg and writhe for the orgasm shimmering before her in all its glory.

He ripped his mouth away again and studied her face. Forest-green eyes delved into hers, sheened with lust and a reverence that filled her up. "You're so beautiful. Come for me, Ophelia."

He rubbed hard over her clit, curled his fingers, and thrust deep.

Her head banged against the door and she cried his name, riding the wicked wave of pleasure as it tossed her around and tore her to pieces. He wrung out every last drop of ecstasy, drawing it out, then scooped her up and laid her on the bed.

She blinked in the darkness, muscles limp.

He leaned over her, gaze raking over her features, his finger tracing the swollen curve of her bottom lip.

"I've dreamed of you for so long, of having you back in my arms. Tell me you want this just as bad as I do. For us to be together again."

The complications of their relationship suddenly hit her full force, but in the dark, in his arms, everything seemed right. "I can't promise you anything but tonight," she whispered.

Pain shimmered in his eyes. His jaw tightened, but after a moment, he slowly nodded. "I'll take it. But you have to promise to give me everything. All of you. No holding back."

The morning meant nothing—a distant time that had no place in this magical moment. It was a bargain that might steal her soul, but right now, nothing else mattered except having him make love to her.

"Tonight, I'm yours."

Resolution beat from the powerful lines of his body. "Then it'll have to be enough."

A sliver of unease crept down her spine, but she was too far gone to have any regrets. In seconds, he pulled off his clothes and stood before her naked.

He was magnificent. Tall and lean hipped, with swirls of golden hair dusting his muscled chest. He stood with his feet braced, head thrown back, the confidence and pride in his body reverberating from his aura. He was pure eroticism. Mouth dry, unable to say a word to express the need coursing through her, she lifted her arms for him to join her.

He lowered himself over her, stripping off her jacket and tank, unzipping her boots, unsnapping the hook on her bra, and tugging down her skirt and panties so she lay naked underneath him. Rubbing his rough palms over her hardened nipples, he spent long minutes stroking, licking, sucking—until her breasts were so sensitive she was once again at the edge. She wriggled and hooked an ankle over his thigh, opening herself up.

He scraped his teeth against her nipple and chuckled. "Oh no, not this time. I'm going slow. I want to see if you have any more freckles."

A groan ripped from her lips. "I don't."

"Shush, I'm counting. And if you interrupt me, I'll have to start all over."

He started with her cheeks, dropped to her shoulders, and traced the dots that peppered her pale skin.

How many times had she cursed the ugliness of those freckles? How many times had he proven how beautiful he thought they were by spending hours exploring each and every one?

He took his time, licking, tasting, his hands roving up and down her body in soothing strokes. He brushed his lips over her throbbing nipples, ducked lower to her hip, and nibbled at the group of freckles that had always fascinated him, telling her they reminded him of the Big Dipper.

His tongue dragged over to her inner thigh, his hands holding her spread open for him to play. She tried to struggle to hurry him up, but his grip tightened and he shot her a warning glance.

"Want me to begin again?"

"No! No, go ahead."

"Twenty-two, right?"

She shook under the strain. Her entire body throbbed with need. "Yes. Twenty-two."

"Very good."

Ignoring her aching core, his head ducked behind her knee. He took his time licking the sensitive skin there, then he moved over to her right calf. He grasped her ankle and lifted it up high so she was completely open to him.

Heat licked at her nerve endings. Her cheeks burned as he looked his full gaze, feasting on every intimate inch, which only made her hotter. When she didn't protest, he pressed a kiss to her inner ankle and then on the top of her foot, flashing her a wicked grin.

"Thirty-three."

She sighed in relief, her hips arching up in invitation. "Good. Can we move on?"

He surged up her body, his head between her legs. "Not yet. Have to make sure nothing is hidden."

Her mouth dropped open. "K-K-Kyle—"

Her cry died in her throat as his tongue licked her slit slowly and deliberately, his hot breath teasing all the sensitive, swollen folds. He used light flicks paired with slow rubs over her clit until she was shaking under those talented lips, reaching again for release.

"I'm going to—oh God, I'm going to—" She shattered for the second time, giving herself up to the delicious release that shook through her body.

The rip of a wrapper echoed in her ears. And then he loomed above her, hands propped up by her hips, his gaze fierce on her face, his dick pausing at her dripping entrance.

"Look at me, Ophelia," he demanded. "I need you to look into my eyes when I make you mine again."

The words pierced, dug, splintered. The years drifted away, and she was once again with the only man she'd ever loved, the man who ruled her body and gave her excruciating pleasure over every other.

He pressed into her sex with slow, steady motions, stretching her to the limit, until she closed her eyes to fight off the slight burn, the agonizing fullness of him taking her completely over.

He didn't stop, but surged forward with implacable determination until he was finally buried deep. She arched up and pushed at his shoulders, caught between needing more and needing him to retreat.

A vicious curse left his lips. "You're so perfect. I've missed you so much."

His admission made emotion rise up within her. The tightness suddenly morphed into an ache that demanded to be filled. Her nails bit into his shoulders and she rolled her hips and her body relaxed and accepted him fully.

"That's it," he murmured, running his hands over her breasts, tugging at her nipples. "Don't hold back. You're safe with me. I won't hurt you ever again."

His words blurred in a haze, lost under the driving rhythm of his thrusts, pushing her higher and higher. He gripped her hips and lifted her to meet him, allowing her no room for retreat or space for hesitation. For one brief second, fear cut through the fog and she tried to resist, fighting the slow spin of pleasure crashing through her, but it was if he sensed it and wouldn't allow it. With a low growl, he lifted her ass higher, pistoned his hips, and hit the spot that made her nerves shimmer and break apart.

She cried out his name.

His fingers bruised her hips, but his mouth was gentle as he kissed her long and deep, his tongue almost reverent. The ruthless, thrilling ride of pleasure contradicted the emotion-filled kiss; she let herself go and fell apart in his arms.

He gave a low shout and stiffened above her, his face a mask of chiseled features, eyes half-closed, full lips drawn back as he emitted sounds of his own release. Then he lowered himself down, his skin damp with sweat, the musky essence of man and sex surrounding her, and rolled her to the side so she was splayed against him.

Boneless, she rested her head on his shoulder and reveled in the imprint of his body on hers, the scent of him ingrained on her skin. She closed her eyes, clinging tight to the moment.

It was enough.

The echo of his promise drifted in her memory.

I won't ever hurt you again.

No. Tonight had to be enough.

Chapter Sixteen

When Kyle woke, she was gone.

Blinking away the dregs of sleep, he rolled out of the bed and checked the shower.

Empty.

The woman had ditched his ass like a cheap one-night stand.

Humor warred with irritation. He'd reached for her three times during the night, and she'd come to him each time with an eager sweetness that humbled him, gifting him her body with no barriers between them.

But his fantasy of them cooking breakfast while they goofily smiled and gazed lovingly at each other was just that.

A fantasy.

Smothering a groan, he pulled on his jeans and shirt and walked into the hallway barefoot. Silence surrounded him.

Hell, it was only six a.m. Did she usually get up so early to prepare for the day?

He wandered into the kitchen and found it empty. Everything was spotlessly clean and organized. It was as if she were a mirage that had disappeared in a cloud of smoke at dawn.

A glance out the window confirmed her car was gone. Unease slithered through him. He'd awoken sated, tired, and happy.

Evidently, she hadn't.

He brewed a cup of coffee on the Keurig, then headed to his room. They needed to talk. After such an earth-shattering night, he couldn't go back to the cool distance between them.

He wanted her in his bed every damn night. Wanted her to admit it was more than something physical between them, because God knows he'd lost his heart to her all over again during those intense hours in her bed. He had to try and show her how things could work between them.

His plan was to return to California to make the big deal, then maybe travel back and forth. A long-distance relationship would be fine for a while, until they worked out a permanent solution.

He imagined a second chance for them—and this time, he'd focus completely on her.

Not like before.

He placed his coffee down and sat down in front of his laptop.

"How did your audition go today?"

He paused from his work and studied her. She'd been a bit more distant these past weeks. He knew it was hard receiving constant rejections, but he also knew how competitive the industry was. It was a miracle he'd gotten his big break and was about to deliver a screenplay and partner with one of the best directors in Hollywood, known for their action movies. They'd made Dwayne Johnson a legend.

"I wasn't flashy enough," she said. Her words came out flat, not like the joyful enthusiasm or positivity she usually showed.

He blinked in confusion. "You? With your coloring and personality? Are they blind or stupid?"

She smiled, but it was weak. "I'm not blonde, or super thin, and I hate dressing in skimpy clothes just to get a second glance. I don't know. Things aren't what I thought they'd be like out here."

Irritation flickered, along with shame. They'd been here less than a year. He'd always thought Ophelia had the grit and determination to make anything work. But lately, she'd been moody and sniping about his work hours—and not being the most supportive. God knows, once the script was done he'd have more time to help or pay more attention. Couldn't she see he was doing the best he could?

Kyle stopped and stared at the page.

Ophelia's words from the other day flashed in his mind in slow motion.

"I already had it all . . ."

"I didn't leave with you to be a famous singer . . ."

"You never chose me."

A realization rolled through him, and the mental light bulb clicked on.

So far, the book had been told from the hero's viewpoint. His story. But with any narrative, there were two sides. Singing hadn't been her priority as he'd originally believed. Her love for him had been the most important, but he'd chosen his career.

What had Ophelia gone through while he was flush with success, getting everything he'd always wanted? What was she thinking and feeling after moving to California, getting married, and struggling to make sense of everything alone?

She'd followed him and taken his dreams on as hers. Had he ever seen the truth of what she really wanted?

No. Because he'd been selfish and so caught up in chasing success, he hadn't taken the time to really listen.

Maybe it was finally time to try and understand her side.

He sipped his coffee and thought for a long time.

She watched him, head bent over the keyboard, golden hair shining under the low light. His jaw clenched and his gaze was fierce as he stared at the page—his new lover and mistress that demanded all of his time.

God, she was a bitch. How could she be so happy and proud of him yet feel so lost at the same time? She couldn't tell him what had really happened at the audition. He didn't need her to bring him down at this critical point when his screenplay was almost done. It was easier to slough the episodes off, but deep inside her soul was beginning to wither.

She began cooking dinner, focusing on the steady chopping of the knife flying over the onions and tomatoes, adding fresh herbs to the sauce. Her expectations of how their life would unfold were fraying rapidly. She didn't like the people Kyle hung out with. Fancy parties where conversations occurred only if favors or connections were being bestowed. Fake tans and bright smiles and empty promises of "I'll call you" or "You'd be perfect for this job" and friends who weren't really friends. The social atmosphere confused her, but her husband had begun to thrive, learning to play the ruthless games with a smile that was slowly turning a touch fake.

She sizzled garlic in the pan and stirred it with a wooden spoon. The audition today had been completely humiliating. The small part on the television show that was supposed to be a reinvented Glee *had been perfect for her, and her singing was top-notch.*

Just not her looks.

They hated her hair and her freckles and said she needed to lose weight. They advised her to change her outfit and smile bigger, adjust her face when she belted out the high notes because she looked "a bit weird."

Her confidence was annihilated. She'd left embarrassed and feeling stupid, beginning to believe television and studios weren't her calling. But even the local jobs of singing at restaurants and clubs were hard to get into. They'd asked her to perform songs in the style of Britney Spears or Pink, but she was more of an Adele or Alicia Keys singer. That didn't seem to be as popular.

But it wasn't even the consistent rejections that were slowly eroding her joy.

It was her husband.

She dumped the pasta in the boiling water and began to slice a loaf of Italian bread. Yes, he was busy and had much less time to be with her, but it was bigger than that. He wasn't present when they were together. His once-focused gaze had drifted off, as if he were waiting for someone more important to walk by or call. He chattered about the producers he met, and his new hot agent, and how they'd be able to get a bigger, fancier apartment once the script was done.

He used to make love to her every night.

Now, he worked. When he did reach for her, he still kissed her with hunger and passion, but there was something lacking. Something she hadn't been able to name until it came to her in the dark of the night, lying alone in the sheets, staring at the full moon while she listened to the furiously clacking keyboard.

Tenderness.

She shook off the clingy melancholy and forced a smile to her face. "Babe, dinner's ready. Take a quick break."

He nodded, worked for another five minutes, then got up from the chair. "Damn, that was a good scene. Hero jumped from a moving car with the briefcase, rolled under a semi truck, and arrived on the other side to confront the bad guy. Rob's gonna love it."

Her nose wrinkled at Rob's name. She didn't like his agent. He had a smarmy-type personality that exuded no loyalty, but she kept her silence. "Exciting. Do you like writing those kinds of scenes now?"

He sat down and dove into his pasta. "What do you mean?"

She shrugged and joined him at the table. "I don't know. You always spoke about writing a literary-type novel for the screen—not action stuff."

"I'm lucky to get this shot. Besides, it's fun." His gaze narrowed. "Why? Do you think I sold out or something?"

"No, I'm just asking. If you're happy, I'm happy."

"Sure doesn't seem that way," he muttered.

She jerked and stared at him. "What?"

"I mean, I get it. Things are hard out there, and the auditions aren't going well, but something will break soon. Robbie told me about this new reality show they're casting. It's called Future Pop Star. You'd be perfect for it."

Her stomach clenched. She poked at her pasta. "I don't think I'm pop star material," she said. "I don't like all that image stuff. I just want to sing."

"Yeah, but first you need to show them you're marketable, or they won't even give you a chance to do what you really want. Things work differently out here, Ophelia. You keep acting like everyone's a sellout."

"No I don't."

He tightened his lips. "Will you please audition for it? Just be more open-minded if they talk to you about image—don't take it personally. Your voice is gold. Once they hear it, they're going to want to make you a star."

The dream. To be a star. Once, she'd believed he wanted fame as much as he wanted her.

Now she realized she'd been wrong. She loved singing, but she loved Kyle more. She just wanted her husband the way he used to be—not this new, shinier version she didn't know how to relate to. What if she told him she didn't want the same things he did? Would he still want her?

The questions whirled in her head, but she nodded, enjoying the smile that lit up his beautiful face. God, how she loved him. God, how she wanted to be what he needed.

"Okay, Kyle. If that's what you want, I'll try out."

"Thanks, baby. You'll be great. I'll call Rob after dinner. Did I tell you they're trying to attach Woody Harrelson to the part of the police officer? Wouldn't that be fucking awesome?"

She nodded and smiled as he spoke—and willed the sick feeling in her gut away.

The phone rang, jolting him out of the scene. Trying to clear his head, he clicked the button and tried not to sound as irritated as he felt. "Yeah?"

"It's Rob. I'm still pissed, you know. We may never get another chance at Jenkins."

Kyle understood, but he was damn glad he'd stayed. Every second with Ophelia was precious. Flying back out to Hollywood would have only given her more doubts about his declaration that he'd changed.

"Yeah, I figured. What'd you tell him?"

"Made up some crap, so if this next thing falls through, we can save face and see if Jenkins still wants help. Speaking of which—when will you have the screenplay ready? I've got a lot of people excited to see this new side of Kyle Kimpton. People got some grabby hands here to read it first."

Satisfaction curled through him. Once they read it, he knew it would be an easy sell. Though *Fifty Shades of Grey* bombed by certain Hollywood standards, it had made a ton of money from audiences made up of loyal readers of the book, so Kyle knew the market was ripe for a decent love story besides the ones penned by Nicholas Sparks. Personally, he'd enjoyed both the Sparks and *Fifty Shades* books and thought the fans supported the films well. Then again, he liked reading romance novels and hated how the industry looked down on them. Kind of like action movies. Everyone wanted to compartmentalize them into a box and call it trashy, shallow fiction. Always pissed him off.

"I'll have it done in two months, by April first. You need to line up the best, Rob. This is important to me—probably the most important project I've done."

"So you've told me dozens of times. I'm not deaf, Kimpton. Give me a ring if you need anything. In the meantime, I'll get the players in play. Now go write."

He clicked off, then rubbed his head and looked over the section he'd just written. He was starting to view the past differently—as if a pair of 3-D glasses had been ripped off his vision and painful memories were now clearer.

Like when Ophelia had left him.

He remembered entering their apartment to find it empty. Her clothes gone from the closet. Her scent lingering in his nostrils. An eerie silence in the air.

He'd been so enraged, so full of raw pain that he'd blamed her for running away and not giving them a chance. Now, looking back, he wondered if she'd given him so many chances, whether he'd broken her trust.

If he had come home that night when he'd promised, would it have changed their entire future?

Her taste still lingered on his lips. His dick hardened at the thought of her sweet body opening up to him as he reclaimed her. Last night had showed him the most important realization of all.

He was still in love with her.

He'd never fallen out of love with her. The past eight years had revolved around doing anything to try and forget what they'd had, but now that he had her back in his bed and his life, he only wanted more.

This time, it would be different. He needed to gain back her trust and get her to understand he wasn't leaving.

This time, he'd choose her.

Ophelia stepped into the house and held her breath.

Straining her ears, she caught the sound of low tapping from upstairs. She sagged in relief. Yes, she was a coward, but she couldn't face Kyle just yet.

There was no way she'd be able to step into her room and see him naked and sprawled out on her bed without jumping him.

She headed to the kitchen and unloaded the bags. She'd been at the Market to greet Fran at opening and score some of her fresh, hot cinnamon rolls and breakfast quiches. It would make her morning easier if she could just supplement them with fresh-fruit parfaits and smoked bacon for the guests. She didn't have the focus to deal with too much this morning.

All she could think of was Kyle.

Ophelia groaned and began making the coffee. Last night had been incredible. Perfect. Soul-stirring.

And it couldn't happen again.

Being back in his arms made her realize her emotions hadn't really changed. He was still the only man who commanded her body and heart.

Oh, how she'd tried desperately to fall for someone else over the past decade.

She'd gone on plenty of dates and had two brief affairs, but no man seemed to interest her.

It became easier to fill her life with other things that brought her happiness.

But Kyle's life was back in Hollywood. That meant, eventually, he'd leave her again. If she opened herself up to him, she didn't know if she'd recover when he left.

"Avoiding me?"

Gasping, she whirled around and slammed into the edge of the counter. "You scared me! Why are you sneaking around?"

He cocked his head and stretched out his arms to prop his palms against the wall. The cotton of his shirt pulled against those hard muscles, then molded lovingly to his lean frame. A pair of jeans hung low on his hips. His hair was still mussed from last night. He was barefoot.

Immediately, her body piqued to attention. Her core heated and softened. Her nipples poked against her bra for release. Her skin got itchy and tight.

And damn if the man didn't give her a half smirk, his lip quirking upward in arrogance. She'd never been able to hide her reaction to him, even after all these years.

"Maybe 'cause you snuck out of bed this morning without a word or even a note. Made me feel all sad and cheap."

She glowered. "I highly doubt it. I wanted to get to the store so I wouldn't have to worry about breakfast."

"I would've helped you."

She crossed her arms in front of her chest. "I can take care of myself and my inn."

He quirked a brow. "Never said you can't. Just wanted the opportunity to show you last night meant more than simply scratching an itch."

She tried not to fidget as she regarded him coolly. "Last night was a way to close a chapter of our past. I don't regret it, but it won't happen again."

"I think it will."

Her mouth dropped open. "What did you say?"

He pushed off the wall and stalked over to her. She hurriedly backed up.

"I said I think it *will* happen again. Hell, I'm going to work my ass off to make sure it happens a few times a day—and all night long."

Heat flushed her cheeks. Her belly dropped. "You can't say stuff like that! Last night was a onetime thing. I figured we'd get back to normal in the morning."

A low chuckle escaped his lips. "Baby, we have never been normal. We eloped at eighteen, and I've never fallen for another woman since. The moment we're in the same room together, all I want to do is touch you."

"No—touching is not a good idea. Let's just try to get back to a normal relationship."

"We're still legally married, and I'm living here for the next two months. What type of normal are you talking about?"

She blew out a breath as her back hit the refrigerator, blocking any further retreat. "A new normal. We go back to the original rules, where we stay out of each other's way. We refile for the divorce and put this whole thing behind us."

He loomed over her. His musky scent hit her nostrils, forcing her to bite back a moan.

Why did he have to be so damn sexy and virile and masculine? Why did her legs buckle and her mind spin the moment he got near?

She curled her hands into tight fists to keep from reaching for him and tried to rally.

"Don't want to put this behind us," he drawled. "I want to offer you something better. A new arrangement."

"No."

He bent his head, and his breath rushed against her cheek. "You didn't hear it yet. You'll like it."

"No."

He laughed softly, his hand pushing her hair back. "God, you're hot when you're stubborn. See, here's the truth. I can't keep my hands off you while I'm here. I don't want to, and I don't think you want me to, either."

"You're wrong. I got you out of my system."

He tipped her chin up and forced her to meet his gaze. Amusement glinted in the forest-green depths. "Did you enjoy last night, baby?"

Oh. God.

She struggled to form words in her suddenly dry mouth.

She wished she could lie or play it casual, but there was no way she could pretend their time together wasn't earth-shattering.

She settled for keeping it short and to the point. "Yes."

His lips tugged into a half smile. "Do you honestly think we can live in the same house together and pretend we're strangers? Pretend I didn't touch you and kiss you and make love to you for hours?"

She hated the weakness of her body and mind. She hated that he was right.

"Damn you," she whispered.

"I don't want to hurt you, baby," he said softly. "I just want to be with you. I'm not trying to play games. I'm asking for a chance to explore this and see if you can give me another chance. Do you want to walk away without ever knowing whether we could have given us another shot? You fill me in a way no other woman can. Is it wrong to fight hard for the only woman I've ever loved?"

Her fingers pressed against her trembling lips as she tried to make sense of his words. Truth lit from his body, his eyes, his aura. This wasn't about just sex. He was being completely vulnerable, standing before her, asking for a chance to see if they had something still worth fighting for. She'd been so focused on battling her body's weaknesses, he'd managed to sneak past her emotional barriers.

"And what happens when it's time for you to return to California? How do we possibly make a long-distance relationship work?"

"I believe if we want it bad enough, we can make it work. Look at Mia and Ethan. They managed."

"They were in the same state. Plus Mia moved upstate to be with him full time."

Frustration shot off him. "Right now, I don't care about the logistics. Right now, I want to see if what we have is real and can grow. I'm looking for you to be open to getting to know me again. We've both changed, and we may not fit in each other's worlds any longer. But, God, Ophelia, I still ache for you. If I don't try, I'll regret it for the rest of my life."

"What about our divorce?"

His jaw clenched. "I'm asking you to wait on the divorce until the end of the winter. Give us some time. I swear to God, if you still want to go ahead with the divorce when I leave, I won't fight you. I'll make sure it gets done. Just give us these next two months."

She turned away and walked to the stove. Her thoughts spun.

Opening herself up for another heartbreak was like playing Russian roulette, right? Why would she possibly consider such a crazy offer?

Because you still have feelings for him, her inner voice taunted. *Because you've never gotten over him or been able to move on.*

Was this a way to truly learn to let him go? Being able to explore every aspect of the man he'd become, beyond the ups and downs of youth?

They'd been practically babies, believing their passion and talent were enough. Married at eighteen in secret like some big adventure, ignorant of what messy reality might emerge. They hadn't been prepared.

Did she owe it to herself to see if their relationship could blossom now that they were older and wiser?

They had a specific timeline.

When it was time for him to leave, she'd know. And if they did agree their marriage could work, they'd be able to see things clearly enough to make the next step. This time with their eyes wide open.

Slowly, she turned to face him. "I don't want to get hurt again."

"Me neither."

"I'll keep an open mind. See how things go. No promises."

He rubbed the top of his head, then nodded. "Fair enough. Let's start with today."

She pursed her lips. "What do you want?"

"Besides dragging you back to bed and waking you up properly?" His grin was very wicked and very male, and her skin peppered with goose bumps. "Spend some time with me today. Let's go for a ride later on."

"A ride? It's freezing. The trails are closed."

"Just a leisurely walk to get the horses some exercise. There's no snow in the forecast, and the wind-chill factor is low today. It'll be good for us to get some fresh air."

She remembered how they'd loved to ride together, racing across the meadow as they chased the sinking sun. Guiding the horses through shaded, woodsy paths while they talked nonstop about everything. Her heart ached at the memory. "Okay. One p.m. works for me."

"Perfect. I'm going to work, then to visit Ethan for a bit. I'll see you later."

She expected him to close the distance and kiss her. Instead, he shot her a devastating grin and disappeared, his bare heels echoing on the stairs.

The breath whooshed out of her lungs. This was uncharted territory. She'd agreed to be open to exploring a relationship with Kyle again. Maybe even to sleeping with him.

No, definitely sleeping with him.

There was no way she'd be able to fight off their intense attraction—and she didn't want to.

The only way to give their relationship a fair shot was be honest and vulnerable enough to fall.

She just didn't know if she was able to give him her whole self anymore.

Her mind whirling, she began to prep for breakfast. She needed to spend the next few hours catering to her guests. She had two new arrivals tomorrow; from their brief phone conversation, she already sensed they'd be divas. They were doing something with the SUNY New Paltz campus and thought it would be cool to stay at a B & B rather than a hotel. She remembered when Mia had first arrived. She'd thrown out a bunch of demands, obviously not thrilled about spending the summer outside of the city. But even from the first, Ophelia sensed a kindness in her, evident after she fell hard for her brother. Maybe her two new guests would prove her initial reaction wrong.

At noon, she decided to make a quick stop to check on Patrick. She was still uneasy about him being alone in that big farmhouse by himself. All those years of misery and boarding himself up couldn't be undone so quickly. He had no social network, and no one else in town gave a crap what happened to him.

But he was still Kyle's father. And he was trying. She wanted to make sure he hadn't had a relapse. If he did, she'd be hit with the guilt that she hadn't made him go to the hospital.

Packing up the leftover breakfast quiche and a cinnamon roll, she took the short drive to his house. This time, when she knocked on the door, he didn't look as surprised to see her. His hawklike nose practically sniffed in anticipation of the goodies she held in her hand, but he pretended it wasn't a big deal when he invited her in.

"I'm feeling fine," he said.

She studied his face.

Yes, his eyes were clear and his throat didn't sound like he was fighting for breath or wheezing.

"You look better. I brought you some breakfast."

"Didn't have to do that," he grumbled as he reached for the bag.

"I know. Just had some leftovers to get rid of. Want some tea?"

"Aren't I the one who's supposed to be offering you stuff?"

She smiled as he sat at the kitchen table and tore into the sweets. "Probably, but I make better tea. What are you doing?"

The table was littered with shoeboxes and scattered papers. A bright blue photo album lay open. Curious, she bent over to examine it, but Patrick quickly slammed the book shut.

"Just some pictures," he mumbled, avoiding her gaze.

She nodded, allowing him his privacy. The kitchen was tidier this time, so she just straightened up and made two cups of green tea, adding a squirt of honey she'd brought over the last time. When she sat down with him at the table, she noticed he'd pushed the boxes and papers to the far corner, away from her prying eyes.

"I'm glad you're feeling better. What are your plans this week?"

He gave a snort. "Plans? Besides my visit to the Queen? Nothin' much. Just cashing my social security check. That's a big day at the bank for seniors. They pretty much have a party."

She smiled at his biting sarcasm, sipping her tea. "Do you go to AA meetings now?"

"Yeah. Three times a week, at least until I've been sober a year."

"Do you have a sponsor?"

"Yeah. Why all the questions? Curious about alcoholism?"

"Curious to know how a man who's been cruel his whole life begins to change."

Respect gleamed from his green eyes, and a laugh ripped from his throat. "Always liked you. Had spunk, and never shied away from protecting Kyle."

"I had to," she said quietly. "He had no one else to protect him."

He winced, and they fell into silence.

She cursed herself for bringing up bad memories, but they were hard to forget—even when she was sipping tea in his house and had brought him breakfast.

Maybe this was a mistake. It felt like a betrayal to Kyle.

"I should probably go," she said, pushing up from the table.

"No!"

She stared in surprise.

"I mean, there's no need for you to go yet. And I'm not trying to defend myself or get smart with you. Old habits die hard, you know?"

She slowly sat back and offered a smile. "Yeah, I know."

They sipped their tea for a while in silence. Then he spoke. "My sponsor checks in daily. Rehab forced me to see things in myself I'd been hiding for a long time. The ugliness of hating yourself eventually takes a toll on a man. It was easy to know why I drank. It was hard to stop, because I knew I had nothing left to hide behind."

"Catherine?" The name of Kyle's mother rolled off her tongue. She'd encouraged Kyle to never be afraid to say her name even though his father had tried to bury her memory.

"Yeah. It's a long story."

"Seems like besides tea with the Queen, you got a lot of time to tell me."

He laughed again, rubbing the top of his head in the same familiar gesture his son used. "Maybe one day. There's definitely more hours in the day when you're sober. I've binge-watched series on Netflix, drank endless cups of coffee, and started to read. Even got myself to church one morning."

"Did an earthquake strike when you walked in?" she teased.

"Nah, it was not that big of a deal. The priest prattled on, but I liked the dark and the quiet. I liked the peace." He paused, crumbling up the empty bag of food he'd finished, then lifted his gaze. "How's Kyle?"

"Good. He's working on his new screenplay."

"I saw him on the red carpet once, on television. It was for that big action flick, *Last Man Down*. It was good."

"He was always a talented writer."

"Yeah, had his nose in a book or scribbled in journals since he was young. Reminded me of his mother. She liked to write."

Her mouth fell open. "Catherine wrote?"

"Yeah, poetry. She loved to read and write poetry. That was her other love, besides horses."

"Did you ever tell Kyle he was like his mother?"

"No. It was something that made me resent him so much." The admission came out raw but truthful.

She thought about Catherine writing poems and stories, like her son. Thought about how the alcohol twisted Patrick's memories; instead of being proud, he only ended up destroying a gift that could have brought joy and healing. She pushed the sad thought aside.

"We're going horseback riding later," she said.

Pain flickered over his features. "Do you still have his horse? Lucy?"

"She died a few years back," she said softly.

"I threatened to shoot her, you know. Her leg was lame. God, how Kyle loved that horse. And I used it against him."

"I remember. He came to see me and asked Mom to take her in. Kyle spent every spare moment nursing her back to health until she was able to walk again." She struggled for the next words. "Why did you want to hurt him so badly?"

He ducked his head. "Don't know. Of all the terrible things I've done to him, that's the scene that replays over and over in my mind. It's on repeat. It's my own personal torture of regret." He seemed hesitant about giving her more, so she was surprised when he continued. "It was my anniversary. The day we had gotten married had been so hopeful. I woke up that morning and swore not to drink. Swore I was going to be clean that day—for her. For Kyle. Instead, I barely got through three hours before the shakes started and I fell back into the bottle. I hated myself. Couldn't stand to look in the mirror because I made myself sick. I took out all that bad stuff on my son. When I heard about Lucy being lame, a switch flicked inside. It was as if the whole thing was another reminder of everything I'd lost." Anguish radiated from his figure.

Ophelia studied his frail frame.

He'd lost so much in pursuit of the bottle. Though his actions had been cruel, she realized he was a tortured soul.

Sympathy flickered.

"Lucy was well loved at my mom's."

"Your mom was good to Kyle. Tried with me, too, but I was too far gone to save. You still in love with my son?"

She jerked. Tea slapped over the side of the mug and splashed on her hand. "What kind of question is that?"

He shrugged. "Just a question. You ran off together, then you came back alone. Always wondered what happened."

"Things didn't work out. We were young. Had no idea what we were doing."

"Sounds like me and Catherine." A faint smile ghosted his lips, and she didn't spot the usual bitterness. "Fell in love with her the moment I saw her. Told her I was going to marry her right then and there. All these years, all these regrets and what-ifs that drove me to drink . . . once I really examined everything, I realized nothing could have changed. I'm grateful for the time I had with her. And I'm grateful Catherine was strong enough for both of us to save our son."

"Kyle doesn't believe that. He thinks you hate him."

Patrick gazed at his clasped hands on the table, trembling slightly. "Don't blame him. I was mean. I wanted to hurt my own son. Never gonna be forgiven for that—by myself, or you, or Kyle, or God. Don't expect it. But I'd do anything to make him see it wasn't his fault his father was an asshole who wanted to destroy everything good around him."

Her heart ached. So many lost opportunities and broken hopes.

"Maybe you can talk to him. Ask him to come see me. Just once. I'd like to give him something important."

She closed her eyes, torn between her loyalty to Kyle and the driving instinct to try and heal the rift between father and son. His quest for fame and success sprouted from Patrick's consistent cutting remarks that Kyle wasn't good enough for anything. To finally hear his father's apology and truth could heal something he didn't even know was broken.

"I'll talk to him," she finally said. "I'll try."

"That's all I want. Just for you to try."

She nodded. "Now I really better go. I'll check on you later in the week."

"No need. I'm better now."

"I will anyway."

She said goodbye and drove back to the inn, thinking about Kyle and Catherine and Patrick and how love could get so tangled and lost along the way. Wrong choices and terrible mistakes had been made.

After speaking with Patrick, she wondered if there could really be second chances—if one was strong enough to forgive. To try again. To take a leap and risk her heart again.

She was beginning to see a bigger picture. Kyle had hurt her, but he'd craved success and acceptance after so many years of Patrick telling him he was nothing. He'd been young and desperate, and lost his way.

But he was here now, fighting to show her he'd changed.

If Kyle could eventually communicate with his father, knowing how he'd changed, could she also give Kyle that type of chance? To start believing they could have a future together and heal all those scars of the past?

The questions whirled in her mind for a very long time.

Chapter Seventeen

Kyle stroked the horse's head and murmured nonsense in a low, sooth-ing voice. Little Foot—another one of Harper's rescues—had a playful personality and liked to butt him off center, then pull back his lips in a snicker. Kyle had chosen him immediately, knowing the horse would be fun to ride. He'd picked out Flower, the pretty gray filly who had spunk, for Ophelia. He'd already brushed and saddled them up, but Ophelia was running late.

He wondered if she'd even show.

"Doing some riding today?"

He turned to see Harper enter the barn. She was dressed in her usual jeans and boots, a black knit cap pulled over her head. Her red jacket was the only flash of color. The horses immediately began to fidget to fight for her attention and her affectionate smile. As she went down the line saying hello to each, he was reminded of how special Ophelia's sister was.

"Yeah, we both need some fresh air. Occupational hazard."

She nodded, stroking Little Foot's nose and patting Flower on the rear. "Did you do any riding in California?"

"Not that much. Most of my friends in the business weren't the horse type."

"You must've missed it. You grew up taking care of them. You saved Lucy single-handedly. She was finally able to walk again because you believed in her."

His throat tightened at the memory of his beloved horse—and his father's cruel actions. "I hated leaving her, but I know you and your mom took good care of her."

"We did. She was family because you were." She tilted her chin, her gaze direct. "Ophelia told me the truth. About your marriage. The big breakup. That you're not divorced."

Shock barreled through him. He prepped himself for accusations and a billion questions, but Harper just kept her silence, as if waiting for him to take the lead.

"Wow, I didn't expect her to tell you. She's been so determined to keep it a secret, but I'm glad you know. I wish I could just tell Ethan and deal with the fallout."

"Yeah, Ethan's a bit on the protective side. Testosterone, I guess, plus the best-friend's-little-sister thing. You still love her?"

Kyle rubbed his head and laughed. God, Harp was a piece of work. Never afraid to ask whatever was on her mind, and she refused to apologize for anything.

But he didn't even think of denying her the truth. "Yeah, I still love her."

She nodded. "I could tell last night. It was like an explosion of chemistry, the way you looked at her."

"That obvious, huh?"

"What are you going to do about it?"

He blinked. "I'm going to convince her to give us a second chance."

She didn't look too impressed. "What's changed from before? You still going to leave at the end of winter? Head back to Tinseltown to make big-time movies? I get it—it's your job—but you know that's not the type of life Ophelia can live."

Jennifer Probst

He shifted his weight. "Yes, but I'm coming back. And maybe she can come out to California for a little while and hire an assistant for the inn. If we want to be together, we can make it work. Look at Mia and Ethan."

"They made some hard compromises." She nodded, then tilted her head and studied him. "Why is Ophelia so wary of trusting you again?"

His temper flared.

Harper certainly didn't seem like she believed that the power of true love could conquer all.

He dug deep and tried to be brutally honest. "I wasn't there for her. Got too wrapped up in my career. Too focused on her being a successful singer to see it wasn't making her happy. It's my job to make sure she knows I've changed." He paused, considering her guarded expression. "Why? You don't think we're good together?"

She surprised him by smiling. "I think you were meant to be soul mates. All these years, it was as if she was just waiting for you to come back. But I don't want to see my sister get hurt again."

"She won't."

She narrowed her gaze thoughtfully. "She changed, you know. When she got home. It was as if a light had gone out in her. She stopped singing. Became quieter, more Zenlike."

Pain tore through him. He hated the idea of how much he'd hurt her.

"After some time, she seemed happy again. Different, but happy. Then I saw you two together at the family dinner, and I realized her light was back—the old Ophelia, who was always so full of life. You bring that out in her. But if you mess it up again, I'm worried she won't recover." She studied him with a probing gaze. "Make sure you listen to her. It's the only way to figure out what you both need and how to make her happy."

The words both puzzled and intrigued him as they floated in the spaces of his mind between memory and the story he was penning.

He'd been wrong about how badly Ophelia had wanted a singing career. What else had he misjudged about her?

198

Harper was right. This time, he needed to listen and make sure he gave Ophelia what she needed.

On cue, she rushed into the barn, her face pleasantly flushed. "Sorry, I got sidelined," she said. "Hi, Harp. You riding with us?"

Her sister shook her head and spun on her bootheel. "No, you guys enjoy the ride. I've got a bunch of stuff to do in the barns."

"Okay. But you're still coming to dinner tonight, right?"

"Of course," she called out. "Especially if Kyle is helping you cook again. See ya later."

Ophelia shook her head and laughed. "Guess you'll be helping me again in the kitchen."

He dropped his voice to an intimate pitch. "Good. We make a great team."

Her cheeks reddened, and she focused on the horses. "All saddled up?"

"Yep, all set." His gaze took in her snug jeans, flannel shirt, short puffy blue jacket, and high riding boots. She'd pulled a knit hat low over her ears, allowing some wild curls to escape. A pair of tortoiseshell sunglasses perched on her pert nose.

She looked adorable.

"Oh good, Little Foot is getting fat. Harper wanted him to get more exercise."

At the sound of his name, the brown horse bumped Kyle again, then gave a snort. Kyle grinned. "Yeah, this one's a comedian. I was dying to try out Phoenix, but Ethan said he wasn't ready for strangers to ride him yet."

"Phoenix has come a long way, but I think he was really abused. Poor thing. Ethan and Harper have done amazing things with him. He's got a resilient spirit."

A cloud of worry passed over her face. She chewed on her lower lip, as if in deep thought. He wanted to ask what was on her mind but decided not to press. They'd have plenty of time to talk on their walk.

"Let's go."

They mounted the horses, grabbed the bridles, and headed toward the side path through the woods. It was mostly flat and relatively clear—like the valley trails the tourists preferred for the spectacular views.

The squeak of the saddles and clump of hooves drifted to his ears. The air was cold but clear, with no wind to steal his breath. His hips rocked gently back and forth, and he stretched his legs in the stirrups, relaxing into position as he had since he was young. He took the lead, guiding Little Foot toward the left on the widening path so Ophelia could flank him.

"Kyle, I have to tell you something. You may get upset."

Dread coiled in his stomach.

She'd changed her mind. She had made a terrible mistake, didn't want him in her bed, and wanted the divorce now.

He tried to remain calm. "You can talk to me about anything, baby. Just tell me."

"I went to see your dad."

It took him a while to process her statement.

He was so fucking relieved she wasn't rejecting him, he didn't know how to respond to her confession. His father?

She hated him as much as Kyle did.

"Why?"

Her breath released into the silence. "Last week, I was driving back from town when I noticed an ambulance at his house. I stopped to check on him."

He didn't like the sudden prickle of worry that skated through him. He'd had nothing to do with his father since he'd left. "Did he go to the hospital?" he asked.

"No, he refused to go in the ambulance, but he was pretty sick. He also told me he'd had a heart attack a while ago, so I've been worried. I ended up making him soup and bringing him groceries later in the week."

He'd had a heart attack?

A mess of emotions began a riot in his gut. He hated thinking about his father and everything that had happened between them. He'd learned long ago to get past the hatred and resentment, but now there was just an empty void that had taken its place.

"Were those the only times you saw him?"

"No, I went again today. To check up on him. Bring him food. He's all alone in that big farmhouse, with no one to talk to. I know he speaks to his sponsors and goes to AA meetings, but the town wrote him off a long time ago, and he doesn't seem to be trying to socialize."

"Do you blame them? Do you blame me?" he asked tightly.

"Of course I don't blame you! But he's changed, Kyle. He's talking openly about how he treated you, and how sorry he is. He's been sober almost a year. I'm not making excuses for him or his past behavior. Neither is he. But he wants to talk to you. I think he needs to tell you some important things face-to-face."

Pain crashed through him. His hands fisted around the reins.

How long had he ached for his father to acknowledge him? To apologize? To explain the shitty way he'd acted was one big mistake that he regretted?

For as long as he could remember—until Kyle realized it was something that would never happen in his lifetime, so he had accepted it and moved on.

Now he wanted to talk.

Rage replaced the pain. His voice felt as stripped and stark as the trees bending slightly in the wind. "No, Ophelia. I'm not going to talk to him. Too much time has passed. Nothing he says will change a thing."

"I understand. He asked me to ask, though."

They walked for long moments in silence. He struggled to move past the conversation but felt stuck.

"Would you talk to him? If it was you?"

Another soft sigh spilled from her lips. "I don't know. I think so. Bad things happen in life, and people hurt others—even people they love. He's the only father you have, the only link to your blood. If he's finally willing to talk candidly, I'd want to hear him out. I think there's something powerful about being willing to forgive someone."

He sifted through her words, choosing not to respond. She'd seen firsthand what he'd gone through as a child, knew how many of his choices were based on his crazed need to prove to his father he was worthy. Knew how he struggled with guilt over his mother's death. A psychologist would have a fucking field day with his family issues, but he'd worked through many of his demons by writing—and talking to Ethan and Ophelia and their mother. That support system had made all the difference.

"Are you going to see him again?"

"Yes. Just to check on him." She cut him a glance. "Unless you tell me not to. I'd never want to hurt you like that."

"Thank you." He reached his hand out, and she took it. Fingers entwined, he squeezed hers tight. It would be easy to tell her to stay away from his father, but there was something in her tone when she spoke about him. As if it were important to her to keep seeing him. "Do you want to see him again, or do you just feel guilty?"

She scrunched up her nose, pondering the question. "Both. He's finally accepting help and being nice. But it's more than that. He shares more of his story each time I'm there, and I can see how he wants to be different. I feel like I should continue to encourage that."

The words stung, but he nodded. Ophelia had a gift with people—a way to make them feel important and cherished.

It was one of the things he loved about her, and he wouldn't ask her to hold back. Even from his father.

"Then I'd never ask you to stop." He forced a grin. "You were always the nicest out of our group."

She made a face. "Nice is the worst adjective ever. I'm not *nice*. I was the one who talked you and Ethan into painting graffiti on the college sign."

He groaned. "God, I'd almost forgotten about that. Judge Bennett handed us both our asses, and when he asked you if you'd been involved—"

"I said you guys were too crazy for me and walked away."

"You left us hanging. We had to scrub that sign with a Brillo pad on a Saturday in one-hundred-degree weather."

She laughed. "I kept you company."

"You hung out eating an ice-cream cone, directing us where to scrub harder!"

"Told you I'm not nice."

He laughed, and their hands fell apart.

Sunlight leaked through the branches and turned her hair to fire. A smile rested on her full lips, her body at ease on Flower. She had surrendered to the gentle rocking motions, heels firmly hooked in the stirrups.

His heart ached as he looked at her, the melding of past and present, child and woman. Harper was right. Ophelia was calmer now. There'd always been a zest and mad energy throbbing in her veins. She'd dash about, ready for the next event or adventure, throwing her entire being out to the world. Now there was a graceful restraint. A quieter sort of happiness that was sensual in the way only a confident woman could be—one who knew her body and mind and accepted herself completely.

"I love seeing you like this," he said quietly. "The way you are with the guests is a humbling experience. The way you give so much of yourself. Your mother would be so damn proud."

She jerked in the saddle, then met his gaze head-on. Those blue eyes turned misty, like the color of smoke, and trapped him helplessly under her spell.

The horses muttered softly, sensing the sudden awareness in the air. His entire body throbbed with anticipation, ready to drag her off that horse, shove her against a tree trunk, and kiss her until his mad lust was finally sated.

She smiled. "I loved running the inn together. She taught me so much. Oh God, how we laughed and complained and giggled together! It was a special time for me, being that close to my mom."

He let his thoughts wander awhile, then asked the question that had been burning inside him. "Do you regret it, Ophelia? Leaving with me? Marrying me?"

Her gaze nailed him, blue eyes flaming with intensity. "I've never regretted running away with you. Everything brought me back to where I belonged."

Pain slapped through him. He barely caught his breath from the hit. "I always thought we belonged to each other. That being together was our safe place."

Regret tinged her voice. "Me, too. But we were too young to know what that really meant."

"And now?"

Was that a flash of hope in her eyes or a trick of the light?

"And now maybe things can be different."

They smiled at each other. His heart bloomed. She was finally admitting there was a chance.

He'd take the small opening and chip away until he created a giant door he could walk right through, back into her life.

Ophelia knew the moment her guests arrived the next day that they'd be trouble.

The duo had matching annoyed expressions. Perfect hair and makeup. Designer luggage. Three-inch-heeled platform Michael Kors boots that were definitely not waterproof. The dark-haired one wore a turtleneck that ended right below her boobs. The blonde had bubblegum-pink lips that could have made her the mascot for Botox. They seemed about twenty-five, with an air of snobby entitlement.

Yeah, this was going to be fun.

Not.

Smothering a groan, she pasted on her smile. "Welcome to the Robin's Nest B & B. How was your trip?"

"Awful," the brunette whined. "The roads suck, and there was, like, no decent restaurant to stop at along the way. Thank God we're only here for two days, or I'd die."

"I'm so sorry to hear that. I can make you some coffee or tea and some snacks while you relax and get unpacked. Let's get you registered. I'll show you the rooms and bring up your luggage."

"We requested a private bath," the blonde threw out. "We're not sharing with strangers."

"Of course. It's all set." She went to the writing desk and pulled up the information on the computer. "Devon Marshall and Margaret Alistair, correct?"

"I prefer Margo." She tossed her golden tresses and pursed those lips in distaste. "I also have a strict list of preferences for breakfast I'll need you to accommodate."

She kept her smile pinned on. "Yes, I'd be happy to tailor the menu to your needs. Can you confirm your address, phone, etc.?"

They got through the check-in process, and she grabbed two keys. She gave them a quick tour of the inn, then led them up the stairs to the rooms. "I've placed you in the Garden and Imperial suites. Both have private baths, a sitting area, king-size beds, and a fireplace. There's instructions on how to work the fire, but I'm happy to help you if you need it."

The girls toured the rooms with matching judgy gazes as if ready to pounce the moment they didn't like something.

Ophelia delved into her spiel, which included everything they both needed to know about the town and the inn's facilities.

"We don't like to share breakfast with strangers," Devon said.

"We only have two other guests right now, but I'm happy to bring up room service."

"Good. We'd like mimosas and fresh fruit—but no pineapple and no apples. Fresh-squeezed orange juice with the mimosas—not the cheap juice in the cartons. Absolutely no carbs. I brought a recipe for oatmeal-banana pancakes we'd like you to make. And we like our coffee with organic Stevia and prefer a dark blend with no bitterness."

Her lip quirked. Guess Margo had no idea oats contained carbs. "Not a problem."

"Is there a gym?"

"No, I'm sorry. No gym."

Devon gasped. "I assumed there was a place to work out! Every facility has a gym!"

She grabbed at the fraying strings of her patience. "I'm sorry, but we are clear on the reservation confirmation and on the website that there's no gym—and that we don't provide dinner."

Margo moaned. "What are we going to do? What if we gain weight?"

"We have a wonderful yoga studio in town that holds classes all day tomorrow. I'd be happy to give them a call and register you."

Devon nodded. "Yes, definitely. I almost fainted."

Margo gave a dramatic sigh of relief.

Ophelia tried to choke back the ball of disgust lodged in her throat. There were always a few guests who made her want to quit the inn and be a file clerk in a big-ass library with no mandate to talk to anyone. But her mother always said the hardest guests to serve brought the most opportunity for growth.

Guess she'd be getting that a lot this week.

"Very good. Let me get your luggage and set up your tea and snacks."

"I only like Barry's tea," Margo said.

"Not a problem." She clicked the door closed and massaged her temples. These next two days were going to be hell, but then she had a nice stretch of isolation until the next group was booked.

She could do this.

She delivered the suitcases and headed to the kitchen to steep some Barry's tea and put out no-carb, low-fat snacks. She reminded herself to run out and grab some champagne. New Year's had cleaned her out, and rarely did guests request bubbly unless it was an anniversary.

Footsteps made her look up. "Can I make some coffee?"

"Already put on a fresh pot. Don't lie. You smelled it, didn't you?"

Kyle rubbed his head and gave her an adorably sheepish look. Sexy scruff hugged his jaw, emphasizing those carved lips she already missed kissing.

"Yeah, I've climbed into the saggy middle of my story. I'd rather scrub toilets than keep writing." He looked hopeful. "Any toilets for me to scrub?"

She laughed, grabbing him a mug and pouring the brew. "Nope. The middle was always the worst for you. You have to stop editing yourself—that's where your block always happens."

"I know! I can't seem to let it go. I fix every few words, think about shit, and then delete the words I put down. I literally spent two hours on my laptop and nothing got written."

"Vomit the words, remember? Think morning pages. Unconscious creative writing. No muse or inner voice telling you anything. Then you can fix it later. It's like hump day—you have to barrel through."

He took the coffee and stared at her with a bit of hero worship. "Yes, this has happened before. You remembered."

She laughed. "You've been writing since we were twelve years old. Every single time you'd bitch and whine and declare it was all over once you hit the middle. No story has beaten you yet, and I highly doubt this will be the one that does."

"You're right." A determined gleam lit up his eyes. "I got this. Why did I forget I've gone through this before?"

"It's like childbirth, I think. Women say no matter how excruciating the pain, the baby is so amazing they have selective memory and decide it wasn't so bad. Then they get pregnant again."

"You're a brilliant woman, Ophelia."

She laughed again and waved her hand in the air. "Yes, I am. Now get the hell out of my kitchen and go write."

"I will. I'm going to—"

"Excuse me! Excuse me, Ophelia? I need some help, please." Devon appeared from the dining room and headed toward them.

Unbelievable.

The kitchen was in the back of the house, so a guest had to walk through a bunch of rooms to get there. This was her private area.

Guess Devon had ignored the big sign at the bottom of the stairs that said to ring the bell for any service.

"Yes, Devon? What can I do for you? I'm just getting ready to bring up your tea."

"Thank you, but we'd also like to request . . . Oh my. Hello. I'm sorry to interrupt." Devon froze, staring at Kyle like Bernie Madoff looking at a pardon.

With pure, undisguised hunger.

The girl dropped the attitude, and her face lit up with a smile. Practically purring, she held out her hand and tossed her head. Glossy dark hair swished past her shoulders. Her gaze roved over his figure like a she-cat appraising her dinner.

"I'm Devon. Are you a guest here?"

Kyle smiled back and shook her hand. "Yes. Welcome to Robin's Nest. Are you enjoying your stay?"

"I just checked in with my girlfriend. We're heading up to the Winter Festival tomorrow."

"Oh, that's a blast. They have great snow tubing, and Angry Orchard usually has a booth."

"How about you?" Devon ran her tongue over her teeth and leaned in.

Ophelia almost groaned at the obvious move. God, she was practically drooling over him.

"Why don't you join us tomorrow?"

"Sorry, I have to work. But thanks for the invite."

"Working on vacation? That's a shame. What do you do?"

Kyle shifted on his feet. Ophelia recognized it as a sign that he wanted to leave but was trying to be polite. "I'm a screenwriter, and I better get back to it. It was nice meeting you."

"A writer for movies? How cool. Name one of your movies."

He looked torn between being polite versus escape. "Umm, *The Bounty* is one."

Devon gasped. Her hand shot out and grabbed his upper arm.

Ophelia felt a possessive howl trapped in her throat, ready to emerge. Why was she touching him?

"I cannot believe this—you're Kyle Kimpton! I'm completely freaking out. Your movies are amazing. I've seen *The Bounty* three times!"

Aw, crap.

Kyle smiled and didn't shake off her touch.

Was he staring at her bare midriff, tanned and tight and on display?

"Thanks, I appreciate that. Always nice to meet a fan."

"Oh, you must join us for dinner tonight. There's nothing to eat here anyway, since Ophelia doesn't cook. It would be an honor." She thrust out her sizable breasts, squeezed his arm, and waited.

Ophelia waited, too.

Slowly, Kyle removed Devon's hand and stepped back, his grin firmly in place. "That's really sweet. Normally I'd love to, but I'm on a tight deadline and I'll be eating in my room tonight. Maybe I'll see you for breakfast?"

Disappointment flickered over Devon's features, but she brightened at the mention of breakfast. "Definitely. Would love to spend some time with you before the festival."

"I thought you required room service?" Ophelia cut in. "Because you don't like eating with other guests?"

Devon shot her a glare, then forced a tinkly laugh. "Oh, I was just kidding. I'm not the diva sort, I'm looking forward to chatting with everyone tomorrow." She tilted her chin and stared at Kyle, dropping her voice to a sexy growl. "I'm in the Garden Room if you need anything *at all*. A break, a chat, another cup of coffee . . ."

Ophelia highly doubted coffee was on her mind.

God, did she have to be so obvious about it? And the man didn't seem to be in such a hurry any longer.

He just smiled back at her, as if he was used to women throwing themselves at him on a daily basis.

Because he probably was.

"Thanks. I'll let you know."

What? He'd let her know? Know what?

"Good," Devon whispered.

Ophelia slammed down the teacup, practically shattering the delicate china. "Tea and snacks are ready," she announced loudly.

With another look at the girl, Kyle left the kitchen.

Devon's smile slipped away, and she regarded Ophelia with pure annoyance. "What time does Kyle show up for breakfast?" she demanded. "I'll have whatever he orders."

"Oh, he likes a woman with a huge appetite," she said, nodding seriously. "I heard him say women who are always worried about their weight and diet annoy him. He likes to eat an omelet, bacon, toast, and pancakes. He adores carbs. Hates fruit and yogurt."

Devon paled, but she was clearly committed. "Fine, make sure I have the same. What room is he in?"

Annoyance surged. "I'm not allowed to give out that kind of information about guests. Sorry."

"Never mind. I'm sure I'll find out soon enough." With a sharklike smile, she motioned toward the tray. "Bring that up to Margo's room, please, and I'll join her. Also, I prefer a down pillow, not that memory foam stuff. Can you get me a replacement pillow?"

Bitch.

"Sure, that won't be a problem," she said cheerfully.

"Thanks." Devon left the kitchen, hips swinging, glossy hair swishing.

Ophelia prayed for the patience not to throw her the hell out of her inn.

There was no way Kyle could be attracted to such a woman. It was just odd seeing up close how his celebrity affected people. He may have craved fame and fortune, but ego had never been his problem. In fact, he'd always wanted approval from the higher-ups, the people, the crowd. It was as if his own success didn't count unless everyone agreed. The more they adored him, the better he felt about proving his father wrong.

Was that another thing that had torn them apart? She'd realized with her singing that it didn't matter if the world termed her successful or a star—she sang for her own pleasure. But growing up with a father who consistently told him he was nothing made Kyle seek approval from the outside world.

If Patrick finally admitted his wrongs, would some of Kyle's demons be soothed?

Her gut drove her to one answer over and over: Kyle needed to talk to his father before he left Gardiner.

She just had to convince him.

"More toast?" Ophelia asked sweetly.

Devon stared at her plate with a touch of panic. Kyle still hadn't seemed to notice the girl's unease with carbs, and he had happily devoured everything Ophelia put in front of him. Margo was perched on the opposite chair, engrossed with her phone. She'd tried talking to Kyle once, but the sharp glance Devon threw her shut Margo right up.

Seemed like Devon had already staked her claim.

The other guests—young marrieds, a thirty-something couple who loved to ski but hated staying at the large resident lodges—had just finished up and were headed back to Windham's slopes for the day. Devon dragged her chair as close as possible next to Kyle and engaged him in lively conversation, stopping intermittently to touch his arm or rest a palm on his knee as she pretended to laugh. Seemed she was a makeup expert who was well known on YouTube and had written some pieces for *Glamour*. She had the nerve to ask if she could interview him for a feature on how to rock the scruffy look with style.

Ophelia couldn't tell if she was more pained or amused by the whole exchange.

"How about I bring home dinner after the festival tonight?" Devon suggested, as if it were a brilliant idea that had just occurred to her. "That way you can work all day and give yourself a break later on."

A frown furrowed his brow. "Aren't you going out with your friend?" He forked up another piece of bacon, seemingly in a happy fugue state from the giant breakfast Ophelia had served.

Devon nibbled on a piece of toast and tried not to look miserable at the thought of carbs entering her pure body.

"Oh no. She has plans. I'll be all alone and would really love the company. How does sushi sound?"

"More coffee?" Ophelia cut in.

"Yes, please. This is an unbelievable spread, Ophelia. Isn't she amazing?" he asked Devon.

"Oh yeah. She is." Devon shoved the piece of toast in her mouth and chewed. "So good. I hate women who turn down food just because they think they're fat."

"Right? I agree," he said, totally clueless.

"We have so much in common. I'll come to your room at seven p.m."

He shook his head. "What? Oh. No, sorry. I can't do dinner tonight."

"Of course you can! You need some downtime. Refill the well, right?"

"I have plans. I'm dining with a . . . friend."

"Oh, okay. Maybe we can catch a drink beforehand."

"Yeah, I'm not sure. I better get to work." He got up, carrying his plates and heading toward the kitchen. "Have a great time at the festival."

Ophelia clamped down a grin when she saw the furious expression on Devon's face. She followed him to the kitchen, where he stood in front of the sink. He grabbed the sponge.

"You don't have to clean up," she said. "I got it."

"No, you've done enough this morning. Let me."

With his tight ass cupped in jeans and a soapy sponge in his hand doing dishes, the scene was total porn. Her knees grew a bit weak. "Thanks. Who are you having dinner with tonight?" she asked.

"No one. Just not her."

Pleasure shot through her. "Not interested, huh?"

He gave her a stunned look. "Are you kidding me? Definitely not my type."

"Oh yeah? What is your type?"

He gave a low laugh, moving the sponge in perfect circles. "Not someone with perfectly manicured fingernails. I like a woman who knows how to get dirty and messy."

Laughter bubbled inside. She glanced at her own hands, which hadn't seen polish in years. "Hmm, interesting. What else?"

"Let's see . . . a woman who doesn't agree with everything I say. That gets old. I prefer a challenge."

"Does a woman who calls you a controlling asshole count as a challenge?"

"Definitely. That just turns me on."

She cocked her hip and pursed her lips. "You are definitely an odd man. Anything else?"

"I do have a fetish not many can satisfy."

"Hmm. Fetish, huh? I hope it's not feet. That's just wrong."

"Nope. Freckles. I love freckles scattered across pale skin. They're like a Picasso painting I can't stop staring at."

Pleasure flushed her cheeks. "More like paint-by-number, but I won't judge."

"Then there's sex."

She stilled. Her heart beat madly in her chest. "Sex?"

"I have certain needs that many would find difficult to satisfy."

An image floated past her vision. His body pressed over hers, his tongue diving deep into her mouth with a tender fierceness that shook her to the core. He'd always had an insatiable appetite in the bedroom. Their sex life had never been an issue—it had, in fact, kept the fragments of their relationship together longer than she imagined possible.

"Kinky stuff?" she asked.

"More like particular. I need a woman who's able to handle me."

Her gaze dropped. "Cocky much?"

"I need the scent of lavender and honey in my nostrils, and the sweet taste of her essence sticky on my lips. I need to look into blistering blue eyes and know I belong to her."

Her vision misted over. She swayed on her feet. He turned off the sink, dried his hands with slow, deliberate motions, and faced her. "I need to slide into her sweet body and be welcomed home. Touch her body and make her moan. I need a woman strong enough to let me fall apart in her arms, then put me back together. Do you understand, Ophelia?"

She tried to speak, but nothing came out. Her entire body was on fire, nerves on edge, ready to explode. His raw words stroked her ears—and between her legs.

"Ophelia? Do you understand?"

"Y-y-yes."

"Good. Then you know why I'm not interested in Devon." He gave her a naughty wink and spun on his heel. "Gotta get to work on that saggy middle. Catch you later."

He left her flushed, off-kilter, and practically throbbing with need. Bastard.

Damn, she was crazy about him.

Chapter Eighteen

"I need your help."

Harper barged through the door, her features set in familiar determination. Ophelia stared at her sister—and at the dog she held in her arms. The once-black shepherd had flecks of gray in his coat, face, and whiskers. His fur was streaked with mud. There was an ugly patch of dried skin toward his rear. His brown eyes rose briefly to meet hers, then quickly dropped.

It was too late, though. She'd already glimpsed the weariness. This dog had seen hard times and was starting to check out.

Ophelia reached out and petted his head with soothing strokes, heart squeezing with sympathy. "Where'd you find him?"

"In the woods. He was half-starved, probably dumped. I took him to the vet. Thankfully there's nothing wrong with him other than dehydration and his paw. I already have ointment for his dry patches."

"What's wrong with the paw?"

"An old injury that never healed. He limps, but the vet said it's nothing she'd fix at his age. I need to get him a bath, some decent food, and a warm place to sleep."

"Are you bringing him over to Ethan's? I have some spare blankets and bowls. What else do you need?"

"I need you to keep him here."

Ophelia stepped back and put her hands up. "What? You know the rules! I can't take any animals at the inn. Too many guests have allergies."

Desperation slowly replaced the determination on her sister's face. "You have to help me out for a little while. I tried to take him to my place, but he began thrashing and howling and totally freaked when he saw my other dogs. Then I tried Ethan's house, but he was terrified of Hei Hei and Wheezy. I don't know what happened, but he needs to be in a place with no other animals."

"What about the vet? Sarah takes them in when we have trouble."

"Sarah's booked up because of the winter. The other kennel I work with is also overcrowded. I made a bunch of calls, and all of them were dead ends. He needs our help, Ophelia."

She groaned and shook her head. "I can't! I don't even have a decent room to keep him in. I'm sorry, I can't help you."

"So we'll just let him go back into the woods?" Harper threw out, anger threading her voice. "It's just a stray mutt, right? Who cares?"

She didn't rise to the bait, knowing this was a sensitive spot with her sister. Every animal meant something special to her, and she swore never to let one suffer if it crossed her path. A great philosophy, but a bit hard to put into practice. Every spare inch of their farm already held homeless animals.

"I care," she said softly. "I'm just saying I can't because of the business I run. There's some guests here who are a bit demanding right now. As much as I'd like to, I can't kick them out."

Harper sagged in defeat. She pressed a kiss to the dog's head as if apologizing. "I'm all out of options. Is there anyone you can think of who doesn't have any pets and can take in a stray, at least until I'm able to line up something else?"

The answer came in a blinding flash.

Oh no—could she? Would he flip out? Then again, if she insisted and brought over all the supplies, how could he say no? It'd only be temporary, a few days at most.

"Actually, I think I do," she said slowly. "But it can only be for a week maximum."

"That's all I need! I'll find him a more permanent place—I just need more time."

Ophelia sighed. "Can you get him in my car?"

"Yes. Where are you taking him?"

She grabbed her coat and shot her sister a look. "Don't ask. Just be grateful I care as much as I do."

"I owe you, big-time!"

Ophelia grabbed some old blankets, rummaged in the cabinets for some bowls, and headed to the car. The poor lab was in the back seat, curled up next to Harper. Her sister was staring at her cell phone screen with obvious tension.

"What's the matter?" Ophelia asked.

"I'm so sorry—what a crap day. One of my rescues is having an issue. I have to get to the barns."

"Go. I can handle this."

"Are you sure?"

"Go."

Harper eased the dog on top of one of the blankets, making a cozy nest for him on the floor. "Thanks."

After Harper climbed out, Ophelia began to drive, making sure she kept talking in a low, calming voice. "The ride is only a few minutes down the road," she told him. "I'm taking a risk, but at least you'll have shelter and food. The quality of the company I can't promise you will be great."

Finally, she got to Patrick's house. She picked up the poor dog, who was shaking, and knocked on the door.

When he opened it, he glanced at her with surprise. "Did you bring more food?" The hopeful glint in his eyes faded when he spotted the dog in her arms. "What the hell is that?" he boomed out, making the poor dog cringe.

She frowned. "Lower your voice. I need you to do me a favor."

His eyes widened, and he backed up, shaking his head. "I'm not taking in a dog. I can barely take care of myself. Have you gone crazy, girl?"

"Probably," she muttered. She kicked the door closed with her heel and walked inside the house. "Look, it's just for a few days. We found him in the woods, half-starved. He's been to the vet so we know he's not sick or contagious. He hates other animals, though, so Ethan can't take him and Harper can't take him. The vet's place is full and, basically, if you don't take him, he's going to die out there in the cold."

He glowered at her, then spit out a few vicious curses. "No."

"You don't need any more crap on your soul, Patrick," she warned. "Didn't AA talk about amends?"

"To people I hurt—not stray dogs!"

"Think of it as an analogy. Or a simile . . . I'm not sure."

Patrick studied the dog. "It's old as dirt. Probably will die soon anyway."

"You're old as dirt and you're still here. How would you feel if someone said that to you?"

He just grunted, looking stubborn.

"Look, by helping this stray dog, you're gaining someone's forgiveness."

"Whose?" he growled, glaring at her.

"Mine. Okay, me. I'll forgive you. Clean slate. Just take the dog."

More cursing. He started to pace. "I have nothing here. What if he shits?"

"He probably will, but I'll head into town right now and get you the supplies you need. I already have blankets and bowls. Will you do this for me?"

"Fuck."

"Thank you!" She placed the dog on the couch and hurriedly backed up. "Just be nice to him. I'll be back soon with the supplies."

"Three days!"

"Five."

"Fuck."

She shot him a brilliant smile. "I'll be right back." Then she took off like Danica Patrick on the racetrack before he could change his mind.

A few hours later, she climbed out of the shower, exhausted. It had taken forever to get the dog set up at Patrick's and convince him it would be okay. Then Margo and Devon came home early from the festival with a whole bunch of requests before retiring to their rooms to get dressed to go out for the night. The ski couple had also returned, wanting to chill in the main room by the fireplace and order takeout. She'd taken care of business, spent some time doing bills since it was the end of the month, and had finally been able to crash. Kyle was over at Ethan's after putting in a full day's work—he probably needed to blow off some steam.

Clad in her comfy yoga pants and oversize flannel shirt, she dried her hair until it was damp, then twisted it into a topknot. She slipped her feet into pink fuzzy slippers and went into the kitchen to pull together a mishmash of leftovers for dinner.

She had a hot date with the television and some yummy carbs.

Singing low, she made herself some cheese and crackers, poured herself some white wine, and settled in with one of her favorite classic movies, *Moonstruck*.

She must've fallen asleep, because when she opened her eyes the movie was over and it was almost eleven p.m. Yawning, she got up and stretched, then took her plate and empty glass into the kitchen.

The main lights were out, and the place was quiet.

Hmm, maybe the girls had come back early?

She'd left the porch and foyer lights on. She wondered if Kyle was home, too. Biting her lip, she fought the impulse to go upstairs and knock on his door, casually ask him how Ethan and Mia were—even though they lived on the same property and she saw them practically every day.

Dear God, it was time to admit it.

She wanted a booty call.

Shaking her head, she went to the front door to check the locks when she heard a door bang upstairs. Moving to the stairs, she strained her ears.

Had he just come in?

Didn't matter. She couldn't stage a seduction dressed in her current outfit. She snorted and started walking back to her room, but she heard the faint creak of the steps. She turned her head to look back and see who was coming down when Kyle suddenly flew around the corner, grabbed her hand, and dragged her inside the bedroom.

"What the . . . ?"

"Save me," he muttered, quietly closing the door tight. He leaned his back against the hard wood, his face etched in the lines of male wariness. "She's scary as hell. Don't let her get near me."

Recognition shot through her. "Are you talking about Devon?"

"Hell yeah. She knocked on my door, but I was trying to get some work done so I didn't answer. Then she started whispering things that made me uncomfortable, begging me to let her in. It was like a bad vampire movie. I had to make a run for it. What if she picked the lock?"

She bit her lip to keep from laughing aloud. "Oh my God. I cannot believe she tried knocking on your door."

"I know. I even told her I was married!"

Ophelia blew out an annoyed breath. "I should say something to her. This is ridiculous."

"No!" His arm shot out to block her. "She'll be gone tomorrow. You don't need her torturing you for the next few hours. I'll just sleep in here. So you can keep me safe."

"Hmm. You think that's a good idea?"

His eyes roved over her disheveled state, hungrily taking in the thrust of her breasts and the curve of her ass. Suddenly, it didn't matter if she was in sweats with her hair in a topknot and no makeup on her face. Suddenly, the way those forest-green eyes lit up like fire made her feel like a goddess.

"Definitely."

Desire flared deep and hot in her belly. "What about your work?"

He rubbed his head as if considering something. "You know, I've been having some trouble writing these love scenes. Maybe some inspiration is in order."

Amusement danced through her. "Sure you don't want Devon to inspire you?" she teased. "Her hands were all over you this morning at breakfast."

He pushed away from the door and placed his hands on his hips. The soft cotton fabric of his T-shirt stretched over those drool-worthy muscles. His hair was mussed. His jaw stubbled. His gray sweats had a hole in the knee. His male hotness made her knees wobble. "I told you she wasn't the woman I wanted." He paused, his gaze fastened on her mouth. "Were you jealous?"

"Did you want me to be?" she threw back at him.

A smile touched his lips. "Maybe a little. You're completely hot when you're pissed and possessive."

Sexual tension flared and pulsed between them. Her nipples strained against the cotton of her shirt. Already, her thighs were trembling with pure need. She thought about Devon sliding her hands over her husband's thigh, and the light of lust she'd seen in her eyes. On cue, a rush of possessiveness flooded Ophelia.

"I didn't like her hands on you," she confessed.

"Why?"

The challenge hung between them. She waited for him to close the distance and take control. Reassure her. Kiss her. Touch her.

But he wasn't budging. He rocked back on his heels, waiting for her answer, like they had all the time in the world.

Frustration nipped. "Because I didn't like it," she repeated.

His voice was a deep rumble of sound. "Gotta tell me why. I can't always be the one chasing you and taking."

She sucked in her breath. Those eyes burned like a forest fire. His relaxed stance hid a fine-tuned tension that stiffened his muscles and carved out the lines of his face. He reminded her of a predator gone still, waiting patiently to jump on his prey until he was sure it was time.

The teasing game suddenly became much more. She fought with the rising unease, realizing he was right. Since he'd returned, he'd been the one to chase *her*. Tell her what *he* wanted. Ask her for a second chance. But now, he was forcing her to choose—and to become a full partner in this relationship.

If she wanted him, she was going to have to tell him.

Ophelia straightened to full height and slowly walked toward him. Each step was a deliberate choice—every pace affected her on a deeper level. She stopped an inch from him.

His body heat pulled her in and tantalized her, his masculine scent of musk and coffee and spice drifting to her nostrils. His jaw clenched with tension.

She trembled, but gave him the words. "I didn't like it because you belong to me."

He devoured her with his gaze, pushing for more. "Truth or dare, Ophelia?"

Her entire body throbbed with delicious, agonizing tension. She dragged her tongue over her bottom lip. "Dare."

His head bent down. His warm breath rushed against her mouth. "Come and take what you want," he growled. "Take what's yours."

The words crashed through her. With a low moan, she fisted his shirt and yanked him close, going on her tiptoes until her lips collided with his.

She kissed him with a ravenous hunger that had no bounds. Her tongue slid between his lips; she was instantly half-drunk on the sexy, spicy taste of him. She hooked a thigh around his hips to get closer, reaching up to tug at his hair and force him to give more, give her what she needed, give her what she craved right now . . .

He lifted her up and slammed her back onto the mattress, never breaking the kiss. She writhed beneath him, and he tugged off their clothes with the fumbling, desperate motions of the young—it was as if he'd die if he didn't get to her naked skin.

The shocking heat of his flesh seared through her. His hard muscles cradled her curves, and she ripped her mouth away, forcing him to roll over.

She dipped her head and tasted him, her hands roving freely over his hard body, her nails curling into his flesh and her tongue licking.

He groaned her name and pulled the pins out of her topknot, tugging his fingers through the damp waves that spilled over his chest.

She was a madwoman. She needed to touch and taste every inch of him, from his flat, hard nipples through the golden whorls of hair over his chest to the lean angle of his hipbone. She dragged her teeth over his flat stomach, blowing her breath over his hardened shaft until he jerked with need.

She closed her hands around his erection, squeezed, sent her tongue darting out to taste his essence, then opened her mouth wide and took him in.

He cried out, fisted his fingers in her hair, and arched his hips. A thrill coursed through her at her feminine power, at the vulnerable need in every jerk and cry and pull of her hair. She pleasured him, sucking deep, swirling her tongue around the tip, using her hands to add more pressure and fist him, until finally he let out a roar and flew upward. He lifted her high above him and slammed her down onto his cock.

Her thighs tightened, and she threw her head back with pleasure. He filled every aching inch of her, driving away her very breath, and she tightened her inner muscles to clutch him even deeper, rocking her hips to take him to the hilt.

He rubbed her tight nipples, flicking them with his thumbs. His green eyes misted with a ferocious hunger that sent a thrill through her.

"Ride me," he demanded. "Take it all. I belong to you."

A primitive thrill shot through her. Slowly, she lifted herself up, dragging his erection over her swollen clit, then rocking herself back down in perfect, deliberate strokes. She rode him and claimed him at once, and when the orgasm finally exploded through her body, she bowed back and screamed his name without restraint.

He let out a hoarse shout, grabbing her hips and forcing her to ride him through her climax, drawing out her pleasure for endless, mind-blowing moments. Then he was coming, twisting his body and dragging her down so he could kiss her, his tongue thrusting as desperately as his cock, exploding inside her.

She collapsed onto his chest, her skin damp with sweat. Moving her head, she slid over to entangle her thigh with his, boneless.

His hand shot out in panic. "Holy shit. I didn't use a condom!"

She almost jumped up in her own panic, but then relaxed back against him. "It's okay, I'm clean and have been on the pill for my period awhile."

His muscles released, and he let out a breath. "Thank God. I'm clean, too."

"You better be."

He chuckled, pressing a kiss to her shoulder. "Thank you for saving me. And giving me inspiration."

She grinned and snuggled in his arms. "It was my pleasure."

"How's your schedule this week?"

"We're half-full, but then we'll be completely empty for a while. Reservations pick up again the first week of March, and they're steady till spring."

"So, very soon, they'll be no guests to bother us?"

"Why? What do you have in mind?"

He rolled over her with a masculine grin that sent delicious shivers down her spine. "To make you be very, very loud. To christen all the rooms in the house."

Her eyes widened. "We can't do that. It will create tons of laundry."

"I'll make it worth your while."

"I don't think—"

He shut her up with his mouth on hers. Ophelia didn't care about anything after that.

Chapter Nineteen

Two weeks later, Kyle headed into the Market to grab some fresh fish for dinner that night. As usual, the owner, Fran, ran over and engaged in the normal small-town chatter that Gardiner was known for. Mia had taken over her PR campaign, and Ophelia was one of her best customers, so he enjoyed the pride that surged from her obvious affection for his family.

Family.

The word caused a warm rush of pleasure. Their Sunday dinners together had become like a treasure. He'd finally met Chloe, and loved watching her interact so closely with Ethan and Mia. They'd all ridden horses together, then curled up with the Disney movie *Moana*.

Hei Hei had even begun to tolerate him.

Chloe was the newest addition to the tight-knit crew. Once again, the inn and farm had made a difference to another person. This place was important, filled with a goodness and warmth he hadn't found in a very long time.

Ophelia had done that by opening her home to guests. His job might seem important because of all the attention, money, and fame, but hers was so much more so. Every time he looked at her, he fell in love with her a little bit more.

He shook his head, then refocused on the conversation with Fran.

"Take the haddock," she insisted. "It's on sale and so fresh, it probably swam over here."

He laughed. "Done. Can you throw in some crab cakes, too?"

"Absolutely. I'm also sending over some of the new Cajun catfish that's new. Tell me what you think of it."

"Thanks." Kyle waited while Fran jumped behind the counter to help get him settled. He nodded at a man who walked over and stood next to him.

"Can you grab me some haddock, too, my love?" the man asked.

Fran's giggle reminded him of a teenager's.

And holy crap—was she blushing?

"Of course, Tony! Anything for you!" She stumbled behind the counter, and seemed to try to rush.

Curious, Kyle studied the giant, stocky, dark-haired man Fran seemed to be crushing on. He sported a scraggly beard, glasses, and was dressed in old jeans and a gray hoodie that stated: DO YOUR STEPS.

Suddenly, the man narrowed his gaze on Kyle. "Hi, I'm Tony. You look familiar."

"Hi. Kyle. Nice to meet you," he said. They shook hands. "Sorry, not sure I've seen you around before."

"That's okay, I just need a minute. My memory is kick-ass."

Kyle grinned, politely waiting either for the recognition or for Fran to get him his fish so he could leave.

Tony suddenly snapped his fingers. "Got it. You're Kyle Kimpton! Patrick's son, right?"

Ice trickled down his spine. He didn't understand why this man seemed happy to see him, but he didn't want to find out. "Yeah. Sorry, I don't know any of my father's friends."

"I'm his AA sponsor. Damn, what a pleasure to get to meet you. Patrick talks about you all the time."

Shock cut through him. "He does?"

"Hell yeah. Told me how you took care of the farm and the animals when he was drunk off his ass. And all about your big success as a screenwriter. He fucking lights up when he talks about you, and Patrick isn't the lighthearted type, you know?"

Kyle's head spun as he tried to figure out how to reply. "Yeah, he's more like John Wayne. The strong, silent type."

"Definitely. So you in town from California?"

"Yeah, I'm working on a new project. Be here for about another six weeks."

Tony nodded. "That's great. Have you seen Patrick yet?"

He stiffened, glancing away. His voice came out cold when he finally spoke. "No."

The man regarded him with a shrewd gaze. "Yeah, I get it. No judgment here, dude. Your dad was really fucked up and did a lot of bad stuff. If you see him, it may be hard trying to reconcile the man he is now with the asshole you used to live with."

Kyle's eyes widened. "Umm, are you supposed to say stuff like that? If he's trying to recover and all, doesn't hearing about your screw-ups make things worse?"

Tony grinned. "Nope. It's about the truth, and Patrick knows it. Admits it. Every day, he let alcohol strip away his humanity and choices. Now, every day, he rebuilds. Remembering who he was is a part of that. It's about balancing the guilt with the intention of making amends."

Kyle stared at the gray hoodie's message in a different light. Do YOUR STEPS. Recognition dawned as he linked it to the organization that had helped so many addicts.

Tony caught his gaze and leaned in, as if his next words were critically important.

"But you know what AA is really about? The crux of it is one simple lesson: we all deserve to give ourselves a second chance. It doesn't negate the pain we put others through, and it's not a get-out-of-jail-free card. Reparations still need to be made. But without second chances, we'd be stuck in the gutter for life."

Kyle stared at him, unable to form words.

Second chances. The same thing he'd been begging for from Ophelia. How ironic to meet a stranger who knew intimate things about him and his father, and preached the same thing Kyle needed from the woman he loved.

Tony continued. "Listen, your dad's one-year sobriety anniversary is April thirtieth. If you can be there, it may be something you want to attend. He'll tell his story, and children of alcoholics sometimes find some healing in listening to parents recall the truth."

The ground shifted beneath his feet, but Tony stared at him with a raw honesty he respected. He hated the lump in his throat and swallowed past it. "I'm sorry. I'll be back in California for a while by then."

"Got it. Well, if you're able to stop by and see him before you leave, I know it'd make a big difference. But I also understand if you can't." He drew out a card from his pocket and pressed it into his palm. "Call me if you ever want to talk, or have questions about your dad, or anything."

Fran appeared before them and handed Kyle the wrapped packages. "Here you go. Tell Ophelia I said hello." Her gaze snagged on Tony.

It was obvious she wanted Kyle to leave, and he tamped down a chuckle.

"Thanks, Fran. I will." He turned to Tony and hesitated. His gut churned. "Bye, Tony."

Tony gave him a grin that lit up his whole face. Kyle noticed his front tooth was crooked and a bit yellow, but Fran didn't seem to mind. She looked pretty smitten.

"It truly was an honor to meet you, Kyle."

He left the store, his mind whirling. His father had talked about him to his sponsor. Told him intimate secrets about their relationship and termed himself an asshole. Was it possible? Could a man get sober and really change? Or was it just another illusion that would suck Kyle in and hurt him all over again?

He pushed the thought out of his mind and drove back to the inn.

Ophelia turned to him and whispered the words in humbled reverence. "They're gone."

He pulled on his earlobe and cocked his head. Silence greeted him. "All of them?"

She gave a squeal of glee and jumped into his arms. He caught her with ease, laughing as he spun her around. "The place is all ours for an entire week. Seven perfect days filled with nothing but laziness."

"Excellent. Let's start our vacation right now."

He began carrying her down the hall toward her bedroom with one obvious purpose, and she didn't intend to stop him. He'd just bent his head, ready to kiss her, when the doorbell rang.

"There's no room at the inn," he growled in warning, glaring at the door. "Let's ignore it."

"No, I have to answer it—just in case." He placed her down, and she peeked through the curtain, frowning when she recognized Albert Townsend, the owner of Crystal's. She opened the door with a big smile. "Hi, Albert. Is everything okay?"

The older man smiled at her, his short gray beard and still-thick hair cutting an impressive figure. With this charming demeanor, handsome suits, and financial success, he was consistently chased by all the single women in town—both young and old. But he still mourned his wife, even after all these years. He chose to spend most of his time at the restaurant. "Everything's fine. I decided I'd make a house call rather than use the telephone."

"Of course. Come in. I'll get you a cup of coffee or tea."

"Thank you." She led him past the crackling fire toward the kitchen, where Kyle was already pouring a mug of coffee. "Oh, I'm sorry. I didn't know you had company."

"Albert, this is Kyle Kimpton. We actually grew up together, but he moved out to California years ago. He's here working on a script till spring."

They shook hands. "Patrick's son, correct?"

Kyle winced, but kept his smile. "That's right. We dined at your place last month, and it was amazing. Some of the best steak I ever had."

Albert beamed. "Thank you. I take pride in the menu and quality. My late wife loved food and beautiful things, so when the Victorian farmhouse it's in suffered a fire five years ago, I decided to rebuild it in her honor and open up a distinctive dining place." Albert turned toward Ophelia. "Which is another reason I've come to see you today."

"Mysterious," she teased. "What can I get you to drink?"

"Coffee. Black, please."

Kyle poured it for her and passed it over, shifting on his feet as if unsure whether he should stay. Ophelia motioned for him to take a seat beside them, not wanting to exclude him from the conversation.

Albert took a sip and folded his hands neatly on the table. His light-blue eyes peered over a pair of smart-looking spectacles. "I'm not sure if you know this, but you've caused quite the stir in our town, Ophelia."

She frowned, puzzled. "What do you mean?"

"I had no idea you were a singer."

Realization struck, and she shifted in her chair. Dammit, she should've known the gossip a small town wouldn't be able to resist. Most of the locals knew she'd left to pursue a singing career, but when she returned home, no one ever spoke of it again. She rarely sang anymore, so that karaoke stunt must have sparked gossip.

"I'm not. I love to sing, but it's just a hobby. I was having some fun, that's all."

He frowned, tapping one finger steadily. "Hmm, I heard your voice. It was quite extraordinary."

"How did you hear it?"

"YouTube. One of the patrons at the Depot recorded you. Haven't you seen it? It's gotten a ton of views, and the number keeps growing."

Horror washed through her. She'd forgotten that social media rarely cared what you wanted to share. The idea of her singing performance being available for the world to watch sent shivers through her. In a way, her singing had become deeply personal—a gift she kept as a secret, when once she'd longed to share it.

As if he sensed her distress, Kyle slid his hand across the table and squeezed her fingers.

"I didn't know it had been recorded," she said.

"I'm sorry, my dear. I didn't know that would make you uncomfortable." A worried expression flickered across his face. "I guess this makes the favor I was going to ask you a bit awkward."

"What favor?"

"I'm in desperate need of a singer for Crystal's. Someone classy, with a pure voice who can offer the patrons something new. I'm completely open on the schedule, since I know the inn is your main career. I was hoping I'd convince you to sing for a few hours, once a week, on a night of your choosing. Of course I'd pay you, and you would be in control of song choices."

A mix of emotions hit her like a sucker punch. A thrill coursed through her at the idea of being able to sing for a small, appreciative audience; to be able to let her voice go free and wild after so many years locked in a cage.

Yes, it was a small, local restaurant. Yes, her schedule and choices would be under her strict control. But she'd already seen how things could blow up. With social media, what if she was inviting chaos back into her life?

"I can't thank you enough for the offer, Albert," she said with a smile, "but I have my hands full running the inn. I'm sure there's plenty of local talent available who would love such an opportunity."

"What if Ethan or Mia helped out at the inn?" Kyle interrupted. "I'm sure they'd be supportive. It's only one night a week, and Albert would probably be understanding if one week didn't work out here and there."

"I would," Albert said. "I just know you'd be perfect, Ophelia. The way you sang gave me goose bumps. It made me happy. It would be an honor to feature you."

She shot a warning glance at Kyle. "Ethan and Mia are heavily involved in the farm and her PR business—they have no time to cover for me. Neither does Harper. I'm truly sorry, Albert, but I have to say no."

The silence hung heavy with unspoken words. Kyle slid his hand away, shoved them in his pockets, then studied his coffee as if it held all the answers.

Albert nodded. "I understand, I truly do. It was a long shot. If you ever change your mind, I'd be overjoyed. Just let me know."

"Thank you."

They chatted a bit about local town gossip, the harsh winter. Finally, he finished his coffee and left.

The tap of Kyle's fingers against his cell phone filled the air.

Maybe he'd let it go. Maybe he'd just carry her back to the bedroom and finish what they started. Maybe—

"Why did you do that?"

She let out an impatient breath and faced him. "Because I didn't want to sing in his restaurant," she said lightly. She went into the kitchen and loaded the mugs in the dishwasher, tidied up the crumbs on the counter.

"Bullshit," he shot back. "I saw your face."

She closed her eyes and fought the waves of energy reverberating from his figure. "I will not discuss this with you. We're not back in California. I run my own life now. I do not want to sing in public, and you'll have to respect my decision."

He muttered a curse. Rubbed his head. "You're lying to yourself," he said. "You've been smothering the need to sing for an audience for almost a decade now, telling yourself you don't need it. But it's a part of who you are. Why can't you take a chance? God, Ophelia, one night of karaoke is burning up the internet. Look." He shoved the phone at her.

The video of her singing was grainy, with flashing lights, but her voice rang true and clear; her red hair was like a beacon on the stage. In disbelief, she saw the number of views had reached 500,000. Comments rolled under it endlessly.

Who is this chick?

F—ng amazing. Why isn't she on iTunes?!

Listened to it a dozen times already. I can't find her anywhere. Who is she?

She should audition for The Voice! She'd def get picked.

With trembling hands, she pushed the phone away. Emotion choked her throat. Strong hands enclosed her shoulders, and she was suddenly surrounded by Kyle's arms. She lay against his hard chest, let his warm breath rush past her ear.

"Baby, I know this is a lot. Just think about it. It doesn't have to be a repeat of the past. This time, you can have it all."

We can have it all.

The words ripped agonizing pain through her. Slowly, she pushed him away, fighting the tears stinging her eyes. She had to get away.

"I'll think about it," she forced out. "Thanks—I have to go to the bathroom."

She left him in the kitchen, shut the door, and dropped her face into her hands.

It might have been almost ten years later, but she was falling in love with him all over again, just as strong as the first time. And seeing herself plastered on the internet brought back the memories that still ached. It had been the final break in their relationship that neither had been able to recover from.

Is that why she'd shut herself away from singing?

Was she still running away from something she loved, believing she could never have both?

And the biggest question of all: Did any of it really matter when Kyle was eventually leaving?

She splashed some cold water on her face and stared into the mirror.

They still had some time to figure things out. She wasn't going to ruin it by dwelling on the past.

The future was enough to handle.

She sat on the couch, knees curled up, and stared unseeingly at the droning television. Past midnight. Again. She'd texted him earlier asking him to come home, saying that she had to talk to him about something important. He'd promised.

His promises were becoming more like scattered offerings with no follow-through.

The door clicked.

She swiveled her head around, noting the too-happy grin lingering on his face, the high sheen in his green eyes. Not drunk—he was always careful about his alcohol intake—but running high on adrenaline. Work parties blurred into ridiculous social functions that had no meaning except to see who could jump naked in the pool, who could bang who, who could cast who. Yet he seemed to not only embrace this new lifestyle but also enjoy it.

She used to think the shallowness of such a world would be something they'd never truly have to deal with, because they were different. They weren't like the others, who needed attention and fame and contacts to fill the emptiness inside. They had each other. Had never needed anyone else.

Not anymore.

She swallowed back the anguish, not wanting to get into another fight, and hoped he was grounded enough to talk. God, how she needed him to listen to her.

"Sorry I'm late," *he said. His words held a touch of defensiveness.* "Got talking to Robbie about the new movie. Listen, I know we haven't had much time together lately, but I'm going to be MIA again next week. Have to be on a location set shoot and available for rewrites."

"You can't do it from home?" *she asked, knowing many of the screenwriters didn't travel with the cast.*

"I want to go. I want them to know when they hire me, I give my all. They deserve that."

"What about your wife? Does she deserve the same?"

She cursed herself the moment the words escaped. Dammit, she couldn't take another round of fighting. It was beginning to drain them both.

Kyle shrugged off his jacket, his features twisted with frustration. "We went over this. I'm the youngest screenwriter to be working with such bigwigs, and I need them to know I can handle it. Anyway, what's the problem? You'll be working nonstop on the* Popstar *reality show, doing plenty of auditions and partying. I heard the network wants you to do a lot of press. So proud of you, baby."

She caught the deflection and wondered when he'd gotten so good at spinning an excuse, or even a lie. But she didn't say anything, just waited while he got a glass of water and slid next to her. His hand rubbed her thigh, but for the first time in forever, she didn't melt under his touch. Lately, even their physical connection was suffering—she felt as if she were watching them from a distance.

"Kyle, I made a decision about something. I really need your support on it."

"Of course. I'll back you up on anything—you know that."

She took a deep breath. "I quit."

He stared at her, head cocked, as if he didn't understand what she said. "What do you mean? Quit what?"

"The show. Popstar. I gave them my decision today, and they weren't happy about it. And since the cast got leaked and I've already done promo, the backlash may be a bit nasty."

He rubbed his head, blinking furiously, as if she'd hit him. "Wait a minute. I'm confused. You quit the show that was your big break? The one that was going to make you a star? You're fucking with me, right?"

She pressed her lips together and moved away from him, not wanting contact. "No. I've been telling you for a while now that I wasn't happy. It's not about the singing. It's everything else—the image makeover and social media followers and political bullshit and other contestants being so competitive and mean, it takes my breath away. It's a world I despise. I couldn't take any more, so I quit."

He jumped up from the couch, choppy waves of fury radiating from him. She sucked in her breath as he jabbed a finger in the air, his voice gritty with emotion. "What the hell is going on with you, Ophelia? Are you that terrified of success you're going to quit the one show that will change your life because it's hard? I used to know you, but lately, you've turned into someone I don't even recognize!"

She stood up, fists clenched, and faced him down. "I could say the same about you. Kissing ass to anyone who has a decent contact, writing what they want rather than what you want, telling yourself it's all perfect because you're the man? You've changed."

"You don't want me to be successful. I've sensed it for a long time. The looks you give me when I go to work functions or come home late or lock myself in a room to write all night. But you knew this wasn't going to be *easy. Chasing dreams isn't supposed to be, and if you're not willing to compromise, you'll never get an opportunity to share your true vision."*

He took a step toward her, hands out. "I get it, baby. I do. You feel like they're trying to change you, and it's freaking you out. But all you have to do is go with it for the show. Get your name out there and get a following. Then you can do anything you want."

She wanted to scream and stomp her feet and shake him so he would finally listen to her. "You're not understanding me. If I do what they say and let them turn me into some puppet, the audience will never know the real me anyway! I'll be trapped—singing their god-awful pop shit, dressed in tight leather pants and a crop top, bouncing my head and smiling like some kind of ventriloquist dummy with no soul! That's not me."

"Just play the game a little bit," he begged. "Why do you have to be so narrow-minded? What's wrong with looking hot onstage and singing Miley Cyrus? Why are you such a damn snob?"

She sucked in her breath. Tension simmered amid a bunch of other emotions too raw to decipher. How had this happened to them? How had they grown so far apart?

"I already made my decision," she said quietly. "I need you to be there for me. Understand this is best for me."

"But it's not," he muttered. "Crap, Robbie is gonna shit—he's the one who got you the audition."

A chill raced down her spine. "That's what you care about? That your agent will be pissed off at you?"

"I'm not like you. I'm grateful for the opportunities I get. Do you have any idea what you want to do next? Got something else lined up besides extra shifts at the diner?"

"I'm not sure. I just want to remember what it's like to sing for me. To enjoy the gift of my voice without all that empty packaging. Maybe I can sing at a restaurant or small club. Maybe even theater."

"But you don't like to act. You did those high school plays because they were fun and no pressure," he said coldly. "And do you really want to sing in front of a chattering crowd who's too drunk to care or listen?"

She flinched at his meanness. "Why are you doing this? What is so wrong with realizing this world isn't for me?"

"Because I like this world!" he shouted. "I like who I'm becoming and I'm afraid of—" He broke off, his face telling her more than his unspoken words. Her heart was beating, but her blood felt so cold it seemed to numb her from the inside.

"Afraid of leaving me behind," she finished.

He didn't say anything, just stared at the carpet for a while as if it held all the answers. "I don't know who we are together anymore," he said. "And I don't know how to get back to the way things were. I feel like every step I take, you're judging me. You're unhappy all the time, but this is what we both signed up for. What we both wanted."

"And I feel like you're slipping away," she said, caught between the desperate urge to go to him and hold him tight, to weep against his chest, to let their embrace take care of all the problems. "I love you. I thought we came to California to get married and be together forever. Yes, we wanted to achieve our dreams, but mine has always been to be with you, Kyle. All the rest is secondary."

She knew that was the moment everything changed.

He looked up and met her gaze, and her world crashed down around her under the startling, raw truth.

He didn't feel the same way.

"I love you," he said softly. "But I'm tired of feeling like a piece of shit for wanting this. I've dreamed of being a famous writer my whole life. I took my father's abuse for years because I knew, one day, I would prove him wrong. I'd be something and make the world take notice. Everything I ever wanted is coming true, but I can't make a choice between you and my career. Don't ask me to."

Because his choice was already made.

He turned. "I'm going to bed."

She watched him disappear into the bedroom. Heard the shower go on. Saw the lights go off. Heard the rustle of sheets and the creak of the mattress. And knew she had to leave.

Kyle stared at the page. His heart was crashing against his ribs, and his neck had crimped, sending a shooting pain down his back.

He stood up and stretched. The words he'd splashed onto the page haunted him, dragging him back into the past to a memory he'd spun so differently.

Is that how she had seen things? Is that why she had finally left?

He'd been so caught up with his own dreams, he'd believed he was giving her tough love. Her refusal to bend to everyone else's demands when it came to her singing frustrated him. Looking back, he realized she'd been the only one who knew who she truly was.

Now, years later, he was famous, but he'd trapped himself in a world where he no longer belonged. He was a robot—the Hollywood scene was shallow and old, his words the same as he drafted script after script of the same formula.

He was coming alive again. Writing this book. Being back home. Loving Ophelia. All of it gave him a deeper sense of peace and belonging he hadn't experienced in too long.

But he knew he had to return eventually. To get the movie made. To secure enough interest and funding to make it a reality. Were they racing toward another climax of him needing to choose between staying with her or chasing after his career again?

This time, would he choose differently?

He had to. Now that she was back in his life, nothing would make sense without her. He had to find a way to claim it all.

But how?

The questions ran on an endless loop in his head for a long time.

Chapter Twenty

Ophelia took a deep breath and prayed she'd be able to convince Patrick to keep the dog a bit longer.

Harper had a friend who'd be willing to foster the shepherd soon, but she had to place her current foster pup first. Ophelia had already begged Patrick for a previous extension, plying him with baked goods to help ease the pain. Now it was way past the original deadline she'd promised. She had a bad feeling he would be cranky about another delay.

Which is why she'd brought him blueberry scones.

She pulled up and was surprised to see a freshly tracked path leading from the front porch to the back. The paw prints beside the boot imprints confirmed he'd taken the dog for some fresh air. She hoped they were getting along. The last few times she'd checked on him, she'd heard constant complaints about the dog's age, his smell, and his talent of pooping on the newly shoveled walkway. She'd threatened Patrick to be nice to the poor thing, terrified if the dog was yelled at he'd die of a heart attack. Enough had happened to cause him to be half-catatonic. When she asked Patrick how she could help him continue fostering and being nice, he'd grumbled a request for banana-cream pie and her lasagna.

It had taken her hours, but she'd baked it and schlepped it over. Now, she hoped her scones would buy her another week.

She traced the path through the towering pine trees. She stopped short a few feet from the duo. Her jaw dropped.

Patrick was *smiling*.

He had some half-chewed tennis ball in his hand, and lobbed it high in the air. The broken-down lab limped after it with sheer joy, barking and shoving his nose in the snow, then bringing it back to Patrick. The dog was slow but steady, his gait awkward.

The older man laughed and patted his head. Patrick's voice echoed in the quiet air. "Good boy. You're a fast learner. Who cares if it takes you longer to get the ball? No rush—it's just there, waiting for you. Now don't forget to look pathetic when Ophelia checks in on us, okay? I'm gonna ask for chicken parm next—with her garlic bread."

The dog barked.

"Yeah, I'll ask for some of those gravy bones for you. Okay, enough play for now. It's too cold out here for me. Let's go, Charlie."

Charlie?

She watched Patrick trudge toward the back entrance. "Charlie" limped behind him, tail wagging. The realization slammed through her, and she leaned against the icy bark of a tree, still reeling from the scene.

He'd only been pretending to hate the dog. Pretending all this time in order to score baked goods and hearty dinners. And that dog was in on the whole thing! They looked like full partners, pretending to dislike each other and looking pathetic.

Oh, she was going to teach Patrick a valuable lesson.

An evil grin crossed her face. She hitched the plate of scones higher in her arms and snuck quietly back to the front porch. Then she made a big production out of stamping her feet and making enough noise to give them a heads-up.

She rang the bell. He greeted her with a stony stare, his gaze dropping to the plate. "Still can't find a place for him, huh? Whatcha got today?"

"Scones," she sang merrily, stepping into the house. Charlie was cuddled up on the sofa. He didn't seem too interested in checking her out. "How's the dog doing?"

"He's a pain in the ass."

"That's a shame. Have you given him a name yet?"

"Nah, I'm not gonna have him for too much longer. Why bother?"

She stared into his face and caught the tiny flicker of emotion in his green eyes.

The man was damn good at telling lies, but now she had him pegged. This would be fun.

"He looks like a good boy. Not too demanding."

Patrick snorted, grabbed the plate from her, and laid it on the table. "You have no idea the work involved with taking care of him." He grabbed a scone and began munching on it with sheer greed. "But I guess I can keep him longer—if I don't have to worry about cooking for myself. I've been thinking about a nice tray of chicken parm. It's one of my favorites."

"Really?"

He shoved the rest of the scone into his mouth. "Yeah. With garlic bread. Might as well throw in some of those nice gravy bones for the mutt. He may like them."

"I really appreciate your willingness to help, Patrick. But I have great news."

"Yeah? What?"

"I finally found a place for the dog. I can take him back now."

Patrick stared at her, a touch of panic lighting his features. "What do you mean? You said he had nowhere to go!"

She shrugged. "We got a shelter to agree to take him. It's really too bad, though. Lord knows what will happen to him there. Wanna pack up his stuff?"

As if he sensed danger was near, Charlie picked up his head and sniffed the air. Regarded his new owner with those big brown eyes.

Ophelia swore if her practical joke didn't work out, she'd bake all the chicken parm Patrick wanted to make him keep the dog.

"Wait a minute. He can't go to a shelter. They'll kill him!"

Harper only dealt with no-kill shelters, but there was no reason to tell Patrick that.

She gave another shrug. "They'll do their best to get him a home before his time expires. At least he'll finally be out of your hair. I appreciate you taking him."

"So you're just gonna let him die? For no reason other than he's old, a bit broken, and has no family who'll claim him? Just lock him in some cage for the last few days of his life and hope for the best? That's your solution?"

Fascinated, she watched a rare bubble of emotion spill over Patrick's usually tightly contained facade. She wished Kyle were there. This is what he needed to see—that Patrick still held the vulnerability of humanity—and that it didn't have to come from lashing out or drowning in drink.

"Well, *you* could keep the dog. It's the only way to ensure his health and safety, but I understand if it's too much for you."

He spun away, cursing.

Charlie let out a whimper, jumped off the couch, and limped over to nudge his master's leg. It had only taken a short time for Patrick to break down the dog's barriers and allow himself to try and love again. Ophelia held her breath and hoped.

"Fine. I'll take him," Patrick said, distractedly patting the dog's head.

She let out her breath. "Thank you," she said.

"Does this mean no chicken parm?"

She crossed her arms and regarded him suspiciously. "Only if I'm asked and not blackmailed."

He didn't even look sheepish. "Of course. I really do like chicken parm. And Charlie likes the bones you use for your gravy."

"I may be able to manage that. Also, they have a great dog park in town. *Charlie* may like it."

She emphasized the dog's name, but Patrick just shrugged. "Had to call him something. Seemed like a good enough name."

She smiled, her heart light. "I'll drop by with dinner tomorrow. Call me if you need anything."

"Has Kyle asked about me?"

She froze, but told the truth. "I tried to ask him to come visit you once, but he refused. He's stubborn. He needs some time to think of you as someone other than a parent who hurt him."

Patrick nodded. "I get it. There's something I want you to give him, though. Something important."

He trudged into the dining room and picked up a cardboard box. "Tell him I should've given this to him a long time ago. Tell him it was all my fault. Okay?"

She blinked, then swallowed the lump in her throat. "I'll tell him." She took the box, called out a goodbye to Charlie, and left the dog and man in the house behind her.

When she got back to the inn, Kyle was waiting for her. He took the box from her arms and set it on the table. "Ethan and Mia want to go to Bea's Diner tonight for dinner. You up for a burger and fries?"

"Sounds perfect. What time?"

"Around seven. Do you need me to bring this box somewhere?"

She shrugged off her coat and squeezed his hand. "It's for you. From your dad."

He blinked. "You went to see him again? Why?"

She let out a breath. "Remember that dog Harper couldn't find a home for? I mentioned it a few weeks ago?"

"Yeah."

"Your dad took him in for me."

Those forest-green eyes hardened. "Why the hell would he have done that? Patrick's not great with animals—or kids. Hell, he's not good with humans. He can barely take care of himself, let alone a dog."

She gave a small laugh. "I promised it'd only be a few days, but it ended up being much longer. Let's just say I bribed him with some home cooking. Anyway, I found him playing with the dog in the backyard. They've obviously formed a bond. Patrick was smiling."

Kyle tightened his lips. "He doesn't smile."

"He was. He was laughing. I told him I was there to take the dog to the shelter, just to play a joke on him. Sure enough, he agreed to keep him permanently. It was sweet."

He turned away from her. The line of his shoulders stiffened. "Why didn't you tell me about this before?"

She reached out and rubbed his arm. "After the last time we talked about your dad, I figured you wouldn't want to know. But he asked about you again. He wanted me to bring you this box and tell you he was sorry, that it was 'all his fault.'"

He spit out a curse. Glanced at the box. "There's nothing he can give me that will take back what was done."

"I know. But talking to him may help give you some closure."

"How many times did I hide at your house because I was afraid to go home? Afraid that in one of his drunken tirades he might actually beat the crap out of me instead of just giving a slap here and there? How about the time he found me in the basement looking at pictures, desperate to see a photo of my mother? Do you remember that?"

Anguish filled her, but his pain was his right. She nodded. "I do."

"He ripped them away from me. Said there'd be no reminder of her any longer because she was dead. She was dead because of me. And then he burned them. I have only one picture of my mother that I was able to steal. I hid it under my pillow every night, terrified he'd take it from me."

She stepped into his arms, offering him warmth and comfort. He took it. Buried his face in her hair and held her tight. The years ghosted away, and she was back to her real home—in his arms—where everything made sense and nothing else was needed.

"I'm sorry," she whispered.

He trembled slightly, and she pressed kisses over his rough cheek, stroking the scruff hugging his jaw, offering comfort with her body and open heart. His lips found hers, and he deepened the kiss, his tongue thrusting sweetly inside her mouth. She arched up, going on tiptoes, trying to get closer to his warm, muscled strength. Then they both fell into the embrace in a slow, glorious, emotional slide of pleasure.

He lifted her, took her into her bedroom, laid her gently on the quilt, and tugged off her clothes with a quiet intensity. She ran her hands over his sleek, heated skin, pushed his jeans down over his hips so he lay bare to her touch.

Whispering her name like a prayer, his gaze delved deep into hers. He held her under his spell as he slowly pressed deep inside her. The stretching, glorious heat ripped a moan from her lips. She half closed her eyes, but he gripped her chin, forcing her to lift her lids, forcing her to share every iota of pleasure he wrung from her body.

The ride was slow and sweet, intense and wild, a crazed combination of soft and hard. The carnality of flesh slapping against flesh, the driving piston of his hips, the panting of breath against damp lips, the musky scent of sweat, sex, and spice lingering in the air. She twisted her fists in the sheet as her orgasm drew near, then shattered her. She refused to close her eyes and hide. She gave him what he'd always had.

Everything.

He came, spilling his seed, jerking helplessly as he gripped her with ferocious need. They fell back on the pillows, still entwined, the afternoon light streaming through the windows—adding to the decadence of their intimacy.

"Best vacation week ever," he drawled, his arm splayed out by the headboard.

She laughed, stretching luxuriously in the tangle of damp sheets. "You still have to make your word count," she pointed out.

"Tyrant."

"How is the screenplay going?"

He propped himself up on his elbow and brushed the hair from her cheek. "It's different from anything else I've tried to do," he said. "Did I tell you I'm writing it as a novel first? I've never done that before, but it's working well. I'm scared out of my mind, but I've never felt better about the work."

"Is it—strange? Writing our story all over again?"

He traced the line of her cheek, his gaze tender. "Yes. And no. Allowing myself to remember the way we loved each other has given me hope. And by finally seeing the missing pieces from your point of view, I understand now how things went so wrong. How I got so caught up in myself that I had nothing left for you."

She smiled and kissed his palm. "Do you have producers and a director attached to it yet?"

A flash of worry glinted in his eyes. "No. My agent is lining up a team who may be interested. It'll be hard breaking out of the regular action stuff I've been typecast into, but my goal is to amaze them with the content so they decide it's worth taking a chance on."

"And if they don't want to buy it?"

"They have to," he said lightly, nibbling on her fingers. "I don't have a plan B."

She pondered his comment for a while. If she knew Hollywood, they didn't like change, especially when an established formula was working.

"Don't let them take away your belief in the story," she finally said. "You have such emotional depth in your writing. I think you're so much more than a car crash or bank robbery."

"What about the hostage situation in *Captured?*"

"Even better than that."

"Aliens?"

She wrinkled her nose. "Tell me you did *not* write a movie about a UFO invasion."

"I didn't. I was asked, but refused. I just couldn't do *War of the Worlds* again, or *Independence Day*—no matter what the pay."

"Good." She kissed him and rolled out of bed. "I have a good hour of computer work, and then we can enjoy the evening. I'd suggest you get back to your writing."

She grabbed her panties and added an oversize sweatshirt. Her jeans were nowhere to be found.

"How am I supposed to work when I know you're strutting around like that?"

She threw him a cheeky smile. "Call it inspiration."

"I think I need one more round."

Her eyes widened at his impressive erection. "Are you trying to cripple me?"

"Just looking to be inspired by you."

She laughed, backing out of the door with her hands up. "Down, boy. I have work to do and . . . No . . . Kyle!"

He leaped from the bed naked, catching her as she giggled, pressing her against the wall while his hands roamed freely. "Come on, baby. You did your job—I'm inspired!"

"What the hell are you doing with my sister?"

They froze. In pure horror, Ophelia stared at Ethan, framed in the doorway, with Mia behind him.

Holy shit.

Slowly, Kyle lowered her to the ground. He opened his mouth to say something, then seemed to realize he was naked. He took a few steps behind her in an attempt to block the full view of his family jewels.

"Ethan, it's not what you think. I need you to calm down before you lose your shit so I can explain," Kyle said.

"Explain that you're banging my sister?" Ethan practically whispered, body vibrating in fury. He took a step toward them. "Explain how I fought to let you stay here so you could betray my trust?"

Ophelia felt as if she were trapped, like her namesake, in some sort of Shakespearean play. She had to remind herself that who she took to bed wasn't her brother's business.

"Look, I appreciate the medieval-style protection and all, but Kyle hasn't done anything wrong. I'm a full participant. How about I make a pot of coffee and we chat?"

Mia sensed disaster looming and quickly jumped in front of Ethan, babbling a mile a minute. "Babe, take a breath. I know it looks bad, but let's just calm down and talk like adults, okay? Ophelia's not in any trouble. Let them put some clothes on, and we'll have some nice scones."

"Sure, no problem."

They all collectively released their breath.

Ethan grinned with a touch of evil. "After I beat the living shit out of him."

It happened so fast, she had no way to stop it.

Ethan jumped right past her and threw Kyle against the wall. Mia yelled and darted after him, but Ophelia staved her off because her brother had her lover pinned with his hand over his neck.

"Don't kill him!" Mia screamed.

"Dude, don't you think this is a bit dramatic?" Kyle tried to reason, one hand protecting his penis. "Or, if you want a fair fight, let me put on some damn clothes."

"You're acting like an ass, Ethan," Ophelia said, pushing at his body to get him off Kyle. "I am so pissed at you right now."

"Well, I'm pissed at him for taking advantage of you. I thought you hated him! You refused to let him stay here, and now you're naked with him. How did he seduce you?"

"Oh, for God's sake, we're not in some romantic drama," she shot back. "He did not seduce me!"

Kyle shot her a hurt look. "Yes I did. Are you going to deny me my skill?"

Ethan muttered a curse and shook him hard. She got the impression Kyle was allowing him to get some of his aggression out in the hopes he'd calm down.

"Go back to your Hollywood hit list and leave my damn sister alone. She doesn't need you using her. I should've listened to her. I should've never let you get near her again."

Kyle had reached his limit. He shoved Ethan hard, and her brother stumbled back. "I'm not using her, you idiot!"

"Oh? You're not gonna leave her behind while you make your big movies? If you wanted some ass on the side here, I could've set you up!"

"Don't talk that way about your damn sister!"

Kyle charged. Ethan dodged, then slammed him to the side.

"I'm going to call 911!" Mia shouted.

"What makes Ophelia different from the others?" Ethan yelled.

"'Cause she's my *wife*—and I still fucking love her!"

Ethan's jaw dropped. Mia gasped. Ophelia stared at her husband in shock, the words echoing in the air like the aftermath of a bullet.

"What did you say?" Ethan asked, confusion soaking his words.

Kyle sighed and rubbed his head. "We eloped in Vegas ten years ago and decided not to tell anyone since we were only eighteen. When she left we filed for divorce, but it never went through. So we're still married to each other. I'd never use Ophelia. I've always loved her."

Ophelia held her breath, stunned at Kyle's admission—and by the feeling of relief at finally having the truth revealed. She'd been stupid to keep it from her family and to try to guard her pain like a secret that had to be shrouded in silence.

Ethan blinked. Took a step back. Then he glanced over, pinning her with his gaze. "Is that true?" he asked slowly.

"Yes. It's all true."

Ethan nodded. Regarded Kyle for a long time. And finally spoke. "Then you sure as hell deserve this."

Ophelia opened her mouth to cry out and stop him, but it was already too late.

He drew back his fist and punched Kyle in the face.

Chapter Twenty-One

Bea's Diner was exactly as he remembered. Down to the cracked red vinyl booths, impressive pie display, and black-and-white checkered floor. The place was still packed, and the scent of burgers, fries, and grease filled the air with temptation. Voices clamored in chatter, and an antique jukebox played oldies from the corner. Kyle tossed away the menu, already knowing what he was going to order.

"That's the second time Mia's seen you naked," Ethan growled in warning. His gaze blasted him from across the booth. "One more time, and I'll beat the shit out of you."

"Think you already did, dude." He touched his swollen eye while Ophelia cooed and pressed a gentle kiss to his cheek. Maybe it wasn't so bad, taking a good hit. The sympathy and coddling were pretty damn awesome. "But it was still a cheap shot."

"You still deserved it."

Kyle shrugged. Yeah, he did.

After he'd crumbled embarrassingly to the floor, Ethan had helped him up and announced his need for a very strong cup of coffee. Spiked.

The women had taken a while to calm down, but Kyle was relieved the truth was finally out so he didn't have to lie to his best friend anymore. He'd gotten a bag of frozen peas for his black eye, and sat down to try and explain their complicated past without giving away too many intimate details. Ophelia had been firm with her brother about one thing: Ethan was required to stay out of her love life and let them work things out on their own.

Mia had backed her up until Ethan agreed to lay off.

Mia shook her head in feminine frustration. "I just don't understand men. If Ophelia and I settled our differences by beating the crap out of each other, how would you feel?"

Ethan grinned. "Catfights are hot."

Mia elbowed him, but he just laughed. "Absolutely hopeless," she muttered, obviously trying hard not to grin. She closed her menu, stared longingly at the case full of fresh pies. "I guess I'll have a salad."

Ethan frowned. "You had a salad for lunch. What about the tuna on whole wheat? Bea makes it with carrots, celery, and onions."

"Okay, that's reasonable."

"Then you can have a bite of my pie," Ethan said, pressing a kiss to her open palm.

Mia stared at him, eyes wide with longing. "The coconut cream?"

"Yes, babe. The coconut cream."

She practically shivered with delight in the booth. "I love you."

"Love you, too."

Kyle cocked his head and stared. "I don't get it. Why are you so freaked about pie?"

Ophelia laughed and tried to explain. "Mia likes to watch her weight, but she also adores food. We call Ethan the gatekeeper. He helps her balance smart choices with occasional indulgences. Including pie."

Mia sighed. "I used to be a size-six Gucci dress. Now I'm in an eight."

"And hot as hell with your new curves."

"Agreed," Ophelia said. "You look absolutely amazing."

Mia blushed. "Thanks, guys."

Kyle watched the couple across from them. They were obviously in love and connected in a way that made everyone else onlookers. Their intimate look gave him hope. Ophelia was the only woman he'd ever imagined sharing his life—the good, the bad, and the ugly. Now that he'd admitted he still loved her, he'd been hoping for some returned emotional exchange. Like an *I love you* back. But she'd been silent regarding his sudden confession.

Now he was getting all freaked out that she was just using him for sex.

Kyle was deathly afraid he was becoming the girl in this relationship.

"Kyle Kimpton! About damn time you came back to my diner."

He looked up at Bea, the proud owner and a well-known face he'd never forgotten. She looked the same, with her famous beehive of gray hair, peacock-blue eye shadow, and hot-pink lipstick. A frilly pink apron wrapped around her hips, emphasizing her brightly colored leggings, tight T-shirt with a pink heart, and high-top Converse sneakers.

"I'm sorry I haven't come in sooner. Been locked up trying to get a project done. But I've been dreaming of your bacon burgers for years."

She stuck her nose in the air and sniffed. "Always been a flatterer. My goodness, I can't believe the three musketeers are back in their old booth. You know the trouble you caused this town when you three ran wild?"

"We kept you young, Bea," Kyle said with a wink.

She laughed with delight. "Oh, you're good. When are you going to stop making those big-time movies and come back where you belong?"

Ophelia stiffened next to him, but kept her smile pasted on her face.

He took her hand in full view and squeezed her fingers. "I've been wondering the same thing lately."

Ophelia's gorgeous baby blues widened at the public gesture screaming of their coupledom.

Bea caught it and whistled. "Always knew you two were meant to be an item," she said. "Had a bet with Amy Hash for years. Gonna call that smarty-pants up and tell her I was right."

Ophelia cleared her throat and tried to take control of the conversation. "Well, we're not really officially together yet. Kyle will be going back to Hollywood soon, and we—"

"We'll work it out. Love always wins. Right, Bea?"

A sharp kick to his calf made him wince.

Yep. She was pissed, and he was going to hear about it later.

"That's right. Now let me get those orders. Mia, I found another client for your PR company. She needs an entire marketing plan and website set up."

"Wonderful."

"Want your regular salad?" she asked Mia.

"Tuna on wheat, please."

"Good choice." She took the rest of their orders and floated away.

For the rest of the dinner, they kept the topics light and airy, but Kyle never let go of Ophelia's hand, and she never tried to let go of his.

It was enough.

Later that night they lay naked, wrapped in a blanket in front of the fire. The scents of wood and smoke and warm apple pie drifted in the air.

Muscles limp with satisfaction, Ophelia stared into the crackling flames and voiced the question she had always wondered about: "Did you ever think about how it ended between us?"

His muscles tensed beneath her, but his voice was steady. "All the time. I went over both of our decisions like a statistician, trying to figure out what move would have changed the outcome." He sat in silence for a while. She waited, sensing he was gathering his thoughts. "I blamed you for leaving, you know. Even though I showed up too late."

"I know. But you'd broken so many promises by that point, I couldn't take it anymore. Couldn't handle one more fight, or lonely dinner, or crying alone in bed because you slept at the production company's office again. I realized then we had grown so far apart, you had no room in your life for me any longer." She paused. "You know what I dreamed about? For days and nights after I left?" she asked.

"What?"

"I dreamed you would come after me."

His voice was a whisper of sound, fluttering against her nerve endings. "And I dreamed you would come back."

He stroked her hair, his fingers tugging through the waves with a sensuality that melted her. "What's going to happen this time?" she asked.

He let out a breath, staring down at her bare breasts with a lusty look of reverence she'd never get tired of. After she'd left California, sex had meant nothing. It was a bodily function she'd indulged in sparingly with partners who never got past the surface. Now it was an all-encompassing need that throbbed through her and demanded she satisfy it with total abandon. It was beyond physical; it reached to long-neglected places she'd thought numb. It was a total rebirth—and it scared the living hell out of her.

"I want to figure it out together," he said. "I don't want a divorce."

"I can't live there again, Kyle," she said honestly. "I'm afraid we'll end up back at the same exact place—loving each other but wanting two different lifestyles."

"Right now, I want to soak in every moment with you without worrying about the future. We still have five weeks left. Let me finish the book and enjoy my time with you. Then we'll make some decisions together. Can we do that?"

She tilted her head and smiled up at him. She was so tired of trying to figure things out in neat, logical order. For the first time, she wanted to *feel* again—to give everything to the moment without regret. Her heart was finally open.

She wished Kyle could give that same chance to his father. She'd been thinking of Patrick lately, and trying to find a way for Kyle to take that first step toward truly hearing him out.

"Yes. But I want you to think about visiting your dad."

He flinched. "Why is it so important to you?"

"I just don't want you to turn your back on an opportunity to heal some wounds. You can't change the past, but forgiveness can affect your future. I've forgiven you, and now we have a second chance. Doesn't your father deserve one, too?"

His voice held the slightest shakiness. "What if I can't forgive?"

She held him tight. "Then at least you tried."

A ragged sigh escaped his chest. "I ran into his AA sponsor in town."

Her eyes widened with surprise. "When?"

"Several mornings ago. His name's Tony. Met him getting fish at Fran's. He recognized me and introduced himself."

Her hands stroked his arm soothingly. "What did he say?"

A rough laugh escaped his lips. "Called my dad an asshole. Told me he has a ton of regrets and talks about me a lot. Then he invited me to attend his one-year anniversary of being sober. I don't know—it was a lot to handle."

"I bet. But it also sounds like the Patrick I've been seeing. He's definitely changed. And though I get why you'd say no, I'm still asking if you'll try. Just once."

She held her breath, hating the thought of hurting him. Her gut instinct told her Kyle needed to see this new version of his dad—even if afterward he decided to walk away and never see him again.

"I have a deal for you. I'll think very seriously about seeing my father if you think very seriously about singing at Crystal's."

Startled, she stared at him. "Why do you want me to sing so badly?"

"Because it's part of who you are. Because I've seen how it brings you joy. And because I think you don't realize it doesn't have to be like

259

the past. With what Albert is offering, this time you can sing for *you*, Ophelia. Not for me, or the cameras, or because you feel you need to prove it to anyone. Just for you."

The memory hit her full force. Being torn apart in the press. Gossip rags writing lies about why she quit the show, citing her thirst for attention and her endless bitchy demands.

"It was so hard," she said softly. "The story blew up and, suddenly, I couldn't even go out. People would yell and make comments, and my social media feeds exploded with cruelty. I was all alone. Every time I tried to tell you, you made me feel like it was my fault for quitting."

Raw pain flickered over his features, along with regret. "I was wrong," he said. "I was more concerned about my damn agent being pissed than I was about what you were going through. All I can tell you is that I see things now I never did before. I would never hurt you again. I swear it, baby."

She studied his beloved face and slowly nodded. Truth rang from his voice and his gaze. "Okay. I'll think about singing for Albert."

"Okay."

A sense of peace washed over her. His answer was a gift, because she knew it would cost him a lot to see his father. And if she was being honest, she'd been thinking of Albert's offer all day, wondering if it was time to truly leave the past behind.

He rocked her gently in his arms, and she heard the distant sound of music like she always did when her mind quieted down—a constant companion since childhood.

"Will you do something for me, Ophelia?"

He pressed a kiss on the bare curve of her neck and she arched, her breasts warmed by the fire.

"Of course."

"Will you sing for me? Like you used to."

The request was bittersweet—a haunting memory of when they'd lain together in the barn, stealing time and kisses, falling into each other. She'd sing to him, wrapping them in a cocoon of beauty as fragile and strong as a spider's web.

She closed her eyes. Her voice rumbled from her throat, spinning out the lyrics of a song that bruised as much as it pleasured, her husky tones blending with a quiet emotion that was somehow more powerful than the crashing crescendos she was known for.

He held her as she sang, her back pressed against his chest, his arms wrapped tightly around her, his chin resting on her shoulder. She sang for their past and for their unknown future, but most of all she sang for the present. She wanted to be in this moment, which she would never forget, with the man she loved.

The final stanza drifted away as quietly as it had begun. And she wondered briefly if Kyle had been right—if she'd been neglecting part of herself that needed to shine before it was lost forever.

"I used to hear your voice in my dreams after you left me. What song did you just sing?"

"'City of Stars.' It's from the movie *La La Land*."

He drew in a breath. "I saw that movie. I didn't like the ending."

"Neither did I. But it was necessary."

His arms tightened around her. He tilted her chin up, and his gaze was fierce, possessing. He was a superhero bent on saving the day and giving her a happily ever after. "We can make our own ending. The one we want."

She touched his cheek. "I love you, too, Kyle Kimpton."

His gaze delved deeper, searching. Then he lowered his head and kissed her.

They didn't speak again.

Chapter Twenty-Two

Ophelia rushed into his room, her face etched with the rare lines of panic. "I'm in trouble. I need your help."

He sprung from his chair, still groggy from being ripped out of the scene he was writing, and clutched her shoulders. "Are you okay? What's wrong?"

"I need your room. I just got a last-minute call from a group of snowboarders who want to book three nights. They're paying top price. I need four empty rooms, but I'm short one. I've never been fully booked in early March. Can you move in with me instead?"

He relaxed, fighting a grin. It was rare to see his woman all hopped up about the inn since she was normally cool and capable, running a tight ship of ruthless organization that left little room for error.

"Of course. We've been spending every night together anyway, and I can write in your room. When are they arriving?"

"Tomorrow." Her cheeks flushed, and curls escaped her topknot to curl wildly around her face. She was dressed in those heavenly, tight yoga pants he adored that showed off the lush curve of her ass and hips. She smelled of lemon polish and that honey-lavender lotion he could easily get drunk on. "I have a million things to do, but this could set me up with a nice cushion for the summer."

"Let me know if you need me to help."

"I'm calling Aubrey to come in for the cleaning and extra laundry. Do you think you can run into town for me and get some groceries? They've requested a March Madness viewing party in the main room. That's basketball, right?"

He laughed. "Yes, but a roomful of men watching basketball sounds a bit scary."

Her brows slammed together. "What happens? What do I need to be prepared for?"

God, she was adorable. And smart. And sexy.

"I'd just have some extra snacks on hand. I'll pick up some hearty stuff that's easy to stick in the oven and heat. Don't worry—you got this."

She dragged in a breath and seemed to calm down. "Thanks." She moved toward the computer with curiosity. From all the time they'd spent together, she knew to never ask to read what he was working on. He had a terrible superstition about leaking creative juices if someone were to read his words before they were done. "How's it going?"

Good. Bad. Past the slogging middle, with the end firmly in sight. He was beginning to slow down rather than speed up, which was his usual routine. It was as if the story had only one place to go, but he was fighting the true ending, forcing the characters into actions that felt foreign. But he couldn't seem to stop it. It was becoming a wicked, tangled mess.

"Been better. But I'll get there."

She picked up the book to his right and smiled. "Whatcha reading, hot stuff?"

He crossed his arms in front of his chest and quirked his brow. "Is there a chauvinistic comment about to emerge from those delectable lips? Something about men reading romance novels?"

She flipped through the pages, her face registering pure delight. "Sorry, I couldn't help it. It's too delicious. This book looks good."

"It is. Jill Shalvis is a master at contemporary romance. Emotion is key, and I like to tap into that segment of readers when I'm working in this genre."

"And this one?" She pointed to another one in his pile. "Kristen Proby?"

"Her Fusion series revolves around a restaurant." He shrugged. "What's better than food, wine, and friendship? She's also good at building in the family element, which is the core of a great story."

"I'm impressed. Sorry, I should have never assumed you were reading them just for the sex. That's narrow-minded."

"Oh, I read them for the sex, too." He gave her a wicked grin. "In fact, I'll demonstrate what I learned tonight."

Her giggle charmed him, even as she backed away. "Later, Casanova. I have too much work to do, and I'm a bit tired."

"Too many late nights?"

"Maybe." She gave him her own wink and sashayed out of his room. "But totally worth it."

Damn right it was.

He sat back down at the computer. The past few weeks had flown by much too quickly, until he realized he'd gotten into a routine. He helped her with breakfast, chatted with the guests, and they shared their first meal of the day together. Then he wrote while she worked, and they reconvened in the early evening to eat, read, lounge by the fire, and make love all night long. The snow and cold shrouded them in a world of their own. Reality was a misty idea that had no place in the now. Because for now, everything was perfect. He almost wished the book would never get done. He had a few weeks left to deliver, and then he'd head west to take the most important meeting of his life.

He rubbed his head, refocused, and got back to the page. Ophelia's words from last month drifted in his mind, reminding him how brutal it must have been to feel ripped apart by the world. The press hounding her, people snickering and writing lies. And the whole time, he'd been focused on his own career—annoyed she'd quit the show and caused a hassle. Shame burned through him, but he took it to the page and began to write.

"We need a rewrite." Solomon threw the thick stack of papers on his desk in frustration. "I still don't like the scene where Cassie and Jack kiss. It's too emotional. I want it lighter and funny."

Kyle frowned and blinked through gritty eyes. He'd barely slept the last few nights. He hated fighting with Ophelia, but it was as if there were a wall of ice between them. Every time they tried to talk, his irritation with her blew up. He was trying so hard to understand why she quit the singing show and didn't seem interested in pursuing her dream any longer. Had she buckled under the pressure? Had she been a different person from what he'd imagined? All they did now was fight, or ignore one another. Still, he needed to find some way to communicate with her. They couldn't go on like this.

He tried to focus on his producer's words. "I don't know, Solomon. I thought the scene had a nice balance and connected the hero and heroine on a deeper level."

"I don't want deep. I want funny, maybe sexy. Have them kiss right before they crash."

Kyle blinked. "That's just stupid."

"No, it's funny. Work it out—I need it quickly, or we'll get behind schedule."

He watched the producer's retreating back and tried not to lose his temper. The rewrites were killing him. At this point, he couldn't recognize his own story underneath the mishmash of opinions consistently thrown at him. It definitely wasn't what he imagined, but he still loved writing for a living and being part of such a thriving, competitive industry. It made him feel alive. Big.

Fucking important.

He grabbed the script and turned to the marked scene, trying desperately to clear his head and map out a scene that didn't suck. He was just getting into the zone when he realized someone was calling his name.

He looked up, torn out of his fog, and stared at Ophelia. Clad in denim shorts and a white ruffled top, hair spilling around her shoulders, he caught his breath as her beauty struck him full force. Even with all this bullshit, he loved her so damn much. They'd work it out.

"Hey, what are you doing here?"

She shifted her feet, looking uncomfortable. "We really need to talk, Kyle. I spoke with my sister. I'm thinking of heading back home."

The tenderness drifted away and was replaced by pure anger. "Are you kidding? Why on earth would you want to run back home? We hated it there. You want to end up running the B & B like your mom? Get trapped for life in a small town with no opportunities?"

"No! Yes! I don't know—I just hate it here," she whispered. She came over to stand beside him. "This thing with the show blew up. The papers are saying crappy things about me—about how I was a diva and wanted all these things and that's why I quit the show. It's all lies."

He gave an impatient sigh. "That's just the press twisting things. It's a new show. By quitting, you gave them a bad reputation. It'll blow over."

She stared at him. "You don't even care?"

He rubbed his head. Stress bubbled over—along with confusion—and he lashed out. "Listen, you can't do this to me right now. I have to get these rewrites to Solomon ASAP, and then God knows what else he'll want me to change to make this movie work. We'll talk later, okay?"

"I need you tonight, Kyle." Her words throbbed with urgency. "Please come home. I'll wait up. I just can't keep going on like this."

"I get it. I'll be home. I promise. I'm sorry, but I have to get this script done."

She took a step back and nodded. "I'll see you at home tonight." Her gaze held a touch of desperation. "You promise, right?"

"Yeah, I promise."

He only had a few flashes of memory of the last time he saw her. The sad look in her blue eyes as she turned away. The click of her low-heeled sandals over the tiled floor. The scent of lavender and soap and honey drifting from her skin. The flicker of light on her left hand from the small diamond she proudly wore, even though he'd promised her something bigger and better soon.

He'd go over them endlessly in the long months ahead as he ached for her.

But he didn't know any of it then.

The shooting ran late, and the producers and director called a meeting to change the ending. He texted her his apologies while he locked himself in a small, airless room with his computer. He typed through the night, finally delivering something the team was proud of.

When he got home, she was gone.

Kyle stared at the pages. So close to the ending. The simplicity and stark honesty of the book humbled him. It was the type of love story stripped to its bare bones: sex, youth, passion, ambition, and what happens to two innocent people caught in the storm. His talks with Ophelia these past two months had helped him understand the nuances and differences between how their individual stories had unfolded, which made the book come alive. Excitement flowed through his veins.

Now, it was time to make the big decision.

The ending.

He swiveled around in his chair and stared out the window. Change was on the way. Most of the snow had melted, leaving a damp, muddy mess, but the ripe scent of spring hung in the air. The evenings began to lengthen, and the sound of the birds exploded in the newly budding trees. Ophelia was already starting her spring planting, including various herbs and vegetables for the garden. Ethan had begun renovation on the bungalow, and Harper had acquired some new spring foals. The red barn doors were now flung open, and the animals began poking their noses from their stalls and galloping in the fields.

Time was running out.

He stood up from his computer and decided to go into town. He'd pick up a few things for Ophelia and grab lunch. Tugging on a thick hooded sweatshirt, he headed out, his thoughts on the past and the present and the promises he needed to keep for the woman he loved.

When he neared the familiar driveway, his hands tightened on the steering wheel. He made the decision last minute—swerving down the path and parking the car in front of the run-down farmhouse. His gut churned, and his palms grew damp. He stared at the sagging porch, the sloped roof still clogged with snow, and the bright-red door that winked at him through the gloom. The barns and chicken coops and shed were tightly closed up and eerily vacant. Ghosts surrounded his childhood home. He squeezed his eyes shut, wondering if he had the guts to go in.

Then with a muttered curse, he shoved open the car door and walked onto the porch. Kyle lifted his hand and knocked. His hands trembled slightly, so he quickly stuck them in his pockets and waited.

His father answered the door. He'd never seen joy in his dad's face before. It was an emotion that was too soft to be shared between them, so it took Kyle a few seconds to realize it wasn't his imagination.

"Kyle. I didn't know you were coming."

"I didn't know I was, either."

Patrick motioned him in. The dog caught sight of him and slowly limped over for a greeting.

He knelt down and rubbed the shepherd's ears, crooning to him. "Ophelia told me she got you to take him in."

A smile ghosted his lips. "Yeah. She's manipulative, that one. But I like him. Named him Charlie."

His throat tightened. "That was the name of my teddy bear when I was young." God, how he'd loved that scraggly old bear. Carried it everywhere with him for way too long, and never even felt embarrassed. He'd wanted to bring it with him to California, but by then it had been lost or boxed away.

"I know," Patrick said softly.

Kyle choked back the emotions, hardened his heart. One nice gesture didn't take away any of the bad. His tone hardened. "I'm surprised you're keeping the dog. You're not really the animal type."

His father nodded. "We're a lot alike. Charlie's not too good with others, either. We don't need much."

"Ophelia said you've been getting her to cook for you."

He winced. "Yeah, I have. Takeout and delivery gets old, and I don't cook so well."

"No shit. I always did that for you."

He nodded. "Yeah, you did. Plus a bunch of other things I never gave you credit for. Probably not even a *thank you*."

Old anger stirred. "No, you didn't," Kyle said coldly. "Other than an occasional slap or the reminder I killed my mother, you weren't into interacting with me."

Patrick flinched but kept his gaze direct, not trying to hide. "Yeah. I gotta live with that. With the shame over the fact that your mother loved you so much she wanted you to live, yet I disrespected her greatest gift of all. You." He let out a sigh that was so weary it was like an arrow through Kyle's chest. "I'm sorry, son. Not that it means anything now, but I am."

An awkward silence fell between them. Kyle waited, not knowing what he really wanted from this little visit.

Patrick cleared his throat. "Umm, want some coffee?"

"Sure."

He petted the dog and watched his father work the coffeepot. "How do you take it?" Patrick asked.

Kyle ignored the shred of pain.

His father truly knew nothing about him. There was something about a parent knowing a child's food and drink choices that created a special bond. Stupid, but he couldn't help it.

"A little sugar."

He gazed around his childhood home, noting the familiar furniture, scarred wooden floors, and the same paintings on the wall. Nothing much had changed, except now the place was neatly kept and a dog bed lay in the corner, along with food and water bowls.

He noticed the framed pictures on the oak tables. Him in his graduation robe from high school. Him at his first Communion. Him at a football game, grinning widely. Him with Ophelia and Ethan in front of Bea's Diner, hamming it up for the camera. All taken by friends. None taken by his father.

He'd barely recognized the most important moments in Kyle's life.

He'd tried to tell his father about taking off to California, but Patrick had been drunk again and hadn't cared. Kyle just packed his shit and left without another word. It had been up to Ophelia's mom to come over and explain what they'd done after they were gone. The jab had felt good, especially since he knew his dad had needed his help with the farm.

Patrick came in with the coffee. Kyle got up and took a seat at the battered dining room table. Charlie padded over and sat next to his father.

"Place looks clean," Kyle said.

"Ophelia helps me out once in a while," he admitted.

"And she took care of you when you got sick."

"She's good to me. Like her mother was."

He couldn't help the sharp edge to his voice. "Don't take advantage of her. She cares about people in a way I've never seen before—people who don't even deserve it. She makes the world a better place."

Patrick didn't even flinch. Just nodded. "I won't. You still love her, huh?"

Kyle stretched his legs out and tapped the table. "Yeah." They sat in silence for a while. "I married her, you know."

His father stared at him in shock. "You got married?"

"Back in California. When we ran away."

"You were only eighteen."

He shrugged. "Didn't matter. It didn't work out, so she came back here. Now we're back together."

Patrick studied his face. "That's good. Always sensed you were meant for each other. You gonna stay?"

Kyle tried not to wince as he took a sip of his coffee. "I have to get back to Hollywood to pitch a new screenplay. But I plan on coming back."

His father seemed to light up. "Yeah? Another like *Conspiracy*? That was good."

"You saw it?"

"Hell yeah. I've seen all your movies. I take a picture on my cell phone when the credits roll and your name is shown. See?" He rose and walked over to the coffee table, grabbing a trio of small, framed pictures Kyle hadn't spotted before. "Printed them out and framed them myself."

Kyle stared at them, his name in big print various times, clad in cheap silver frames. Emotion choked his throat. "I didn't know you even knew what I did."

Patrick sat back down, hands on his knees. "Because I'm an asshole. I get it. But even before I finally stopped drinking, I was proud of you. I think leaving me was the best thing you ever did for yourself. I ended up letting the farm go to hell, drinking myself into almost nothing, and I became the town drunk. If you had stuck around, I would've ruined more of your life."

He sat in silence for a bit. "I ran into your sponsor in town. Tony."

"Yeah? Tony's helped me a lot." He watched in shock as Patrick's eyes filled with shame. "Did he try to guilt you into coming to see me?"

Kyle shrugged. "Not really. Just said you'd changed." He ran his thumb around the corners of the frame, turning it around in his hands. "I came here because Ophelia asked me to see you. I'm doing this for her."

Jennifer Probst

Patrick nodded. "Makes sense. I'm glad you found her again. You deserve some happiness. God knows you had none as a kid. God knows what I did is unforgivable, but I'm saying I'm sorry anyway."

Kyle looked him straight in the face. "I hated your guts. I wished you were dead."

Grief touched his father's green eyes. "I know. Did you look in the box I sent over?"

He shook his head. "Not yet. I couldn't."

"Maybe you'll open it one day."

"Maybe." Kyle took another sip of coffee and stood. "I gotta go." He patted the dog's head, turned, and headed toward the door.

"Kyle?"

"Yeah?"

"Thanks for seeing me."

He couldn't answer, so he just nodded and left.

He headed into town, stopping at the Market to fill up on some appetizers for the March Madness crew, and tried not to think about the conversation with his father. He was just pulling back into the inn when his cell rang. It was his agent.

"Robbie. Been wondering when you were going to call with some news."

"I finally have some, but it depends on how fast you can get me the script."

His gut lurched. "What do you mean?"

"Alan Bell said he may be interested. I told him this was a script no one else had seen yet, and it was going to rock the industry."

Kyle winced at his agent's normal dramatics, but the mention of Bell made his breath stop. The hot new director storming Tinseltown was known for his Academy Award nominees and a talent for hitting the audience with tearjerkers. "Are you fucking kidding me? Bell would give it a read?"

"Only if you can get me the script ASAP. He'll be out of the country for the next few weeks, so if you want him, we need to schedule the meeting for Tuesday. How close are you to wrapping up?"

"Close."

"Then get it done so I can send it to the team in the next day or two. Who the hell knows if Bell will still be interested after returning from overseas? You know how hard it is to keep the attention of directors of his caliber, or even score a meeting at all. You in?"

No.

He wanted more time here. He wasn't ready to leave her yet.

But this opportunity needed to be grabbed. "Yes, I'm in. I'll get it done. Thanks, Robbie." They exchanged goodbyes, and he clicked the phone off.

Kyle wanted these last few weeks with Ophelia, uninterrupted. But if he could sell the script early and nail down the project of his dreams with the director of his dreams, he needed to give his all.

It was different this time. He knew better what he wanted, how to manage things, and had rediscovered who he was. All he needed to do was convince Ophelia they wouldn't be separated for long.

This time, he'd come back for her.

Chapter Twenty-Three

The next evening, Ophelia was prepping dinner when the phone rang. She hit the speaker button with her elbow, her hands covered in flour. "Hello?"

"Ophelia? It's Patrick. I need help."

"Hi, Patrick. Are you okay?"

"It's not me." His voice caught in a strange way. "It's Charlie. I think he's sick. I have to get him to the vet."

She didn't question why he was calling her, just stumbled to the sink, turned on the faucet, and rinsed off the powder. "I'm on my way. I'll call Sarah and tell her it's an emergency."

"Okay."

She grabbed her coat and raced to her room, where Kyle had settled in to make room for the snowboarders. He had been working nonstop and was probably deep into the zone, so she knocked a few times before saying through the door, "Babe, I have to run out for a while. Be back soon."

The door flung open. He blinked as if emerging from a dark cave. "Want some company? I need a break."

She hesitated. He'd finally gone to see Patrick, and though the visit had gone relatively well, he hadn't told her he wanted to see him again. "I'm going to your dad's. Charlie's sick, and he needs help getting him to the vet." A flicker of emotion crossed his face, squeezing her heart. She reached out and touched his cheek. "I think you should come with me."

He stared at her for a few moments, then slowly nodded. "Okay."

"Let's go."

They didn't speak on the drive over. Patrick was waiting outside for them, with Charlie hooked to a leash. When she neared the dog, she could see from his glassy eyes and slumped head that he was out of it.

Kyle got out of the car, nodding at his father but not speaking. Patrick stared at his son, obviously shocked by his presence, but didn't seem to know what to say, either. Kyle picked up the dog and settled him in the back seat of her car. Patrick climbed in next to the dog.

"It could be the flu," she said to Patrick, pulling onto the highway. "I've heard animals can get it, too."

"He hasn't been eating. Not even the chicken or the gravy bone he likes. He's just been laying there, and his breathing sounds funny. That's not good for his age."

"Let's not panic until the vet sees him. You can be old as dirt and still tough as nails."

A half laugh echoed from the back. Kyle stared out the window silently, his face set in a hard line.

Within ten minutes, they arrived at the vet and got Charlie checked in. Kyle waited outside the office while she stood next to Patrick as the doctor examined the dog. After a thorough exam, Sarah turned to both of them, her brown eyes kind. "I think it may just be a virus, but with his age, I can't rule some other things out. I'd like to keep him overnight and do some blood work."

Patrick stared at her. "You talking about cancer?"

"Possibly. He's definitely dehydrated, so I'd like to get some fluids in him, run some tests, and take it from there. I'll take good care of him. Is that all right?"

Patrick nodded. "Sure. Will I know tomorrow?"

"Yes, I'll rush the tests to the lab. I should have them by noon."

"And you'll call me?"

"Yes, as soon as I know. Do you want to say goodbye before I take him in the back?"

Patrick flinched. She watched as the older man gently laid his hands on the dog and whispered something in his ear. Then he walked out of the office without turning back.

Ophelia followed him out. "Patrick, he has all the symptoms of a virus or a cold. Don't panic yet."

"I'm good. Can you take me home now?"

Kyle glanced back and forth between them as if trying to figure out what might have happened in the exam room. She nodded. They checked out at the counter, then got back in the car and drove home.

The silence was terrible—full of pain and memories that seemed to pulse and throb in the tight interior of the car. Biting her lip, Ophelia tried to come up with something to say, anything to break the tension, but soon she was back in Patrick's driveway.

Kyle turned to glare at his father, his words coming like a gunshot. "I guess you're gonna open up a bottle and get drunk now, right? 'Cause that's how you handle what life throws at you. Or maybe the dog being sick is somehow my fault, too?"

She pressed a fist to her lips to strangle her gasp. She cringed, ready for the explosion.

Patrick looked his son right back in the eye. "I would've. Lived my whole life by that philosophy, but I've been fighting for my humanity for the past year, and I'm not ready to give that up."

Ophelia cut in, her voice shaking with fierceness. "And you don't have to. You've learned a different way to deal with pain now."

"Yes, I work on that every damn day." He paused, letting the words penetrate. "But I'm a poison. I seem to ruin or kill all the good things in my life. I'm not even worth the love of a dog, but if all I got was a few weeks with Charlie because of Ophelia, I'll be grateful. Good night, son. Thanks for coming with me."

He climbed out of the car and walked into the house.

Kyle stared at the cardboard box for a long time. The edges were yellow and crumbled. A large water stain took up half of one side. Written in black marker were the words FOR KYLE.

He didn't recognize the man he'd seen the past two days. He'd only known the harsh version of his dad and rarely spotted any tenderness beneath the abrasion. But his father's expression when he'd looked at the dog stirred something inside him. Patrick looked like he *cared* about the dog. And yesterday, his father had apologized for his crappy actions. He'd looked Kyle straight in the eye without giving him some bullshit excuse about what he'd done.

I'm a poison . . .

God, why did those words cause pain in his chest?

He would've laughed them off and accused Patrick of being dramatic to get attention, but it hadn't been uttered like that. It had been uttered like total truth and deep regret.

Slowly, he lifted the cover off the box and lay it on the bed. A musty scent drifted up toward his nostrils. He stared at the three photo albums bound in maroon fake leather. With a trembling hand, he picked one up and cracked open the cover.

Pictures of his mother filled the pages. Pictures of his father. Pictures of them together.

He flipped through the precious treasures, studying their wedding day and their happy, smiling faces. Saw them kissing and eating cake and dancing with guests. Saw them on a beach, his mother in a bikini, splashing in the waves. Saw them at parties all dressed up in fine suits and dresses.

As he turned the pages, he watched their life unfold together. His mother pregnant. Glowing, hand on her belly, grinning at the camera. The nursery. His father kissing her belly. The beautiful, intimate way they gazed at one another.

Before he was born.

He spent a long time poring over the pictures his father had told him were burned. His view blurred, and he fisted his eyes to clear them. The past was finally given to him to cherish and savor and ponder.

He closed the book. When he went to replace all of the albums in the box, his gaze caught on a piece of folded paper at the bottom. He reached for it.

A letter. In his father's familiar scrawl. A few short paragraphs filled the lines.

Dear Kyle,

I wanted to say this in person, but you don't want to talk to me, and I don't blame you. I would want to move on with my life and forget my past, too, if I were you. I don't deserve a second thought, but I needed you to know some things.

First, your mom saved you because you were a precious gift—not a sacrifice or loss or anything but pure love. I was an alcoholic when you were born. I know that now, but I didn't then. Your mother and I fought a lot about my drinking, but I didn't think it was a big deal. After she died, I drank more. I became someone I couldn't recognize anymore.

The alcohol turned me into a monster. Sickened my brain. It drained my blood and kept me in a cycle of need. Sometimes, I'd wake up in the morning and swear I'd change. For your sake. And then all day I'd dream about the bottle and how bad I needed it, and it became even bigger than you. God forgive me—alcohol was more important than my own son.

Your aunt did her best to help the first few years after you were born, but I drove her away. Soon, my family and friends couldn't help me anymore. I'll regret my actions till the day I die. Regret what I did to you.

Being sober is its own form of torture because there's nowhere left to hide. In spite of me, you succeeded in everything. But most of all, you succeeded in life because of your mother and her capacity to love. That's the greatest gift she left you.

I told you I burned the pictures because the sight of them killed me with guilt. They are yours now.

I do love you, son. Always have.

Dad

Kyle crumpled the letter between his fingers and bent his head, wondering if some endings were too late to change.

Ophelia clicked off her phone and slumped against the washer in relief. Charlie was going to be fine. He was already feeling better, and all tests had come back negative.

Thank God.

She put the cell phone down and finished folding laundry. The memory of Patrick and Kyle's exchange in the car tore at her heart. She knew Patrick was trying, but she was also the one who'd witnessed what he'd done to his son on a daily basis.

Forgiveness was such a twisted, thorny thing—easy to preach and hard to practice. But she knew if Kyle could find a way to forgive his dad, he'd heal a broken place inside and be stronger.

She knew, because forgiving Patrick had helped her forgive Kyle and their broken past.

Now there was nothing she wouldn't do to fight for the only man she'd ever loved.

These past two months, he'd been completely focused on their relationship. They'd learned to love each other all over again, and she was ready to face the future. Yes, he'd be going back to Hollywood soon, but they still had some precious time left together. She intended to use every moment to strengthen and deepen their bond.

She jolted as strong arms closed around her, then relaxed as the familiar scent of cotton, coffee, and man hit her. "Hey, baby," she murmured. "You need anything?"

"Just you. Always you." He lifted her up and placed her on top of the dryer, right on a pile of folded towels and sheets.

A giggle escaped her lips, and she snagged her arms around his neck. "Love in the laundry room, huh? That the title of your script?"

He laughed, nipping at the vulnerable curve of her neck. "Brat. I wanted to know if you'd heard anything from the vet yet."

She ran her fingers over the rough scruff hugging his jaw, loving the ferocious sexiness of his face. "Your dad just called. Charlie's fine—it was just a virus."

"That's great."

She took in the shadow flickering across his face and tapped on his chin to make him look up. "Then why do you look sad?"

"I opened the box. It was full of photo albums of my mother and father."

She sucked in her breath. "I thought he'd burned them."

"He lied. Wrote me a letter, too, trying to explain how his alcoholism changed him. Said he was sorry."

"I think he is. I think he's trying desperately to change and have some sort of relationship with you before it's too late."

"Isn't it already? How do you change the past?"

She gazed into his forest-green eyes and told him the truth. "You don't. But you can change the ending if you want. You can choose to forgive him, to open the door, and see if he respects your heart enough not to hurt you again."

He leaned his forehead against her chest. She held him for a long time, giving him comfort. "What else is bothering you?"

Before he spoke the words, she sensed what he needed to tell her.

Their path was careening to a familiar fork in the road, but this time, she had to be strong and trust him. They'd come too far and given too much to each other to close down over what-ifs. These past two months had taught her something precious.

The power of second chances.

"I have to leave soon." He lifted his head. Pain carved out the angles of his face. "My agent called two days ago. Alan Bell is interested in reading my screenplay."

Her eyes widened. "The director who won the Academy Award with Meryl Streep?"

"Yes. He spoke with Robbie, and he wants me to meet with him. Bell's going overseas soon, so I need to finish the screenplay and send it . . . by tomorrow." Regret flickered in his eyes. "I should've told you sooner. I'm sorry, baby. I just didn't want to think about having to cut our time short."

Even with her newfound resolution to trust him, the familiar dread rose up, choking her throat. She tried to keep her face and voice calm. "When do you have to leave?"

His pause told her everything. "Monday."

Raw emotion attacked her from all sides. She dragged in an unsteady breath. "I see. That's too bad. Chloe's father is joining us for dinner next Sunday, and I really wanted you to meet him."

"I know."

"Oh, and I bought tickets to that spring dance they're holding in town. I thought it would be fun for us to go to, but I'll just sell my tickets. It's not a big deal."

"Ophelia, I'm coming back." He leaned forward and cupped her cheeks, his breath rushing against her lips. "I know I sprung this on you last minute, and it's hard to believe me when this is the same scenario that tore us apart the first time, but I'm coming back. I won't sacrifice anything for you again. I love you."

Her eyes stung. She hated herself for being so emotional. He'd never hidden the fact that he'd eventually have to leave. She just hadn't prepared herself for it yet. She forced a smile to her lips. "I know. Sorry. You just surprised me."

"I'm going to take this meeting. If Bell likes what I wrote, we'll put a team together. I have a clear vision of what I want this time, and I'm not going to compromise. No more crazy rewrites night and day. I'll make sure I don't have to be on set so I can work from the inn. It won't be like before. I don't have to prove myself any longer. I choose *you*. Okay?"

She swallowed back the doubt and nodded. "Okay," she whispered. "I just need you to promise me something."

"Anything."

"If you love this screenplay you wrote, don't let them take away the heart and soul of your story, no matter what they promise. It's too important for both of us. Okay?"

"I won't. This time it's going to be different. They either like the story as is, or it's not going to work out."

"Good. Can I read it?"

He scratched behind his ear and looked away. "I still need to write the ending."

"Are you stuck?"

"Big-time."

"Wanna talk it out?"

He seemed to ponder her question. Stared into her face while he stroked her thighs through her jeans.

Knowing it was their story made her feel vulnerable. Would he write them a happily ever after? Or would it end on more of a cliffhanger?

"I feel like I'm forcing it," he finally said.

"Because you don't really believe it can work?"

He frowned and gripped her shoulders fiercely. "No, baby. There's only one way this story ends—and it's with them together. Forever. I'm just torn about which way to write it."

She smiled, her heart a bit eased. "Well, you need to figure it out today." She jumped off the dryer and faced him with a stern expression.

She needed to keep things light. There'd be plenty of time to digest his leaving later, on her own.

"I'll bring you up coffee and a sandwich, but you know the golden rule . . ."

He grinned, and her heart stuttered. "Vomit out the words. Go with your gut. Fix them later."

"Exactly." He moved to kiss her, but she backed away. "No fooling around until the ending is done."

"That's just mean."

"I'll give you a sneak peek of your reward." She lifted up her shirt and flashed him her naked breasts.

"You're not wearing a bra," he said, voice strained.

She threw him a cheeky grin. "That's right. And no panties. Happy writing, baby. Get it done."

She sashayed out of the laundry room, smiling at his groan.

He stumbled into the empty apartment and waited, hoping to catch her scent, or hear her voice, or catch a glimpse of those strawberry curls. Instead, the silence ate at him slowly, devouring him with gleeful intent to drive him insane.

He didn't know if he could live without her.

The past three weeks, he'd tried to drown himself in work. It wasn't hard, especially since the movie was about to be wrapped up and he was already being tapped to write a new screenplay to spec. Everything in his career was perfect.

But would it be enough? Success was empty without sharing it with Ophelia. Nothing seemed to be able to take away the throbbing ache in his heart and his gut.

He cracked open a beer and drank, moodily staring at his cell phone. She hadn't called. Not once. She was his wife, yet she'd left him.

He'd call her right now. Tell her he could change, if she'd just give him one more chance. This time, he would choose her first every time.

He reached for the phone. At the same time, there was a knock at the door.

Growling in frustration, he strode over and flung it open.

And stared at Ophelia.

Dressed in jeans and a simple yellow T-shirt, faint shadows and exhaustion lining her face, she stared back at him. Endless moments dragged on. They were both caught up in the sight of each other, both having so much to say yet not knowing where to start.

"I can't leave you," she finally whispered, reaching out her hands, palms turned up. "I tried. But I'm not . . . whole."

"Neither am I." He pulled her into his arms and kissed her deeply, his tongue thrusting inside, claiming his wife as his own. "This time, I'll be different. I'm never going to lose you again."

"And I'm going to give singing another chance. This time on my own terms."

"We can do it together."

She smiled so sweetly his heart ached. "I love you, Kyle."

"I love you, too."

He pulled her into the apartment and shut the door behind them.

This time, they'd have a brand new ending.

This time, love would be enough.

The End.

Kyle stared at the final words on the page, then read the last paragraph again.

God, it was shit.

He rubbed his head and groaned. It was so fucking saccharine sweet he felt like he'd just given himself a cavity. But every damn movie in Hollywood prided itself on happily-ever-after endings in a big-assed way. Unless you killed someone. And this wasn't that type of story.

He got up and paced, growling at his muse.

Couldn't you give me original material, you bitch? I've been on my ass for the last six hours and haven't moved.

Fuck you. I gave you what you needed. They made it. They didn't break up, and they're together forever. Plus, I gave you some of that Jerry Maguire *stuff that works so well.*

He stopped talking to his muse. He never won an argument with her anyway.

No, this was the ending he'd always dreamed they'd have. A way for them to be together and to work through their problems instead of spending nearly a decade apart. This was the type of ending Ophelia deserved. It worked.

Pushing away his doubts, he spent the rest of the evening converting the final chapters into a script format, then emailed it to his agent. He knew Robbie would read it ASAP and get any major changes back to him before sending it on to the team. That would leave him a day or two for quick revisions before he got on the plane.

He'd done it. Both the book and the script were finished. He was back with Ophelia.

Things were finally perfect.

Two days later, he fielded a call from his agent and got the news. "They fucking love it," Robbie crowed. "Ate it up as the next big Hollywood chick flick. Bell wants in."

Joy shot through him as he gripped the phone. "Are you kidding me? They liked it? Do they want revisions?"

"Not now. They wanted to talk about it face-to-face. Meeting's at nine a.m. Tuesday morning. I'll meet you there a little early to talk about a few things."

He grinned at the phone. "Sounds good."

"Why didn't you tell me you were a closet romantic? Holy shit, it gave me memories of some of the chick-flick classics. Congratulations, Kyle, this one is going to cement you as one of the best writers in Hollywood."

He clicked off and allowed himself one short fist pump.

Guess the ending had worked. Guess it was so good they were willing to take a chance. Somehow, he'd stretched into a new genre and nailed it.

He couldn't wait to tell Ophelia, even though it meant he was leaving in two days.

Chapter Twenty-Four

Ophelia poured two glasses of wine and rechecked the table she'd set.

Kyle had finished the script. Usually, he experienced elatedness mixed with a touch of depression when he handed off a project. She always pegged it as mourning the goodbye to characters he'd given his heart and soul to. For a brief time they belonged only to him, but once the story was finished, they belonged to the public.

The guests were settled in various activities—either retired to their rooms or out to dinner. The scents of freshly baked bread and home-made sauce wafted in the air. She spooned out two generous bowls of pasta with sauce and added meatballs, then sliced the crusty bread open and set out a tub of fresh-churned butter. The lights were dim, the candles were lit, and she was dressed in a royal-blue shift dress. With her hair pinned up and actual heels on her feet, she looked ready to celebrate.

Yes, they only had two more nights together, but she refused to mope around until he got on the plane. She'd grab every precious second with the man she loved and not waste any of it.

His footsteps echoed on the stairs. He walked in, studying the beautifully set table, and gazed hungrily over her figure. "What is this?"

She smiled. "You finished the script, and we have a big meeting to celebrate. I wanted to cook you a special dinner."

Those forest-green eyes lit with a fierce love and adoration he didn't try to hide. "You didn't have to do this." His voice came out husky.

She walked to him and pressed a kiss to the curve of his lips, breathing in the spicy scent of musk. "I wanted to," she murmured. "The end of a story was always an important event. As you once told me, beginnings are necessary and cherished, but it's the endings that will make a person remember you forever."

He jerked, his gaze flashing a gleam of emotion. "Yes, I guess I did say that." He reached for his wine, handed her a glass, and they clinked the crystal together in a toast. "To our own happy ending."

She took a generous sip, then slid into the chair. "Shall we?"

They feasted on the meal while they gave each other long, heated stares laced with the realization that their time was limited. "Ethan wants to have a family dinner tomorrow night to give you a proper send-off."

"I'd like that."

"Are you going to say goodbye to your father?" she asked.

"I'm not sure. I'm still thinking about it." He wiped his mouth with the napkin. "I keep going over what his sponsor told me. That AA was about second chances—not as much for the other person, but for yourself."

She nodded and reached across the table for his hand. "Yeah, I never thought about it like that. But if you can't forgive yourself for your own mistakes, how can you possibly be ready for a true second chance?"

Their gazes met and locked. "You're right," he said softly. "Having you back in my life is everything. And if you hadn't been willing to try, I would have lost the only woman I ever loved."

The connection between them surged to life, crackling around them like a lit fuse. She sucked in her breath at the sheer intensity and watched him rise from the chair. He never let go of her hand.

"I need you, Ophelia. I need to make love to my wife."

Without a word, she followed him into the bedroom. He kissed her long and slow and deep, with a shattering sweetness that made tears burn her eyes. Her arms tightened around his neck, and she fell into him and the kiss, letting her body take the lead and show him all the things in her heart.

He undressed her slowly, lovingly. He laid her out on the mattress, and his hands ran over her naked body, his tongue following the path of his hands to linger between her thighs. He tasted her in slow, long licks that coaxed shudders from her body. She grabbed at his shoulders, ready to explode, desperate for him to slide inside her, but he only lifted her higher, opened her wider with his thumbs, and devoured her whole.

The pleasure was sharp and bold, and it simultaneously ripped her apart and put her back together again. His lips sucked on her swollen clit, and his fingers sunk deep inside her, urging her over the edge.

She gave in, writhing her hips, spilling his name into the darkness.

He rose up and pressed inside her with slow, deliberate precision, his possessive gaze pinned on hers. He buried himself to the hilt until there was no space for anything but him in her body, and heart, and soul. Then he began to move.

He was both sweet lover and wild warrior. Each deep stroke pushed her further toward oblivion as he gave himself to her with his mouth and tongue, with his fingers and body, wringing out every last ounce of pleasure, those burning forest-green eyes never leaving her face.

The orgasm shattered her, claiming the very last of her soul. He followed her over, shouting her name, gripping her hips with a fierceness as he claimed her for his wife.

They drifted down together. Still shuddering with the aftereffects, she pulled the sheets around them and held him tight.

"The time we've spent together has changed me, Ophelia," he said quietly. "I need to know you trust me and believe I'm coming back."

She propped herself up on an elbow and stared into his beautiful face. Her fingers traced the soft scruff hugging his mouth, the sharp line of his cheekbone, the ridge of his brow. She sensed the truth radiating from his figure, could see the intensity of determination in his eyes.

How she ached to believe him. But deep inside, there was still fear. Fear that, if faced with the choice between producing the story of his own heart and coming back for her, his career would win again.

Her hand dropped to his chest. Right now, in the quiet of her bedroom, with his heart beating under her palm, she gave him the words. She needed to take the final leap and let him go. She needed to believe he would come back.

"Yes, I trust you."

He kissed her. She kissed him back, pushing away the worry that they were doomed to repeat the past all over again.

For the second time in a week, Kyle knocked on his father's door.

This time, he recognized the open pleasure on Patrick's face when he opened the door and saw Kyle on his front porch. The responding rush of satisfaction told him no matter how deep he'd buried his resentment regarding their relationship, it felt good to have his dad finally welcome him.

"I'm glad you stopped by," Patrick said, motioning him in.

Charlie trotted over. Kyle got down on his knees to rub his head. "He looks better. How's he doing?"

"Good. He's eating and drinking again. Doc cleaned out his ears, too, so he seems to hear better." His father gave a quick grin. "He's a tough one. Manipulative, too. Stands by his jar of gravy bones and gives me a pathetic look, but I know his game."

"You still give them to him, don't you?"

"Hell yeah. At his age, he should eat whatever he wants. He deserves it."

The affection on his dad's face hit him hard in the chest. His open love for the old dog was so unlike anything the man he once knew would have shown. He unfolded himself from the floor and cleared his throat.

"I came to tell you I'm leaving."

Disappointment flickered over his father's face. "Back to Hollywood, huh? For the new screenplay?"

Kyle nodded. "Got a big meeting to try and sell it." He paused. "Alan Bell."

Patrick gasped. "No shit? He won an Academy Award, right? Wow, this is the big time. You're a hell of a writer to get that kind of respect. Congrats."

The rush of pride he felt from his father's praise was foreign, and it took him a few moments to even recognize the emotion. "Well, I haven't sold it yet, so fingers crossed."

"Don't worry, you will. How's Ophelia taking it?"

Kyle rubbed his head. "Fine. She knows I'm coming back. It's just a short trip to get things in order."

"So you'll move back permanently? Help run the inn with her?"

"Yeah, I can do my writing anywhere. There's really no need for me to be stuck in Hollywood full time at this point."

"So you have everything you ever wanted." Patrick laughed. "That's amazing, son. Well done."

Kyle turned away, not comfortable with his burgeoning emotions. He hadn't told the full truth.

Yes, Ophelia had given him the words, but already he sensed her pulling back. A distance in her eyes. As if she didn't truly believe he'd put her first this time.

"I had it all before," he finally said. "But I lost it."

"You were young. You weren't sure yet about what you wanted. Now you know."

"Yeah." He gave him a tight smile.

"Did you look in the box yet?"

"Yes. I read the letter. Looked through the pictures."

"They should have been with you in California. Keeping you from your mother's memory was sick. I was sick. I'm sorry, and every damn day I ask for your forgiveness. I don't drink. I do my best. That's all I got left."

His heart squeezed in his chest. Hearing the truthful words helped soothe a bit of the raw wounds, allowing extra space in his lungs to breathe. He rubbed his head and shifted his weight.

"I never thought I'd be back in this house, talking to you. I'm not ready for most of this, but I wanted to see you before I left. Tell you I'm glad Charlie isn't sick. And that I appreciated the letter."

Patrick nodded, clearing his throat. "That's more than I imagined. Thank you."

Kyle bent and patted the dog's head. "Bye, buddy. Take care of each other."

Then Kyle drove away, feeling lighter than he had in a very long time.

Ophelia lay in his arms and tried desperately to hide her heartache.

In a few hours, he'd be gone. His stuff was cleaned out. His luggage packed and waiting at the door. Their final dinner together with Ethan and Mia and Harper was full of chatter and laughs, and an emotional goodbye. He kept promising he'd see everyone soon, once the script was accepted and finalized. A few weeks, tops. Then he'd be back.

If only she believed him.

"Do you want me to go to the airport with you?" she whispered.

"No. I want you to sleep—no need for you to wake up at four a.m."

"I'm glad you spoke with your dad."

He grabbed her hand and kissed her palm. "Me, too. Somehow, it felt right."

"Make sure you call me when you land."

"I will."

"I made you some scones for the trip. Just press the button on the coffeemaker when you wake up and you can take a fresh mug of coffee with you."

"Okay."

"I also left that Airborne stuff out, because the last thing you need is to get sick. Planes are horrible with germs. And I—"

He kissed her hard and deep, his lips curved upward in a smile. "It'll all be okay. I left you a copy of the book on my desk for you to read. Not the script. I want you to read the full book—the way it was originally written."

"Thank you."

"Call me after you read it. I want to know what you think."

"I will."

He stared at her for a while, as if glimpsing her real worry. "Truth or dare?"

She forced a smile. "Truth."

"Do you believe I'll be back?"

She tried to avert her gaze, but he held her chin and forced her to look at him. Finally, she gave him the only truth she could. "I hope you will be."

"I'll just have to prove it to you, then."

Her heart ached, so she pressed a kiss to his full lips. "Truth or dare?" she whispered.

"Dare."

This time, her smile was real. "Prove it to me now."

With a low growl, he reached for her, pinning her body with his, taking the kiss deep and long and slow.

Afterward, she slept.

When she woke up, he was gone.

Chapter Twenty-Five

Kyle sat back in his chair in the lush conference room and rested his hands on the polished mahogany table. His agent flanked his right, and Alan Bell joined two producers to his left. The script was open on the desk, along with scattered laptops, cell phones, pens, and a crumbled pack of Marlboros because Bell had failed with the patch and reverted to his old ways.

"I love it," Bell said simply, shaking his dark head. The powerhouse looked more like a blue-collar guy who eschewed fancy suits and too much coddling. He was well known for showing up at the most prestigious functions in jeans or leather pants. His energy whipped like a mini cyclone around his body, sucking everyone else in, and he was reputed to be a bully on set, but brilliant. "When Robbie told me it wasn't an action flick, I was intrigued, but this surpassed my expectations. I think we're poised to make something fresh and exciting."

Kyle grinned, muscles relaxing in relief. Though his agent had parroted the same sentiments, until it came from the director's mouth, nothing was real.

Robbie smoothly cut in. "We're not interested in an option at this point. We want a straight sale with a team in place. Plus producer credits. Who are you thinking of?"

In all his years of work, Kyle had never been able to secure producer credits. It would change the entire project and bump up both his expertise and responsibility. He'd have a bigger hand in his own movie, instead of being stuck on the sidelines.

Carlson—the red-headed producer who was known to be a real shark—spoke up. "I heard through the grapevine Liam Hemsworth is looking to delve into a romance and beef up his credits. He's a big draw."

"You think he'd be able to bring enough sensitivity to the role?" Kyle asked doubtfully. "I have a list of suggestions for the cast here." He passed over the papers. "What did you think of the ending?"

"Loved it," Bell said. His hands stroked his pack of cigarettes, and his leg jiggled up and down. "Very *Jerry Maguire*. I like that she was the one who came back to him."

"You don't think it was cliché?" Kyle ignored the scathing look Robbie shot him.

One of the golden rules was to never doubt your work. You needed to have a big dick in this business, and if you didn't, you'd better be the greatest bluffer in the world.

Bell waved his hand in the air. "No way. People like cliché with their romance. I think with a few tweaks we can get this deal going before I take off. We just need to amp it up."

Carlson flipped a few pages of the script. "Definitely. It's too straight-up love story to carry now, but all the elements are there. You thinking a murder, Bell?"

Bell slammed his fist on the table. "Fuck, that's brilliant. We have the drunk father murdered when they're out in California so they have to fly back together for the funeral. This gives time for the heroine to miss her farm, and the hero to realize he hates the place and belongs in Hollywood. Ratchets up the tension, too."

"Who murdered the father, you think?" Carlson asked with a frown, his pen furiously scribbling notes.

"The girl's mother?"

"I don't know—could you make that work, Kyle?"

He stared at them. Was he suddenly writing a fucking sci-fi movie? Were they honestly telling him they loved the script, a full-on love story, but wanted to add a murder to it?

"No, I'm not making that work," he snapped out. "I'm not looking to turn this into a murder mystery."

Robbie shot him a glare and jumped in. "Kyle's not interested in having the purity of his vision muddled," he said. "You can't go screwing with the genre and audience this is meant for."

"I hear you. I do," Bell said. "But unless it's *Fifty Shades*, with sex, or someone dies, a straight romance needs a bit of a bigger element. Plus, this isn't a rom-com. We don't want to change your vision, Kyle. We just need to tweak it to add a subplot that can interest the audience. I did the same thing with my last two movies and got an Academy Award. See where I'm going with this?"

Carlson agreed. "We don't want it unless we can bring it to the next level. It's perfect, but Alan is right. If we're even thinking about offering producer credit, we need you to work with some bigger elements. We'll work with you on it, and we can be open. Maybe a close friend gets murdered and the heroine goes back alone, then decides she wants to stay?"

"Or we add in a love triangle," Bell suggested. "The girl goes back to the inn because of her friend getting murdered, meets a guest there, and begins to fall for him while she's away from the hero. Now she has to choose one. Another spin on *The Choice*, right?"

Carlson nodded. "I love it. Kyle?"

He shifted in his seat. A warning voice whispered deep inside his gut, telling him to close out the meeting now and walk away. Already, he realized it would not be the story he'd originally conceived. Of course, he also knew they changed everything in Hollywood, and he needed to be reasonable. Maybe if he came up with his own revisions he could live with, it would be a win-win.

Ophelia's voice echoed through his mind. *"Don't let them take away the heart and soul of your story, no matter what they promise. It's too important for both of us."*

"You willing to work with us on this?" Bell asked. "'Cause if not, I gotta know now. I'm getting on a plane soon. You give me what I want in a reasonable way, we'll get it done. I'll give you producer credit."

Something he'd been wanting for years. Something no other director had been able to offer him.

Reasonable. Compromise. Wasn't that the necessary element to turn creativity into true success? Was he willing to scrap the best script he'd ever written and a chance to change his reputation? He could still do it on his terms. He could make it work.

Robbie rapped his knuckles on the table. "Let me talk to Kyle. We'll get back to you in a few."

Bell shrugged. "You got it. But make it fast."

They left the conference room. Robbie made some notes on his pad and looked up to study his face. "What do you think? You'll never get producer credit from anyone else. Bell is willing because he sees something big in you."

"I think it's bullshit," he said. "I don't want to change a damn thing."

"You know that's not how it works here. It never has."

"I know." He rubbed his head and spit out a curse. "I need to have final say in everything. Can you get me that?"

"Difficult, but not impossible. What about cast?"

"Right to reject in a reasonable way. I'll work on the pages right away and find a compromise I can live with."

"Then I'll get it done." He thumped Kyle on the shoulder. "You're making the right decision. Starving artists are starving for a reason. I'll let them know."

Kyle watched his agent disappear back into the conference room. He leaned against the wall and wondered why this time felt different.

The thought of telling Ophelia and having her be disappointed bothered him, but he had no other recourse. He was determined to make it work.

It had to.

♥ ♥ ♥

"How bad do you miss him?"

Mia sat across from Ophelia in the booth at Bea's Diner. They'd decided to take some time and go to lunch to catch up. Plus, Ophelia desperately needed some girl time. She was feeling a bit moony, and there was nothing better than being able to bitch to one of your people. "It's terrible," she admitted. "I can't believe in the span of a few short months it was like we were married again."

"Well, you *are* married." Mia laughed. "And going to stay that way, right? What's the plan?"

"He's got this big meeting today for the new script. It depends if it sells, where it shoots, how much he's needed on set. But . . ." she trailed off, still swamped with doubt.

"But?" Mia prodded.

"But I know how Kyle gets when he's passionate about a project. He says he's coming back, but if they need him on set twenty-four seven? Or if they demand constant rewrites? He may decide not to come back for a while."

"He loves you. That's evident," Mia said. "You don't think things have changed?"

"I guess I'm still scared he may not choose me." Ophelia lifted her hands in surrender. "At this point, I have to just trust it will work out for us, because I love him."

Mia reached out to clasp her hand. "I've never seen you so happy before. It was really hard for Ethan and me in the beginning, but once you realize the other person is the priority, choices are easier to make."

The words hit her directly in the gut, like a sucker punch. Mia had called out the very depth of her worry.

"Yes." She paused, then decided to tell her friend everything. "I read Kyle's script."

"Did you like it? Was it good?"

"It was about us. Our story."

Mia gasped. "No way! He wrote about you?"

"Yeah, and I mean, he included *everything*. How we fell in love. Our life on the farm. His ups and downs with his dad. Our running away to California, and how it unfolded. It was so strange reading about us, but my God, it was good."

The emotions that seeped onto the page had her up late at night, unable to put it down. It was heartbreaking and real and honest. It was everything she always believed he could write.

"Did he give you guys a happy ending?" Mia asked with a grin.

"That's the strange part. He did, and I expected to swoon and love it. But for some reason, it didn't feel right." The end had felt false—the first lie within the truth—and it had left a lingering bitter taste in her mouth. "I don't know, maybe it was just me."

She heard her name being called, and turned. Albert walked over, dressed in his usual smart suit and wool hat, a beautiful carved cane in his hand. "Don't want to interrupt a ladies' lunch, but wanted to say hello," he said, smiling and greeting them.

"What are you doing here?" Ophelia asked. "Are you buying Bea's pies?"

It was well known Crystal's had a pastry chef who was brilliant but very temperamental. Albert shook his head mournfully. "Alas, as much as Gerard keeps the restaurant at the top of its game, I've never been able to say no to Bea's famous pies. But please don't tell him. I'm afraid he'd quit."

She laughed with Mia. "What happens at Bea's, stays at Bea's."

"Please let me know that you'll be dining with me soon. And Ophelia, I'm still holding out hope you'll sing for me. Let me know if you've changed your mind."

"I will, thank you."

He tipped his hat and left. Ophelia tried to concentrate on her salad, but she felt Mia's gaze piercing into her.

"Are you gonna tell me or make me ask?" she finally said.

Ophelia sighed. "Somehow, some idiot posted my karaoke on YouTube, and it went viral. Albert asked me to sing at his restaurant a night or two a week. I promised Kyle I'd think about it, so I'm still considering."

Mia dropped her fork and crossed her arms in front of her chest. She looked pissed. "I've been meaning to talk to you about this for a while, but Ethan said you're sensitive about the subject so I backed off. Now I regret it, because some things need to be said."

She frowned, puzzled. "What are you talking about?"

"For starters, *I'm* the idiot who uploaded the video to YouTube."

Ophelia gasped. Shook her head. "No! You wouldn't do that to me!"

"Do what? Show off the amazing talent God gave you? I wanted to upload it the night you sang, but I decided to back off. Then I over-heard some people in town raving about your singing, and how they wish you'd do more appearances. So I just did it. Within hours, the stats went crazy. Last time I checked it had a bajillion views. Yet you still stubbornly hide yourself away and pretend you don't want to sing."

Uneasiness flared. Kyle's words had been haunting her, but she'd pushed them aside for a while, choosing not to think about it.

"I like to keep my singing private. That video opened up a whole bunch of chaos and questions for me. I get stopped in town and asked if I'm going to record some songs, or if I'm singing locally. It makes things awkward."

"Why?" Mia demanded. "What are you so afraid of?"

She stiffened. "I don't want to deal with anything like what happened in California. I dropped out of a reality show because they were making me feel more like a piece of meat than a singer. They judged me and disapproved of me and poked me to see what they could do to make me look better, act better, be liked more. It was about everything but the singing."

Mia tilted her head. "You never told me about this."

Ophelia sighed. "I know. It's just that, after I quit, everything blew up. There was a ton of gossip about me and I was written up in all the magazines. It was so humiliating. They called me a diva and tore me to shreds."

Mia gasped. "That's terrible! Dammit, if I had been your PR rep at the time, I would've beaten them at their own game!"

Ophelia smiled. "I would've loved that. Anyway, I swore I'd never sing in public again. It's not about fear, Mia. I just don't need that kind of stress in my life ever again. It made me question myself and my singing."

"But this is an entirely different situation. This happened when you were young, in California, pursuing stardom." Mia sighed. "You're so stubborn. Just like Ethan."

"Am not!"

"Listen up. You stopped singing to protect yourself from the crap being thrown at you. I totally get that it was necessary at first, but now you've closed the door to any future opportunities, too. Why are you denying people the chance to enjoy your voice? Taking care of people is part of your calling, Ophelia, and your singing uplifts everyone. I don't think you'll ever be truly whole without expressing that love for singing to the world. But it doesn't have to be on television or Broadway. It can be done quietly, right here, where you belong."

She stared at Mia, hearing Kyle's voice echoing over and over with the same mantra. She'd been fighting public singing for so long, thinking it was the road to ruin, she'd never allowed herself to think outside the boundaries.

She remembered the amazing freedom and pride she'd felt after singing karaoke; the flush of pleasure she'd gained from the audience's enthusiastic response.

She imagined herself at Crystal's, in front of the piano. Singing songs she chose, the way she wanted, for the people she loved. In her mind, there would be no judgments or opinions. Just a quiet evening to share her voice.

"You're right," she said slowly. "You and Kyle are both right."

"Of course we're right. Just try it once. If you hate it, I won't push you again. But I think you may find a piece of yourself that's been missing."

"You training part time to be a shrink?" she grumbled, stuffing a cucumber in her mouth.

Mia beamed. "I'm PR, babe. I counsel people all the time to be the best versions of themselves."

"Damn, you're good at your job. Okay, I'll do it. But no more videos unless I know you're recording."

"Fine."

They gazed at each other and laughed.

A few hours later, Kyle called. The sound of his smooth, rich voice made her heart ache with longing.

"I miss you."

"Miss you, too. It's too sunny here. I never noticed how many fake tans people have—why don't they just go outside and get a real one?"

A giggle escaped her lips. "What happened at the meeting? Did it go well?"

"They liked the script. Want to buy it. They just had some . . . tweaks."

His hesitation spoke volumes. Immediately, her senses pricked up. "Big tweaks that change the story? Or little ones?"

"They want me to add a subplot, which is standard for the industry." Defensiveness poured over the line. "I don't like it, but they're making a reasonable request." The tension in his voice painted a picture.

Oh, he definitely wasn't happy. Was he going to do it again? Let a bunch of studio executives tell him what his story should be about?

"Did you agree?" she asked softly.

"Yeah. I did. They're also offering production credit. I've been trying for years to be listed as a producer, and now I finally have the opportunity. It would be crazy to turn it down for just a few changes."

Sadness coursed through her. She felt like she was reliving the past, but she refused to let this define what they'd discovered again with each other. "I read the book, Kyle. It's beautiful and gut wrenching, and I cried. It's everything." She didn't tell him about the ending, not wanting to discourage him.

"I'm glad."

Why did his voice sound so distant? As if even this phone call was perfunctory, and he was itching to get back to work?

Nausea roiled through her gut. She swallowed and tried to remind him about what they had discussed in the intimacy of their bedroom. "Remember what I said? Don't let them take away the heart and soul of your story, no matter what they promise."

She waited awhile for his answer. When it finally came, she closed her eyes in disappointment.

"I made the right decision. I want to see this story made, and Bell is a star director. They want to cast Liam Hemsworth! I'd be nuts to walk away."

She closed her eyes against the anguish, but kept her voice light. "Sounds like you got exactly what you wanted. I'm glad. How long do you think you'll be out there?"

His pause vibrated with tension. "Just a few weeks. I'll try to fly in for a long weekend, but they'll need me to stay close for a while as we get things moving. Maybe you can come out and visit while I'm stuck here?"

"I'm moving into high season for the spring. The inn will be booked steadily for a while."

"Right." Silence hummed over the line. "Well, I have to get to this party in a few hours. Don't worry—we'll make it work. Call you later. Love you."

"Love you, too."

She rested her forehead against the wall. Why did this whole conversation seem so damn familiar? She couldn't be the one to make him walk away. It had to be his decision, on his terms, or she'd always wonder if deep inside, he blamed her.

The familiar worry gnawed at her nerves, and an inner voice reminded her how, once Hollywood called, it was hard for him to say no.

Mia's words drifted in her mind, reminding her she'd made her own choices based on the past. She thought about her promise to Kyle, his urgent plea to share her gift.

Wasn't it time to challenge herself, too? She had a responsibility to be real with herself and admit she loved singing. It was time to stop hiding behind her past experiences and move forward—on her own terms.

She had no control over whether Kyle came back to her, and she didn't know if this second chance with their marriage would work. Though it would tear her to pieces to lose him again, she deserved to give herself her own second chance. To do something she'd always loved.

She picked up the phone and punched in the number before she changed her mind.

"Hi, Albert. I wanted to talk to you about your offer to sing." She dragged in a breath and took the leap. "I want to do it."

Chapter Twenty-Six

Kyle parked his car and began walking down Rodeo Drive. The hot sun beat down ruthlessly on his shoulders, and the stink of money drifted in the humid air. His mind sifted through the past few days, and he thought about how everything had changed.

The other night, he'd attended his first party since he'd left. It was the usual potpourri of useful contacts and glam squads. Robbie had introduced him to the hot new casting director they were using to try to score Hemsworth. Endless women flirted and hung on his arm. Drinks got pushed into his hands, urging him to get drunk. Conversations swirled around surface niceties, and subtle cutting insults were shared with hidden glee.

God, he'd hated every second.

He longed for the scent of fresh hay and earth, the vision of clean blue sky and white clouds hovering over the majestic Gunks. He longed for the bite of cold air dragged into his lungs. Ophelia's face haunted him, carving out an empty ache in his soul that cried out to be filled. Everything he looked at was shiny and fake—like empty calories gobbled up only to make him feel more ravenous.

He was lost. He missed home. Missed his wife. Missed the old life he'd rediscovered.

Could he grit his teeth and bear being in this lifestyle for the next few weeks? Maybe months? Traveling back and forth, caught between two worlds? Was the film worth it?

All he'd worked for his entire life was finally being offered to him.

The script of his dreams. Producer credit. Academy Award–winning director and a stellar cast. After this, everything would change.

He thought of all the upcoming battles and stress, the endless nights of revisions while he fought to have his original vision remain. He thought of the love story he'd written that meant something to him and how, once again, he'd have to compromise to put it on the big screen.

Then he'd steeled his resolve and made the only decision that made sense for him. The decision that his heart cried out for, no matter what he was giving up.

He'd called off the entire deal.

A small laugh escaped at the memory.

Holy shit, Robbie had flipped out. Called his career dead in the water. Begged him to reconsider. Funny, it was so much easier than he'd thought to walk away and explain he was done with compromise.

He didn't know what was going to happen to the book or screenplay, or where his career would end up. There was only one thing he knew he wanted.

His wife.

He wanted to go home.

The bell over the door tinkled merrily. The sharply dressed staff bolted to attention, exhibiting the perfect balance between anticipating questions and not seeming too hungry for a sale. He didn't need to play games today, though. He walked up to the gleaming counter and spoke to the gentleman standing with perfect poise in front of the signature robin's egg–blue wall of Tiffany's.

"May I help you, sir?"

"Yes. I want to see your wedding rings, please."

"Of course. Follow me." The man walked to the next case. The gleaming sparkle of exquisitely cut diamonds winked at him and temporarily blinded his view. "We have a varied selection here. Is there a particular style you prefer?"

His gaze swept the display, then stopped on a stunning platinum band encrusted with diamonds. His heart stopped, then resumed beating. His finger tapped the shiny glass. "That one."

"A perfect choice."

The man took it out of the case and laid it on the thick black velvet cloth. It screamed elegance rather than extravagance. It beat with pulses of romance rather than glitz. It was everything he'd always dreamed of in a ring for the woman who was his soul mate, and who'd refused to replace the cheap, tiny ring he'd scrimped and saved to give her when he was eighteen years old.

"I need it in a size seven, please. Gift wrapped."

"Of course, sir. Just a moment."

Kyle dragged in a deep breath, thinking over his last conversation with Ophelia. Thinking over the past two months they'd spent together.

Finally, after all this time, he'd gotten it. Even to the very end before he'd left, he'd been selfish—telling Ophelia over and over that he'd choose her over his career, as if it was a gift he was finally able to give her. Every claim and reassurance he'd uttered had always revolved around him.

He shook his head with a touch of shame. He'd never asked her the most important question of all.

Would she choose him?

It was time to find out.

"How do you feel?" Mia asked, adjusting the final pin in her hair.

"Like I'm going to vomit. I can't believe I agreed to perform so soon. I figured I'd have a month to plan."

Mia laughed and stepped back to survey her handiwork. "You got this. Just remember this is low-key, and everyone out there is a friend. We're all here for you." Mia gave her a brilliant smile. "Go and enjoy yourself, sweets. Sing your heart out."

Ophelia smiled back, her muscles unlocking a few fibers. Mia was right.

She was doing this for herself because she loved it. The venue was perfect.

She looked at herself in the mirror, pleased with her appearance. With her hair pinned up and just a few curls spilling over her shoulders, and wearing a simple black dress with an elegant, square neckline, she felt like herself.

Albert stuck his head around the corner and motioned her out. "Ophelia, you're up. I just announced you."

"Thanks, Albert." She took a deep breath, squared her shoulders, and walked to her spot at the piano. The chandelier drenched her in light, and it took her a few moments to adjust her vision before she introduced herself at the microphone.

The tables were packed. Generous applause hit her ears. Ignoring the jumble of nerves in her belly, she dove right into her first song—an easy favorite by Barbara Streisand to warm up her vocal cords. Her fingers flew across the keyboard, her voice melting into the strains of harmony in a way that emphasized, not overpowered. Soon, she fell into the beauty of the music.

The hour drifted by like a misty dream, until before she knew it she came to the last song of the evening.

"I've always had a weakness for musicals," she said to the audience, "and since we're in the no-judgment zone here tonight, I'd thought I'd share this lovely song from *La La Land*. It's called 'City of Stars.' Enjoy."

She closed her eyes and steeped herself in the memory of that night. Lying naked in Kyle's arms, wrapped tight in his delicious body heat. The trickle of moonlight seeping through the curtains. The crackle and pop of firewood as shadows danced over the walls. The sound of her voice as she sang to the man she loved, offering her heart for the second time in all its fragility and beauty.

Her eyes stung with silent tears, so she blinked and refocused on the crowd.

And saw him.

He stood in the back of the room. Dressed in black pants and a matching jacket, his snowy white shirt opened at the neck, his burnished hair falling over his brow. That gaze burned from across endless tables, encouraging her, supporting her, loving her.

Claiming her.

The final words uncurled from her tongue and shimmered in the room, slowly fading to nothingness.

She stood up, gave the audience a *thank you*, and began moving toward him.

Applause thundered. She moved past each table with a single purpose, weaving her way through the crowd until she reached him.

The world around them faded away.

"What are you doing here?" she asked.

He closed the distance between them. Smiled. Her heart stopped, sputtered, and relaunched at top speed at his masculine beauty.

"I got everything I ever wanted, so I came here to tell you."

She choked back her sorrow even as pride filled her at his success.

He'd come back to tell her he needed to stay in Hollywood. He'd come back for a proper goodbye.

This time, tears filled her eyes unchecked. "You look so happy," she whispered. "I'm glad your work gives you that type of feeling."

"It has nothing to do with my work."

She tilted her head. "What do you mean?"

"It's you. This. Us." He ran a finger down her cheek with sweet tenderness. "It's everything," he said simply.

She began to tremble, the truth unfolding before her. He lowered his head, his mouth inches from hers. "Truth or dare?"

Emotion tightened her throat. "Truth."

"Do you love me enough to forgive me for the past and my mistakes? To build a brand new ending? Because I've outgrown my old life, baby. I'm done with Hollywood, and writing screenplays, and living with my heart half-dead. I want to come home and be with you. I want my wife."

"And I want you," she whispered.

"Then there's one thing left to do." Slowly, he removed a small robin's egg–blue box from his pocket.

Her heart stopped, blasted forward, and stuttered. He snapped the lid open, and a thousand prisms of light danced before her. She sucked in her breath as she stared at the gorgeous ring—a ring he'd promised over and over to buy her one day, even though she'd said she never needed it.

He dropped to one knee.

She heard gasps of breath and endless chatter, but her world narrowed to only the man she loved and the ring he held out to her. His smile was joyous and full of pure love.

"I told you these past few months that I would always choose you. But I never asked the most important question of all. Will you choose *me*, Ophelia Bishop? To be your husband? Your lover, protector, supporter, and best friend? Will you stand before our family and friends and renew our vows?"

The word spilled from her lips in a gasp of breath. "Yes."

He slid the ring over her finger, and she reached out. Suddenly, he was kissing her. A large cheer rose up around them, and she laughed, clinging to him.

Ethan and Mia and Harper cut in, giving them hugs and congratulations and welcoming him back. Finally, their relationship blossomed in the light, among family and friends, and among dreams both shattered and reborn.

And everything was perfect.

Epilogue

Five Weeks Later

"Is this Kyle Kimpton?"

He juggled the phone as he moved around the room, searching for his favorite black T-shirt.

Damn, he was already running late.

He had picked up the call automatically. "Yes. Listen, I don't have time for a telemarketer right now. Sorry."

A low, husky female laugh spilled into his ear. "I'm not a salesperson. This is Presley Cabot from LWW Enterprises. I'm calling about the manuscript I was sent, *A Brand New Ending.*"

Since he'd passed on the whole screenplay with Ball, he'd taken some time to decide what he really wanted to do next with his career. LWW Enterprises was a huge media conglomerate with branches all over the United States. They had a stellar film and book division, but he didn't have any contacts there. He frowned.

"I don't remember sending you my book. How did you get it?"

"Robert Cavanaugh forwarded it to me. Said it was worth a look."

He finally found the shirt in the back of the top drawer and pulled it out, trying to ignore his rapidly beating heart.

Robbie had sent it over?

His agent hadn't contacted him since the walkout, and Kyle figured he'd have to find new representation.

"I'm not sure where you are with the book yet, but I'm very interested in acquiring it. Simply put, it's brilliant. I couldn't put it down."

He sat on the edge of the bed and tried to keep it together. "Thank you. I'm sorry—are you interested in buying it for the screen, or as a book?"

"Robbie sent me both formats, and I think this was made to be a novel—not a movie. I'm looking for a fresh voice to launch our beach reading line, so there'd be a ton of marketing behind you. I have very good instincts, and right now, I sense this will be a huge seller."

He rubbed his head, trying not to let out a shout of victory. *Yes.* His own instincts kept reverting back to the novel, too, where he could develop the emotion and characters as he wanted—not be tied to the vision of a director.

He tried to remind himself to play it cool and not jump on the offer because he was desperate.

God knows, he'd finally learned his lesson about protecting the work.

"What did you think of the story?" he asked. "Do you see any big editorial changes at this point?"

The sound of papers being shuffled echoed over the phone. "It's tight, well written, and grounds the reader immediately into the world. The only problem I had with the book was the ending."

"What's wrong with it?"

"It doesn't fit. The heroine comes back to the hero, but there was no real growth arc for either of them that way. It was too easy—especially for him. I think it would work better to have the hero leave Hollywood for the love of his life. It's bigger stakes, and a bigger payoff. Does that make sense?"

Immediately, he knew Presley was right. That was what had been bugging him about the book. He'd been so insistent on making things right, he'd forgotten the story wasn't about the heroine returning to have everything magically happy again. It was the hero who had to make the leap, and it was the ending he and Ophelia had finally achieved.

No one had truly seen the bigger vision of the story until Presley Cabot—which told him she might be the perfect person to handle his book.

"I agree," he said. "I'd love to meet to discuss it further."

"Wonderful. I'm in New York—in a town called Port Hudson. It's close to Manhattan."

"That's not far from me—I'm in the Hudson Valley."

"Does next week work? I can have my assistant send you an email to arrange a meeting."

"Yes, that'd be great. Thanks for calling. I'll see you next week."

He clicked off and jumped in front of his laptop. He brought up the website for LWW Enterprises, focusing on Presley Cabot. Head of the publishing division, and one of the main owners of LWW Enterprises. She had an impressive client list—all popular bestsellers and a nice assortment of various genres. Many had gone on to be adapted into successful films with well-known directors. She looked young to head a multimillion-dollar empire, which made her even more impressive.

"Kyle! Babe, are you ready? We're late!"

"Coming!" He pulled his shirt on, grabbed a casual jacket, and headed down the stairs. "Are we picking him up?"

Ophelia grabbed his arm, and they raced out the door. "No, he had to go early, so we'll meet him there. Are you nervous?"

"A little. I've never gone to one of these before."

She smiled and squeezed his hand. "It'll be fine. Who were you talking to?"

He ignited the engine and turned to face his wife with a big grin. "You're not going to believe this, baby. I think I'm going to sell my book."

Her eyes widened. "Tell me everything."

And he did.

The small room was crowded. Folding chairs were neatly lined up, and the scent of coffee and doughnuts drifted in the air. The walls were dull yellow. Water stains spotted the ceiling. The linoleum floor was slanted and cracked, but there was an energy that burned in the room that made the surroundings fade away.

Patrick stood on the small podium and stared at the large group. Kyle noticed his hands trembling slightly. For a brief moment, Kyle wondered if he'd be able to go through with it, but Tony flanked his left side and gave him an encouraging nod.

"My name is Patrick Kimpton, and I'm an alcoholic."

"Hello, Patrick," a chorus of voices responded.

He began to speak. Kyle sat motionless, holding his wife's hand, and heard the truth about his father—raw and unfiltered. How he'd started drinking at twelve years old to avoid his parents' abusive fighting. How he felt funnier, and braver, and bigger when he drank. How he'd met Kyle's mother in a bar, and they'd fallen in love during endless weekend parties and over constant cocktails. At one point, his father stopped, wiped his sweating brow, and dragged in a breath. Kyle swallowed past the lump in his throat and wondered if he would quit.

But he didn't. He pushed through.

Kyle learned how much his father loved his mother, and he realized for the first time how much he'd been wanted. But alcohol had become just as important.

"My wife got pregnant. We were so happy, because we'd been trying for so long. She begged me to cut down on my drinking. Finally, I agreed. I figured it would be easy. A little detox, like a juice diet to take off some weight.

"I got the shakes within hours. But even worse were my thoughts. I needed that drink more than my next breath. I knew I could do anything, be anything my wife wanted, if only I had a few drinks. The cycle began again. And again."

Grief ravaged Patrick's face. His hands shook harder, but he seemed to hear the low murmurs of approval from the group, the whispered encouragements surrounding him, and he continued.

"When my wife went into premature labor, I was at the bar getting drunk. When she started bleeding out on the floor, calling out my name, I told my friends she was only tracking me down to nag me. When she finally crawled to the phone half-conscious and called 911, I was playing darts and belting back shots of whiskey. And when I got to the hospital where my son was being born, I was smashed out of my mind.

"I held her hand, smelling of liquor. When she began to crash, the doctor said they'd have to take the baby by C-section. She turned to me, gripped my hand, and told me if there was a choice to be made, to save the baby at all costs. Then she smiled at me with such peace and happiness. I didn't understand what was going on. It was like she knew. She said she loved me. She told me to take care of our son. And then they got her into the operating room, and she died on the table."

Tears stung Kyle's eyes. He shook his head hard, trying to clear his thoughts. The retelling of his father's life and his mother's death was tearing Patrick apart. Yet he pushed on.

"I raised my son as a drunk. Somehow, in my twisted-up head, I blamed him for Catherine's death. A baby. My baby. The son we had tried so hard for and prayed for—my precious baby boy. I treated him like a piece of garbage, secondary to the bottle. I had people help me raise him, and I kept him at a distance. I told him regularly that he'd caused his mother's death. One time, I found him looking through old photo albums. He asked me so many questions about his mother, I went nuts. The guilt was too much for me, so I punished him by taking them away and lying, saying that I burned all the pictures. I watched my son cry, and I betrayed him every day. I watched him grow up without a father and was haunted by my wife's sad pleas in the dark of the night.

315

"My son learned to hate me. At eighteen, he left to make his own life, and I was alone with my memories. I became the town drunk. I lost the farm. I lost my friends. I lost everything worth having, but I had my precious bottle.

"And then one night, I had a dream. Catherine came to me and said it wasn't too late. I remember the words clearly: 'Our son may never forgive you, but you owe it to yourself to try and get your life back. Be worthy of your family. Of yourself. It's never too late.'

"I woke up and looked at my nightstand. There was a bottle waiting for me. Then I got out of bed, got dressed, and drove down to the church. I sat in the pew and prayed for strength. I prayed for my son. I prayed for the dead wife I'd betrayed. I sat for hours on that hard bench, not moving. When I finally got up, I went to my first AA meeting.

"The next day, I went to another. Sometimes I went two or three times per day. And I haven't stopped. That was a year ago."

Men and women nodded. Some cried. Two walked out, raw pain carved into their features as they faced their own demons. In that small room, people shared their pain and vulnerability and ghosts of the past and present. In that small room, there were not only acceptance and understanding. There was forgiveness.

There was the power of second chances.

His father cleared his throat and looked straight at Kyle. Those familiar green eyes were clear. Full of regret. And full of love that emanated across the room in waves.

"My son, Kyle, is here tonight with his wife, Ophelia. Somehow, their hearts were big enough to come hear my story. To hear my apology. I submit to a higher power and believe I am worthy of forgiveness. Every day, I choose not to drink. Every day, I choose life. I love you, son. Thank you."

He stepped off the podium. Tony whispered to him, clapping him on the shoulder, then made the announcement that everyone should help themselves to doughnuts and coffee. The buzz of conversation rose in the air. Hugs were exchanged. Support given.

Kyle sat with Ophelia, feeling as if his world had spun on its axis, then finally righted itself.

His father made his way through the crowd and stopped in front of him. Vulnerability and exhaustion carved out the features of his face. "Thank you for coming," he said, his voice a bit choked.

Kyle stared at his father for a long while. The memories of the past rose up, full of bitterness and pain; they mixed with fleeting images of love and joy with Ophelia, and at the inn.

A man stood before him, asking for some form of forgiveness for so many sins.

"I'm glad I came." He leaned forward and gave his father a hug, and Patrick hugged back, his frail frame gripping him with a fierceness that pulsed with emotion.

Ophelia smiled and embraced them both. And in that moment, Kyle realized the most important thing of all.

Sometimes, it wasn't about endings at all.

Sometimes, it was all about new beginnings.

ACKNOWLEDGMENTS

I've learned as an author that some books are easy to write.

Some are not.

This book was a particular struggle, and I need to thank many people who helped me through a difficult time, and cheered me to the end. This book holds so much of my soul.

Thank you to the team at Montlake, especially Maria Gomez, for all the support and expertise. Thanks to my agent, Kevan Lyon, for always being there whenever I need her. A special shout-out to Kristi Yanta, my fabulous developmental and line editor, who polished this story with so much love, it can only sparkle like a diamond.

Big hugs and kisses to my writing sisters, who supported me and showered me with love. The Ladies Who Write: Melissa Foster, Sawyer Bennett, Jill Shalvis, Kristen Proby, Marina Adair, and Emma Chase. Also to my email buddy, the beautiful Lauren Layne, who keeps me sane. Kudos to my assistant, Lisa Hamel-Soldano; the Probst Posse reader group, for loving and shouting about all my books; and my family, who puts up with my craziness on a daily basis because they know I'm a writer. It takes a village, guys.

I'm so grateful my village is full of love.